INTRIGO

HÅKAN NESSER

INTRIGO

*Translated from the Swedish
by Deborah Bragan-Turner
and Paul Norlen*

MANTLE

First published in Swedish 2018 by Albert Bonniers Förlag, Stockholm

First published in the UK 2019 by Mantle
an imprint of Pan Macmillan
20 New Wharf Road, London N1 9RR
Associated companies throughout the world
www.panmacmillan.com

ISBN 978-1-5098-9216-7

Visit www.panmacmillan.com to read more about all our books
and to buy them. You will also find features, author interviews and
news of any author events, and you can sign up for e-newsletters
so that you're always first to hear about our new releases.

Contents

Foreword

Foreword

Intrigo is a cafe located on Keymerstraat in central Maardam.

It is also the collective name of three films directed by Daniel Alfredson, shot in 2017, with international premieres in 2018–19: *Death of an Author, Samaria* and *Dear Agnes*. The films are based on some of my stories – the last four in this volume – and have previously been published in Swedish. The novella that opens this collection, *Tom*, is newly written and is published here for the first time.

A book is a book, a movie is a movie. Stories must often be redirected, find new forms of expression, when transferred from one medium to another. They can even get a whole new ending. In the case of *Intrigo*, all differences between book and film are both necessary and to the highest degree intentional.

But, of course, the resemblance, the very essence of each story, what it is truly about, is well preserved.

TOM

Translated from the Swedish by
Deborah Bragan-Turner

ONE

Maardam, 1995

The telephone call came a few minutes after half past three one Thursday morning. The number was unknown, evidently foreign, and under normal circumstances she wouldn't have answered.

Clearly she wouldn't, but she had just woken with a start from a dream and although it was pitch-dark inside the room and outside the window, where a branch of the huge walnut tree whispered intimately against the glass, she felt wide awake. Maybe it was just the dark, in some kind of mysterious pact with the rudely interrupted dream – the contents of which she was unable to recall, either then or later – that made her lift the receiver and take the call.

'Hello?'

'Judith Bendler?'

'Yes.'

'It's Tom.'

Silence ensued, apart from a slight interference on the line. A faint thrumming scratch, barely audible, like spent waves breaking on a pebble beach. Afterwards, once she had replaced the receiver, that was what she could picture in her mind. After their long journey, the waves finally coming to rest as silent white foam in a sheltered but stony cove.

Strangely enough, she wasn't often haunted by images. She

didn't fall for that kind of cheap analogy, or whatever it's called. She wasn't religious and she detested poetry.

'Tom?' she eventually asked. 'Which Tom?'

'Do you know more than one?'

She thought about it. No, there was only one Tom.

Had been.

'I thought maybe we could meet. It's been a few years.'

'Yes . . .'

She felt a shudder sweep through her body and perhaps she even lost consciousness for a moment. Had she tried to stand up, she might well have fainted and hit the floor.

But she didn't, thank goodness; she lay in the dark on her side of the king-sized bed and when the brief attack was over, she automatically reached her hand out for Robert. It took another second for her to remember he was in London. He had left on Monday and would be back on Friday evening, Saturday afternoon at the latest. It was a film project; he had mentioned the names of various famous actors, but she had forgotten who they were. He had even asked if she fancied going with him, but she had said no. London was not one of her favourite cities.

'Hello?'

She suppressed a sudden impulse to hang up.

'Yes?'

'So what do you say?'

'About what?'

'About meeting.'

'I . . . I don't quite understand.'

She could hear him drinking something.

'You know what? Think it over and I'll get back to you in a few days.'

TOM

'I don't really think—'

There was a click and the call ended. She put the receiver back and lay on the bed without moving, her hands clasped over her chest. She closed her eyes but then opened them again; there was something she needed to figure out. The slow waves that still seemed to emanate from the darkness must mean something, she thought; they would reveal something to her, and whatever their significance, it involved *distance*. An inordinately vast distance in both time and space. And not only that, his voice was still there, deep inside this fog, so distant yet so utterly close. Slightly gruff and slightly . . . Well, what? she thought. Ironic? Confident?

Tom?

Think it over?

She counted up and concluded that it had been twenty-two years.

Twenty-two years and two months, to be precise.

The therapist was called Maria Rosenberg. Her rooms were on the second floor in one of the old pommerstone houses on Keymerstraat, and Judith Bendler had been one of her clients for almost a decade. Not endless, heavy sessions, it's true; but they met once or twice a month, usually on Thursday mornings, when Judith generally had things to do in the centre of Maardam anyway. Afterwards she would enjoy lunch with a friend, take the opportunity to do some shopping and maybe spend some time in one of the galleries in the Deijkstraa district. Or Krantze's antiquarian bookshop on Kupinski Street, if it happened to be open. The train from Holtenaar took just over half an hour, and with each year that passed she was aware of a slowly mounting reluctance to leave their beautiful house and its even more beautiful garden by the river. Why leave paradise when you had your own place right in the middle of it?

So that absence could make the heart grow fonder, maybe? That had been Robert's suggestion when she had raised the subject with him. And of course, he had a point. Robert often did; he had a way of putting his finger on the crux of a matter in all sorts of situations, she would give him that.

Perhaps there was some quiet pleasure in seeing Maria Rosenberg again as well. Every single time. The world might rage, the human race might wage wars, burn cities to the ground and slaughter its own children, but Maria Rosenberg stayed put. Sitting in her wing chair in the room with the weighty curtains and the thick, blood-patterned rug from Samarkand.

And listening. She had been old when Judith met her the very first time, a week or two after the business with Robert, and she was the same age today. The reason she used to give for her changelessness was that she had reached a juncture on life's turbulent path when the years no longer touched her. One day she would presumably be dead, but until that final journey, regardless of whether it lay a few months or several years ahead, she had no intention of ageing. Perhaps a little wiser, chastened somewhat by experience; that sort of thing was hard to guard against.

But of course the conversations in that hushed, dark room were not about Maria Rosenberg.

'Welcome, Judith. I hope your journey here went well.'

'Thank you. At least I managed to get a seat.'

'Well then, shall we treat ourselves to a pot of rooibos?'

'That would be lovely.'

More or less the same opening remarks as always. While Maria Rosenberg made the tea behind a curtain in the kitchenette, Judith took off her coat and shoes and made herself comfortable in the corner of the sofa, the tartan blanket over her legs and a cushion for her back. As she waited she felt the anxiety ticking inside her and there was no doubt as to its cause.

'I think I can detect a certain disquiet. But correct me if I'm wrong.'

She hadn't decided if she was going to talk about the telephone call, but when Maria peered at her over the rim of her teacup, the decision was made. If ever there was a look that brooked no resistance, it was Maria Rosenberg's. That was the acknowledged situation, and maybe she had already known when she set foot on the train an hour earlier that she would tell.

'Something's happened.'

'Yes?'

'I received a really odd telephone call.'

Maria Rosenberg nodded, sipped at her tea and put the cup down.

'Last night. Someone rang at half past three.'

'Half past three? And you answered?'

'Yes. For some reason I'd just woken up. Thirty seconds before the phone rang, I'd say. It was strange. And afterwards I found it quite difficult to go back to sleep.'

'Who was on the phone?'

'I don't know.'

'You don't know?'

She drew a deep breath, straightened the blanket and fixed

her eye on the painting hanging between the two narrow bookcases, a miniature reproduction of Caspar David Friedrich's *The Monk by the Sea*. The figure, turned away, surveying the grey ocean. She had often speculated on why her worldly-wise therapist had chosen to hang that particular painting in her consulting room – it was the only picture there – but up to now, after more than a hundred sessions, she had never asked.

'He said he was Tom.'

'Tom? Do you mean . . . ?'

She nodded, but her gaze didn't leave the painting. Out of the corner of her eye she saw Maria Rosenberg take another sip of tea and then fold her hands together on her knee. Waiting.

'He wanted us to meet.'

The monk on the seashore didn't move and neither did Maria Rosenberg.

'But?' she said.

'I find it hard to believe it was him.'

She had spoken about Tom, but that was a long time ago. It had come up during the course of one of their earliest meetings. They had returned to the sad story a few times at the beginning, but as far as Judith could remember, they hadn't discussed him for four or five years. It might have been even longer since his name had been mentioned. There had been no reason to.

Tom was a closed chapter. A bleak, forgotten part of life there was no point in analysing or trying to resolve. She didn't talk about him with Robert either; even if their agreement was a silent, unwritten one, neither of them broke it. She couldn't recall the subject of Tom being raised once since they moved out to the house at Holtenaar.

'I think it would be best if you could recap a little. If you don't mind. I only remember the gist, but it must be ages since it happened . . .'

'Twenty-two years,' Judith answered. 'Twenty-two years and a few months.'

'And so then he was . . . ?'

'Seventeen.'

'Carry on. Or maybe you don't want to talk about it here? It's completely up to you. I'm just a listening ear and I respect your confidentiality utterly. But I don't need to remind you of that.'

Judith sipped her tea, undecided. But the hesitation was a pretence. She had said A, and since that was clearly a decision – either conscious or subconscious – she had obviously already lifted that particular lid. That's why I'm sitting here, she thought. To talk about B as well. If I don't raise it now, I'll dwell on it forever more.

'Yes, Tom was seventeen when it happened,' she said. 'He'd just had his birthday, even though it had been no time for cele-bration. I remember he'd had a watch from Robert, quite an expensive wristwatch, but by the next day he'd sold it.'

'He'd sold his birthday present?'

'I'm afraid so.'

'Because?'

'Because he needed money for drugs. Or maybe to pay for drugs he'd already injected. We didn't know the extent of his debts or the criminal activities he was mixed up in. Perhaps we had a sneaking suspicion, but it wasn't until later that we got the whole picture. Or the major part of it, at any rate.'

'A young man in dire circumstances?'

'To say the least. He'd had a tough time ever since puberty. Well, actually, it went further back than that. School had never really worked out. He was always getting into trouble with his classmates and teachers. They'd done tests and I don't know how many diagnoses he'd had. And of course, when drugs were part of the picture, it all went rapidly downhill. His father once used the expression *he's racing headlong towards the abyss*, when we were talking to some kind of social worker, and it was quite a good description of how things were.'

'He was Robert's son from a previous marriage, wasn't he?'

'Yes. His mum died when the boy was only two. I came on the scene a few years later. Robert and I got married the year before Tom started school.'

'And you adopted him?'

'Yes. I signed a document assuming full parental responsibility. Robert wanted it to be that way . . . and I did too, of course.'

'Of course?'

'Yes.'

Maria Rosenberg raised an eyebrow but made no comment. There was a pause while a motorbike sputtered past down in the street. Otherwise very little noise from the city made its way into the room; the building was old and built well and the window behind the heavy curtains had thick double glazing. The therapist had actually alluded to this once at the beginning: while most of the time it was desirable for conversations to be wreathed in silence, it didn't do any harm to be reminded of the existence of the outside world now and

again. Judith cleared her throat and tried to straighten the delicate question mark that seemed to be hovering in the room.

'I really didn't have any doubts,' she explained. 'Not at the
beginning. I wanted to be Tom's mum. His real mum was dead
and I don't think he had any memory of her. But naturally, I
did start to wonder when he grew up the way he did.'

'Several years later?'

'Yes. But it didn't make any difference. I suppose I might
have had other feelings about the boy if he'd been my actual
birth child. I haven't discussed this with Robert though, obviously not. It was . . . well, a bit too sensitive, really.'

'Quite understandably. Certain things are better suited for
a therapist's ears; it's worth remembering that. Your husband
is how many years older than you? Is it ten, or am I wrong?'

'Nearly eleven. He'll be seventy this summer. He's not in
the best of health – we've already talked about that – but getting him to stop working is out of the question. He reckons
film-makers are at their peak between seventy and eighty. I
don't know how much truth there is in that.'

Maria Rosenberg laughed. 'It's exactly the same with ther-
apists. We reach our zenith just before we turn up our toes.
But what happened to that poor, aimless seventeen-year-old?
He disappeared without trace, if I remember correctly?'

Judith sighed. 'Absolutely right. He melted into thin air.'

'Hmm. And there was a proper search for him?'

'We searched high and low. And not just Robert and I. The
police had more than one cause to look for Tom. Not only
because they thought there might be criminal involvement in
his disappearance, but also because he was suspected of
a number of offences. If he hadn't disappeared, he'd probably
have been looking at a few years in a young offender institution.

They actually showed us a list of the things he'd been mixed up in, and it didn't make happy reading, I can assure you.'

Maria Rosenberg nodded again. 'What do you think happened to Tom? I remember what you said last time, but opinions can change.'

'I haven't changed my opinion. I'm convinced Tom's dead. Either someone murdered him . . . bumped him off, stuck a knife in him, whatever. Or he did it himself.'

'Without leaving any clues?'

'These things happen.'

'Undoubtedly. What's the current situation? Has he been officially declared dead by the authorities? Doesn't that usually happen after someone's been missing for ten to fifteen years?'

Judith shook her head. 'No, he's not been declared dead.'

'Why not?'

'Because Robert's against it. As long as there are close relatives still living, it's up to them to submit an application.'

'Yes, I know that. But why won't your husband take that step? It is because he still has hope?'

'I suppose so. But we don't talk about it any more. And a declaration of presumed death would just be a formality in any event. Tom had no possessions, Robert and I would be his only heirs . . . but won't it happen sooner or later anyway? I'm sure society has its efficient procedures even for this kind of thing.'

'Let's assume so,' Maria Rosenberg agreed, leaning forward and adopting her gentle but rather insistent smile. 'But then here comes a telephone call from someone purporting to be your son . . . in the middle of the night. A son who has been missing for more than twenty years. I must say you appear more composed than most people would be in your situation.'

Judith Bendler gazed at the monk for a few seconds before she replied.

'I'm not composed at all. I threw up my breakfast this morning and got off at Zwille station instead of Keymer Plejn. That's why I arrived five minutes late.'

The therapist maintained her discreet smile. 'I didn't say that you were composed. I said you *appeared* composed. So what do you think, then?'

'About the call?'

'Yes.'

'I don't just think. I *know*.'

'Know what?'

'That it was an imposter.'

'And what would he be after? Imposters are usually in pursuit of some kind of gain.'

Judith shook her head. 'I don't know. I actually have no idea.'

'But he's going to ring back?'

'So he said.'

Maria Rosenberg leant back in the armchair and thought about it for a moment.

'Forgive me for asking, but have you considered the possibility you dreamt the whole thing?'

Not only had she considered the possibility, she had been expecting the question.

'Oh yes. But I looked at the telephone before I left the house this morning. We've got caller ID and the number was still there.'

'I see. Did you write it down?'

'No, I intended to, but I couldn't find a pen. And just at that moment Robert rang from London and I had other things to think about. But it was a number from abroad, I know that much. And it . . .'

'Yes?'

'It would explain why he rang at that time of the night.'

'A different time zone?'

'Yes.'

'Quite a distant imposter, in other words?'

'Mm.'

Judith found it hard to decide whether Maria Rosenberg was being sympathetic or mildly sarcastic. Or whether she had the capacity for both at the same time; a combination, if so, that was inherent in her increasing wisdom.

'What did Robert think about the call? I assume you told him about it when he rang?'

'No . . . no, I didn't.'

'Why not?'

'He was in a rush. On his way to a meeting. He only rang to say good morning.'

'I see.'

Maria Rosenberg rose to her feet and took a turn around the room. This was one of her routines, something to do with the circulation in her legs. But it was also a way of achieving a break in the conversation. At least that was what Judith supposed. A kind of pause for breath and a subtle hint that it might be time to change tack. She waited until the therapist had resumed her seat in the armchair. Waited for the change of tack.

'Do you want to carry on talking about this telephone call, or should we turn to life in general?'

It was as close as you could get to a rhetorical question. For a moment Judith thought about the waves on the pebble beach again. Distance, the immense distance.

'That's enough, thanks.'

'Sure?'

'Yep. If he rings back, we can deal with it next time?'

'Excellent. That's decided. How's the dog after its operation?'

She didn't mention the telephone call when Robert rang on Thursday evening. He sounded tired and breathless, and she wondered whether the illness was taking a greater toll on him than he was willing to admit.

But she didn't raise that subject either. It would only have irritated him, and after she had replaced the receiver she began to question whether he would actually survive until the seventieth birthday she had referred to in conversation with Maria Rosenberg. Maybe he would, maybe he wouldn't. The thought of one day living in this beautiful house as a widow had been playing on her mind for some time, and it wasn't an idea she found particularly disturbing. It would be too much to say she was looking forward to it, but solitude, *relative* solitude, was a condition that seemed to offer more appeal and satisfaction the older she became. Perhaps it was because she had no brothers and sisters and had grown up without the irksome intrusion of others, aside from her mother and almost perpetually absent father. Few friends, used to looking after herself, happy in her own company; these were certainly influencing factors. He who makes a friend of solitude is never disappointed, she had read somewhere, a truth she could unreservedly acknowledge.

So it didn't matter that Robert had been obliged to stay in

London an extra day. It really didn't. She slept well all night; she had naturally felt slightly apprehensive that the telephone would ring again in the hour of the wolf, but it kept as silent and uncommunicative as the rest of the house. Django lay on his bed under the bench in the kitchen as usual. As she had said to Maria Rosenberg, his operation had gone well, but he was eleven and obviously the days of this once splendid dog were numbered too. Judith knew that she would never remarry or indeed enter into any sort of relationship after Robert had gone, but she would certainly get a new dog. Probably a Rottweiler, like Django. Self-sufficiency had its limits, both in emotional and practical terms. A woman alone in a large house is quite different from a woman alone in the same house with a loyal guard dog.

She walked Django after breakfast, through the sparse wood up to the water tower, then down and along by the river, over the old wooden bridge and back on the other side. Just short of an hour; in the past, with a young dog and a mistress who had not yet reached fifty, the same stretch would have taken half the time. The trees had started to yellow, but the leaves had not yet begun to fall; it was one of those beautiful, clear autumn days and she tried to keep Tom and the telephone call as far from her thoughts as possible.

Which wasn't easy once they had started to worry her. Images from that day twenty-two years ago came back to her too, as if someone – she herself, who else? – had discovered a forgotten photograph album and couldn't help opening it and flicking through.

But the pictures were moving, like something from an old film archive rather than an album. Herself. Tom. Then Robert.

The apartment on Kantorsteeg in Aarlach.

In the month of July.

That last night.

The violence. The panic. The deed.

How could someone so young be so terribly damaged? So arrogant and so hateful to everything and everyone, and above all to his own parents.

This was what she had asked herself then and still asked herself today.

She remembered scenes from further back as well. When he bit Robert in the calf because he couldn't have his own way – and wouldn't let go, almost like a fighting dog whose jaws had locked. He was five years old and Robert had to hit him with a heavy book to get him off.

The anger in him that was almost impossible to control. She remembered one of the psychologists at school had said that Tom, and boys of his sort – she had actually used the expression *of his sort* – usually quietened down at the onset of puberty. Where in the world did that kind of knowledge come from? In any event, this turned out to be the case, at least partially. Tom had changed when he turned thirteen, but not really for the better. He had become more introverted, distant and difficult. Although admittedly he had started to acquire some friends, they were the sort that would have terrified any parent. She remembers one of them in particular, a boy called Shark – that was the name he went by at any rate – who had a swastika tattooed on his forearm. More than three years older than Tom, and with a father and older brother in prison for murder and grievous bodily harm respectively. And Shark hadn't been the only one.

A time of evil: when she looked back, this was the phrase that often sprang to mind.

She opened the gate and let Django into the garden. Enough of that, she thought, it's all dead and buried. Whoever rang, it wasn't Tom. If you're going to rise again, you do it on the third day, not out of the blue after twenty-two years.

She spent the whole of Friday afternoon working at her desk. Her major biography of Erasmus of Rotterdam was planned for next autumn and she had promised the publisher a first completed manuscript before Christmas. She had been working on the project for nearly four years, having originally estimated it would take three, but that was before she fully understood what a colossus Erasmus was and how much had been written about him. And *by* him. But the publisher was reasonable and solvent, and her name and her previous works were a guarantee of the quality they sought and for which they were renowned. Better a good book every five years than a mediocre one every two.

Robert called again about seven. He sounded more upbeat than in the morning, all the meetings and bizarre problems that always beset every new film project had been resolved, at least temporarily, so she felt it was time to tell him. To avoid complications, she shifted the episode forward twenty-four hours; it couldn't possibly make any difference.

'Something happened last night. I wanted to tell you about it this morning, but I knew you had a demanding day ahead.'

'Oh yes?'

'I received a telephone call.'

'Mm?'

'Half past three in the morning. It was someone masquerading as Tom.'

'What?'

'Yes. The telephone rang and I answered . . . without thinking. He claimed he was Tom and said he thought we should meet.'

'What the hell?'

'Exactly. I was utterly speechless. I'd had a strange dream immediately beforehand as well.'

'What . . . what did he say?'

'Hardly anything at all. Just that we should meet. Said he would ring back. Then he hung up. We can't have been talking for more than a minute . . . or less.'

There was silence on the line, but she could hear Robert's breathing. It suddenly sounded laboured again, as it had that morning. I shouldn't have said anything, she thought. Not mentioned it to him at all.

'Where was he ringing from?'

'Somewhere abroad. I don't know where.'

'Didn't the caller display show the number?'

'Yes. But it had disappeared by the time I checked.'

'Disappeared?'

'Maybe I pressed the wrong button. I don't know, it wasn't there anyway.'

Because that was true. When she returned home after her visit to the therapist, she had looked for the number, but it had gone. In which case she must have mistakenly deleted it when she spoke to Robert.

Unless . . . ?

But she dismissed the thought.

'How did he sound?'

'He sounded . . . well, there wasn't anything in particular. Quite a normal man's voice. Not especially deep, not especially high . . . slightly hoarse, maybe. We didn't exchange many words.'

'And he was going to ring back?'

'So he said.'

'You . . . you didn't think you recognized his voice at all?'

'Good Lord, Robert, of course not.'

'I'm sorry. It's just come as a surprise. We're obviously dealing with an imposter, someone impersonating Tom . . . But why? That's the question.'

'That's what I've been puzzling over all day, and I haven't come up with an answer. He has to be after something . . . unless it was just a prankster.'

'A prankster?'

Robert suddenly suffered a coughing fit; she could hear him turn away from the telephone and ask someone for a glass of water.

'Aren't you alone?'

He took a few gulps before answering.

'I'm ringing from down in the hotel bar. Don't worry, it's not being tapped.'

Tapped? Why would it be tapped?

'I'll be home tomorrow afternoon and we can talk about it then.'

'Of course, that's fine.'

'But if he rings again, make sure you get the number. And call me at once, even if it's the middle of the night. What time did you say you received the call?'

'Half past three in the morning. A couple of minutes after.'

'Christ.'

'Yes. But as you say, we can discuss it tomorrow. Maybe it was just a nutter who thinks this kind of thing is funny.'

Breathing heavily, Robert gave this a moment's thought.

'Yes, let's settle for that, at least for the time being. The world's crawling with idiots.'

'I can tell you have experience from the film business, dear.'

It was a standing joke. He laughed and then hung up.

She was reminded of one of the police officers too, one of the investigators working on Tom's disappearance. He popped into her head just as she turned off the television after the nine o'clock news.

He was quite a young detective inspector, who she seemed to remember was called deJong, or possibly deJung. Or maybe just Jung. He came to speak to them several times in the month after Tom disappeared, on one occasion with a female colleague and the other times alone. He had impressed her, and Robert too, with his measured, courteous tone. He had in fact been questioning them, but neither she nor Robert interpreted it as such: that his intention was to trip them up. Or at least satisfy himself that they weren't involved in Tom's disappearance in any way; they might have worked out the precariousness of the boy's situation and consequently arranged safe haven for him in some gloomy place on a foreign continent, beyond reach of the long arm of the law. Or the long arm of the Maardam police, at any rate.

But the realization that this had been the aim, or at least partial aim, of the conversations didn't dawn on them until afterwards, and she remembers them both shaking their heads at their naivety.

On one occasion deJong/deJung/Jung had asked if it would surprise them if Tom had somehow got hold of a large amount of money and decided to use it to go on the run, change identity and stay away for the rest of his life.

'Are you implying he might have robbed a bank?' Robert had asked.

'I didn't say that,' the quiet detective had replied. 'But since you've suggested it, what do you make of that theory?'

'Highly implausible,' Robert had said after a moment's thought. 'Tom is a drug addict and a small-time crook, not a criminal genius.'

She had thought it wasn't a particularly flattering verdict to pass on his own son, but deJong/deJung/Jung had just nodded and afforded himself a discreet smile.

She wondered if he was still working on the force, this nice detective, and whether it would be possible to ask for him, in the event the imposter made good his promise to ring back.

Absolutely not, she decided, draining the last drops from the glass of wine that had accompanied the television news. Under no circumstances should the police be involved.

But he didn't ring back.

He didn't ring on Saturday or Sunday, or any time the following week, or for the rest of the month. She and Robert discussed the matter more than once and she soon sensed he had reservations. Put differently, this meant she might have dreamt the whole thing, and there had never been a nocturnal telephone call. He didn't push this argument very hard and she

didn't bother to refute it. But she recalled that Maria Rosenberg had suggested the same thing, and as the days passed and
nothing happened, she too began to experience some doubt.

A telephone call in the middle of the night, over in thirty
seconds.

From a person missing for twenty-two years.

The number deleted from the caller display.

What was there to suggest it didn't all boil down to this?
She had imagined it, she had dreamt it, it had seemed completely real, but it had never happened.

She regretted telling her therapist about the call.

She regretted talking to Robert.

Time passed, the trees lost their leaves and she became
more and more absorbed in the sixteenth century and Erasmus of Rotterdam.

The second call came one week in November.

On a grey, rainy Tuesday afternoon she was going through one of the most difficult chapters in the book – about the complex relationship between Erasmus and Martin Luther – and wasn't going to answer at first. Normally she had the telephone switched off while she was working, but she had been talking to her publisher at lunchtime and had forgotten to press the button.

Later, after she had hung up, she wondered whether she might have had a premonition, and, if so, whether it was the premonition that made her lift the receiver. But probably not, she thought, it was too easy to dream up warning signs and omens with the benefit of hindsight. Our need to see clearly in the rear-view mirror when the future looks increasingly uncertain; she remembered she and Robert had been talking about related phenomena not so long ago, about seeing patterns and so on, about simplistic solutions.

'Hello?'

'Judith Bendler?'

'Yes.'

'It's Tom.'

A sudden tremble passed through her body, from her toes upwards, just like seven weeks ago – an observation that

surprised her – and for a second her field of vision shrank to a
tunnel. A narrow tunnel, tinged with yellow, with walls that
seemed to pulsate and move. But she recovered at once and
even had the presence of mind to look at the caller display for
the number.

Unknown.

'Hello?'

'Yes, I'm still here. What do you want?'

He gave a short, rasping laugh.

'What do I want? I want us to meet, naturally. As I explained
last time.'

'Who are you?'

'Tom. Don't tell me you've forgotten me.'

'Which Tom?'

'Tom, your son. You're my mother. What are you trying to
suggest?'

'I . . . I'm not suggesting anything. But I find it hard to
believe you're telling the truth.'

'And how do you reach that conclusion?'

She thought about it for a moment. Now he sounded
ironic, almost teasing, as though it amused him to be talking
to her like this. She swallowed, finding the strength to continue.

'My son Tom went missing more than twenty years ago.
Both my husband and I are convinced he's dead.'

'I'm not dead.'

'No, apparently not. But neither are you the Tom you're
masquerading as.'

'Shame on you!'

'Pardon?'

'I said shame on you! Don't you realize you should be ashamed to talk to me like that?'

'No. Not if you're an imposter.'

'I'm not an imposter.'

'How can I know that?'

'By meeting me. That's why I'm ringing. I promised to last time, have you forgotten?'

She gave it another moment's thought.

'And why do you want to meet me?'

'Is it strange for a son to want to see his mother?'

'Yes, if he's kept himself away for twenty-two years.'

'He had his reasons, as you know.'

'No, I don't know what reasons you're talking about.'

'I'll explain everything when I see you.'

'I might not have any desire to see you. Or any desire to continue this conversation.'

For a few seconds there was silence. No breathing, no distant waves. Please, God, let him give up, she thought. Make him admit defeat and never get in touch again.

He cleared his throat. 'I think you'll regret it if you don't agree to meet me.'

A threat? She couldn't decide, but he had lowered his voice and spoken more slowly.

'Where are you?' she asked.

'Here,' he replied instantly. 'Here in Maardam. We could meet tomorrow.'

'Tomorrow?'

'Why not?'

'Robert's away. He won't be back until Sunday.'

'You and me, that'll do. What do you say?'

Why? she thought. Why didn't I hang up long ago?

And, as if it were already too late, she said: 'Where? Where did you have in mind?'

'Cafe Intrigo. I suggest Intrigo tomorrow, at three o'clock. There's usually lots of room there in the afternoon.'

'OK,' she swallowed. 'But I've got a meeting in town at four, just so you know.'

'An hour should do it. Fine, see you tomorrow.'

I have a meeting at four o'clock. Why had she made that up? A kind of insurance she'd plucked out of the air, but after she had pushed all her papers about Erasmus and Luther to one side and was sitting with her chin on her hands, looking out at the rain and the bare trees, she considered it an allowable lie in the circumstances.

But Robert? Should she inform Robert? He had left for Geneva that morning and wouldn't be back until Sunday. Exactly as she had said to the imposter, not twisting the truth in that instance.

No, she decided. Robert will have to wait. He thinks I'm imagining it anyway, and if I do manage to persuade him to the contrary, he's only going to get worried and inundate me with a lot of pointless instructions. Better to tell him what happened when he's home. I'll have to . . . have to play this game alone.

For the time being, at any rate.

Game?

It must have been at least ten years since she'd last set foot in Cafe Intrigo, but it looked exactly as she remembered. From the outside, at least: rather run-down and slightly sad and yet somehow intact. A little forlorn, she thought, since the tables and chairs usually on the wide pavement had been brought inside; it was November, after all, and the season for sitting outside was over.

Yes, everything comes to an end one day, she thought, dismissing the platitude as soon as it entered her head. She had taken the half past one train from Holtenaar and there was still almost an hour before the rendezvous. It might have been her intention to be out in good time, but now that she was standing in the drizzle on the other side of the street, she found it hard to see the point in having to wait. To be forced to while away fifty aimless minutes before it was time to sit down with her dead adopted son . . . no, that was definitely not the soft option.

I have to think about something else, she realized. I have to pull myself together, or this is going to get out of hand.

She started walking, making her way down the narrow lanes to Langgraacht and continuing along the canal in a northerly direction. All at once she recognized where she was: forty years earlier, when she had arrived in the city and started at the university as a student of literature and philosophy, she had shared a small flat on Leuwenstraat with two other girls. They had only lived up there under the roof for three terms, but it had been an exciting and important period of her life. It was difficult to believe Robert had arrived on the scene less than a year later, and that her time as a student, which had seemed so full and rich in promise, both at the time and afterwards, had in fact been so short.

And life with Robert had been so long, was the inevitable sequitur. Thirty-seven years, she thought. I've been with the same guy for nearly four decades, my entire adult life. What happened there?

It wasn't the first time the question had reared its head, of course, but right now, as she dragged her feet past Bachtermann's, the old cheesemonger and wine merchant on the corner of Leenerstraat and Kuijverstraat, it felt more emotionally charged than it had for some time. What was it in a person's life that sometimes made time intensify, fill with meaning and substance, and sometimes dilute and cool? Slow down? she thought. Like a plane coming in to land, on the landing strip called Death.

Another bizarre image. Waves on the pebble beach? Landing on a graveyard?

Shaking her head, she folded her umbrella. There was a temporary break in the rain and a sudden ray of sunshine streamed through the naked branches of the trees along Wilmersgraacht. Surely it must be Wilmersgraacht? The small sign she caught sight of on the corner confirmed she was right in her assumption.

I know where I am, she observed. At least in a spatial dimension.

She checked the time next. It was quarter to three and she realized she would probably be at Intrigo a few minutes late.

That was excellent. It would be he who was waiting for her, not the other way around.

She pulled the door open, went inside, took a couple of steps into the narrow, elongated cafe and stood still. Her gaze wandered along the rows of tables, straight ahead and to the left, as she waited for someone to notice her.

Waited for *him* to notice her. As far as she could remember, there was nowhere else to sit in Intrigo, no hidden corners where you could be a bit more private. The customers who were there could be seen from the entrance, from the position where she had just stopped.

It was quite empty, apart from a quartet of elderly ladies to the left and three gentlemen spread out in the main part of the room, two at their separate tables by the window and one by the wall on the other side of the counter. All three were facing the entrance and all three – she formed the impression they did this in turn – raised their eyes to look at her. Briefly, before returning to their respective pursuits: a pasta dish, a book, a beer and, if she wasn't mistaken, a race card. She looked at her watch. Seven minutes past three.

A waiter appeared and half smiled at her.

'I – I'm waiting for someone. I don't think he's here yet.'

'Maybe you'd like to take a seat while you're waiting?'

She sat down at the table nearest the door but didn't order anything. The waiter disappeared. The three men remained in their places, immobile, and as none of them appeared to be taking any notice of her, she was able to observe them more closely.

What struck her immediately was that all three appeared to be the right age. Forty, give or take five years. Had Tom been alive, he would have been thirty-nine. Is it one of them? she thought. In that case, why . . . why is he just sitting there? And why didn't we arrange some sort of sign to identify one another? Even if he were Tom, he couldn't expect me to recognize him. And what is there to say he knows what I look like?

On the other hand: they had agreed to meet at three o'clock and there was only one woman alone in the whole place. In other words, she thought, in other words, he hadn't yet arrived. For some reason.

Unless?

She studied the men a little more carefully, one at a time. They were remarkably similar in appearance too. Not one of them had a beard or moustache, not one of them was wearing spectacles. All three had quite short hair, though when the one furthest away momentarily turned his head, she could see he was actually sporting a ponytail. All three looked in good shape, normal build, no excess weight. A charcoal-grey jacket and dark shirt, a white shirt with knitted waistcoat, a dark-blue polo neck. Nothing that stuck out. Three European men of standard model and in the beginnings of middle age.

Which one? she thought again. If she had to choose.

Perhaps the one sitting nearest to her? At a window table with a cup of coffee and apparently deep in a thick, well-thumbed paperback. But his face didn't match her memory of what Tom looked like as a seventeen-year-old. The eyes were a little too close together and the jaw too long. The mouth was too thin.

But in God's name, she thought. It can't be him. Why am I sitting here speculating like this? Tom is dead.

While she was engaged in these fruitless reflections, the waiter had taken payment from the ladies' quartet in the section on the left and now came back to her table.

'Are you sure you won't have anything?'

She looked at her watch again. Quarter past three.

'No, thank you,' she said. 'I do believe there's been a misunderstanding. My friend is obviously not coming. Thank you for letting me sit down.'

He gave a non-committal nod and withdrew. She stood up, pushed the chair back under the table and left Cafe Intrigo.

'Strange, isn't it?'

Maria Rosenberg looked genuinely worried. As if for once she had come up against a form of human behaviour that fell outside the range. Her personal, very broad range.

'I think so too,' Judith Bendler said, adjusting the cushion behind her back. 'I honestly don't understand what this is about.'

'I'd be surprised if you did,' the therapist said. 'I must say I'm rather concerned on your behalf.'

It was Thursday morning and the appointment had been scheduled for some time, but Judith thought she would have made sure she had a consultation regardless. In any event, the evening and night following the futile visit to Cafe Intrigo had been difficult. She had just about held it together on the train journey back to Holtenaar and for the first few hours after she got home. But after she had given Django his short evening walk and the dog had settled down on his bed in the kitchen, it was as if something inside her snapped. A crack opened up and from it welled a torrent of nameless fear. When Robert rang about nine, she had already drunk three glasses of red wine. He could undoubtedly hear in her voice that she had been drinking and it was with tremendous self-control she managed to keep the real reason to herself.

Yes, she'd had a couple of hot toddies, she explained, because she felt a bit under the weather. But drunk? Of course not.

What he would have said if she had told him about her

failed meeting with their dead son, she didn't like to contemplate.

'But why?' Maria Rosenberg wanted to know. 'Why is it so important to keep Robert out of this? Can you please explain that to me?'

She thought for a few moments but could find no mitigating explanation.

'He thinks it's in my imagination. And the fact that this damned individual didn't turn up at the cafe would just confirm his opinion. Don't forget that . . .'

'Yes?'

'Don't forget there've been couple of episodes in my past.'

'Do you mean Majorna?'

'Yes, of course I mean Majorna. For someone once a psych patient, the road back is short. You know that better than most.'

Maria Rosenberg nodded, pursed her lips and muttered about the way of things and people's stupidity and then took another mouthful of tea. 'It's a delusion.'

'Delusion?'

'Robert's, I mean. I don't believe for a second that you're imagining it. You weren't when you were admitted either. As I recall it's ten years ago. Correct me if I'm wrong.'

It was true. In both respects. Judith had started therapy in conjunction with her discharge from Majorna, and whatever had been wrong with her then, twelve years ago and subsequently ten, she had never suffered from hallucinations again. No matter how Robert viewed it. And she hadn't been kept in more than two weeks each time.

'It doesn't matter, anyway,' the therapist continued. 'For

the moment, let's leave Robert out of this. But let's at least try to be rational. What do we know with certainty?'

Judith shrugged. 'Carry on.'

'With pleasure. Well, we know with certainty there's a cuckoo out there aiming to frighten you. He's phoned twice and impersonated your son, who's been missing for twenty-two years and is probably dead. You agree to meet said cuckoo at a cafe but he doesn't turn up. The question is . . . the question is, of course, what does he want from all of this? Is this an accurate summary?'

'Totally accurate,' Judith said.

'Another question is whether we should be taking any precautionary measures.'

Judith noted she had started using the pronoun *we*, and she felt a sudden rush of gratitude. It wasn't necessarily about being looked after, but at least she had a confidante. Someone who knew and who cared. Who was ready to join her so that together they could solve the problem that had arisen.

But measures? *Precautionary measures?*

'What do you mean?' she asked.

Maria Rosenberg removed her spectacles and began to chew on the arm.

'What you need to do next time he gets in touch. That's the question I suggest we need to discuss.'

'I lay awake for four hours last night thinking about that,' Judith said. 'Unfortunately I didn't come up with anything.'

The therapist shook her head worriedly. 'There was a quite a long period of time between his first approach and his second. It makes you wonder whether the same thing will happen again. Nearly two months, wasn't it?'

'Almost,' Judith said. 'Seven weeks by my reckoning.'

'Hm. What do you think about contacting the police?'

'No,' Judith replied instantly. 'Naturally, I thought about that possibility while I was awake last night, but decided against. What could they do? There isn't a single lead for them to follow. No telephone number. Nothing. And he . . .'

'Yes?'

'He hasn't actually made any threats. Just said he wants to meet me. That's not illegal, as far as I'm aware.'

'Presumably not,' Maria Rosenberg sighed. 'No, we need to focus on settling this without recourse to law enforcement agencies. At least for the moment. Can you manage to live and work as normal?'

Judith considered for a second. 'I'd really like to have closer contact with you. If I could ring, for example?'

'Of course,' the therapist exclaimed, flinging her arms wide, almost as if she wanted to embrace her client – if they hadn't been sitting so comfortably and if the distance between them had been less than a metre and a half. 'You can ring me twenty-four hours a day. And even if nothing happens, I suggest we meet once a week. More often if you feel you need to. How does that sound?'

'Sounds good,' Judith said.

'And what about Robert? Are you intending to inform your husband about the state of affairs?'

'I don't know.'

'Where is he now?'

'Geneva.'

'Is it a film?'

'Yes, he's coming home on Sunday.'

Maria Rosenberg gave it a moment's thought. 'In that case

you have a few more days to decide. But maybe it's tending towards . . .'

'Towards waiting until I get another call,' Judith Bendler said. 'Yes, I think I prefer that alternative.'

'All right, that's agreed,' the therapist concluded.

And yet, she thought when she emerged onto Keymerstraat an hour later, and yet Robert obviously had to know.

Eventually, anyway; because after all they were the only two who knew what had actually happened that night. She could discuss all manner of things with Maria Rosenberg, but there was a line that couldn't be crossed. A line it was safest not even to come near.

She realized she'd left her umbrella upstairs in reception, but the rain had stopped and it was only 200 metres to the station.

It didn't take seven weeks.

It took three days.

Counting from her wasted trip to Cafe Intrigo. Saturday afternoon, a few minutes after half past two, and this time she definitely had a premonition. The caller display again showed that the number was unknown and when she lifted the receiver she would have been surprised if it had been anyone else.

'Yes?'

'Judith Bendler?'

Just as on both previous calls, he began by asking if it was her. A sudden thought flashed through her head: what if she were to say she was someone different? A female police officer, for example, working on harassment cases and allied crimes who was drafted in where appropriate. What would happen then?

But she rejected the idea.

'What do you want? I don't have time.'

'I think you do. After all, you had time to come to the cafe.'

'How do you know? You weren't there.'

'I was there.'

'Nonsense. I waited for a quarter of an hour and you didn't come.'

'I was there. Of course I was there.'

What is he talking about? she thought, recalling the images of the three men at their tables. The book, the pasta, the race card; the polo neck, the jacket, the knitted waistcoat. Their total lack of interest in her existence as she sat waiting. Almost antipathy, she thought, now she had had time to recover. Even so, could one of them . . . ?

'You were wearing a light beige coat and a blue scarf. You hung your coat over the back of a chair and sat by a table quite close to the door. Do you really not remember me?'

She didn't respond. She could find no words and all of a sudden it felt as though her mind was starting to lose its balance. Or splinter. Or both. No thoughts surfaced and she wondered whether she was actually in the grip of a mental breakdown.

Several seconds of silence passed.

'Why don't you remember me?'

Put the phone down, she tried to tell herself, you must put the phone down. This is a dead man who's ringing you. You're taking leave of your senses.

But she couldn't bring herself to and instead, clutching the receiver tightly, she lowered herself onto the chair in the hall. She had taken the call here, on her way out with Django, and now the dog was standing by the door, giving her a reproachful look, wagging his tail dolefully.

He's dead, she thought. Tom's dead. That's why I didn't see him.

The silence continued. No waves. No breathing.

The dead don't need to breathe.

He's come back to punish me.

'Why aren't you saying anything? You talked to me at the cafe.'

She found the strength to make a weak protest.

'I didn't talk to you at the cafe. You weren't there . . .'

But almost before he said it, she understood.

'No, members of your social class don't generally notice people who wait on them.'

The waiter.

She replaced the receiver, rose to her feet and picked up the dog's lead.

A problem that can't be resolved on a long walk with a dog is best avoided.

It was Mr Klimke, her philosophy and religious studies teacher at grammar school, who had written these words of wisdom on the blackboard in a lesson once. He went on to explain that it was a practical illustration of another classic problem: *how to pick one's battles.*

The slow walk with Django that Saturday took nearly two hours and, had she followed her old teacher's advice, this is one battle from which she would have withdrawn. She had no solution and consequently should have discounted the whole thing; ignored the imposter, who, for some mysterious and probably quite bizarre reason, was intent on subjecting her to this unpleasantness.

The snag was, it was impossible to opt out of this battle. In theory perhaps, but not in practice.

The realization that it was the waiter who was the villain of the piece meant one good thing, at least: she could extract herself from the supernatural morass. That was not where the explanation lay. It wasn't a dead avenger she was facing, or a ghost. Whoever this irritating idiot was, and however twisted his intentions, he was a person of flesh and blood.

That's something at least, Judith Bendler thought as she knelt to dry Django's paws in the same cosy, safe and welcoming hall in which she had spoken to the imposter for the third time. That's something. Tomorrow I'll ring Cafe Intrigo and get a name. I do actually remember very clearly what he looked like.

She couldn't really account for why she was procrastinating until the following day.

It might have been because the waiter, in common with the three male customers, had been in his forties.

And it might have been because there seemed to be – at least with the benefit of hindsight – something vaguely familiar about his face.

A young woman's voice answered.

She apologized for her unusual request, but said she wanted to contact a waiter who worked at Intrigo, the reason being that he had helped with a little problem when she had visited the cafe a few days previously and she would really like to thank him personally.

It had been Wednesday afternoon, to be more precise, at about three. A man in his forties, short dark hair, polite, considerate; and helpful, as she'd said.

The young woman hesitated, but not for long, before asking her to wait while she looked at the rota. In thirty seconds she was back.

'I think it would be best if I could take your name first.'

'Of course. Judith Simmering.'

She had been prepared for the question and had her maiden name at the ready.

'Thanks. The waiter in question must have been Tom Bendler. He was working on Wednesday.'

Bendler. She swallowed the impulse to hang up.

'Thank you. Do you by any chance know how I could contact him? Or when he'll be on next?'

'He won't be back. He finished on Friday.'

'He finished on Friday? How . . . how come?'

'He was only employed for a month, temporary cover. The regular waiter's back now.'

'I see. But maybe you have his telephone number? Or an address?'

'Only an address, actually. 25B Armastenstraat. I have to get on with my work now, but I hope you find him.'

'Thank you. Thank you very much for your help.'

'Not at all. Hope to see you here again soon.'

The idea of hiring a private detective came to her out of the blue, and yet it was perfectly obvious. She could see it was precisely the right measure to take under . . . what was it called? . . . *current circumstances.* She couldn't appeal to the police and she didn't want to involve Robert, not yet, at any rate. Maria Rosenberg was ruled out; she was a seventy-two-year-old therapist, not a snoop. And heading off to Armastenstraat on her own in an attempt to do something struck her as the least attractive option of all.

Forget the whole thing? Not choose this battle?

Out of the question. In for a penny, in for a pound. She had taken the bait at Cafe Intrigo and in so doing had committed herself. To what was unclear, but in any event she felt it was high time to take the initiative. Up to now, in the two months since the whole thing started, it had been the imposter in charge, fooling with her, calling the tune. Now it was time to adjust positions somewhat. High time.

Before the seeds of doubt could be planted she went into action, unearthing the thick business section of the telephone directory and finding eight firms listed under *Private Investigators, Detective Agencies*. She decided on number seven, for reasons she couldn't explain. Maybe just because she liked the name. Her very first boyfriend had been called Herbert.

Herbert Knoll. Private detective. Discretion a point of honour. Maardam 500221.

She dialled the number, and although it was Sunday morning, the call was answered. He was a man of around her age, at a guess, and despite sounding rather tired and rather vacant, he assured her he was happy to listen to her summary of what she required help with. If she could take five minutes to explain the facts, he undertook to tell her whether or not he would accept the job.

And explain the facts she did. It possibly took a little longer than the stipulated five minutes, but Herbert Knoll hmmed and listened and, judging by his short supplementary questions and interjections, he sounded increasingly interested. When she had finished, after telling him about that morning's conversation with the waitress at Intrigo, he declared the case to be within his area of expertise. He suggested they meet as soon as possible and they arranged an appointment at his office for the following day. 6 Ruydersteeg at eleven o'clock. Would that suit her?

Judith Bendler said it suited her perfectly.

After putting the phone down, she was left with a feeling of triumph akin to the success she felt when finally making an appointment at the dentist's, and for the next four hours she devoted her full concentration to Erasmus of Rotterdam.

She hadn't promised to pick Robert up at the airport, but decided to anyway. Maybe because she owed him something, a little gesture of goodwill to show she loved him, despite choosing not to inform him about recent developments relating to Tom.

Since he would never be in a position to interpret or understand this gesture, it was on the face of it a muddled way of reasoning, but that didn't bother her. A marriage was like a pair of scales, Maria Rosenberg had once suggested; it never did any harm to put good deeds into the balance, even if they were not immediately recognized or appreciated.

These were the thoughts occupying her mind as she waited in the arrivals hall, but they melted away the moment she caught sight of her husband.

He looked terrible.

As though he had lost ten kilos and shrunk as many centimetres. She knew Robert didn't like flying, even if she did sometimes feel he spent more time in the sky than he did on the ground. It was something to do with poor oxygen intake – the dry air inside the plane had a bearing on it – and the problem hadn't improved over the years.

But on this Sunday evening she was conscious of something more: this haggard old man, who was actually her husband, apparently wearing a suit two sizes too big, in all likelihood did not have long to live.

In accordance with his wishes they had never spoken in great detail about his illness, but all the same it had played a part in their relationship over the last few years. A kind of invisible presence, she used to think, something you knew was there but avoided talking about, or even referring to. In several discussions with Maria Rosenberg about this approach, they had both taken issue with it, but since Robert was the one who was ill, he had a certain edge when it came to strategic choice.

But now he was not simply ill, he was dying.

His breathing, when he gave her his usual quick kiss, told its own story.

It became all the more evident on the car journey back from Sechshafen.

'I have to make a confession,' he began. 'There is no film project in Geneva. Well, there might be. But not that I'm involved in. I've been to see a specialist.'

'A specialist?'

'A doctor. I've been in hospital for observation for four days. They've done thousands of tests and it's led to . . . it's led to a prognosis.'

She didn't answer. I know, she thought. I knew it.

'Six months,' he said. 'A year at the outside. There are ways of prolonging the suffering a bit, but I don't intend to go down that route.'

He placed his left hand on her knee.

'You'll have to forgive me, Judith. I'm going to leave you.'

'Robert, I don't know what to say. I'm sorry,' she sobbed as she stroked his hand.

'You don't need to say anything at all. I think we can

celebrate one last decent Christmas together, at least. And start a new year. Dr Celan reckoned I would remain pain-free . . . relatively pain-free . . . for another two or three months. Then . . .'

'Then?'

'Then it will probably get worse. How's it going with Erasmus? I'm really looking forward to having the time to read your manuscript and discussing it with you.'

How typical of Robert, she thought. He wanted to deal with the subject of his own impending death in three minutes, but would doubtless be able to sit dissecting her 600-page text for days on end. That's how it was, and she realized that in truth she was thankful he was made that way.

But was he also ready to talk about Tom?

Good question, Judith Bendler thought, as she turned off towards Holtenaar. But in view of current circumstances, I'll put that off for a few days.

Knoll's private detective agency occupied no more than twelve square metres.

A desk with a swivel chair, a filing cabinet and an armchair for visitors. That was it.

Apart from two framed diplomas on the wall to the right of the desk, dusty and illegible, and a small, dirty window facing a brick wall, letting in a minimum of sombre daylight.

Her guess as to his age seemed accurate: the same as her own. His weight was about twice hers, and he filled up the room in a way that was rather impressive. Faintly tinted spectacles pushed up onto his forehead, bulbous nose, shaved head, unshaven cheeks and chin.

'Welcome to Dr Knoll's Think Tank,' he began. 'Whatever your first impressions of my spartan surroundings, I wish to inform you that I solve ninety per cent of the cases I accept. That's more than any of my colleagues in this city can claim, considerably more, I can assure you. Please sit down.'

Judith sat down on the unadorned leather chair. *Doctor?* she thought. She had a sudden impression of a scene in one of Robert's films, in which the man in front of her was actually a famous actor, not a real private detective.

But maybe it doesn't matter, she thought in confusion.

Maybe it's what he always claims, that film is life condensed, as simple as that.

'Let's go through everything one more time, to make sure I haven't missed any important detail,' Herbert Knoll continued, opening his notebook at a new page. He clicked the end of his ballpoint pen a few times, squinting at her. 'Please go ahead, and I'd rather have ten pieces of information too many than too few.'

She began her account. About the three telephone calls, the visit to Cafe Intrigo, the three men and the waiter.

That he reportedly no longer worked at the cafe, that he was masquerading under the name of Tom Bendler and his address was 25B Armastenstraat.

And the background. Tom's disappearance in July 1973; not in detail, obviously, she hadn't divulged that to anyone, but the official version, the one the police followed and the one she still knew by heart after all these years and all the occasions she had repeated it.

'All right,' he said after she had finished, and he went on to ask for clarification on a number of points: the imposter's appearance in detail; Tom's appearance when he went missing; her opinion on what was really at issue; what her husband thought; how she wanted the investigator to handle the imposter when he had tracked him down (was he just to be kept under surveillance or had she considered other measures?); how she would like to receive the reporting; and whether she was prepared to pay for the first few days' work immediately, and thereafter according to the tariff, subject to unforeseen expenses and complications.

Judith answered the questions to the best of her ability, requested a report on developments whenever there was something to report, preferably daily, and paid for three days' work in advance.

Herbert Knoll held out his hand to her across the desk and promised to ring her within twenty-four hours, regardless of the situation.

'Who is he?' Judith said. 'That's clearly the most important question. And what does he want?'

'I've understood,' Herbert Knoll said, as she took her leave. 'You can rest easy and count on me.'

On the train back to Holtenaar she unexpectedly burst into tears.

For Maria Rosenberg it would probably not have been unexpected, but for Judith it was. She never wept; she couldn't remember the last time she had, but it must have been many years before. Maybe at the time of her second stay at Majorna, although she didn't associate her bouts of depression in any way with tears.

So why was she sitting on a suburban train, crying? Fortunately, there were very few other passengers so early in the afternoon; no one noticed the state she was in and she made no effort to hide it. To her surprise she felt better; something strained and tense had been released and she supposed that was the whole point of weeping. That's why people did it.

She didn't really know what she expected from the private detective. He might not achieve very much of any value, but the least one could hope for was that he found the bogus Tom and uncovered a few things about him. If he could somehow establish his real identity, there was every chance she would soon be rid of the matter. Wouldn't she?

But in fact, her tears had little to do with Herbert Knoll or the imposter. She soon realized it was Robert at the heart of the knot that needed to be loosened. In a year's time he wouldn't be around. They had lived together for an awfully long time; admittedly, they had no children together and without a doubt their relationship in recent years had not been especially close. Their sex life had ceased when her periods did, but neither of them regretted it much. Sometimes she thought he might as well have been a congenial cousin she happened to share a roof with. And things could have been worse. They didn't argue, they didn't get on each other's nerves, they almost always behaved with kindness and consideration to one another and they shared a dark secret.

That was roughly how it was, and as the last phrase took shape in her head, she did wonder if she could hold her silence about the last few days' developments with the imposter. The troublemaker, the phoney Tom, or whatever label you wanted to put on him. Didn't Robert have the right to know, when all was said and done?

Or should he be spared?

When she got off the train in Holtenaar, she still hadn't decided, but she had dried her tears and blown her nose.

It was a glass of champagne that tipped the balance.

Maybe not the first or the second, but probably the third. Robert had been down in the cellar that afternoon gathering samples and had found a couple of bottles he was adamant she shouldn't have to drink alone while he was pushing up daisies and consorting with worms. Or alternatively floating around on a cushion of cloud playing the harp.

So that led to a seafood dinner, champagne and candles, even though it was an average grey Monday in November. Damn it, was Robert's thinking, much as I would wish to, I'm not going to die of cirrhosis.

He also said he had refused all film assignments, every single one, awaiting the big day. He wanted to stay at home in peace and quiet for his remaining time, be it three months or ten. Reading, listening to music, drinking wine for as long as he could, and being close to his kind, beautiful, clever wife.

Above all he wanted to immerse himself in her weighty manuscript on Erasmus of Rotterdam. Surely she wouldn't deny him these simple but sublime pleasures now, in his swansong?

Of course she wouldn't.

The prawns were good. The lobster was divine.

She knew she could manage two glasses of wine, but she shouldn't drink any more if she wanted to stay in control.

Why should I stay in control? she thought, nodding to Robert when he plucked the bottle out of the ice bucket to top up her glass. I've been far too careful all my life.

And that is how it came about that, half a glass later, when Robert wondered if anything special had happened while he was in Geneva, she told him.

At length and in detail, the only thing she left out being Private Investigator Knoll.

'For Christ's sake!' he exclaimed when she had finished. 'Why didn't you say something?'

'You came home with sad news. I'm saying something now.'

'It sounds completely insane.'

'You thought I was imagining things. That I'd dreamt the

first telephone call . . . and then, I don't know, you were away when it happened in September and again this week. Anyway, I know it's not my imagination. There's someone pretending to be Tom and he's after something.'

Robert frowned and sat in silence for a moment. Then he knocked back what was left in his glass, rose from the table and walked over to the French windows. As he stood with his back towards her and his fists clenched, she guessed he was beset with the same frustrating thoughts she herself had been for the past few days and nights.

She let him stand where he was and waited for him to return to the table and draw up a plan of action. But the only thing he said when he sat down again was:

'God damn it, I think we'll open the other bottle as well.'

She nodded. If she had drunk three glasses of champagne, she might as well drink five or six.

'Have you really not cottoned on to what he wants?'

It was some time later and they had moved over to the armchairs by the fireplace. Robert had lit the fire and she felt more drunk than she had been for a long time. But she was sitting here with a husband who would die within the year, her Erasmus manuscript was to a large extent completed, so what did it matter?

'What? What did you say?'

'I asked you if you hadn't grasped what he's after.'

'Really? No . . . I've thought about it, but . . .'

'The inheritance.'

'What inheritance?'

The minute she asked the question, it dawned on her what

an idiot she was. Robert looked at her, shaking his head with concern. Bloody champagne, she thought. My head is spinning even though I'm sitting down.

Spinning and . . . panic-stricken?

In any event, something dark and sinister was taking hold of her; it was unmistakeable. Damn it.

'The inheritance I leave when I'm dead,' Robert spelt it out. 'I'll go and put the coffee on. You seem a bit . . .'

'Thank you. That's a good idea.'

After he had gone out to the kitchen, she stared into the glowing embers of the fire. Inheritance? Clasping her hands, she tried to calm herself down and hold back the flood of thoughts assailing her like a swarm of hornets. The house? *The house.* She didn't know how much there was in the bank, but everything they owned, they owned together – and it was undoubtedly the house, this wonderful house, where they had lived for nine years and which she loved more than anything else, that had the greatest value. No doubt about it; they had purchased it for a million, and today the price was definitely two or three times that. All the mortgages were paid off . . . she had assumed, almost from the day they moved in, that this would be her home for the rest of her life, until her time too was up. And now . . . and now? Bloody hell! Expletives crowded her drunken head. So, did the imposter, that damned caller, that bloody waiter, intend to grab half the inheritance from Robert? Was this his plan? Was this what he had his sights set on?

But . . . he wasn't Tom. How could he be under the illusion he could carry off such a shameful trick? It was almost laughable . . . but it wasn't.

Robert came clattering in with the coffee pot and cups on a tray.

'He can forget that,' she said. 'I mean, inheriting from you. Tom's dead, we both know that. Isn't that right?'

With a degree of difficulty, he placed the tray on the small glass table and sank into the armchair. When she glanced at him she noticed how tired and wretched he looked. Smaller too, as she had observed at the airport. As if he was going to leave this life by shrivelling away.

What an odd thought. Bloody champagne, again.

'We know Tom's dead,' she repeated, when he said nothing. 'We know because we killed him.'

He nodded and sighed deeply.

'There's a complication.'

TWO

Aarlach, 1973

There is a thunderstorm.

She is standing by the living-room window, looking at the angry sky and thinking that it reflects her inner feelings rather well. It is quarter past eleven at night and neither of them has come home yet.

Neither Robert, nor Tom. Actually, Tom hasn't been home for the last two or three nights, she has lost count. But there have been glimpses of him during the day, and twice the police have rung and asked for him. A few hours ago Robert got in touch and explained that he had been in contact with the boy: he's coming in.

Coming in? Like a delayed train or flight. Robert himself is filming out by the lakes around Zingen and has promised to be home about ten, half past at the latest. Three quarters of an hour late so far; it doesn't surprise her.

The thought of running away has been hovering at the back of her mind for several weeks, maybe longer. Yes, definitely longer; the present situation has not arisen overnight. On the contrary, it is a process that has gone on for years and has slowly and inexorably worn her down to the extent that she is grateful if she gets three hours of continuous sleep a night.

I am thirty-seven, she thinks, and I feel like fifty-seven. If I could get away with murdering Tom, I would.

There is nothing new about this. Would she have felt the same if he had been her own flesh and blood? Good question. But there is no time to formulate an answer before another flash of lightning illuminates the whole area. The crash of thunder that follows after only a few seconds makes the house vibrate. She goes out to the kitchen, where she pours a glass of wine, takes a mouthful and sets in motion the verbal merry-go-round of grievances.

Tom is a failure, a malevolent idiot.

He is due in court in two weeks.

He is not my son. He is on drugs, he is a criminal and he plagues the life out of us.

I will never have children of my own.

My marriage with Robert is going to be destroyed.

Is being destroyed.

If Tom didn't exist, everything would be all right.

I am worth more than this. Robert is too.

The wine tastes sour. She pours it down the sink and mixes a gin and tonic instead. She takes a cautious sip and decides she needs a slice of lemon. She takes the last lemon out of the fruit bowl and cuts a slice with the large meat knife, the only one that is not in the dishwasher. Just as she is tasting it again, the front door opens and someone falls into the hall.

That same someone slams the door shut, kicks off his shoes, laughs at something and belches.

Tom. She looks at the clock. Twenty minutes to twelve.

And why isn't his father here to receive him? she thinks. Why should I have to be here alone with an inconsiderate, inebriated slob I am so tired of I can hardly bear the sight of him.

He enters the kitchen.

'Hello, Judith!'

He has never called her mum, or even mother. He is sniffing and there is something strange about the look in his eyes. Drugged, she thinks. Definitely high, on some cheap trash he has bought down on Klejne Markt with money he has stolen . . . and the way he is looking at her? What the hell is the matter with him?

She soon finds out.

'Nice dress, Judith. And short. You're not wearing any knickers either . . . are you?'

In shock she drops the glass she is holding in her hand; for some reason it doesn't break when it hits the floor. She desperately pulls at her dress in an effort to make it longer, bringing it to halfway down her thigh, at least.

Anything but this, she thinks. Anything!

'Tom, go to bed.'

He comes nearer, a broad grin on his face. His eyes glazed, manic. His hands outstretched. His hair sticking to his forehead. He is stronger than me, she thinks. Twenty kilos heavier and twice as powerful . . .

'Turn round and take your pants off . . . if you've got any on. It's time for you and me to have a fuck, Judith!'

She makes a bid to get past him, but he catches her and throws her against the worktop, her hip rammed into the edge as he pushes hard from behind. They stand like that for a second until he pulls her dress up, rips apart her dainty knickers and forces his hand between her legs. She tries to break free, but he grabs hold of her hair and pushes her face into the fruit bowl, from which she has just taken the last lemon; and somehow he has removed his erect penis from his trousers and is trying to thrust it into her. She clenches her muscles and is about to scream, but she can't, because with his hefty elbow on her neck, he is pressing her face into the fruit and suddenly she finds it difficult to breathe. He mustn't come inside me, she thinks. He mustn't. Anything but that . . . and out of the corner of her eye she sees the carving knife she used to slice the lemon. It is lying where she left it on the chopping board, only half a metre to her right. In a flash she has seized it and in an even quicker movement she stabs at random. It is a clumsy effort, directed backwards at an angle, but thanks to some unknown guardian angel, it has the intended effect.

She feels it hit home, and instead of Tom's penis thrusting into her, the huge knife penetrates soft flesh. She hears him groan and his hold on her slackens until, with a heavy thud and another moan, he lets go completely and falls to the floor. Her empty gin and tonic glass starts to roll, the slice of lemon still perched on the rim. As she turns round and tries to straighten her dress, she hears the front door open and close.

Three seconds later Robert is standing in the kitchen. Before either of them has time to say anything, there is another flash of lightning and almost instantaneous thunder-clap. The whole house shakes.

The world is falling apart, she thinks.

'He tried to rape me.'

'I can see.'

'You should have come home five minutes earlier.'

'I'm so sorry.'

Hold me, she thinks, and he does. He takes her into his arms and for several long moments they remain in the embrace, while they contemplate Tom their son, Tom the rapist, lying on his back on the floor, his trousers and under-pants pulled down to his knees, his sex exposed, flaccid and harmless now, the carving knife still stuck in his waist right under his ribs. A thin trickle of blood drips onto the kitchen floor, his mouth hangs open, like an idiot, his jaw has dropped and only the whites of his eyes can be seen through the half-open lids.

But his chest is rising and falling.

'He's alive,' she says. 'But if we just leave him, he'll die.'

Letting go, Robert stares at her.

But he doesn't fall on his knees beside his dying son. He doesn't pull the knife out of his side. He keeps staring at his wife, who stares back without blinking; and during this silent conversation, the rest of their lives is determined. He sees it and so does she. And each of them sees that the other sees it too. Nothing will change it.

He has come home with one of the film company's vans. A convenient stroke of luck.

It is also a stroke of luck that they live on the ground floor. Robert can reverse the van right up to the tiny patio; it takes less than a minute to carry the body out, wrapped in four sheets, and get it in through the back doors. It is past midnight and all the neighbours' lights are out. The storm has not abated.

'Take the sheets off and leave him in the forest. I'll wait for you.'

Robert nods. Before he shuts the doors she can see that the boy's chest is still rising and falling, but his vital signs are weaker now.

Tonight we are saving our marriage, she thinks.

She kisses her husband.

He returns her kiss and then drives off into the darkness.

Hours pass. She has mixed a fresh gin and tonic and is sitting at her desk, waiting. In front of her is the new electric typewriter, papers lie strewn all over, and the windowsill serves as a home-made bookshelf for a row of reference books.

This is her most important work to date: a biography of Catherine de' Medici. She has received an advance so large she has taken leave from the grammar school where she has worked for six years. Her hope is that she will never need to return. This is not an unrealistic hope, as both her previous books have been well-received, but sales didn't reach expected levels; this time is different. She has moved to a larger, more prestigious publishing house and her publisher has more or less promised her more commissions in future. Her life has taken the direction she wants it to.

On this particular night it is impossible to focus on Catherine de' Medici. Her husband is out there engaged in an undertaking of almost unfathomable magnitude. He is going to dump their dying son in a forest, after she stabbed him, following his – the son's – attempt to rape her. If it were a television programme, she would switch off. But if she didn't, would she understand both parents' actions, or would she feel sympathy for the son?

Of course it would depend on how the director wanted to

present it all. But if his intention was to keep to the truth, to the material facts – how Tom had terrorized his mother and father over a number of years, what a selfish, delinquent, arrogant, drug-taking brute he had been, what trouble he had caused them – then sympathies would no doubt lie with the right people. The stabbing had been an act of self-defence and desperation, and in all probability she would have been acquitted in court. But to go through a trial, regardless of whether Tom's life was saved or not – with the publicity, humiliation, shame – would have been impossible. This was the truth that she and Robert read in each other's eyes out there in the kitchen a few hours earlier and this has become the cornerstone of their new alliance. For their marriage to continue, it is the only way out.

When she hears him return, a few minutes past four, she goes to meet him in the hall and hugs him. He is unimaginably wet and dirty and immediately bursts into tears. Violent, unstoppable sobs rack his body and when they don't subside she guides him into the bathroom. She undresses him, puts the clothes in the washing machine and her husband in the bath. After a while she slides in with him and there, in the warm embrace of the water and his wife, he finally begins to talk.

'I buried him,' he says. 'He was dead by the time I reached Zingen. I didn't want anyone to find him.'

'Zingen?'

'Not at any of the places we're filming, obviously, but there's lots of forest out there. I put a spade in the van, but it wasn't easy to dig. This weather as well, I nearly . . .'

'Yes?'

'. . . I nearly broke down. What have we done?'

'He tried to rape me,' she reminds him. 'Tom was going to destroy our lives, Robert.'

Trying to stifle the sobs, he nods. 'I know. He'd already destroyed his own.'

They remain in the bathroom for several hours. In the morning Robert rings his assistant director to say he has suddenly been laid low by an upset stomach and has to stay at home.

They spend the whole day scrubbing the kitchen and cleaning the van. They wait for two days before calling the police to report that their son has gone missing. He left the house on the night of the storm, very upset, probably under the influence of drugs, and they haven't heard from him since. They have settled on this account, in view of the fact there could be witnesses. One of the neighbours might have seen Tom come home just after half past eleven that night.

They will have to assume that no one observed a van belonging to the FFF film company drive off into the night forty-five minutes later.

Over the next few months the police make a half-hearted search for the missing seventeen-year-old, but find no trace of him. Robert finishes his eighth film, *The Woman in the Forest*, and Judith completes her book on Catherine de' Medici.

THREE

Maardam, 1995

Judith sat in silence, waiting.

There has to be something else. You can't utter the word *complication* and then neglect to clarify of what the complication consists.

Not even Robert. Not even Robert in his present condition.

She took a gulp of the strong, sweet espresso and looked at him again. He reminded her a little of Humphrey Bogart, she suddenly noticed, but even shorter and more like a rodent. A dying rodent, an endangered species, perhaps. Not a rat, he was cuter; and forlorn. It might have roused her maternal instincts, had she possessed any.

'Well?' she said finally.

Robert straightened up in the armchair, bent forward and threw a log onto the fire.

'About the inheritance . . .'

'Inheritance?'

'Yes, if that's what he's after. In any case, I think it's a possibility we have to allow for.'

She considered this for a moment. *Tried* to consider it, but the champagne bubbles were still in action.

'I hadn't thought it through. But maybe you're right . . . though if that is the case, why would there be a complication?'

Robert cleared his throat. 'Err, well, if it's a question of establishing his identity. He is, I mean, he never was my . . . Tom, that is.'

Confused, she drained the rest of the coffee.

'What are you saying? I don't really follow.'

'Tom had a different father.'

'What?'

'Minna and I tried for years to have children. When nothing happened, we went to a doctor. I'm sorry, Judith, that I never told you this, but I was . . .'

She suddenly felt dizzy, as if the room had keeled over. As if she was on a roundabout and needed to be sick. She swallowed, clenched her fists, composed herself.

'Carry on. What are you saying, Robert?'

He sighed heavily, exhausted.

'I – I was afraid you wouldn't want me if you knew. You were so young and I assumed you wanted children.'

'I did.'

'But we had Tom, and Minna was dead.'

'Your sperm are good for nothing, is that what you're saying?'

He nodded. 'I'm sorry . . .'

The five seconds that passed seemed like five years.

'Why the hell are you telling me now?'

'Because . . . if there's a paternity test. On the basis that Tom and I should have the same set of genes . . . but we haven't. We didn't have, I mean.'

'Wait, can you be quiet for a second. I need to think.'

Which indeed she did. She leant back in the armchair and gazed into the fire. Why does everything have to happen at once? she asked herself. Why?

Because this was the situation, more or less. A fraudster

starts to harass her, claiming to be Tom. Robert comes back from Geneva and informs her he is dying. Then he tells her he is not Tom's father at all and therefore there can be no question of a paternity test . . . But wait a minute. What did that actually mean? In the worst-case scenario? Didn't it mean . . . ?

'Who knows about this?' she asked.

Robert shrugged. 'Nobody.'

'So the whole world thinks that Tom is your rightful son, produced with the aid of your excellent sperm?'

Sorry, she thought. That was below the belt. But she didn't say it.

'I took on fatherhood,' Robert said. 'In the same way you took on motherhood a few years later. That means he should have inherited from both of us.'

'If he'd been alive.'

'If he'd been alive.'

She tried to concentrate. In the coffee's battle with the champagne, the coffee won a meagre victory.

'I understand. If the imposter wants to get his hands on a share of this house . . . and a share of everything else . . . proving a blood relationship will never be an option, because neither one of us has left any trace in Tom. Have I properly understood?'

Robert nodded again.

'But if no one knows about it, surely that's a good thing? Everyone believes you're Tom's father, so in actual fact, we can demand a paternity test. Can't we?'

'It's not quite so simple. There's a document.'

'A document?'

'Yes. With the authorities . . . the court, I think. It states that I'm not the real father.'

'What . . . what does it say then?'

'Father unknown.'

'Father unknown?'

'Yes.'

'But why? Why did you do that? If no one knew?'

'Because . . . because I wanted it that way. Minna did too. It was stupid, but we were young.'

'Idiotic.'

'Yes.'

'And that means that any Tom, Dick or Harry can come along and claim he's Tom Bendler?'

'There's no genetic proof he's wrong, at any rate.'

'Who is the father then?'

'I don't know.'

'Don't know?'

'No. Minna never told me and I didn't want to know.'

'And there's . . . there's nothing left of her?'

'Ashes. In the sea. Thirty-seven years ago.'

The next day, after a short morning walk with Django, she considered everything again. She sat at her desk with a cup of tea and mildly throbbing temples, trying to comprehend what was happening.

And what Robert had told her.

And what it meant for . . . for the man claiming to be Tom Bendler, their son; their erstwhile son, dead for more than twenty-two years.

She felt beleaguered, not to say *assaulted*; both by what had been, and by what was currently taking place. Why hadn't Robert told her before that he wasn't Tom's real father? Why now? Was it because he believed it really had some bearing . . . that it could make a difference? That there seriously could be an inheritance dispute after he had gone. A dispute that this bloody waiter could even win? That she would be forced to sell the house if she didn't watch out. Watch out and take appropriate steps.

It was absurd. Totally absurd, in the true meaning of the word.

Or . . . or was it just because he was dying and wanted to get a secret off his chest before it was too late? Was that why he had chosen to break his silence?

She glanced at the clock. Quarter past nine. Robert was still in bed asleep. It wasn't like him, but perhaps he too had had a drop too much the night before. And maybe the illness was taking a firmer hold now he had relaxed, resigned to the fact that his days were numbered. He had dedicated most of the previous day to ringing people and explaining the situation, cancelling all his film commitments, present and future, with immediate effect.

The reason: Death's waiting room. He enjoyed using that expression.

I'm sorry, Franz, but I'm sitting in Death's waiting room so I'll let this one go now.

You know what, Clarice. In Death's waiting room you have different priorities.

On the other hand, she thought, on the other hand, we said everything that needed saying last night. I'll let him sleep.

★

But she very much wanted to speak to the imposter again. Today was Tuesday; the last call, after the visit to Cafe Intrigo, had been last Saturday.

Three days. He didn't seem to be in any hurry, anyway, but she could see no possibility of accelerating progress on her part. If that indeed was what she wanted.

Progress, come to that. What progress?

She sighed, picked up the telephone and dialled Herbert Knoll's number.

Four hours later she was sitting in his office again.

The office was no bigger and the private detective no smaller. But he looked pleased with himself, even if he did try to disguise it under an outward appearance of professional gruffness. Perhaps so that she wouldn't get the impression the assignment she had given him wasn't big-league, that his fee could easily be reduced a little.

'There are many details still outstanding,' he began. 'Nevertheless, we can present a picture of the subject in broad outline.'

She wondered what lay behind the word *we*. An inflated ego or a partner? Or several? But she didn't ask. It was of no consequence, obviously.

'It seems he really is called Tom Bendler. At least that is the name he uses and the name on his passport. He has been in the country just two months and has been renting a one-room apartment on Armastenstraat since the first of October.'

'A passport? It's not possible.'

'It could be false. We haven't had time to investigate the circumstances yet.'

'I understand.'

But she didn't. On the contrary, she was overwhelmed by the sense that the whole situation was beyond comprehension.

She had thought that in hiring Herbert Knoll she would be rid of a nuisance, but now the nuisance was back with teeth bared.

'It's also correct that he worked at Cafe Intrigo for a month,' the detective continued. 'He's worked as a waiter before and they needed a temporary replacement for a short period. They have no complaints about the way he carried out his duties and would consider employing him again, if he so wishes. Though probably not in the winter months, when business drops off a little.'

'Where did he work as a waiter before?'

'A few places. But all in New Zealand.'

'New Zealand?'

'Yes. Apparently he's lived there for at least twenty years. But we need to check that too.'

'How . . . how did you find this out?'

Herbert Knoll pushed his spectacles up onto his forehead and placed a substantial forefinger over an equally substantial pair of lips.

'That's not a question you should ask. In the intelligence community we don't reveal our sources, it's part of our professional integrity. But you can probably work some of it out for yourself, if you think about it. There's nothing strange in this case.'

She did as he suggested and thought about it.

'Intrigo, of course. And neighbours, maybe? I assume he doesn't know that . . . that he's being investigated?'

Herbert Knoll shrugged. 'We can only hope not. But if we don't talk to people, it's almost impossible to obtain evidence. I'm sure you realize?'

'I dare say. But why did he arrange to meet me and then not come forward? I was there waiting, after all.'

'What do you think yourself?'

'I don't know. It seems both strange and illogical . . . does he or does he not want to have any contact with me?'

'A serious question. We can't answer that one for the moment, but there is a possibility you might not have thought of.'

'What possibility?'

'Maybe he didn't know what you look like. Now he does.'

'Why would he . . . ?'

But she could find no words. The turmoil in her head obstructed them and it was impossible to formulate sensible questions or even absorb the information Detective Knoll was delivering: it seemed the waiter really was called Tom Bendler; he had a passport confirming that fact; he had lived in New Zealand.

He might have arranged the meeting just so that he could get a closer look at her; it was so calculated it made her scared to think about it.

She herself had confirmed that he was the right age, and how could they prove he wasn't the person he said he was?

'Hang on,' she said as something occurred to her. 'What country was the passport issued in?'

'In New Zealand. By our embassy there . . . Wellington, if I'm not mistaken.'

'So he's a citizen of this country?'

'Apparently. As long as the passport isn't a forgery. But that's a detail still to be confirmed, as I said.'

'How long will it take?'

Herbert Knoll shrugged again. 'Give me a few days.'

She sat in silence for a moment, before standing up and thanking him. On her way out, the door already open, she thought of one more question.

'By the way, what does he say about being in touch with me? What comment does he have on what he's doing?'

Herbert Knoll had also risen to his feet, with a certain degree of difficulty, as there was scarcely room for him between the desk, the chair and the wall.

'Dear Mrs Bendler, we haven't spoken to him yet. We've not been working on the case for more than twenty-four hours. But would you like an answer to that question? Would you really like us to confront him?'

In a matter of seconds, she had thought it over and replied. 'Yes, please. I would.'

Without having made a deliberate decision to do so, she found herself heading towards the canal district and Armastenstraat. It wasn't a great distance from Herbert Knoll's office on Ruydersteeg, only a couple of kilometres, and for once the weather was fair, despite it being November, the most inclement and depressing of months. She wished she had Django by her side, but he wasn't happy in the noise and commotion of the city; it was years since she had bothered to take him along when she had things to do in the centre.

But she would have appreciated his calm, dependable company and she recalled that during the last of her two stays at Majorna there had been a dog in her unit. It was some kind of experiment; they wanted to establish what influence an animal's presence had on patients, and as far as she could see the experiment had nothing but positive effects. She also remembered a play she and Robert had once seen, something about the Eye of the Horse, in which the message had been the same. In times of darkness and mental turbulence, we are well advised to focus our minds on an animal.

Provided, of course, there is an animal available. A dog or a horse, or maybe a donkey.

Am I being an ass? she asked herself. Am I behaving like one?

Not really. A headless chicken was nearer the truth; and having arrived at this point in her self-analysis, she realized she had actually reached Armastenstraat. She came to a halt, her eyes following the row of buildings in search of the house numbers. Above the door where she had stopped was the number 8A; odd numbers were on the opposite side of the street, and she started to walk in the direction of increasing numbers.

25A and 25B proved to be in a five-storey council-owned mansion block built at the beginning of the century, or perhaps the end of the last, like many others on Armastenstraat. Russet brick, rather down-at-heel, slightly shabby; a lot of graffiti that had clearly been there a few years. Further on towards Grote Graacht, west of Fourth of September Park, the housing stopped altogether, she knew; factories and warehouses took over completely and it was hardly an area where a woman walked alone after dark, as they used to say. But this was at the start of the long street; there were still a number of shops here, a post office and some fast-food places, and besides, it was still several hours before autumn darkness would descend over the city.

She looked up at the row of windows above 25B. She counted twenty, but it was difficult to ascertain exactly where the dividing line was between 25A and 25B. In any event, he lived behind one of these silent rectangles – or perhaps behind a couple of them. But probably only one, she thought; Herbert Knoll had said he was renting a one-room apartment. There were no lights on in any of the windows above 25B, but, as she had already noted, there was still some moderate daylight and people didn't want to pay unnecessarily high electricity bills.

I could go in through that door, she thought, to see where a certain Mr Bendler lives . . . and confront him.

Why leave that to a private detective? Provided he's at home, I could be looking him right in the eye in less than a minute, she told herself.

The chances of him being in the apartment were uncertain, but at least he didn't have a job to go to. Unless he'd already found a new one?

Why not? Why not take the bull by the horns and give it a try?

But she knew this was hypothetical. A move like that required decisive action, and if there was anything beyond her current capabilities, it was decisive action. The little spate of energy that had brought her to the canal district was running out, and before the feeling of hopelessness could overwhelm her, she turned on her heels and began the weary walk back the way she had come.

Back home, she thought. To the garden. Erasmus of Rotterdam. And safe with Django.

After a couple of blocks, as she stood waiting for the green light at a crossing, she realized she hadn't included Robert among the immediate objects of her anticipation.

By accident or design? That was the question.

★

'Why hasn't he been in touch? It's been four days, hasn't it?'

'Three. And I don't know. How could I know?'

They had gone to the Red Ruby, a local restaurant on one corner of Holte Markt, for dinner. According to his own account, Robert had slept half the day and he seemed brighter than on the previous evening. It was at his suggestion they were sitting here at their usual table, under a Piranesi print, waiting for their risotto. One seafood, one mushroom. The Ruby had opened at virtually the same time as they had moved into the house and they must have been to the simple but very pleasant restaurant at least a hundred times. She wondered whether she would ever come here after Robert had gone.

'But it's weird, isn't it?' he insisted. 'Do you think he's watching us somehow . . . or you? That he might be sitting here, for example?'

She couldn't help looking around. 'No, he's not in here.'

'Sure? What did he look like?'

'Like a normal forty-year-old.'

'Dark? Fair?'

'In between.'

'Tall? Big?'

'Not especially.'

'Don't you want to talk about this?'

'Not really.'

'Why?'

'I don't know. Maybe I hope it's over. That he won't be in touch again.'

'Do you think that's the case?'

'I said *hope*.'

'OK. I understand. You're furious because I never told you about Tom. That he isn't my real son . . . *wasn't*.'

She gazed at him for a moment before she replied, wondering whether he really believed that just because he had brought it up, that was the end of the matter, there was no need to think about it.

'No,' she said. 'Actually I don't think you do understand. It doesn't sound like it. Tom wasn't my child and he wasn't yours. He was produced by two completely different individuals and he's been dead for more than twenty years. Now a horrible person appears, claiming to be your son and heir. Perhaps his aim is to take from me my last vestige of security, as you suggested yesterday. In a year's time I'll have no husband, no dog . . . and maybe no house. Why should I be furious?'

'But . . .'

'Had I known Tom wasn't your son, I would never have adopted him, it's as simple as that. But I would still have chosen to live with you. Just so you know.'

The breath was visibly knocked out of him and he didn't answer. He refused to meet her gaze, his eyes darting between a young couple who had just come in through the door and his own hands resting on the edge of the table. He looked lost and suddenly she felt sorry for him.

'I'm sorry. It probably wouldn't have changed the inheritance situation, but it's difficult for me to accept that you could keep something like this to yourself. How do I know you're not harbouring more secrets?'

'I . . .'

But he fell silent.

Why has he stopped? she thought. What did he intend to say?

He cleared his throat and straightened his back. 'OK,' he

said. 'I'm the one to be sorry. And we'll do as you say, we won't talk about this imposter any more . . . at least until we see how things develop. Now I can see our food on its way.'

She nodded, realizing she was actually rather hungry.

The fourth call came just after nine o'clock the following day, and this time she was ready. She knew it was Tom before the first ring had ended. *Unknown number*, as usual. She drew a deep breath, allowed another ring to sound and then picked up.

'Hello.'

'Judith Bendler?'

'Yes.'

'It's Tom.'

'I hear what you say. But you're not Tom.'

'Of course I'm Tom. What makes you doubt me?'

'Everything. The way you're behaving, for example.'

He gave a laugh, short and hoarse.

'The way *I'm* behaving. I don't know what you're getting at. All I want is to see my mother . . . and my father . . . again after such a long time. While you disown me and even put a private detective on my tail. If anyone needs to examine her behaviour, it's you, dear Mother, not I.'

Her heart missed a beat at the expression 'dear Mother'. I've never been your mother, she thought, nor the real Tom's mother either, even in those days. And the real Tom happens to be dead.

'What do you want?'

He paused a few seconds before answering.

'First of all I want to prove to you that I am who I say I am.

So I suggest we meet face to face. This time I don't intend to be your waiter.'

'Good,' she said. 'I didn't think much of you in that role. But it's pointless anyway.'

'You'll change your mind.'

'Rubbish. When and where? And it will only be this once.'

'I don't think so. But I suggest Intrigo again, if you don't have any objection. How about three o'clock Friday?'

Three days to wait, she thought.

'Why not today or tomorrow?'

'I've got things to do. But Saturday would suit me too.'

'Friday at three o'clock will be fine,' she said with decision. 'Intrigo, right. That seems to be your home ground, not that it matters to me.'

His rasping laugh again. 'Excellent. But I think you should get rid of that gumshoe. He's got nothing to do with you and me.'

'Let me think about it,' she promised, and hung up.

Herbert Knoll, however, was not going to be dismissed out of hand.

'Think twice, Mrs Bendler,' he recommended shortly afterwards, when she rang to explain the situation. 'Your adversary is not someone to be trifled with. If you're going to meet him again, we need to take some security measures.'

Security measures, Judith thought. Maria Rosenberg had talked about *precautionary measures*. Sometimes the difference between a detective and a therapist was less than you might imagine.

'And what measures would they be?' she asked. 'Specifically?'

'We should have a man present in the cafe.'

She didn't really understand. 'Why?'

'To listen, for example,' he explained patiently. 'Maybe record the conversation as well. It might be useful with regard to . . .'

'With regard to what?'

'With regard to the future.'

She hastily considered. 'I don't see what purpose that would serve. Besides, I could record it myself. No, I don't want a spy around when I meet him. You'll have to forgive me.'

'It's your decision,' the detective said in a measured voice. 'Can I therefore expect that our services will not be required henceforth?'

'I'd like to know what happened when you . . . confronted him.'

'Of course. Not very much happened. One of my colleagues stopped him when he left his apartment yesterday evening. Told him he had a blue belt in karate and was a good friend of yours. Asked him to stop harassing you. Standard procedure, as they say on the other side of the Atlantic.'

Good God, she thought. I'm playing a role in a gangster film. 'And how did he react?'

'According to my colleague, he raised an eyebrow, that was all. That's why in my judgement you need to be careful. He might not be someone to mess around.'

'I never imagined he was,' Judith declared. 'I'll get in touch after the meeting on Friday. I don't want you to take any . . . any measures, until further notice.'

'As you wish,' Private Detective Knoll answered. 'I'll prepare your invoice in the meantime.'

After the call ended she wondered about the new-found strength she had gained in both the conversation with the imposter and with the detective. In any event, it didn't hang around, it abandoned her like . . . like a rat deserting a sinking ship.

Infernal mental images again, she thought, as she went up to the bedroom to see if her dying husband had woken.

He hadn't. But after coming home from the Ruby the previous evening, he had settled down with a bottle of brandy and a number of film cassettes, so she wasn't surprised that he was still snoring. She went back downstairs, put Django's lead on and set out on a long walk.

At last it was Friday, and eventually Friday afternoon.

But it had been a long haul. Work on Erasmus was slow; she didn't have the extra concentration, vital in the weeks before the submission date of the first complete version of the book, and after a series of vain attempts to make some progress on the text, she decided to take a break from it for a few days. After the meeting with the imposter she would still have almost a month, that would have to suffice.

The fact that Robert was at home all day – sitting in front of the television looking at old films, to be more precise, films he had directed and produced, in total about fifty – constituted a disruption. If Django had been in his prime, she could have spent half the day outside with him, but when all was said and done the poor dog was probably as moribund as his master, and the weather was as to be expected for this time of year: rainy, windy, gloomy.

They hardly spoke to one another, she and Robert, and of course Tom was the elephant in the room. It ought to have vexed her, the lack of words and interaction, but for some reason it didn't. His unexpected revelation about paternity and his worthless sperm had changed something essential; it had shifted a central pillar in their relationship. But she didn't want to discuss the matter with him, not now, in this period of waiting. Maybe afterwards, after she had actually looked into the face of the man who claimed to be Tom Bendler. Though even of this she wasn't sure; maybe the silence had come to stay.

She contemplated telephoning Maria Rosenberg and asking for an appointment on Thursday, but decided against it. Better to defer this as well. Having discovered a couple of unread crime novels on the bookshelf, by a writer called Henry Moll Jr, she spent a number of hours lying under a blanket on the sofa in her study endeavouring to take an interest in storylines that seemed to grow more obscure the further she read.

Unless she could no longer understand people's motives and intentions. In that case, she thought, it was entirely consistent with the world in which she was currently living.

Nonetheless, Friday arrived.

Cafe Intrigo was considerably more crowded than it had been on the previous occasion. Two large parties, one Japanese, the other of uncertain origin, filled most of the cafe, but at the far end in a corner, alone at a table, sat the fictitious Tom Bendler. She had had difficulty in remembering exactly what he looked like, having focused too much on the other three men during her last visit, but when she caught sight of him, she was in no doubt.

He rose to his feet and walked towards her. They shook hands without a word and sat down opposite each other at the table.

He was quite slim and of above average height. Longish, dark-brown hair, greyish green eyes, regular features. Wearing a white shirt under a V-necked blue pullover. Slightly drawn, perhaps, posture a little poor, but he looked quite good; she noted this despite herself, unable to dismiss the thought that Tom might look rather like this.

Might have looked. If he hadn't died twenty-two years previously. Twenty-two years and four months.

'A pleasure to see you, Judith Bendler,' he began.

'I wish I could say the same,' she replied.

He smiled. 'Would you like anything?'

She shook her head. There were two glasses and a jug of water on the table. Without asking again, he poured some water, while at the same time saying hello to a waiter passing with a pile of plates for the Japanese party. Yes, of course, she thought, he was a colleague of everyone working here. *Home ground*, as she had said.

'You look younger than I thought you would.'

A compliment. Which she ignored. Instead she gave a disdainful sigh and stared at him with a look of what she hoped was neutral indifference. She folded her hands on the table in front of her.

'I haven't come here for polite conversation. I don't know who you are, but I do know one thing. You're not who you say you are. I've known that from the start, right from the time you rang me in the middle of the night.'

He gave no reply, just drank some water and smiled again.

'I've considered calling the police several times, but didn't. I hope you have the sense to stop what you're doing all the same. Neither my husband nor I are amused by your behaviour and frankly we don't understand what you're playing at. You haven't been particularly forthcoming on the telephone, so now I want an honest explanation. And a promise that you'll stop this foolishness. And if not, well, you'll have to face the consequences.'

She leant back. That was it. That was all she had to say to him, and she had done it in more or less one single breath.

He gazed at her without moving. The smile had faded somewhat, but he still looked amused. Or at least unperturbed.

'Why are you so negative?' he said. 'I don't remember you being like that.'

'You don't remember me, full stop.'

'Of course I do. In the same way you remember me.'

'Don't you realize how simple it would be for me to prove you're lying?'

'Go ahead. Be my guest.'

How can he be so confident? she thought. As if he held some kind of trump card he could play whenever it suited him.

'I could ask some questions that you can't answer. But the real Tom would be able to. Do you truly not grasp that?'

'Go ahead,' he said again. 'I'm not stopping you. By the way, do you remember the last time we saw each other?'

'The last time . . . ?'

But words failed her.

'That evening in the kitchen. I was a bit high, but you were irresistible. You were standing there with a drink in your hand and you were wearing that terribly sexy short dress. Black with little red dots. Do you still have it?'

FOUR

Queenstown, New Zealand, 1994–95

The farm was called Promised Land and Daniel Freemont had ended up there by pure chance.

Or perhaps it was fate. He really wanted to believe in fate, but there was little in his life up to now which suggested the existence of anything on such a grand scale. At least nothing on such a grand scale that was benevolent. Most of it had been a complete mess, especially the last twenty-five years. And since he had not yet reached forty, there were grounds for assuming it had been shit from the outset.

But what had happened at the beginning of September up in Auckland was the absolute nadir. Operating with an idiot from Tonga, Daniel had robbed a security van. They got hold of a small bag of notes that were worthless the moment they opened the bag, as the action triggered an ink tag, and the Tongan idiot shot the van driver. Daniel didn't even know he was armed, and when the driver, a forty-year-old father of five, died a few hours later in hospital, both of them were wanted for murder. To the best of Daniel's knowledge, the Tongan had managed to board a bloody cargo boat and sailed home to his bloody island, where he had holed up in his family of 180 people, all of whom looked the same and none of whom had any identity papers. And the police had no idea which of the two robbers had been holding the murder weapon.

Daniel had gone underground, as they say, though not on Tonga. By various means, often under cover of darkness, he had made his way south. Down to Wellington and eventually over to the South Island. He let his hair grow, stole some spectacles and stopped shaving. When he reached Queenstown in the middle of November, he didn't look in the least like the photograph in his passport, which he had set fire to anyway on the edge of a campsite one night, the week after the infamous heist in Auckland.

He stayed in Queenstown for two months, into the new year, and actually earned some money, working in bars, backpacker hostels and a launderette. But one evening he got into a fight with a German tourist who accused him of stealing his wallet, which was a complete fabrication, and Daniel decided it was time to leave town. Early one morning a sheep farmer from up in Glenorchy gave him a lift and after a few hours on the winding road snaking north along the side of Lake Wakatipu, they got a puncture. While the driver, with seasoned though rather slow-moving hands, changed the wheel, Daniel took advantage of the break to have a look around; and there he discovered his new abode.

He bade farewell to the sheep farmer, hoisted his rucksack onto his back and started up the narrow track in the direction shown on the disintegrating sign.

PROMISED LAND

NEW TRUTH SEEKERS WELCOME

The first impression was a sorry one, even for someone like Daniel, and if he hadn't been climbing uphill from the main road for nearly two kilometres, he might have turned round.

The main building appeared to be a large, barn-like shack, painted in half a dozen different colours, most of them peeling off. On the surrounding expanse of rather swampy grassland a motley collection of around thirty caravans and tents stretched out. A few huts, cobbled together from various pieces of board and corrugated metal, nestled close to a thinly wooded area, and in and around these rudimentary dwellings were a number of mucky cows, a few scrawny horses, a large flock of rather fatter Merino sheep and a smaller flock of children. The latter looked as though they were between five and ten in age and were just about as dirty as the cows, possibly as a consequence of trying to play football on ground that would have been better suited to speedway or potatoes. Sitting in a rocking chair on the sagging veranda of the multi-coloured barn was a huge person, presumably a man, sporting a straw hat, kaftan and flip-flops, taking a draw on something that appeared to be an uncommonly large joint.

Maybe I've come to the right place after all, Daniel thought.

Two hours later he was installed in a small caravan without wheels, but with a roof over his head, reasonably intact walls and a floor that didn't give way beneath his feet. There were three bunks; one was free, one was occupied by soiled clothes, bottles and rubbish, and on the third lay a creature under a pile of blankets, snoring. At about three in the afternoon this creature woke, coughed up phlegm for a few moments and then asked if he could have a cup of coffee and a litre of water.

Just as Daniel was thinking it was a long time since he had seen a person in worse shape than this roommate, he was struck by another thought: this bugger looks like I'm going to look in a few years. If I'm not careful, I'll end up the same.

He managed to fulfil the order and five minutes later they were each sitting with a mug of coffee, looking at one another.

'If you're going to stay here, you'd better tell me your name,' the creature said. 'If not, it doesn't matter.'

'Daniel Lipkens.'

It was a surname he had borrowed from a pretty teacher he had had in seventh grade and he had been using since the fiasco in Auckland.

'Tom Bendler.'

They shook hands.

'You don't happen to have anything in your pocket fit for smoking?'

It was Tom Bendler who asked. Daniel shook his head.

'Not at the moment. I'm trying to keep off it.'

'You've come to the wrong place.'

'I'm not fanatical about it.'

'Then you've come to the right place. Where are you from? I have a feeling I recognize the accent, if you don't mind me saying.'

'Born in Maardam. Not been home for ten years.'

Tom Bendler erupted into laughter, which rapidly turned into a protracted fit of coughing. 'What do you know!' he said, when the cough subsided. 'I came into the world in Aarlach. We're fellow countrymen, for fuck's sake.'

'So it appears,' Daniel said.

'And now we're both sitting in the same swanky caravan on the other side of the world. Someone up there must like us.'

'How long have you been round here?' Daniel asked.

Tom Bendler pondered this with wrinkled brow. 'Over twenty years, I'd say. I've smoked away most of my little grey cells, but I think that's a fair estimate. Yeah, at least twenty years. But now you'll have to excuse me, I need to go out for a piss.'

'By all means,' Daniel said. 'Just tell me if you need any help.'

His reply was met with another burst of laughter and subsequent fit of coughing. Poor bugger, Daniel thought. But I'll stay a few nights and see how things shape up.

They shaped up tolerably well. Promised Land didn't deliver quite what the name suggested, but it was good enough. About sixty people were living there, fifty adults and ten children, roughly. The commune – that was what they called it – had been set up on a small scale at the end of the seventies by a moonstruck pastor and his two wives. The pastor and one of the wives were dead, but wife number two, a mysterious woman in her fifties who bore the name Madam Holy, was still there. She was happily remarried to the present leader of Promised Land, Dr Brutus Hotchkiss, the very same character Daniel had observed in the rocking chair on the veranda when he arrived. The doctor was a former chemist and in a special room in the large barn he and some assistants cooked up drugs; these were sold at a handsome profit in Queenstown, where demand was great, particularly in the summer season. There were other possible lines of vocational activity at Promised Land. Some people helped with looking after the horses at a couple of ranches nearby, further up towards Glenorchy, but most people had different kinds of jobs within the commune itself. Cooking, tending the sheep, growing potatoes, vegetables and marijuana, renovating dwellings in danger of collapse and so on. On certain mornings children of school age were sent on the bus to the school in Glenorchy; when Daniel arrived it was the school holidays, however, and in any case it was a moot point whether they actually learnt anything of value out there in the so-called civilized world.

A general meeting was held each week, or a few times a month at least, in the Rainbow, as the barn was called, led by Dr Hotchkiss and Madam Holy. First, 'We Shall Overcome' was sung in unison, then the doctor gave a sermon, after which matters of common interest were discussed; it culminated in the pleasant partaking of an enormous meal accompanied by a constant flow of home-made wine. These meetings often lasted until dawn and the following day was the Sabbath, with strict prohibition on work.

Not everyone participated in the general meetings, however. About a third usually stayed away – not necessarily the same third and not necessarily for the same reasons, but normally illness- and drug-related. Non-attendance was accepted unreservedly. Promised Land was a republic of freedom, where each and every one may not quite pull their weight, but where enough did to enable it to function satisfactorily. It had been in existence nearly fifteen years and as far as Daniel could see, the authorities had stopped interfering. If indeed they ever had, here in the outback. They bothered no one and were left in peace.

He carried on living with Tom Bendler in the little caravan.

It soon transpired that not only were they from the same country, they were the same age, with only seven months between them. Neither of them was particularly inclined to be sociable and they could go for days with scarcely a word exchanged, an arrangement that suited them both perfectly. Broadly speaking, there was far too much bullshitting in the world already.

All the same, one evening as the sun was setting and they were sitting with their backs against the wall of the caravan, each with a beer in his hand, Daniel did ask a question:

'Are you wanted by the police for anything?'

'Don't think so,' Tom answered. 'I was before I wound up in this country, but that's presti . . . presbi . . . What the hell's it called?'

'Prescribed?' Daniel suggested.

'That's it. It's been a hell of a long time, so it's definitely . . . pre . . . that.'

'I understand,' Daniel said.

They sat in silence for half an hour or more, drinking beer, smoking, watching the sun go down.

'I've got a crazy story about how I got here,' Tom said. 'Is there any more beer?'

'I'll have a look,' Daniel said, and returned a few minutes later with a six-pack. 'What kind of story?'

Tom Bendler sighed. 'I can't bear to talk about all that crap. Another day perhaps.'

'OK,' Daniel Fremont said.

They drank three more beers each, crawled into the caravan and turned in.

*

But after a week, or possibly two, Daniel raised the subject again.

'What was your story about?'

'Bullshit,' Tom Bendler said. 'But since you're so bloody interested.'

And so he proceeded to tell his story, which, exactly as he had said, was crazy; and it actually took three evenings, or possibly four, before Daniel had heard the whole tale. If Tom Bendler hadn't been the screwed-up, hash-smoking deadbeat he was, he might not have given any credence to what he learnt, but that his buddy might have the energy or the where-withal to fabricate such a sick story seemed highly unlikely to say the least.

'Twenty years ago?' he asked.

'What year is it now?'

'Nineteen ninety-five.'

Tom was quiet as he did the mental arithmetic. 'Then it's twenty-two.'

'Bloody hell, that's all I can say,' Daniel exclaimed. 'And you're not planning on going back?'

'Shouldn't think so,' Tom Bendler said, and belched.

It was a few weeks later when Daniel was searching in the clutter under the sink in the caravan that he found the canvas bag. It was tied up with a criss-cross of blue nylon cord and after battling with his conscience for a few seconds, he decided to take a look at the contents.

They proved to be a passport and an ID card. The passport was issued by the police authorities in Aarlach in 1972, the ID card by a post office in Christchurch, New Zealand, thirteen years later. The passport photograph of the then sixteen-year-old Tom Leonard Bendler gave him something of a shock.

It could have been one of his own school photos.

The same hair. The same narrow nose and the same mouth. The same weak chin and sullen expression in the pale, close-set eyes.

Holy shit, Daniel Fremont/Lipkens thought, and at the same instant something else occurred to him. To do with fate. And that it might not have been pure chance that brought him to this godforsaken farm. Perhaps there was a purpose.

A deeper purpose and a pointer to the shape the years to come might take.

Why not? He took charge of the passport and ID card, put the nylon cords back and returned the canvas bag to its place under the sink. That same evening, he started to formulate a plan.

Step one was to get Tom Bendler to tell him more. Draw more details out of him, especially about that last evening in Aarlach; obviously it wouldn't be easy, but with intelligence and patience a man can go far in this world. It was a truth that had possibly eluded him thus far in life, but one it was now high time to embrace and use.

Step two was to head north. If you found yourself at the southernmost tip of New Zealand's South Island, there were not many directions to choose from.

He took his leave of Promised Land and Queenstown in the middle of August. Among the things he left behind were a few kilos of old underwear and his name. His *names*, strictly speaking, both Fremont and Lipkens. As well as Daniel, of course.

From now on he was called Tom Leonard Bendler and in a lightweight bag hanging by a leather cord round his neck he kept a passport and an ID card to corroborate this.

At the embassy in Wellington, which he reached five days later, an official explained that they couldn't issue a full passport in such a short time, only what was called a temporary passport. It was valid for three months, but there would be no difficulty in getting a better document when he was back in his own country.

It was the best they could do, and given that his mother was dying, it was of course an entirely acceptable solution.

He obtained his new passport the following day and one week later, with the help of income from the sale of products from Dr Hotchkiss's laboratory, plus the contents of an American wallet, picked from a similarly American pocket, he was able to purchase a one-way plane ticket from Auckland, via Singapore, to Sechshafen International Airport outside Maardam. The Fates smiled upon him, like Uzbek carpet dealers.

A few days before his departure, he made a telephone call.

FIVE

Maardam, 1995

'Can you please explain to me how all this makes sense?'

'Hmm.'

'Is that your answer? *Hmm?*'

Staring at her husband, she tried to keep calm. Robert looked anything but calm; she got the impression he wished he were already dead. In that case she sympathized with him, but it wasn't a feeling she could share. Before he shuffled off this mortal coil, there was something he needed to disclose.

There, you see, another infernal image, unbidden. She was reminded of the waves and the foam. The landing strip called Death. *Pick your battles.*

And there was a war being waged this evening. Django stood between them whimpering like a failed mediator. Robert was silent, knowing he would lose, or that he already had. That the decisive battle had actually taken place more than twenty-two years earlier, but only now had the smoke thinned enough for them to see clearly.

For *her* to see clearly.

But that was precisely what she couldn't do. She could only see red, and that was what caused the dog to put his tail between his legs and leave both the room and his self-appointed diplomatic role – because she was speaking to her husband in a way she had never done before. Like a . . . like a very large, hungry feline versus a defenceless rat, who had lost all resemblance, probably non-existent anyway, to Humphrey Bogart:

'Robert, for Christ's sake tell me how the imposter can know what I was wearing that night!'

Robert didn't reply.

'And how he can remember what Tom was trying to do before I stabbed him! I want an answer now, and no more bloody hmm-ing!'

'Calm down!'

'No, I'm not going to calm down. There are two people with knowledge of these things. They are the two people sitting in this room now, two people who have had a pact for twenty-two years. One of them hasn't kept his mouth shut, and it isn't me.'

There was a grimace on Robert's face. As if his illness sent a jolt of pain to some part of his frail body, or as if he wanted to feign a jolt of pain – she couldn't determine which.

'I have kept my mouth shut.'

She was quiet. The old pendulum clock on the wall started to strike seven and she let the sounds fade away. He had more to tell, it seemed. Now he's going to say there's another complication, she thought, and she was filled with an unwelcome, oppressive sense of déjà vu. Clasping her hands and closing her eyes, she tried to force it away, without success.

'There's a . . . how can I put this?'

She gave him time to find the right word.

'Another factor.'

'A factor?'

'Yes,' he cleared his throat. 'I'm afraid I kept you in the dark, Judith, but I . . .'

'Yes?'

'But I believed I was doing the right thing. In both respects.'

'What bloody respects?'

'Both with regard to Tom, and with regard to you.'

She waited. Something stirred deep in her subconscious, the faintest inkling.

'That evening. It didn't happen the way I said. I didn't bury Tom out in the forest. He . . .' In a fraction of a second, the inkling grew to a certainty. '. . . he didn't die in the car. He was still breathing, still alive. I couldn't simply . . . Can you understand this? I couldn't simply . . . finish him off.'

He fell silent. She reached for the jug of water and noticed her hand was shaking as she poured herself a glass. She raised the glass and drank, two large gulps, not caring about the trail of drips she spilled on the table.

Can you understand this?

'Carry on.'

Robert stared at her, his gaze blank.

'Do you remember Eric Shapiro?'

'Your old school friend? The doctor?'

'Yes. I went to his house, and we made a . . . well, we made an agreement.'

'You made an agreement?'

'Yes. We took Tom to Eric's clinic and he saved his life. I can't go into all the details, but one month later Tom was on a plane to New Zealand. On a one-way ticket to Auckland. He agreed to it all; he had some money in his pocket and had to promise never to come back. I'm sorry, but that's what happened. I'm not going to ask for forgiveness, because I know I'm not going to get it.'

A pause for thought, before she said: 'Because you don't deserve it.'

'Because I don't deserve it. I'm tired and I have to go and lie down. You can let me know in the morning if you want me to move out.'

'It must have cost you quite a bit.'

'Yes, it cost me.'

'Didn't Tom get in touch after you packed him off?'

'Never.'

'You didn't consider letting me in on your plan, you and Dr Shapiro?'

'Yes. But he had nothing to do with it. It was I who decided to keep you out of it. As I said – I thought that was the right thing to do.'

'How the bloody hell could you think that was the right thing to do?'

With the air of someone truly nearing his end, Robert shook his head. 'I don't know. I was wrong, and then, quite soon, it was too late to put it right. I'd already compromised myself and given my story. Told you I'd buried him . . . I'm sorry.'

'I don't give a fuck if you're sorry. I want to think about this overnight. You've laid waste to a great deal, just for the record.'

'I know,' Robert said and stood up, his legs shaking. 'Believe me, I know.'

But she hadn't finished.

'One more thing. You said I was imagining things after the first phone call. You can't have believed that?'

'No, maybe I didn't.'

'You're a good liar.'

'I've mixed with actors all my life.'

With that, he stumbled painfully out of the room. Away from the ashes of a burnt-out marriage.

It was past twelve when she went to bed in the guest room. She had spent the whole evening sitting in the bay window, facing the damp November garden. She didn't put a light on, but let the darkness wrap around her, and from this darkness a certain clarity emerged. It was remarkable. She should have cursed and raged; everything that had happened recently had threatened her existence. No, that was putting it too mildly – it had driven a lance through her life.

But lance wounds can be healed, and the hallmark of a human being is that she can adapt to new conditions, in circumstances where a donkey or a hen, for example, would fail. The past was over; Robert would soon be dead, but she still had who knows how many years left. She mustn't throw them away. Or let anyone else steal them.

Right? she asked herself.

Yes, she answered. Too right. I have the leading role in my life.

As for Robert's question – Can you understand this? – of course she could. It was totally conceivable she wouldn't have been able to bury her son that night. What was inconceivable – and unforgiveable – was that he had lied to her. Lies don't diminish with time, they grow. Maybe you can turn a blind eye to what someone confesses he did a few days ago, a month ago, or even six. But twenty-two years? Impossible.

Right? she asked herself again.

Of course, she reaffirmed.

But so to the future. Out with the old. What was she going to do?

And slowly, like ice creeping over the canals on the first frosty night in November, like faltering moments of dawn in the hour of the wolf, a plan began to form – and when she finally pulled the blanket over herself in the guestroom, without turning off the light because it wasn't on, she was well on the way to finding a solution. The only solution.

After about ten minutes in the car with Robert Bendler, the man who was supposedly his father, Daniel Fremont began to change his plan.

He had been thinking of a nice round sum – maybe a hundred thousand American dollars – with the promise that he would never again darken their door. But this old man was under sentence of death – he couldn't have much time left in this vale of tears, anyone could see – and when Daniel realized that, it also dawned on him there was probably more to be had. Considerably more.

If he played his cards right, that is. Robert and Judith Bendler were well off, of that there was no doubt. Maybe they weren't exactly wealthy, but if what Tom had said in the caravan in Promised Land was correct – and why shouldn't it be? – they had no other children. And unless Daniel was very much mistaken, that meant there was an inheritance in the offing. And a handsome inheritance, at that; with an eye to the day, presumably not too far away, when Robert Bendler pegged it. His wife would obviously have half, but surely to God the other half would have to pass to the son? Who, just at the right time, happened to have returned home after several years abroad. What had been mentioned in the caravan? Twenty?

Slightly more than that, if Daniel's memory served him correctly.

How much this small, rat-like man slumped behind the wheel was good for was hard to say. But there must be more than a hundred thousand to collect, a bloody good sight more.

Playing his cards well, that was the thing. He was quite confident he had convinced Judith Bendler that he was her son, albeit adopted. All that remained was to get this decrepit old geezer to think the same.

That shouldn't be a problem.

'It's a long time since I was in Aarlach,' he said.

'Twenty-two years, I imagine,' Robert replied.

'Ha ha, that's right. It'll be great to be back, anyway.'

'We'll see,' Robert muttered. 'Aarlach's a dump.'

'That may be,' Daniel agreed. 'But when you've grown up there, it's special.'

'Though your growing up wasn't much to shout about, was it?'

'That's true,' Daniel said. 'So in a way it was lucky you sorted it out. Got me away to New Zealand, I mean.'

'That's the way it happened.'

He doesn't seem very keen on chatting, Daniel thought. I just hope he doesn't fall asleep behind the wheel. Or breathe his last.

They had joined the motorway and had a two-hour drive ahead of them. Should he offer to take over at the wheel? He considered it for a moment, but then decided it was safest to leave things as they were. He didn't have a driving licence; of course, he had stolen cars and driven them as well *down under*, but if they encountered a police check, there could be trouble. Although his plan was far from finalized, trouble was something to be avoided, even a Merino sheep could grasp that.

He reclined the seat, thinking that if the old chap didn't want to chat, he might as well shut up too. He would lie back and consider what strategy to adopt, today and in the future. And what he would do with all the money he would soon be in possession of. When the old man delivered.

Travel the world, perhaps? A house in the West Indies? Las Vegas?

Gratifying thoughts. Nice to chew over, and even nicer when you shut your eyes, he noted. Might as well have a kip, and if the old boy suddenly gets talkative, he'll have to wake me up.

Vegas, he thought. A green roulette table surrounded by beautiful women. Plenty of chips and cash in the pockets of his Armani suit. A drink in his hand, a slender cigar in his mouth. Well I'll be . . .

He was woken by the old man saying something.

'Hm, yes,' he said, setting the seat upright. 'What did you say?'

'Nothing. You must have been dreaming. Snoring, anyway.'

'Oh. I'm sorry. Whereabouts are we?'

He looked around. They were on a narrow road running across barren countryside. No buildings, just ugly, low-growing pine forest. Surely this couldn't be the road to Aarlach?

'I thought we'd make a little detour,' Robert Bendler said. 'You've no objection?'

'Detour?' Daniel said. 'Why? Where to?'

'The quarry in Kerran. You liked it last time you were there.'

'Oh . . . did I?'

Should he or should he not remember this? Was the old man calling his bluff? Was it a test? The safest thing was not to reply at all.

'Yes, you can't have been more than seven or eight. You might not remember it at all. We were on a little outing, you and I and your mother.'

'Ah? I don't really know. We'll have to see when we get there. How far is it?'

'Only a few minutes. It's no longer in use, you know. It wasn't then either. A bloody great hole in the ground, fifty metres deep . . . a little bit like the Grand Canyon, if you know it?'

'Of course I do,' Daniel said. 'It's near Las Vegas.'

Robert Bendler didn't answer. He carried on driving, hunched slightly over the wheel, and suddenly the landscape opened up in front of them. Straight ahead was a crater, hundreds of metres from side to side and breathtakingly deep. It was actually precisely as he had said: a bloody great hole.

'Christ,' Daniel said. 'There's been some rock hewn around here.'

'That's right. It operated for a hundred years until it became unprofitable.'

Daniel nodded. They were approaching the quarry at some speed and he had the impression the old man might have been accelerating instead of braking and coming to a stop.

'Don't get too close. Are we supposed to get out and have a look?'

'No. We're going to take a little flight. You're up for that, aren't you?'

And at that point, before Daniel Fremont had time to grasp what was about to happen, they were only fifteen or twenty metres from the edge of the quarry. Robert Bendler kept the accelerator pedal pressed to the floor, a shower of gravel and stones flew from the spinning tyres while his passenger tried in vain to grab the wheel; and, as if projected from a cannon, they carried straight on, out into the void.

'I'm not Tom Bendler,' Daniel screamed. 'I'm someone else.'

'Someone else? And now you tell me?' Robert Bendler had time to say, before they hit the ground in an explosion of stones, splintered glass, metal, burning petrol and body parts. A landing strip called Death.

The monk by the sea was standing in the same place.

Turned away, perhaps so that he didn't have to see. Maybe the ocean he was surveying drowned out the sounds of what was being said in the dark consulting room too. Was that what Maria Rosenberg was thinking when she chose the painting? Not beyond the bounds of possibility.

They drank tea as usual. The therapist had hurt her hand and Judith had helped with serving it. It was the fifteenth of December and their first meeting after the funeral.

'You must be feeling dreadful. Your husband and your missing son . . . both at the same time. What happened?'

'I think they'd made a deal. It must have been something like that.'

'A deal? What kind of deal?'

Judith looked at the monk. 'I don't know. I didn't even know they'd gone off in the car.'

'But it was your husband who was driving?'

'Yes. There wasn't much left, of the car or their bodies . . . but yes, at least that could be established.'

'And no skid marks? I'm sorry . . . I've been reading the papers.'

Judith drank some tea. 'No, he must have done it deliberately.'

'He took his own life and your son's at the same time?'

'Apparently.'

'Would you like to talk about it? We can save it if you like.'

She shook her head. 'No, I don't want to save it. I want . . . I think I want to get through it and move on.'

'That's good. It's important for you to be able to look forwards.'

'Thank you. I'm trying, at least.'

'Are you sleeping at night?'

'So-so.'

'Are you eating properly?'

'Not much, but sufficient.'

'That's good enough. You've been through an enormous amount recently and it's important for you to be able to concentrate on simple, everyday things. And to get some rest. Would you like me to ask you one or two questions, or would you prefer to hold the conductor's baton yourself?'

The therapist gave her kindly smile.

'You're welcome to ask.'

'All right. Which is the harder to bear, that Robert is gone, or that your son turned up and disappeared? If you can separate them?'

Judith considered the question.

'When all's said and done, that Robert's gone.'

'Are you sure?'

'Yes, even though I knew he was dying. When I try to think about Tom, I just get confused . . . I thought he was an imposter when he arrived. I was quite sure he was dead. And suddenly he is . . . properly dead. Sometimes it feels as though I dreamt it all. And then . . .'

'Yes?'

'And then, I can't understand what happened . . . It's difficult. Why Robert did what he did. And I'll never get an answer.'

Maria Rosenberg nodded.

'Probably not. But you ask yourself all the time?'

'More or less.'

'It's not been a month yet. There's an old method for dealing with questions that have no answer.'

'A method?'

'Yes. Stop asking them . . . the questions.'

She smiled again. Deep in thought, Judith drank more tea.

'What are you thinking?'

'That Robert never agreed to have him declared dead. He was right on that point. And then Tom comes home after twenty-two years, and . . .'

'. . . is pronounced dead,' the therapist filled the pause. 'You know, Judith, many things have been discussed in this room – I've been sitting here listening for over forty years – but your story surpasses almost all of them. I'm glad to see you coping so well, despite everything.'

'I have a very good therapist, that makes it easier.'

'Thank you. But are you intending to stay in the house?'

'I think so.'

'Don't do anything hasty. How's the dog?'

'He's old, but I hope he's still got a year or two left.'

'Excellent. And Christmas?'

'I've had a few invitations, but I think I'll stay at home.'

'You're not afraid of being lonely?'

'No. I've got a big edit to get through.'

'Of course. What's this one? Erasmus?'

'Yes.'

'Well then. As for me, I'm going away over the festivities, but I'll be back in the new year. Shall we book another session for the beginning of January?'

Judith gazed at the monk again. His enigmatic figure and his absolute integrity.

'No, thank you. I think maybe we should have a break. Please don't take this the wrong way, but I'd like to see if I can manage on my own.'

Wrinkles appeared on Maria Rosenberg's brow, but were instantly smoothed away.

'My dear friend, that sounds like an absolutely excellent suggestion. But you must promise me one thing. Get in touch if you ever feel you need a cup of tea.'

'I promise,' Judith Bendler said.

SIX

Wanaka, New Zealand, 1996

The treatment centre was on the side of a hill with a view over Roy's Bay, and it was his third.

Both of the previous establishments had been on the North Island, one on the outskirts of Auckland, and the other in Hastings. Neither of them had worked; he had run away from one and been thrown out of the other. But they were a long time ago, at least ten years before he ended up in Queenstown.

This third place was called My Brother's and Sister's Keeper, a somewhat biblical name, and the reason he had finished up here was that he had met an angel. She was called Norah and one morning when he opened his eyes in the hospital in Queenstown, she was sitting by his bed. At first he thought he was dead and had, by some procedural error, been sent to heaven, but then he felt a sudden stab of heartburn and realized he was still alive. Whatever went on up there with Our Lord, it didn't include heartburn.

How he came to be in hospital was rather unclear. He remembered nothing about it, but someone had supposedly found him in a ditch somewhere near Promised Land. When he eventually regained consciousness, a bearded doctor informed him that if he didn't immediately give up all forms of drugs, including alcohol, he would be dead within six months.

At which point he would not be rubbing shoulders with angels; the bearded doctor didn't mention that, but he worked it out for himself.

But then one day – he must have been in for at least a week, detoxed and cared for as well as possible and soon to be discharged – she was sitting there. Angel Norah Perkins. She was around twenty-five, with blonde, slightly curly hair and skin that looked as though it were made of marzipan and porcelain. And eyes as blue as lavender.

The first thing she said when she opened her rose-red lips was: 'I've come to help you find the narrow road. You've been travelling too long on the broad one.'

He tried to reply, but could only emit a sorrowful wheeze. When she handed him a glass of water and her fingers brushed his, he almost fainted, but recovered himself.

'We have a home up in Wanaka. I've been sent to collect you.'

He took a deep gulp of water and said: 'I'm a bad person.'

She smiled. 'Through faith you'll become a better person. But it's up to you whether you want to come with me or not.'

He considered it for a second.

'I'll come.'

'Hallelujah,' said the angel.

That was in February. Now it was November; he had been staying at My Brother's and Sister's Keeper for more than six months and it wasn't an exaggeration to say he was a new man. A better person. A humble believer.

Drug-free for the first time in twenty-five years. It was Norah Perkins who had saved his life, just as she had promised she would. He knew that if she had been an overweight sixty-three-year-old cripple with a hairy wart on her cheek, instead of the lovely creature she was, he might never have gone to Wanaka. But the Lord moves in mysterious ways, and even if he had fallen in love the moment he saw her, he had been released. She was an instrument of God, and you don't flirt with an angel.

The treatment centre really was a home. He thought that in some ways it was his first home. He had recounted his life story at the meetings that were held three times a week. With honesty, repentance and as well as he could remember. Other residents had told their stories, each worse than the one before, but that was the way to move on. The narrow road had no shortcuts; the only way to be forgiven and born again was to open one's heart.

He would have liked to stay on the green hillside overlooking Roy's Bay for the rest of his life, but that was not to be. He knew he had to venture out into the world, perhaps bear witness to the Gospel, and one evening he had a conversation with Norah herself about what he should do and how.

Not least about where he should go. She was familiar with his background in detail – apart from a certain stabbing, which he had kept to himself for the sake of everyone involved – and she offered a tentative suggestion.

'How would it feel to go back?'

'I don't know,' was his honest reply. 'But I suspect there's only one way to find out.'

'Go where your heart takes you,' Norah Perkins instructed him. 'For God lives in your heart and He will not fail you.'

He nodded, and so it was decided.

'You need to get in touch first and find out how things are,' said Norah; there were times when she sounded less like an angel than others.

'Will you help me find the telephone number?' he asked. 'If I can borrow the phone, that is?'

She nodded. That was no problem. There were generally no problems at all at the treatment centre My Brother's and Sister's Keeper.

He made the call one morning in the middle of September, without considering the time difference. There was a slight interference on the line. Like waves breaking on a pebble beach.

'Hello?'

'Judith Bendler?'

'Yes.'

'It's Tom.'

REIN

Translated from the Swedish by Paul Norlen

Adapted into the film *Death of an Author*

ONE

I had two reasons to travel to A., perhaps three, and because my intention is to recount everything as precisely as I'm able, this is the starting point I choose. The journey to A.

As I see it in this unwritten present, of course there is a risk that things will run together, become unclear. That perhaps I haven't fully succeeded in separating all the events and connections, and then of course it's a good rule of thumb to use the chronology that is available anyway. Even if – at least this is my hope – I have not yielded to the temptation to venture too far back in the warp of time.

Who can say when something actually begins?

Who?

The first reason was thus that radio concert. Beethoven's Violin Concerto; as commonly known it is in D minor, probably written in 1806, originally for the violinist Franz Clement, and it is said that Beethoven himself considered it such a masterpiece that he never bothered to write anything else in that genre. Unsurpassable, in other words.

True to habit I had curled up on the Barnesdale sofa with a couple of blankets over my legs. A glass of port was within comfortable reach on the table, accompanied by a bowl of nuts and a single wax candle. I recall that it struck me how the slightly flickering cone of light somehow seemed to embody the distance between myself and the music; the impenetrable land, that fuzzy but definite boundary between me and it. Outside, a persistent rain lashed against the window. We had arrived in the middle of November and the weather was the way it usually is this time of year. Dark, wet and gloomy. Gusts of wind swept through streets and alleyways, and in the past few weeks the temperature had alternated between zero and a few degrees above. At the most.

The broadcast started a few minutes after eight o'clock and I soon found myself in that state which encompasses both strong concentration and relaxation, and which is so character-istic, possibly even unique, of a good experience of music. Perhaps I also fell asleep for a few minutes, but I am nonethe-less certain that I did not miss out on a single note of Corrado Blanchetti's superb playing.

The cough came right at the end, during the very quietest part of the rondo, and thus it gave me something of a shock. I have reflected a great deal both on the sound and on my reaction to it, and I know that actually no doubt prevails in either respect. It was an electric shock, to put it simply. Electro-emotional; I was immediately sent into a state of trauma, and it went on for some time while I numbly listened to the final chord of the concerto, to the subsequent applause and to the announcer who explained that we had just enjoyed Beet-hoven's Violin Concerto in a recording made by the radio symphony in A. The soloist had been Corrado Blanchetti and the date of the event was 4 May that same year.

I don't want to deny that there was still some intellectual doubt from the very first moment. In no way was I foreign to the possibility that I could have heard wrong. That I was mis-taken. I truly reasoned and rejected and contrafabulated quite

a bit about this momentary auditory memory; I am not really
a person who likes making decisions on the fly, but deep down
– in the protected space of emotion – I knew of course that I
was not at all mistaken.

It was her. It was Ewa's cough. Somewhere in the audience
during this more than six-month-old recording my missing
wife had been sitting, and through a slight throat irritation she
was unable to suppress, I got the first sign of life from her in
over three years.

A cough from A. One and a half minutes from the end of
Beethoven's Violin Concerto in D minor. Of course, it may
seem peculiar that something like that can happen at all, but
in the light of much else, of what had affected me both earlier
and later, for example, it does not seem particularly sensational.

It took me over a week – nine days, to be exact – to get hold
of the recording from the classical music station (my tape
recorder had unfortunately not been turned on during the
broadcast, because I forgot to buy tape), but to the degree
doubt had managed to sink its claws in me during this waiting
period, they immediately released their hold when I sat down
and listened again. Four or five times I wound backwards and
forwards over the place in question, and each time I tried both
to be neutral and to sharpen my attention before the sound.

Of course I can't describe it. Are there even words for
something like a cough? It strikes me what a small part of our
reality and our impressions of it actually fall within the
domains of language. So while it is completely possible for me,
by means of a single brief auditory impression, to distinguish
what is characteristic in a specific person's cough – among
millions – I hardly have an adequate word or expression to

describe this sound. I assume that a precise distinction could be achieved by means of comparative audio frequency graphs and similar technicalities, but as far as I am concerned, from the very beginning this aspect has been both superfluous and uninteresting.

It was Ewa who coughed. On 4 May she had been sitting down there in A., listening to Beethoven's Violin Concerto; I had known it at once when I heard it, and I knew it just as strongly after having listened again.

She was alive. Alive and somewhere. At least she was six months ago.

And that gave me a shock, as I said.

The other reason to travel to A. turned up about two weeks after the radio concert. Early one morning my publisher, Arnold Kerr, called me up and reported that Rein was dead, and that he had just received his new manuscript.

Naturally this sounded both puzzling and a bit contradictory, and the same day we met at the Cloister Cellar over the lunch hour to discuss the story.

Discuss the little there was to go on at this point, that is. Yes, Rein was dead, Kerr noted, poking a little apathetically at the fettuccini with his fork. Unclear circumstances, but he hadn't been particularly healthy in recent years, so in a way perhaps it was no surprise. I tried to find out the details, naturally, but Kerr mostly sat shrugging his shoulders defensively, and it soon emerged that he didn't know all that much about what had happened. He had only received the news by phone; Zimmerman had called the night before from A. and reported the fact, and Kerr assumed that all the detailed circumstances would come out in a press release, which admittedly seemed to be unusually long in coming, but which would probably show up before evening. Rein had been a well-known figure after all, both in his homeland and here and there in other parts of the civilized world.

Austere and considered a little difficult perhaps, but read and appreciated, to be sure. And translated into a dozen languages. It was here I came into the picture; or had come in, rather. Rein's earlier works – *The Tschandala Suite* and the essays – Henry Darke had still interpreted and translated into our language, but as of *Kroull's Silence* I had taken over. Darke's illness put a stop to all translation assignments, and in several conversations I had also understood that he had never really been satisfied either with his final texts or with the relationship with Rein himself. At one of our last meetings – only a month or so before Darke's decease – he actually stated that Rein inspired a sense of repugnance in him; at that time I had not yet met Rein personally and thought of course that sounded a bit peculiar, but over the years I have come to understand Darke's standpoint more and more, I don't want to deny that. True, I have not met Rein on more than four or five occasions, but I have been undeniably struck by something hard to digest in his personality. I have never quite managed to clarify where it came from, but the feeling has been there nonetheless.

Yes, in any event, not until that day when Kerr and I sat at the Cloister Cellar and pondered over why not a word had yet been mentioned about his death, either in the newspapers or on radio and TV. Even though more than half a day must have passed, more or less.

'What was this business about a manuscript?' I asked.

Kerr reached down and dug in his briefcase, which was leaning against the table leg. Took out a yellow folder, held together with rubber bands this way and that.

'This is what is so damned strange,' he said, wiping the edge of his mouth a little nervously with the napkin.

He removed the rubber bands and opened the folder. Took out a sheet of paper, the top one in the bundle, and handed it over to me. It was handwritten; black ink, rather sweeping handwriting. I recognized it.

> A. 17.XI.199–
>
> Sending you my final manuscript for translation and publication. Forbid all contact with my publisher and others. The book may under no circumstances come out in my native language. The utmost secrecy is necessary.
> Sincerely
> Germund Rein
> P.S. This is the only copy. I assume that I can rely on you.

I looked at Kerr.

'What the hell does this mean?'

He threw out his hands.

'Don't know.'

He explained that the folder arrived the previous day, with the afternoon mail, and that he tried several times to make contact with Rein by phone. His attempts, as he expressed it, had come to a natural end when Zimmermann called and told him that Rein was dead.

After these clarifications, we sat silently and turned our attention to the food for several minutes, and I recall that I had a hard time keeping my eyes off the yellow folder, which Kerr placed to his right on the table. Naturally I felt an ever-so-strong curiosity, but also a certain distaste. My last meeting with Rein had taken place six months earlier in connection with his most recent book having come out in my translation.

The Red Sisters, it was called. We had met up at the publisher just very briefly, and as usual he had been very secretive, autistic in a way, even though we followed his instructions for the press conference to the dot. We had toasted with both champagne and sherry, Amundsen expressed his hope that the book would be a success, and Rein just sat there in his disintegrating old corduroy suit and looked as if the only emotion he could possibly foster with respect to it all was contempt. A grey, indifferent and disinterested contempt, which he had no intention of trying to conceal.

No, it would be a lie to maintain that I harboured any warm feelings for Germund Rein.

'Well?' I said at last.

Kerr finished chewing and swallowed deliberately before he raised his head and looked at me with his pale publisher's eyes. At the same time, he set aside the tableware and started lightly drumming his fingers on the yellow folder.

'I've spoken with Amundsen.'

I nodded. Naturally. Amundsen was head of the publishing house and the one who had ultimate responsibility.

'We're in complete agreement.'

I waited. He stopped drumming. Folded his hands instead and looked out the window down towards Karl's Plaza and the trams and hordes of pigeons. I understood that through this simple gesture he wanted to grant the moment the weight that it rightly deserved. Kerr was not one to neglect an effect.

'You can take it. We want you to get started immediately.'

I did not reply.

'If it contains as many references as the last one, it's probably best if you stay down in A. too. You have nothing that binds you, as far as I understand?'

That was obviously a completely correct presumption. For three years I had not had anything that kept me here on the home front other than my dubious work and my own inertia, and Kerr knew that damned well. Of course I could not decide just like that; perhaps I felt that I wanted to keep them on tenterhooks a few hours, so I asked for time to consider. A couple of days at least – or until the details about Rein's death had been properly explained. Kerr went along with my request, but when we parted outside the restaurant I could clearly see how the suppressed excitement was brimming inside him.

That was naturally no surprise. While I wandered homeward in the biting wind I thought about the matter and tried to clarify the conditions a bit more closely. If what Rein had written in the letter was true, then this concerned a completely unread manuscript. Unread and unknown. It was not difficult to imagine what a sensation it would provoke in publishing circles and among the book-reading general public if it came out. Germund Rein's final work. First edition in translation! Why not on the anniversary of the author's death, even?

Regardless of content, the book would surely climb to the top of the bestseller lists rather quickly and bring much-needed money into the publishing house, which – it was hardly a secret – had been going through some lean times the past few years.

One prerequisite, naturally, was that Rein's conditions of confidentiality and secrecy had to be respected. Exactly what the circumstances were around this peculiarity was of course hard to know at such an early stage, but if it was as Kerr hoped, then there were perhaps only four people in the world who knew of the manuscript's existence. Kerr and Amundsen. Myself and Rein.

And Rein was dead, evidently.

While we sat there at the Cloister Cellar I had never asked to look more closely in the folder, and Kerr had not invited me to either. Until I gave a positive response I, of course, had to accept hovering in ignorance of the contents. It was with almost ritual precision that Kerr put on the rubber bands again and stuffed the manuscript back down into the briefcase. When we put our coats on out in the cloakroom he also secured the handle with a chain around his wrist, and I realized that he truly took the whole thing with the strictest serious-ness. I also realized that both he and Amundsen had presumably taken note of Rein's request and not made an additional copy.

What I have now reported occurred on Thursday, the week before the first Sunday in Advent, and to the extent I had not already decided, the matter was settled the next day when I came to my job at the department.

Schinkler and Vejmanen met me with gloomy faces and I understood immediately what had happened. Our request for additional project funding had been rejected.

I asked, and it was confirmed through a long oath from Vejmanen. Schinkler waved the letter from the Ministry of Education that had arrived half an hour earlier and looked generally despairing.

The situation was clear to all three of us. Even if we hadn't spent very much time discussing it, we knew what that meant.

We had to cut back. There were three of us and we had project funding for two.

One full-time and two half-time. Or two full-time and one dismissal.

Schinkler was oldest on the farm. Vejmanen had a wife and kids. When I look back, I still think that I didn't have much choice.

'I think I can get a translation grant,' I said.

Vejmanen looked down at the floor and scratched his wrists nervously.

'How long?' Schinkler asked.

I shrugged.

'Six months, I would think.'

'Then let's do that,' said Schinkler. 'We'll probably be able to dig up some money for next autumn.'

With that, the matter was settled. I spent the morning cleaning my desk and drinking my rightful share of the whisky bottle that Vejmanen went down and bought in the store on the other side of the street, and when I got home I called Kerr and asked if he had heard anything more about Rein's death.

He had not. I explained that I had decided to take on the assignment in any event.

'Excellent,' said Kerr. 'It does you credit.'

'Under the assumption that you pay for six months in A.,' I added.

'We had intended to propose that,' Kerr stated. 'You can probably stay at Translators House, I assume?'

'Presumably,' I answered, and because I was feeling the whisky rather clearly in my temples, I ended the call. I decided to take an afternoon nap. It was 23 November, and before I fell asleep I lay there awhile and thought about how quickly life can switch onto a completely new track.

This was not a new thought, but it had been lying fallow

for a couple of years. Whether it then followed me into the illusory world of dreams, I have no idea. In any event I have no memory of that. Generally I am unable to recall my dreams, and the few times that I have, it has almost always had a complicating effect on my mental state.

And it is certainly the case that forgetfulness is a much more reliable ally than memory; that I've learnt from one thing and another.

The third of January was a dreadfully cold day. The temperature stayed down towards fifteen degrees below freezing, and out at the airport a hard, tempestuous north wind was blowing, which meant that most departures were delayed several hours. Personally, I was forced to spend the whole afternoon in the cafeteria waiting for my flight, and I had plenty of time to think about what I was really getting myself into.

Maybe it was only natural that this old feeling of interchangeability came over me. The sensation that all these people who were sitting and waiting around me, or pacing impatiently between the various duty-free shops – all torn out of their normal contexts – in reality could have changed place and identity with each other as easily as anything. That it would simply have been a question of setting our passports and travel documents in a big pile on the floor and letting chance – represented by some bored, anonymous security officer – peel off new lives for us. Arbitrary and just, and completely without preferences or engagement.

I tried to read, too. Not Rein's manuscript, which Amundsen and Kerr had solemnly delivered at a little ceremony the evening before – I had decided to wait for a better moment before starting on it – no, what I browsed in and tried to concentrate on were a couple of dubious crime novels that I'd bought in the after-Christmas sales, but neither of them was able to capture my interest sufficiently for me to follow the plot.

Instead, I mostly sat and thought about the situation, as I said. About Ewa, of course, and about how I would organize the search for her down in A.: whether I should try to manage it on my own, or if it would be wiser to make contact with some kind of private detective. At that moment I was leaning towards starting alone, and then engaging help later on to the degree that it seemed necessary.

I don't think I had any great illusions that it was not going to be necessary.

Mostly I was still wondering about Rein. It was hard to keep my thoughts away from him, even if I truly had no desire to go over his damned death in my head every day and every hour. I had done that for a while; there were a number of question marks, and they would no doubt remain until they at least located the body.

If it ever were to show up. News of Rein's demise had taken almost four days to come out after Kerr got the phone call from Zimmermann. As far as we understood, this was because the author's widow refused to give credence to the authenticity of the suicide note, and demanded a lot of analyses and investigations before she accepted it and it could be released to the press. It was not until the abandoned motorboat was found, and all other indications pointed in the same unambiguous direction, that she gave in and the message was cabled out over the world.

From the viewpoint of dragging, the place he had chosen – or, rather, the probable place – was not favoured by either winds or underwater currents this time of year, and so there was much that indicated the body had been carried out to sea. If it was true besides that he had been weighed down in some way, there was ever so much that argued that the remains of the great neo-mystic Germund Rein were presently somewhere at a depth of between three and four hundred metres, twenty to thirty kilometres out to sea. This was the cautious assessment made by C. G. Gautienne and Harald Weissvogel in *den Poost*, the newspaper that went furthest in its attempts to determine a probable resting place.

In some way all of this was typical for Germund Rein, and I had no difficulty imagining him lying down there in the depths with his contemptuous smile on his lips, while the fish nibbled on his flabby old man's flesh.

Much too sublime, that is, to let himself be put down in the earth by ordinary mortals in the customary manner. Untouchable to the end.

Naturally, I also realized that thoughts like this hardly made a good platform for the work I had to perform in A. If there is anything that has all the prerequisites for upsetting a translation assignment, it is a feeling of hostility and animosity towards the author.

But I hadn't started yet, as I said, and perhaps it was just as well to get rid of this aggression before it was time.

I think I tried to convince myself of that anyway.

My plane took off at ten o'clock, exactly six hours delayed, and when, after a rather bumpy flight, we landed at S–haufen outside A., it was already past midnight. The airline offered all passengers an overnight at the airport hotel, which I – like the majority of the others – accepted, and it was thus not until the morning of the fourth that I could step off the train at the central station in A. I don't really know why I take up space with these basically irrelevant time indications, maybe it's mostly a question of control. The feeling of control, that is: what Rimley designates as *Movement's necessary time and space load*, or something similarly sententious. I don't know if you, Reader, are familiar with Rimley, but once I had spent some time in A. – in the stationary space – I soon noticed in any event how inessential it seemed to me to keep track of concepts such as date and time. While I sat in the library and worked, they often had to tactfully shoo me out when it was time to close for the night, and I remember that on a couple of occasions – during March or April, presumably – I pulled uncomprehendingly on the door of the neighbourhood shop long after closing time or at an early Sunday hour.

But thus, on 4 January, I arrived. In the morning. And it wasn't exactly spring in the air here either.

With two heavy suitcases and my worn briefcase (containing the yellow folder, some dictionaries and a large envelope with countless photographs of Ewa), I took a taxi to Translators House. Of the six rooms for rent, four were occupied: two Africans, a Finn, evidently, and a ruddy and puffy-faced Irishman who I met on the stairs – he smelled of cheap whisky and addressed me in some kind of German. I turned down his invitation for a drink at the bar on the other side of the street, took possession of my room and decided to try to find something better as soon as possible. I discussed the housing issue with Kerr and Amundsen, and a certain unanimity prevailed that Translators House was perhaps not the best solution after all. Presumably my stay at such a place would sooner or later come to Rein's publisher's knowledge, and we had decided not to compromise the great one's final wish. Discretion a point of honour. My work in A. should be done without anyone's attention being brought to what I was occupied with; the commotion and articles after Rein's death had continued all of December, and there was of course a lot of money to be made on reissues of this and that old book. Not to mention what an echo his last, posthumous book could achieve. A posthumous first edition in translation. Absurd as anything, undeniably.

It was still lying there between the yellow cardboard sleeves. I'd been forced to swear, before both Amundsen and Kerr, to guard it with my virtue and my life. Even so, they had made a copy and placed it deep inside the publishing house's most sacred safety deposit box – there still had to be some measure to risk-taking, Amundsen had let it be understood. My steadfastness against starting to read the manuscript while still on the home front may perhaps seem a trifle extreme, but it is due to the method I apply when I translate. Like so much else, I inherited it from Henry Darke, and I have understood that it is not particularly common in the guild; the main idea is that the interpretation, the translation, must start immediately on first contact with the text. To make doubly sure of this I take great pains to read as little of the text in advance as possible. Preferably only a sentence or a line; at most half a page. I know that other translators work in exactly the opposite way; preferring to go through the whole work two or even three times before they get started with their own writing, but Henry Darke recommended his model and I soon discovered that it suits me better. Especially when it concerns an author like Germund Rein, where you quite often get an impression that in the moment of writing he himself is not really clear what is going to come two pages further along.

Besides rooms for rent, at Translators House there is a common kitchen with stove, fridge and freezer, and a rather well-stocked library (especially where dictionaries are concerned, naturally enough) with a number of somewhat separate and basically appealing workspaces. This first day, however, it all seemed rather deserted. In the refrigerator I found a couple of beer cans, half a stick of butter and a piece of cheese that must have been there since long before Christmas. The library looked dusty and hardly inviting; at three of the workspaces the lamps were broken. I realized that it was out of the question for me to sit down with Rein's manuscript in this lugubrious environment. The coffee machine in reception was out of order, and Miss Franck, who sat at the so-called reception desk four hours a day, told me that a new one had been ordered in October, but the delivery had evidently been delayed. She also started going through the laundry and cleaning procedures with me, but I interrupted her and explained that I had stayed here before and was already familiar with them, and that I would only stay a week.

Apparently I managed to offend her through this simple information, because she blew her nose ostentatiously and returned to her knitting without another word.

I left her to her fate and made my way out into the city. Even though it was an ordinary Tuesday, there were ever so many people in motion, I could see, at least in the city centre and along the tourist thoroughfares. The cold was tangible, several of the canals were frozen and a biting wind came in from the sea. I slipped into a couple of bookstores and music shops, mostly to get a little warmth. Sat in some cafes with beer and cigarettes too, stared at people, and I soon noticed that it was Ewa I was searching for. All women with dark, straight hair immediately drew my eyes to them, and the thought that I actually could find myself eye to eye with her again felt both stimulating and a trifle alarming.

I thought about our last morning together in that little mountain village, before she took off on the final journey, and about what infinite tenderness I felt for her as she got into the car and drove off to meet her lover. I remembered how I stood on the balcony and resisted the strong impulse to call her back, while she crossed the courtyard and waved at me through the rolled-down side window. Warn her. Get her to stay behind instead of taking off on this fatal journey. When she disappeared behind the stone wall I was unable to hold back a cry, but naturally it had no effect. It only became a vain expression of the double-edged tension that was pulsing inside me. Not even the old caretaker who was raking leaves out of the flowerbeds below seemed to have heard it, and after having seen her start up the winding road along the mountainside, I went back into the room and took a long, refreshing shower.

No, first I crawled into bed awhile and tried to read, that's how it was . . . but naturally that was a completely hopeless enterprise.

In this way – by stepping in and out of shops, and by sitting in cafes and thinking about Ewa – I moved slowly through the central parts of A.: down towards Vondel Park and the public library on Van Baerlestraat. From my last visit I had the idea that their doors didn't usually open until sometime during the afternoon but in return stayed open until rather late in the evening, which would suit me extremely well. I have never been a morning person. Having to perform any important tasks before noon has been something of an Achilles heel ever since my teens. The evening and early night-time hours are my morning air, that is when my capacity is at its peak, both mentally and physically, and if you happen to be in circumstances where you yourself can determine your daily rhythm, there is naturally no reason to deny yourself those early morning and forenoon hours in bed.

That was correct. Monday–Friday from 2.00–8.00, it said on a notice on the door. Saturdays 12.00–4.00. Quite excellent, accordingly. I didn't go in this first day, but decided on a visit the next one. As I had no great longing to go back to Translators House, I decided to while away the rest of the afternoon in town. After having wandered around more or less aimlessly for an hour or two, at the corner of Falckstraat and Reguliergracht I found a small housing agency. I stepped in and explained my wishes: a more or less centrally located room, preferably in the vicinity of Vondel Park. Shower and cooking facilities. Six months approximately. Not too expensive.

The dark-skinned girl browsed in some binders and made two calls. There might possibly be something that was suitable, she explained; if I had the opportunity to stop by in a couple of days, she would investigate in the meantime.

I thanked her and promised to return no later than Friday.

It was not until fairly late that I came back to Translators House that first evening. Thought it was just as well that I live it up a little before getting down to business, so I indulged myself both in a proper dinner at Planner's and a few hours at the bars around Nieuwe Markt. As it was I probably spent most of the time thinking about how I should proceed with the search for Ewa, but I don't think I managed to find any particularly viable plan of action. In any case nothing that I could later recall, and when I finally tumbled into bed towards midnight, I could tell that I still had not started to part the veils of either of the two sinister affairs that caused me to travel to A.

But I was on the scene. The foundation was laid, and on the other side of night it was of course high time to get started. I also remember that I liked imagining this untouched future. A tabula rasa, a snow-white field that I still had not entered and where all possibilities still rested side by side.

With these thoughts I fell asleep.

'I know that I'm hurting you, but I have to go my own way.'

Her words came out just like that, they could have been taken out of any contemporary melodrama, and I carefully stroked a strand of hair from her cheek. It was the first time and it wasn't the first time. We were lying on our sides, face to face in our comfortable double bed, and I remember that I thought about that dubious thing with the eyes. That suddenly, when you get too close, they turn completely blank. The expression, the oft-mentioned mirror of the soul, disappears as if by magic at a distance somewhere between ten and fifteen centimetres. Within this boundary there is nothing. No way and no promises. Not even the dormant hostility of cat eyes.

When we get right next to another person only this cell accumulation remains, this bitter thing. It is a hard experience to go through, naturally, and then it's not always easy to find your way back to the right distance. Maybe it's the sort of thing you learn over the years. I assume that you, Reader, know what I'm talking about.

In our case, I understood, of course, that she would not manage very long on her own, but the thought of simply letting her run was enticing anyway, that I must admit.

It was an August day. In the late morning, warm and promising as a sun-ripened plum. We had three weeks of holiday ahead of us, and it was in the next moment that she declared that she had a lover. I suppressed an impulse to laugh, I recall it as if it were yesterday, and I don't think she noticed that. She had been in therapy all summer, it was less than six months since she was released from the institution and yet it was too soon to start planning for the future.

Much too soon.

'Do you want me to get breakfast ready?' I asked.

She hesitated slightly.

'Yes, thanks,' she then said, and we looked at one another in mutual understanding.

'We're leaving tomorrow?'

She didn't answer. Didn't change expression at all, and I got up to go through to the kitchen and prepare the tea tray.

That first night in A. I dreamt about Ewa, an ever-so-erotic dream evidently, because I woke up with a strong erection. It quickly passed and was replaced by a headache and nausea; while I sat on the toilet with my head in my hands, I tried to tally up how much alcohol I'd consumed the night before, but there were a number of uncertainties that would not become clear. I showered for a long time in the miserable stream that was offered at Translators House, and embarked into the cold sometime around lunch. With my briefcase firmly clamped under my arm I managed to get on board a tram that I hoped was going in somewhat the right direction. It was, it turned out, and when it reached Ceintuurbaan I jumped off. Slipped into a bar and got myself a couple of sandwiches and a cup of black coffee. Then wandered the remaining blocks over to the library; the wind that blew through the streets and across the open canals was murderously cold and I understood that I must at least see about buying myself a proper scarf, if it was my intention to stay healthy in this cold metropolis.

When I arrived at the library, there was only a thin woman in her sixties behind the counter, and I waited while she served a dark-skinned gentleman in ulster and turban. When he had his books stamped, I stepped forward and introduced myself. Explained that I was working on a translation project and that I needed a place where I could sit in peace and quiet for a few hours every day.

She smiled obligingly and a little shyly, and took the trouble at once to come around the counter and escort me over to the work tables, which stood four by four in rows in the reference department. She asked if I wanted to have a table reserved for my use – there was always plenty of room anyway, she maintained, and if I wanted to leave behind books and materials, or simply have paper kept there, there could of course be an easy solution.

I thanked her and chose a place furthest to the left, only a metre or so from the high, leaded window, through which you could look out towards Moerkerstraat and one of the entrances to Vondel Park. For the moment, besides the woman and me, there were only two other people in the place, and I assumed that this was how it usually appeared. She nodded, wished me good luck and returned to the counter. I sat down and placed the yellow folder to my left on the table. To my right I placed the spiral notebook and four newly acquired pens. Then I removed the rubber bands and prepared to get started with Germund Rein's last book.

When I left the library it was dark. I must have been working for many hours and yet I hadn't got more than three pages into the manuscript. It was a heavy, mysterious text and it resembled none of what Rein had written earlier, I could immediately determine that. If I hadn't known that he was the one behind it, I presumably never would have guessed it. Yet it was too soon to make out either a setting or plot. The only sure thing seemed to be that there was a person with the designation R, in whose consciousness these first pages took place, rendered in a kind of interior monologue, where a woman, M, and another man, G, also seemed to play a certain role. I could sense that the whole thing would possibly develop into some sort of triangle drama, there were signs that indicated that, but the text could just as well take other turns and when I put a stop to the day, I felt that I still didn't have much of a grasp on the whole thing.

The first paragraph alone must have taken me almost an hour, and when I later read it again (while I sat and waited for food inside De Knijp), it still seemed to me that I had missed the core of Rein's text. Or the tone, rather: naturally it's the chord that's the important thing, then the individual words and expressions may be handled with a certain freedom, that's one thing I've learnt over the years.

> The totality *[it started]* of R's time in the world is growing no longer, still exists, but merely, yes merely vanishingly thin, a gaping and a screaming for footholds and roses, always these roses, dew and dew, perishable as dew, a burning and a panting and M. Where is M keeping herself these days? Her profile always stays behind a moment even after she twisted her head and left the room, a bewildering woman. Stays behind also in R, image is added to image, edge to edge and overlapping, all these moments are

always there in parallel, even the present. He has struck her, sure he has raised his hand, but as a tree lives from the rain and the storm, she is also his, the pain and the anger and the fire that purifies and heals and solders them together, and it was he himself, R personally, who introduced them to each other, M and G, years ago, still edge to edge that too, side by side and as the drop finally hollows out the stone now this too has come to this, this is what all this will be about. When R wakens in the morning he is confused. For some time now everything seems changed.

My food arrived and I closed the spiral notebook. While I ate I also felt the emptiness inside me, the feeling that always seems to appear after hours of concentrated work. As if the world and my surroundings no longer reached me; the people, the murmur and the quiet movements in the rather crowded place could just as well have been going on somewhere else – in another medium, another time; I sat in a deaf-mute aquarium and looked out towards an incomprehensible world.

Two, three glasses usually help, and so they did now. When I stepped out onto the street I felt like a normal person again and wondered whether it wouldn't be just as well to slip into a cinema before I made my way home to Translators House. I had no great desire to spend more than the hours of sleep I needed in my gloomy room, and I decided to visit the girl at the agency again the next day, to see what they had to offer.

I was unable to find any particularly enticing film, it had got a bit too late, so instead I spent the rest of the evening at a cafe with South American music, while I brooded over how I should actually take on the problem of Ewa.

Just strolling around the city, hoping to catch sight of her somewhere in the throng, undeniably seemed futile, but it was hard to get a grip on what other paths of action were open to me. At least I had a hard time discovering any on my own. When all is said and done, there was probably only one situation in this city where she could certainly be expected to show up sooner or later.

Concerts. Classical music. As far as I knew there were two concert halls in A. with consistent classical repertoire. Concertgebouw and Nieuwe Halle. I had never been to either of them, but while I sat there with my beer and listened to the muffled flutes from the Andes, I decided it might be time to become acquainted with their programmes.

No further ideas showed up in my head that evening. Apparently Rein's text had pretty much taken the steam out of me, and perhaps I also had one or two glasses too many. I left the bar around midnight, but still didn't feel so intoxicated that I couldn't go on foot all the way over to Translators House. The Finn – a massive guy who reminded me more than a little of some pre-Christian thunder god with a big, bushy beard and a voice like a bassoon – was sitting with the Irishman in the kitchen. They were entertaining each other with drinking songs and obscene stories, and through the floor I could hear their volleys of laughter and astounding oaths well into the night.

The wind from the sea. Temperature around zero. Occasional thin snowfall or rain turning to ice. January continued as it began. On Saturday of the first week I changed residence; through the agency I got hold of a small two-room apartment on Ferdinand Bolstraat, only ten minutes' walk from the library. The owner was a young photographer who had just received a six-month commission in South America from *National Geographic*, and our agreement included care of house plants and a cat.

The latter was an indolent, spayed female by the name of Beatrice, who, besides a half-hour stay on the balcony overlooking the courtyard (where she passively and without any real interest sat and observed the pigeons) and a couple of walks to the food bowl and the litter box in the kitchen, barely did anything other than lie in front of the gas heater and sleep.

The smaller room was equipped as a darkroom and I never used it; because of the poor insulation I spent as good as all my time at home either in bed or in the armchair in front of the same heat source as Beatrice. It was the only one in the apartment, but I want to stress that I was completely satisfied with the situation anyway.

Perhaps, above all, the surroundings. On the street below there were all kinds of shops: an Albert Hijn, some bars and even a laundrette. I soon found that I could hardly have wished for a better location; the traffic and street life out there were busy and varied during most hours of the day, and if I just dressed properly, I could stand in the window and observe the dynamics from my lookout point on the third floor. Undeniably this gave me an illusion of control: standing there, admittedly separate, but yet not without contact with the movements in time and space.

With regard to the rent, it was reasonable; certain adjustments had been made considering the flowers and Beatrice, and when I spoke with Kerr on the phone, it turned out that the publishing house had no objections to the little extra expense this nonetheless entailed compared with Translators House.

After the move my days also acquired a more uniform and routine character. I often slept late, preferably until eleven or eleven thirty. Showered, got dressed and went down and bought a newspaper and fresh bread. Had a leisurely breakfast in the armchair with Beatrice across my feet, while I read the news about the world and my previous day's translation. Made any corrections, and towards quarter to two I left the apartment. Walked first through a couple of small alleys sheltered from the wind, then out into the breeze over Ruysdalegracht, along Kuyperlaan and Van Baerlestraat, to arrive at the library a few minutes after the doors had opened.

Most often it was Frau Moewenroedhe who was sitting there – the woman who had taken care of me the first day – but sometimes one of the two younger women, the one dark with a slightly alluring, shy beauty, the other ruddy and a bit overweight. Neither of them spoke to me, would just nod at me in some kind of unwritten mutual understanding; I did not exchange many words with Frau Moewenroedhe either, but as of the third day I always got a cup of tea and some biscuits at four thirty, which evidently was the time when they allowed themselves a little break.

During these first weeks I still had some control over the hours of the day, I notice that when I look back. In a way it was, of course, necessary too. Once I had gone through the programmes of both concert halls I made a schedule that meant that I attended four or five events a week, which in turn assumed that I departed from the library soon enough to have dinner before it was time for Concertgebouw or Nieuwe Halle.

By and by I realized that my treasury would hardly allow me to run to expensive concerts several times a week, and I changed instead to simply appearing in the foyer to see the audience arrive. Sometimes I watched the audience stream out instead, but no matter which method I applied, during these cold January evenings I never saw so much as a glimpse of Ewa, and even if I didn't exactly start to despair, it was clear that I had to think of something better.

Otherwise I gladly spent a few evening hours at the cafes, especially a couple of rather motley ones that were located along my natural walking route home – Mart's and Dusart respectively. Sat there in a corner and now and then struck up conversation with people, especially older and slightly worn gentlemen, who had lived most of their lives and achieved a degree of scepticism that I found liberating and gladly shared. I guess I also ran into women on these evenings, but even if there were certainly one or two who wouldn't have had anything against spending the night with me, I never took any initiative in that direction. Anyway, it was unusual that I went to bed before one o'clock.

Even if my thoughts this first month revolved a great deal around Ewa, and what it could mean that she had actually been sitting at that Beethoven recording here in A. six months ago (I had checked that it really did take place in the Concert-gebouw), it was still the work with Rein's text that more and more came to monopolize my concentration.

It was heavy and sluggish, the first pages had been no exception, but despite this there was something that soon started exerting a certain control over me. Something hidden, almost: as if the manuscript contained a message or a subtext that he had made every effort in the world to try to conceal. I didn't really know what, but sensed early on that there must be something. The text was dense and tangled, sometimes downright incomprehensible, but the feeling that under it all was something that was simple, pure and clear became in-creasingly undeniable the further into the whole thing I got.

It was not particularly extensive either, the manuscript. Just a little over 160 pages, and if I managed to maintain a pace of fifteen pages a week, I ought to have made my way through it sometime around the end of March or beginning of April. A first draft, that is. Then naturally a period of refining and corrections would commence, but there could hardly be any doubt that I would be done in June as agreed.

But the subtext captured me. Enchanted me and baffled me. None of Rein's previous works had contained this degree of complication, and at the same time, of course, there were also the peculiar circumstances and restrictions concerning the publication itself. There must be some reason that he abso-lutely wanted to bring out the book in translation instead of his native language; both Kerr and Amundsen had scoured the annals, but were unable to find anything similar – certain texts smuggled out from various dictatorships, naturally, Solzhenitsyn and others, but nothing in this style. I know that I tried to abstain as much as possible from thinking and starting to speculate about the matter, but the more time passed, and the deeper into the book I penetrated, the more convinced I became that it was there, in the text itself, that these circumstances would be explained. The answer to the question of why Germund Rein's book must come out in translation was in the book itself and nowhere else.

Despite this growing insight, I still resisted reading ahead. Steadfast and unswervingly faithful to my method, I moved ahead line by line, paragraph by paragraph, page by page. The temptation was there, but I overcame it without particularly great exertions.

It is hard to describe Rein's text. The primary stylistic device was without a doubt the interior monologue, which seemed to wander between the protagonist R and the author himself, sometimes also to the woman M. The only other character in the book, at least in the beginning, was a certain Mr G, and in dense, more or less dream-like sequences, Rein depicted some kind of relationship between these three figures. As I already mentioned I could early on discern a triangle drama between the two men and the woman; certain incidents – or situations in any case – recurred now and then, reproduced in widely diverging registers and terms. That the relationship between R and G was not the best, as well as that R seemed to be very close to the first-person narrator who was sometimes glimpsed, I could hardly avoid noticing.

Throughout January, this was also all I really managed to

be clear about. It is possible, of course, that I would have realized the true relationship much sooner if I hadn't had Ewa to think about and devote my energy to besides, but that is merely speculation. Perhaps both of my projects were needed as relief from each other; when I think back I am often struck by how wholeheartedly I must have devoted myself to either the one thing or the other during this time. Either I found myself deep inside Germund Rein's text, or else I was searching everywhere for my missing wife. I never mixed. I kept my missions separate, like oil and water, which I think was completely the correct method.

By the very last days of January I was extremely tired of my one-sided and hardly productive concert monitoring, and I decided to seek new paths. Under the heading 'Private Detectives' in the phone book I found no less than sixteen different names and bureaus, and after my work at the library one evening I had arranged a meeting with a certain Edgar L. Maertens at his office on Prohaskaplein.

'Will you describe your problem, sir?' he began after the introductory preludes were over with and we had sat down, each with a cigarette and a glass of beer. He was older than I had thought, almost sixty, with close-cropped grey hair and gentle blue eyes that inspired a certain confidence.

'Have you been in the business very long?' I asked.

He smiled weakly.

'Thirty years.'

'That long?'

'It's a world record. You can safely confide in me. Well?'

I took the photographs from my inside pocket and spread

them out in front of him on the table. He observed them hastily.

'A woman.'

It was not a question, just a tired statement. He took a puff on the cigarette and looked at me. I chose to remain silent.

'First, I have to ask if you're sure that you really want to go through with this.'

The tone of resignation in his voice was bitter and unambiguous. I nodded.

'Surveillance or missing?'

'Missing,' I said.

'Good,' he said. 'I prefer disappearances.'

'Why is that?'

He didn't answer.

'When did she disappear?'

'Three years ago. A little more.'

He made notes.

'Name?'

I provided it and added that it was unlikely she still made use of it.

'You've checked that?'

'Yes. There is no one by that name in A.'

'And you have reason to believe that she is here?'

I nodded.

'Will you please tell your story in brief terms.'

I did so. Naturally omitted certain decisive parts, but made an effort to include everything that might otherwise be essential. When I was done, he did not reply immediately. He leant forwards across the table instead and studied the pictures of Ewa a bit more carefully.

'All right,' he said. 'I'll take on the case.'

It had not occurred to me that he might decline, but I realized now that it was hardly a dream job that I was asking him to perform.

'Of course I can't promise any results,' he explained. 'I suggest that we give it a month, and if we haven't tracked her down by then, I'm afraid we'll have to write off the matter. I assume you want discretion.'

'Full discretion,' I said.

He nodded.

'Concerning the fee,' he started to wind up, 'I take only half if I fail.'

He wrote two sums on the pad in front of him and turned it around so that I could read. I understood that I would not feel inclined to continue using his services after our agreed month.

'What do you think about the chances?' I asked.

He shrugged. 'If she really is here in the city we'll probably catch sight of her. I have a small staff.'

'Baker Street Irregulars?'

'More or less. Does she have any reason to lie low? Other than what follows from your story, that is.'

I thought.

'No . . .'

'You hesitate.'

'No reason I know of, in any event.'

'And you haven't seen her in three years?'

'Almost three and a half.'

He put out his cigarette and stood up.

'Are you really sure you want to get hold of her?'

His persistence on this point was starting to irritate me a bit.

'Why do you ask that?'

'Because most people manage to get over a woman in three years. But not you, I gather?'

I stood up too.

'No, not me.'

He shrugged again.

'You can give me a couple hundred up front. I assume that you intend to stop by now and then to hear how things are going?'

I nodded.

'I suggest Mondays and Thursdays. If anything acute happens we can be in touch, naturally.'

We shook hands and I left him. Back on the street the rain had picked up again, and I quickly decided to slip into the first available bar.

It was called Nemesis, it turned out, and while I sat there and sucked up my dark beer, I didn't really know if I should interpret the name as a good or a bad omen. In any case, I thought I could sense a feeling of movement after the hopeless tramping in the same spot of the past few weeks. For the time being I decided to put my hope in this vague impression.

Because the rain kept up, I also remained sitting at Nemesis for several hours before I was able to make my way home more or less dry-shod. I do not have the faintest idea what time it may have been when I crawled into bed, but when I woke up by and by, it was February and there was a red-haired woman lying by my side.

I never found out what her name was, and she didn't seem particularly eager to introduce herself. Without making much fuss she showered and left. All she left behind her were a few strands of hair on the pillow and a faint scent of Chanel No. 5.

I stayed in bed until twilight had descended properly. Then I got up and gradually took off towards the library, but out on Ruysdalekade the wind was so strong that I turned around completely. Returned home and made cinnamon coffee instead. Sat down with Beatrice in the armchair. Turned up the heat to max and listened to Bach's Brandenburg concertos in the cassette player the photographer had left behind.

Listened to Bach and thought about Ewa.

It was 15 August that we set off. Exactly as planned, we gave ourselves a few days to get through Germany and I felt that I truly loved her. We had been married for almost eight years at this point, but never before had I experienced this love this strongly. Something had matured between us, and I knew that things could actually not be better between two people than they were for us during this trip. It is hard to specify what the feeling actually stemmed from; I seemed to discover features in my wife that I had never seen before, but whether in reality the change was in her or inside myself I could not figure out. Not then and not later.

Because of this change in my attitude, her recurring talk that she had a lover and that we had to separate was rather a great strain for me. I also tried several times, in a number of different ways, to talk her out of her illusion, and at last I asked who it was.

'Mauritz,' she answered simply.

It was at a rest area along the Autobahn. We were eating egg sandwiches and drinking coffee, the weather was beautiful. Black and white cows were grazing on a clover meadow that sloped down towards a waterway, I recall. An unusually beautiful rest area overall.

'Mauritz Winckler?'

'Yes.'

'You're out of your mind,' I said. 'All women fall in love with their therapists. You have to forget that nonsense.'

She looked at me seriously.

'I know that I'm hurting you,' she repeated. 'But my honesty is the only thing I have. He's going to meet me down in the mountains. We've agreed on that.'

Then I struck her and then we didn't talk any more about it for several days.

It was during this first week in February that I started to catch sight of the hidden message in Rein's text. Or one aspect of it, at least. Late one evening, a few minutes before closing time, I was still sitting at my usual table and studying what I had got down during the day. The last sentences read:

R's entire obsession with the total moment, this instance where all crooked shortcomings and failed ascents are tumbled over, will perhaps nonetheless never see the light of day, an insight that has long been found in M. To live side by side, or parallel or for his neighbour; the doubt has never existed in the woman, nothing has been questioned; there on the shore she is simply there on the shore, simply there, solely. A present heavy thing *in* the stone-dead security of the sea, the shadows and the screeching gulls. Oh, sterile mother vanity! Cold fish, cold fishes; seaweed, rotting seaweed, a wind that does not struggle, does not speak, does not invite, has nothing to report after a long, long journey. Such is M.

The word *in*. I stared at it. Reread the short section of text a few times and could not for the life of me see any sensible reason to italicize this insignificant preposition, and then I remembered a couple of other italicized words or phrases that had seemed unwarranted to me.

I browsed back. There were only two places. On page four the word *like*. On page sixteen the words *the poet*.

like the poet in

Just at that moment, Frau Moewenroedhe came into the reference department and coughed discreetly. I packed up my papers and left the library. Once home on Ferdinand Bol I took them out again and browsed ahead in the text. After perhaps ten minutes I had skimmed through it all. In the whole manuscript only two more phrases were italicized:

the earth's on page 63
ashes on page 158
like the poet in the earth's ashes

It took a few seconds before I understood the connection, but it was stark once I saw it. 'The Earth's Ashes' was the name of one of the stories in the collection *The Dream Cupola*. A rather short and tragicomic story about an author who, at the height of his literary career, is struck by compulsive thoughts and thinks that his wife wants to murder him. I pushed the papers away from me. Then two rather contradictory feelings appeared.

The first was anger. Or irritation bordering on anger in any case, about something so incredibly silly. Why bake something like that into this frightfully heavy, in places almost unreadable text? Something so cheap! My barely suppressed antipathy towards Rein flared up, and I know that for a few seconds I toyed with the thought of sending the manuscript back to Kerr and Amundsen and asking them to burn it. Or find another, less fastidious translator.

The other emotion is harder to describe. Something related to fear, perhaps, and I soon realized that my agitation and my anger probably mostly arose as a defence against this rather threatening sensation. One of these automatic, but arbitrary, Band-Aids for the soul.

Like the poet in 'The Earth's Ashes'?

It must be ten years since he wrote it. Five since I translated it. What the hell was the meaning? I tried to recall exactly how the story ended, but could not get it clear in my head.

I went over to the window. Turned off the light and stood and observed the reality outside. For the moment it consisted of a lead-grey sky, a dark building exterior with a row of illuminated shop windows on the ground floor – Muskens Slaapcentruum, Hava Nagila Shawarma Grillroom, Albert Hijn. Some people on bicycles. Parked cars. The sound of a tram rattling past. Cars that came and went and street lights that were swaying in the wind.

Objects that stood there and objects that dissolved. I remember what I thought, and I remember that there were no words for these thoughts, then or now.

I don't believe that my contempt for language was ever stronger than right then, as I stood in the window that evening with Rein's italicized words grinding in the back of my head. After a while I went back to the armchair, put Beatrice on my lap and sat with her in the darkness a rather long time.

After that I went out. Got intentionally drunk at some of the cafes in the immediate vicinity; my worry sat the whole time like an irritating flicker under my skin, an unreachable itch, and it was not until later, much later during the night, when I staggered up and vomited in the toilet, that it let go to some degree.

The next day the sun was shining. Instead of going to the library I continued on to Vondel Park, where I then wandered around as long as the light held. Made a number of decisions concerning the immediate future, and in the evening I called Kerr.

'How's it going?' he asked enthusiastically, but not without a trace of worry in his voice.

'Excellent,' I explained. 'I just need some information.'

'Yes?'

'What is the name of Rein's wife?'

'Mariam. Mariam Kadhar. Why?'

I did not reply.

'Can you send an account of his death?'

'Whose? Rein's?'

'Naturally. I need a detailed summary, don't want to root in this myself. It might attract attention.'

'I understand.'

I could hear that this was just what he hadn't done.

'If you could go through the newspapers rather carefully?'

'Does this have anything to do with the manuscript?'

'It's not impossible.'

'I'll be damned.'

'As soon as you can, then?'

'Of course.'

We ended the call. I left the phone booth, and I understood of course that against my will I had fired up Kerr's and Amundsen's enthusiasm for the Rein project. In my mind's eye I could see them rubbing their hands together. And why shouldn't they? A publisher that came out with a posthumous book by the great neo-mystic, a book that cast new light over his death. What more could you really ask for? If you didn't succeed in selling such a morsel, it would be just as well to change your line of business altogether.

Personally, I did not feel particularly eager to take on the threshing at the library again, but knew I had to go further into the text. It attracted me and repelled me at the same time, but perhaps it was mostly a question of beating down the reluctant curiosity I had started to feel with respect to the circumstances around Rein's death. It struck me that I ought to have asked if there was any G in Rein's vicinity too, while I had Kerr on the line anyway, but I decided to postpone that to some later occasion. When all was said and done my supposed suspicions at this stage were nothing other than loose, unfounded fancies. By and by more light was shed on the case, but at that point

– even during the next few days while I continued struggling with the inaccessible formulations in the manuscript – I was probably prepared to dismiss it all as rather fantastical. An instance of over-interpretation in peculiar circumstances, and not much more.

My contact with private detective Maertens was regular, as we had agreed on. On Mondays and Thursdays I took the route past his office on Prohaskaplein after my work day at the library, and each time he just shrugged a little apologetically and explained that no leads had yet been discovered.

After a series of such visits, I had undeniably started to lose heart. Maertens never seemed the least bit embarrassed that he hadn't achieved any results, and the arrangement had already cost a fair amount. At last I asked him flat out if he thought there was any prospect at all of succeeding, but he only answered that it was impossible to make a prognosis.

When I left the detective bureau that evening – it must have been sometime in mid-February – I had a grinding sense of discouragement. I had single-mindedly and slowly worked my way up to page ninety in Rein's manuscript, over halfway in other words, but the past few days' progress had been sluggish. The language was virtually impenetrable in numerous places, and even if I was now rather easily finding the right expressions and formulations, I often thought that the text did not give any meaning at all. No meaning that I was in a position to discover, in any case. Just a hopeless uncontrolled inner monologue, most often placed with the protagonist R, dream-like here and there, constructed of words and text masses instead of images. My suspicions of a hidden message increasingly seemed to amount to nothing, and the only thing I had to look forward to, I assumed, was an additional seventy pages of the same mush. It can't be denied either that I started wondering what readers this subjective, concrete prose could actually find, and whether Kerr and Amundsen were actually making a fuss about nothing and rubbing their hands together too soon.

The 'Like the poet' sentence was of course still there to brood about, but that these seven words would constitute the whole point of this posthumous text seemed rather unlikely, to me anyway.

When I stepped into Nemesis that evening – yes, I am rather certain that it was just 15 February – I know that most of all I had a desire to tell Rein to go to hell. Upon closer reflection, however, I realized that was probably exactly what he'd already done.

I had two beers standing up, then I continued straight home. My mail was on the stairs, consisting for the day of a single, rather thick letter, and when I saw the return address I understood that Kerr had finally sent the account of Rein's death I had asked for. (It was only long afterwards that I found out about the accident with his daughter, which naturally was the reason that he took so long.)

Sometime later, I was sitting in the armchair with a cup of tea and Beatrice over my feet, reading Kerr's account. It was six pages long, he had undeniably exerted himself to some extent, and when I was done, I immediately went through it all one more time.

There was no particularly noteworthy information as such, nothing I didn't know already, but now when I had all the circumstances served up in this compressed way, I thought

I sensed one or two points in common with the text I was in the process of translating. Nothing I could immediately put my finger on, but I decided to go through what I had written down so far as carefully as possible the next day, to see if that possibly might produce something.

Externally, at first glance, not much mystery rested over Rein's death. On Friday 19 November he had gone with his wife and his publisher to the couple's house out by Behrensee. After an evening and night of rather heavy drinking, the wife had woken up at some point around lunchtime the following day, and sometime later found a farewell letter that was still in the typewriter. It was brief and perhaps not completely unambiguous (the exact wording had not, however, been leaked to the press), but when Rein's motorboat was found the following evening, abandoned and striking against the stones in a bay a dozen kilometres further north along the coast, the connection, of course, started to be sensed. The police were contacted, but it took, as stated, almost a week before Mariam Kadhar went along with the fact that her famous husband actually made his way out to sea that night, or early in the morning, and then took his life by putting himself in the embrace of the water. The only passage of the letter that leaked out was: 'I am carrying our old bronze woman with me, so at least I avoid coming up to the surface and embarrassing you all . . .'

The old bronze sculpture, a piece weighing almost fifteen kilograms, was indeed missing, and it was thus presumed that Rein had tied it firmly to his body somehow before he heaved himself overboard.

It was thus based on the position of the found boat, prevailing wind and current conditions, plus the combined weight of Rein and the bronze woman, that one then tried to make calculations about where the physical remains of Germund Rein had probably found their final destination. The margin for error was great, naturally, and the prognosis that dragging him up would be successful was about as good as finding the sunken Atlantis. Consequently, they had refrained from trying – other than as much as was required to show a little goodwill, anyway.

Concerning the reasons for Rein's suicide, there were different reactions and theories, but at this point none of them showed any major deviations from what usually comes out in such circumstances.

Why had he done it? Should someone have understood? Hadn't he sent any signals? And so on.

But what do we actually know about what goes on inside those nearest to us and about their deepest motives? This byline of Bejman summarized general opinion in *Allgemejne*. Nothing at all.

That was it, the extent of Kerr's account. He had some questions too: in particular, of course, he wanted to know what I would do with it. Because I hardly knew that myself, I had no intention whatsoever of doing as he wished and sending a written report. Instead, I put the sheets of paper back in the envelope, got up and stood by the window, and yet again observed the decreasing movements out on Ferdinand Bol. A feeling of the enormous emptiness and futility of everything hung over me for several minutes, I recall that I smoked a cigarette and thought about whether it actually was possible to kill yourself if you simply jumped head first down onto the pavement. I hardly believed it. Presumably I would only inflict some kind of depressing and lasting disability on myself, which there would truly be no point to.

When these feelings ebbed out, in their place came a little wave of energy, and I decided to make cautious contact with Mariam Kadhar. Whether there would be any point to this was of course written in the stars, but it is just when we make these decisions, whose consequences we cannot foresee, that we feel dynamism bubble a little in our sclerotic veins.

I know that I'm quoting, don't recall who.

When we arrived at Graues, our village in the mountains, it was early morning and we'd been driving all night. More correctly, I had been driving all night, while Ewa was lying in the back seat asleep under our blue-checked blanket from Biarritz. At least for the past few hours, while I listened to Poulenc and Satie on the car radio and saw the darkness rise out of the valleys.

It was a beautiful morning, without a doubt. The houses, the narrow alleys, the mountains and the whole world were washed clean and innocent. I parked on the sloping, uneven pommerstone square, got out of the car and rinsed the fatigue out of my face in the quietly purling fountain. The sun was just coming over the ridge in the east and cast a gentle glow across the sleeping facades. I stood and looked at them while the water dripped from my hair and I thought that, when it's early morning, you can feel a sense of homecoming in any place whatsoever in the world. Then I woke Ewa, and I remember my disappointment that she wasn't able to step out of her own tiredness and experience this eternal, quickly passing moment just as strongly as I did.

We found our way to our hotel, which was located a bit outside the community itself, clinging to the middle of a rather steep mountain slope and with an endless view of the peaks on the other side of the valley. We checked in, Ewa went back to sleep and I did too, after a while.

It was a tourist village, naturally, but mostly with an emphasis on winter and when, a few hours into the afternoon, we made an initial reconnaissance tour, we discovered that there were blessedly few Germans and bleating Americans. We had dinner at one of three Gasthof, and when we were done Ewa said that it truly pained her that we couldn't continue to be together. I asked a little sarcastically when her lover could be expected to show up, and she explained that he was already on the scene. In a little village in the next valley, to be more precise, and she had promised to call him that same evening.

We paid and went back to the hotel. Shared a bottle of wine on our balcony, and while we sat there she left me for a few minutes to make a phone call from down in reception. She soon came back and I now noticed that she was surrounded by that kind of transfigured light that I had sometimes seen in her in the time after we were first together. I poured more wine in the glasses and swore to myself that I would never, never ever, let any other man have her.

Somewhat later we made love. Hard and brutal, as we did sometimes, and afterwards, when she returned from the bathroom, she said, 'That was the last time. I know that I'm hurting you, but that was the last time we made love.'

Suddenly I felt simply tired and irritated, especially at that meaningless nagging that she was hurting me.

'You're mine, Ewa,' I said. 'Don't imagine anything else.'

She did not reply and we lay there silently for quite a long time before we fell asleep. Perhaps I sensed already that she really meant what she had said, and that I actually was already a loser. I know that now of course, but the way you choose to lose is not inessential.

After approximately ninety-five pages, Rein's text suddenly became clearer. On one of the grey days of pouring rain around 20 February, I translated the following paragraph:

R's obsession, to with thought and word divest every situation of its content, its facticity, its essence, is not only this simple. Is also to conquer and to subdue reality. The disclosure, the capacity to put it under the pen is to conquer it. M and G. To be able down to the last letter to describe and expose what it is that is going on, is to make them into nothing. So he believes, in this frenzy he makes notes day and night, with these weapons he objectifies and kills; kills and kills, and nonetheless they stand there. M and G. Stand there, things-in-themselves, two things, one thing, everything, and this cursed obsession only turns the spear and the knives against his own sunken chest. They and he. He and they. He knows. She knows. G knows. He must get out of his head now. Out of his heart. Must find a cliff for perspective, must get clear, understand. What do they intend to do? What are the plans, what kind of future are they chiselling out with this endless watchful carefulness? Suddenly, one evening at Dagoville, his fear gets a new name. An infernal name. He fears for his life. R fears. He picks up the pen and starts writing, it is now he gets started in earnest and this night and coming nights he is anchored in this fear.

I leant back. Looked around the room. The lamps were on at only two of the other tables; it was the usual old visitors –

an elderly Jew with a white beard and skull cap who always sat here on Thursdays and Fridays and seemed occupied with some sort of Cabbalistic texts, and a woman in her forties who would come in now and then and with gloomy sighs sit over thick anatomy books for a few hours at a time.

Outside the window the rain came down steadily, across the street the yellow lanterns at Cafe Vlissingen had been lit. Of all the infinite cafes in this city, I think it was Vlissingen that had become my favourite place, I don't know why. Nothing other than a subtle balance between a series of inessentials, presumably, but I understood that if I were ever to come to live permanently in A., this is where I would be a regular. I packed up my books and left my work table. My thoughts needed a beer and a cigarette, I felt that clearly, and when I looked back I realized that I hadn't eaten anything the whole day other than the four biscuits that accompanied my daily cup of tea.

R is afraid? I thought while I crossed Moerkerstraat. *They and he? He and they?*

I experienced a sudden feeling that I was out walking on thin ice.

Mariam Kadhar was a chain smoker.

She was a thin, dark little woman with Levantine features and a sensuality that was felt in the air. Presumably she was making an effort to restrain it. Without success: with or against her will, she was the sort of woman who gives an impression that she was naked twenty seconds before you met her. And of being so again twenty seconds after you've left. I introduced myself.

'You were the one who called?'

'Yes, I hope I'm not disturbing you, as I said.'

'Have we met before?'

'I don't believe so. I wouldn't have forgotten that.'

She took that in without blinking, and started showing me further into the house. In what must have been Rein's library and study she had set out a tray with port wine, nuts and dried fruits on a little smoke-coloured glass table. The walls were covered with bookshelves from floor to ceiling, through a large panorama window you could look out towards the over-grown garden, which sloped down towards one of the canals. I tried to orient myself and decided that it must be Prinzen-gracht.

We sat down, and suddenly I wished that I was somewhere else. Or that I was sitting here, but that I was *someone* else. The sensation was rather strong and I remember that I closed my eyes hard and quickly to shake it off, which I won't maintain succeeded very well.

'You've translated my husband's books?'

'Yes.'

'Which ones?'

I listed the titles. She nodded weakly several times, as if she remembered them one by one as I mentioned them. As if each book were also a part of her own life, it struck me. It was not unreasonable to assume that it really was that way.

'You were married a long time?'

'Fifteen years.'

I cleared my throat.

'Well, I was in the neighbourhood, as I said. Wanted to convey my condolences. I liked him a lot . . . his books, that is. We only met a couple of times . . .'

Blather. She nodded again and lit a new cigarette. Poured the port, we toasted vaguely and without a word.

'He talked about you sometimes,' she said. 'I think he appreciated your translations.'

'Really? That makes me happy . . . it must be hard for you?'

She hesitated a moment.

'Yes,' she said then. 'I assume that it's hard. But I probably haven't got used to it yet . . . even though several months have passed. Don't know if I have the desire to get used to it either. You have to be able to live in darkness, too.'

'Is it painful for you to talk about him?'

'Not at all. I keep him alive that way. I've reread several of his books too. It's . . . it's as if they've gained a new meaning, I don't know if it's just personal . . . because I was so close to him, I mean.'

I understood that no more opportune moment would come up.

'Forgive me for asking, but what was he working on before he died? What was he writing, that is?'

'Why do you ask that?'

I shrugged and tried to look apologetic.

'I don't know. Just thought there was a line in his works that pointed ahead towards something . . . but there wasn't anything else?'

'Yes, of course he was writing.'

'Yes?'

'We just don't know where it went.'

'What do you mean?'

She hesitated again. Took a few quick puffs on her cigarette. I happened to think that the nerves of a person who chain-smokes like this could naturally not be in such great shape.

Perhaps in reality she was more tormented by the conversation than I was. It was a thought that carried with it a sensation that I still had control. Vague and quickly passing, I think.

'He was occupied with a manuscript the whole autumn, all the way until . . . well, until his death. It's not around. Perhaps he destroyed it. Burned it or . . . took it with him.'

'What was it about?'

She sighed.

'I don't know. He was secretive, he always was, but I think he was satisfied with it, because it occupied him. It showed on him.'

'He was a great author.'

She smiled quickly.

'I know.'

I drank a little port. Wished I had been in a position where I could continue asking questions. About why he had taken his life. About why she refused to accept it.

If she possibly had a lover whose name was G.

Naturally that was out of the question. Instead we talked a while about some of his books, primarily the two most recent ones, which I translated during an intensive eight-month period a couple of years ago and still had fresh in my memory, and we both expressed our regret that he had taken his last book with him into death. After approximately twenty minutes, it felt clear that she was bothered by my presence, and I understood that it was time to leave her alone.

At the door she stopped me a second.

'I still don't understand why you wanted to see me. Was there really nothing else?'

'I've bothered you.'

'No, not at all. I just got an impression . . .'

'What kind of impression?'

'That you had something more important on your mind.'

I tried to smile.

'Excuse me. Not at all. I'm a great admirer of your husband's writings, that's all.'

She looked up at me, she must have been twenty-five centimetres shorter than me, and as we stood there in the doorway rather close to each other, I suddenly understood how it would feel to press her head against my chest. She held my gaze an extra second; then she took half a step backwards and we said goodbye without making contact.

Out on the street there was snow in the air. Big, heavy flakes floated slowly down between the dark houses, and I remember that I tried to catch a few of them with my outstretched hands, but they didn't even seem to tolerate the nearness of my skin.

No contact here, either.

My head was naturally full of Mariam Kadhar, would have been no matter what the weather, but there was also something about these snowflakes that seemed to say something about her. Far beyond the words, I tell myself, where so many connections are hidden.

Yes, in the big, fresh silence beyond language and signs and other glitter. To speak like Rein.

If I remember right, it was only two days after my visit to Mariam Kadhar that I discovered that someone was watching me.

The first sensation came one morning when I was on my feet unusually early – I took a walk over to the grocery at

Waterloo Markt – and the impression was registered by my brain without my knowing it. Not until the same afternoon, when the pursuer came in and sat down at one of the rear tables in the reference department where I spent my time, was the first image developed, and I knew that it was the same person who had been waiting for me outside the tobacco shop on Utrechtstraat while I bought cigarettes. A tall, slightly stooped man roughly my own age, with dark, thinning hair and brown-tinted glasses. Inside the library he had hung his coat over the back of the chair and when I noticed him, he was browsing in a book that he appeared to have taken from a shelf more or less at random. Naturally I could not turn around to observe him, but when I went out to the toilet a little later with my folder under my arm, I passed him at a distance of only one metre and had time to study his appearance rather carefully. Thoroughly enough, in any case, that I would surely recognize him if he showed up another time.

Obviously I was still not a hundred per cent convinced that it was as I suspected – that he was actually following me. However, I became so that same evening; when I stopped for the day I walked over towards Maertens' office on Prohaskaplein, because it was a Thursday, and after only a hundred or so metres I had a feeling that there was someone moving in my tracks. I picked up the pace, took a short cut across Megse Plein and Verdamm Park, made my way around the same block on the north side of the park a couple of times and at last slipped into a narrow alley, where I waited, crouched behind some bicycles. After only ten seconds he passed by on the street.

I stayed behind in the alley another few minutes before I continued the two blocks over to Maertens' office. The whole thing seemed bizarre to me. Whoever it was who was assigned to shadow me and watch my doings, and whatever purpose there was behind it, the whole thing mostly left an amateurish impression. I had a little difficulty seeing any point to it either; what seemed most probable – in any event it was what first popped up in my head – was that it had something to do with my visit to Mariam Kadhar. Or that something about Rein's manuscript had leaked out somehow.

At this stage no other alternatives occurred to me.

As I stepped into Maertens' office, it also struck me that the simplest explanation for the shadow's clumsiness must be that it was intentional. Their idea was that I would become aware that someone was watching me, but there was no time to brood over what design might lie behind such a thing.

In any event, there wasn't time right then. You see, for the first time since I engaged him, Maertens had something to present. True, he stressed that it might very well be a wrong track, and he warned me not to get my hopes up too much.

Then he shoved a little brown envelope across the desk. I opened it and read a street address that I didn't recognize.

'One of the suburbs,' Maertens explained. 'You get there by train in half an hour.'

'So, have you seen her there?'

He executed his usual shoulder shrug.

'Not me personally. Just one of my employees.'

'When?'

'Yesterday. Saw her go into one of the high-rises, but she took the lift up and he wasn't able to see what floor she got off on. He's a bit lame and has problems with stairs . . . well, we've been watching the front door today, of course, but she hasn't been seen.'

'Are you sure that it's her?'

'Not at all,' he said with a smile. 'The birthmark matches, but who can say what a woman looks like three years later?'

I stuffed the envelope in my inside pocket and left him. When I came out on the street the bells in Keymer Church were just starting to strike nine and I understood that I might as well delay my visit out to the suburbs until the following day.

We had dinner at our hotel the second day, and it was while we were drinking coffee and smoking a cigarette afterwards that she explained that she was going to leave and meet Mauritz Winckler the next morning.

It happened that way too. I stood out on the balcony and watched her drive away in the car up the winding road that went over the mountains to the valley and the villages on the other side. Could follow her progress all the way up to the pass between two dark massifs, where the white Audi suddenly dissolved and disappeared as quickly as a snowflake in water.

The day was tuned in the same key; overcast, with threatening cloud formations that hung over the mountaintops. I decided on a hike up the mountain in the very same direction. Had no desire to be out among people and buildings, actually had no desire for anything at all except for my wife, but I recognize these occasions when it is necessary to get away. I always have. When the disquiet of the soul is too strong and must be converted and watered down in something physical, and right after twelve o'clock I set off with a few bottles of beer and a sack of sandwiches that had been prepared for me down in the kitchen.

After an hour, the rain was over me. I soon found a grotto

however, and I spent the whole afternoon there sitting on a stone and gazing out through the curtain of water towards the landscape, which had lost all outlines and much of its beauty that day.

Sat there and finished my bottles of beer and slowly chewed the sandwiches, while I rejected one plan after the other. Also thought a bit about the strangely smooth skin on the inside of my wife's thigh; other women's too, of course, but mostly about Ewa's. It seemed to me, in any event right then, so paradoxically innocent, this soft flesh, and I wondered whether it was possible by means of sensation alone, with the light touch of the fingertips, to decide where on the body a certain section of skin is located.

These thoughts naturally distracted me a bit, and the ultimate solution did not appear until I was on my way down again but even so, by the time I stepped into the hotel reception again it was clear to me. Not in the slightest detail with every step worked out, but in broad strokes, and it was with a feeling of grim satisfaction that I got into the shower and let hot water replace the cold sprinkle that had soaked me during the entire hour-long return hike.

I think I got the idea from an old movie that I had seen in my youth, probably on TV, but I never remembered the title, either then or later; although perhaps my plan only derived from one of the many archetypes of crime, with an origin as unclear as the soup the innkeeper chose to offer me in my solitude that same evening.

It was a great solitude and a hopeless soup.

When Ewa returned it was past three o'clock in the morning and I pretended to be asleep. I am quite certain that she understood that I was only pretending, but she played her role anyway and padded carefully around in the dark room, exactly as I used to do myself, six months earlier.

I have forgotten the name of that woman.

The suburb was called Wassingen and consisted of two dozen high-rises and a shopping centre. I didn't see any older construction and I assumed that it all originated from the late sixties or early seventies.

From the station I followed the winding snake of people who, via some foul-smelling pedestrian tunnels covered with graffiti, emerged into the reluctant light of day on a grey, heartless square. Shops and various service establishments fenced the square in from three directions and from the fourth a relentless wind was blowing in from the sea. I remember thinking that if Hell had been built in our day, they might well have used this architecture.

I found my way to the relevant building. It was a greyish-brown, damp-stained concrete affair with sixteen storeys. I made a quick estimate and calculated that it ought to house somewhere between a thousand and twelve hundred people. On the directory inside the front door where Private Detective Maertens' emissary supposedly saw my wife go in, there were seventy-two different names. I left the building and sat in a cafe in the shopping centre. Thought about several alternative strategies while I tried to keep an eye on all the women walking past in one direction or the other.

No acceptable plans of action showed up in my head, only a growing feeling of despair and futility, but then my gaze fell on the newsstand that was across from the cafe. I finished my coffee, went over and browsed the selection for a while, and finally bought six copies of a Christian weekly magazine called *Wake Up*. After that I made my way back to the building and got started.

Just over an hour later I had rung sixty-four doorbells. Because it was getting to be rather late on a Friday afternoon, I had also got answers at the majority, forty-six of them; I had sold two copies of *Wake Up* and not had so much as a glimpse of Ewa.

I threw the remaining copies of the magazine in a rubbish bin and returned through the tunnels to the station. Twilight had now descended; the feeling of alienation was starting to sink its claws into me in earnest, and while waiting for the train I had three glasses of whisky in the bar. Tried to initiate a conversation with the bartender too, an almost gigantic bodybuilder type with tattoos both high and low, but he only muttered dismissively and never raised his eyes from the computer game in front of him on the bar. I noted that he moved his lips a little while he read.

I returned home to Ferdinand Bol and called Maertens from down in the cafe, but as I said it was Friday evening and I got no answer. Thus it had to wait until Monday to settle the bill and decline future use of his services.

I continued drinking whisky the whole evening. Remember that I almost got into a row with a ruddy Norwegian at a bar in the vicinity of Leidse Plein, and on the way home stumbled over a bicycle on the pavement and got a couple of sizeable scrapes across the knuckles.

The most lasting negative from this evening, however, was that I managed to lose the list where I had checked off all the apartments I peeped into out in Wassingen, and when I look back I understand that this alone was probably what made me wait so long to pay my next visit.

In any event, I know that at this stage I had in no way given up the idea of actually finding Ewa; my evident depression that afternoon and evening was only a temporary resignation prior to the task.

Temporary and, as I see it, understandable in some ways.

On Monday I settled my bill with Maertens. I visited him before I went to the library; there was a little dispute about whether the Wassingen lead should count as a substantial result or not, but at last he gave in and we went by the lower rate.

He did not wish me good luck when we shook hands, and I understood that he was still of the opinion that I would do best to forget the whole thing and devote myself to something more meaningful. I had a few critical viewpoints on the tip of my tongue concerning lack of interest and engagement, but I held back and left him without further comment.

During the whole weekend, ever since the Wassingen lead was on the table, I had more or less managed to repress the question of the person who was tailing me, but just as I stepped through the doors to the library, I happened to think about him again. He showed up in my awareness like a will-o'-the-wisp without warning, and I remember that it felt as if I could conjure up his presence in the reference room.

For that reason it was almost with a feeling of disappointment that I found the premises completely empty. During the whole afternoon, as I continued working with Rein's manuscript, I only had company for half an hour, when two students sat and whispered about some common assignment at one of the tables in the very back.

I never saw a glimpse of any pursuer.

None of this will amount to anything, I thought several times this Monday. It will all fizzle out, as usual with all intentions and purposes in this accursed life.

And nevertheless I knew it was not that way. Nevertheless I knew that sooner or later everything would yield, and it was only a question of showing a bit of patience and persistence. There are signs and there are signs.

Rein's text was not particularly sensational either, at least for the first days of that week. If I remember correctly it was not until Thursday that I encountered something that forced me to start speculating anew: after a number of pages of rather unclear flashbacks of someone's childhood – probably R's own – suddenly the text opened up, and while the tea was cooling in my yellow plastic mug I translated the following paragraph:

> Documentation. During those fleeting moments when the anguish let go R started thinking about documentation. When all is over the wound must not simply close up like a footstep in water, from the dictatorship of oblivion and the continuous present. One morning she is on the square shopping for vegetables, always these vegetables that must not be a day old, her memento mori, he searches through her belongings, she knows that he would never do this and has not bothered to hide. Finds letters, four letters, three are clear enough, the fourth a conspiracy. They are conspiring, they are actually doing that, he feels drops of

sweat break out on his forehead when he understands this, they are conspiring against his life. R goes out on the beach, fills his lungs with uncontaminated sea air, continues out into the water, all the way to his waist he continues, stands there in the indolent swells and sees his life just as fleeting and just as vainly struggling as the slimy blue jellyfish who have drifted too far in and are never going to escape again. Returns to the house, she is still there among the vegetables at the square, it takes time, perhaps she is in bed fucking G too, he puts the letters in a folder, drives into the city and copies them, she is still gone when he returns. R hesitates. Copies for posterity? Goes halfway and replaces two among the panties in the bureau, places two originals plus two copies in a plastic bag, wraps it in canvas, very deliberate and very meticulously he goes about these assurances for posterity. Goes out to the shed, gets a spade, looks around and chooses. Out in the middle of the soft, pitted lawn stands this monstrously ugly sundial, and in the loose earth on its north side he buries his treasure and his will. Drinks several glasses of whisky. M not back yet, she is in bed fucking G, he knows that now, between wildly parted thighs she receives G's viscous semen, two sweaty animals in a hotel room in the city. Belvedere, presumably, or at Kraus in the neighbouring city further away, because they are so damned careful, M and G; but R drinks more whisky and he can picture them anyway. How they are fucking and batting around his life, raised above all doubt now, he sits down to write, his countermove becomes these words as always, these thin and bloodless abstractions in order to ensnare the sweaty homicidal bodies, an implacably

growing cocoon of words around the stinking flesh.
R fears and R knows, but R writes.

Pages 122–23. That evening I finally violated Darke's rule.
Without bothering to translate I simply read the rest of the
manuscript.

Yes, in the glow of the heavy cast-iron floor lamp and with
Beatrice resting across my feet, I read the last forty pages of
Germund Rein's writings. The very last lines were a quotation
from one of his first books, *The Legend of the Truth*:

> When one day we no longer understand our lives, we
> must still continue as if we were a book or a film. There
> are no other instructions.

I set aside the papers. The time is a few minutes past eleven
and I notice that my body is tense as a spring. I stand up and
try to relax, pace back and forth in the apartment awhile and
finally stand at the window with a cigarette. Turn off the lamp
too and observe, like on so many evenings, the sparse movements out there in the darkness. Thoughts get stuck in me,
glide in and out of each other and remove the words at a safe
distance. Even so, I understand that I must do something. I
have come to a point where all defences are cut off. I cannot
understand why he turned it over to me, but as of now it is too
late to buy your way out of taking action. It does not fall on
Horatio to harbour doubt.

After a while the tension eases. I go down to the cafe, but
I only have a couple of beers and it is with a fairly clear head
that I decide what strategies I must adopt.

These are, of course, nothing remarkable. I see no alternative solutions now, and I won't later either.

I had not seen Janis Hoorne in two and a half years, but he was in the phone book, and when I called he had no difficulty recalling our most recent meeting.

It had taken place in connection with a little book fair up in Kiel and we had spent a few evenings together at the bars. He was the same type of lone wolf as me, it turned out, and there had been a lot to talk about, even if his rather consider- able alcohol consumption of course placed a few obstacles in the way.

Obstacles to the kinds of things that perhaps could have been said. From other quarters I knew that now and then he would spend time at various clinics, but when he answered now – it was around lunchtime the first Sunday in March – he sounded both articulate and energetic. He was busy right then with a project for television about various extreme right-wing movements, he explained; found himself in the middle of an intensive work period, but even so seemed almost enthusiastic that I had called.

It was actually just a simple piece of information that I wanted from him – I had not managed to find the address to Rein's summer house through open channels, and because I knew that Hoorne had been there – he had talked about it during that week in Kiel – that was the first possibility that came to mind.

Anyway, he insisted on getting together and we decided to meet at Suuryajja, a little Indonesian restaurant in the Greijp-straak neighbourhood, on Monday evening.

It was a long session with both food and drink and conversation about existential matters in that particular, slightly sarcastic tone that I remembered from those evenings two and a half years ago. Hoorne expressed no surprise whatsoever at the fact that I planned to go out to Rein's house by the sea – my cover was that I was working on a number of personal notes that might perhaps result in a biography at some point – and when we parted well into the wee hours, I had both the address and a meticulously drawn route map in my inside pocket. The house often went under the designation 'The Cherry Orchard', I had also been told, but he did not know why. Something to do with Chekhov, naturally, but exactly what the connection was neither of us could establish, despite certain speculations. Cautiously I had also tried to pump him a bit concerning Rein and his marriage – after all, Hoorne had known him a little – but I had not produced any information that might indicate that there were suspicions about the death. On the contrary; for Hoorne the suicide had not come as a surprise at all. Rein had been in the right stage, he thought – in one of those low points in life, when it is actually only a question of whether the pendulum will swing back or not.

The most natural thing in the world.

I did not press him further either. I did not know what circles he moved in and what people he associated with – to the extent he had any associations at all. The simple control I had to perform was at this point not particularly dependent on more or less informed speculations. At my wondering whether he believed that the marriage between Rein and Mariam Kadhar had been happy, he simply dismissively shrugged and countered by asking if I had possibly heard tell of something called woman's nature. Evidently he considered this both ingenious and exhaustive, and I dropped the subject.

We parted late, as stated. Because I had a few months left in A. in any event, we also decided to be in touch in a couple of weeks, when he figured that his work for TV would be completed. His idea was that perhaps we could spend a week-end out by the sea in Molnar – only a couple of miles from Rein's house – where he evidently had inherited a small cottage from his father, the not entirely unknown military historian Pieter Hoorne.

I said that I looked forward to such an arrangement, but at the same time I had a feeling that in a few weeks things might well have taken such a turn that it would likely not happen.

The day after my meeting with Janis Hoorne I devoted an hour to investigating the train and bus connections out to Behren-see, the town that was closest to Rein's house. After that I gave up. If I wanted to take public transport, it would involve a number of complicated transfers and a four-kilometre-long walk along the coast. Consequently I decided to rent a car for a day instead.

Right before closing time at a Hertz office at Burgisgracht I reserved a little Renault for all of Wednesday, and it was when I came out of this office that I once again ran into my pursuer.

He was standing on the other side of the narrow canal, apparently trying to look as if he was observing something down in the black, motionless water. He had exchanged his long coat for a leather jacket with fur collar and had a dark woollen hat on his head, but even so I could immediately see that it was him. The same long horse face, the same hunched shoulders and bad posture. The same glasses.

For a brief moment I hesitated about what I should do, and perhaps that was enough for him to understand that I had noticed him. I started slowly walking towards the city centre and he dutifully followed me, but somewhere on Kalverstraat he turned into an alley and disappeared.

Even though I wandered around a good while I never caught sight of him again, and at last I gave up and took the trolley home to Ferdinand Bol. Swore to myself too, while I stood there dangling from the ceiling strap, that I would not let him get away next time, but whether it would then be best to simply confront him or try to reverse the roles, I could not decide.

I had a hard time in general getting a handle on what was actually going on these first days of March. The weather had suddenly switched over to pure spring warmth, and in some way it seemed as if this also involved a shift in quite different respects. In the game that was going on around me (I know that I formulated it just that way) my own positions seemed to constantly shift between various moves and pieces, and if there was any feeling that took hold during this time, it was one of being manipulated. The illusion that my decisions and actions were truly being governed by some kind of free will of my own was without a doubt hard to maintain, and I remember that more than once I decided that this was also probably just what the whole thing was about.

An illusion.

'But don't you understand that this is a delusion?' I said.

'It's no delusion,' Ewa said without even looking at me.

We got no further while we sat at the restaurant at Gasthof number two. We ate in silence instead, and I felt that language and words had suddenly become heavy as lead, and that neither of us would be able to pull them up from the deep mire we had ended up in. As before an imminent war, we found ourselves very close to the point where all negotiations break down and then only naked action remains.

Afterwards we took a drawn-out walk in the village. Then sat for a long time under one of the chestnuts alongside the schoolhouse, closed for the summer, and observed the black-clad, elderly gentlemen who were playing boules a little ways further down towards the river.

'I have had other women,' I said.

Ewa did not say anything. A squirrel jumped down from the chestnut, stopped a moment in front of our feet and looked at us, before it continued. I don't really know why I remember this little animal and the brief second when it stood quite still and looked at us from only a metre away, but I do and I understand that I am never going to forget it either. Perhaps there is something about the animal's eyes and about the unformulated question that is always there that I cannot cope with, I think that is it.

'It never meant anything,' I explained.

She took a breath.

'That's exactly what the difference is,' she said.

'What is that?' I asked.

'I have only had one, and it means everything.'

I did not answer and after a while we got up and started back to the hotel.

The next day, our fourth in Graues, I explained to Ewa that I wanted to spend the day on my own to think things over. I said that I needed the car too, our white Audi that we rented for the summer, and she did not make any protests. It struck me that Mauritz Winckler had a car of his own in his village on the other side of the pass, so if they intended to meet again, there were no obstacles.

I set off immediately after breakfast and my attention was intensely directed on all the details of the drive up to the pass. It was a clear day with only light wisps of clouds in the sky, and when I reached the pass I could see that it truly was just as I had calculated. The only critical point seemed to be right at the exit from the hotel, but assuming that you did not need to stop for any vehicle that came out on the road, there was no real reason to put the brakes on here either. The ten-minute-long drive up included a few hairpin curves, but the climb was so steep that I never even thought about removing my foot from the accelerator.

I drove over the crown and stopped at a little parking spot with an expansive view of the landscape on the other side. A tourist plaque informed that the elevation above sea level was 1,820 metres and that the surrounding peaks were close to 3,000. I sat on the guardrail while I smoked a cigarette and tried to follow the winding asphalt ribbon down towards the town, which I could more sense than see far below me. The road appeared and disappeared behind rocks and outcrops; it was naturally a question of the same lengthy descent as the one I had just come up. Some way below me, at a distance of only a kilometre or two, I could glimpse the artificially level surface of the Lauern reservoir, a gigantic dam that I had read about in the tourist brochures. The colour was an impenetrable green and, if I remembered correctly, the brochures had said that it could store up to a billion cubic metres of water.

I put out the cigarette. Closed my eyes and tried to visualize the whole thing. It wasn't particularly difficult.

Not difficult at all.

Instead of continuing down towards the dam and the town, I decided to first check the ascent one more time. I drove back down to Graues, had a beer at the cafe on the square, and then set off upwards again. Thus I happened to pass our hotel two times, but I refrained from stopping and examining this critical point at the exit – I did not know of course if Ewa was still in our room, or if she was already in the arms of Mauritz Winckler.

There was nothing to contradict the thought that she was doing both.

Lying in his arms in our room, that is.

My second attempt confirmed the conclusions from the first one. From the hotel up to the pass between the mountain massif took just under eleven minutes, and I was not in the vicinity of the brake pedal a single time. So far all was well, but of course the decisive part still remained.

The descent.

It took me almost three hours to figure out the most probable scenario, and during that time I drove the same stretch down and up no less than eight times in either direction. Sat up at the viewpoint several times too, while I smoked and thought. In order to get as realistic a picture as possible of it all, I tried to make my way down as far as I was able without using the brakes, and the last two times it was with obvious risk to my own life that I rushed through the curves in lowest gear. I also checked that there were no arrester beds or other conceivable safety islands along the road, and it was with grim satisfaction I was able to dismiss all such possibilities.

The furthest I managed to make my way down was just over a kilometre along the road, but then I proceeded with the utmost preparedness and in first gear from the start. The first four curves were not at all impossible to manage; I got the idea that even a driver in a state of shock ought to be able to get around them, and there was no question of any hairpin curves affording a chance of achieving a relatively soft stop into one of the rock walls. What then followed was even worse – an almost hundred-metre-long, sharply descending stretch with vertical rock face on the right side and an equally vertical drop to the left. No matter what I did it was impossible, without using the brakes, to lower the speed enough before the right-hand curve that followed at the end of the stretch. When I went into it, the car was irresistibly pulled out towards the drop-off on the left; an almost thirty-centimetre-high stone guardrail, eroded away in places, was the only protection, and I gradually came to the conclusion that it was here, right here, that it was going to happen.

So the drop was almost vertical, and about fifty metres deep. Below that an incline began, sharp cliffs and boulders, but no vegetation – and then, the best of all: the motionless dull surface of the Lauern reservoir.

A combined drop from the road of perhaps a hundred metres. An occasional blow on the side of the mountain, and then *plop*, down into a billion cubic metres of green meltwater.

No, it was not difficult at all to visualize.

I had dinner in Wörmlingen, the first village in the valley below the dam. Wrote a few postcards to friends and acquaintances, and told them about what a marvellous holiday we were having. To L and S I revealed that both Ewa and I experienced this trip as a kind of second honeymoon, and that it truly was no problem to find secluded love nests up in the mountains.

When I drove through the pass for the last time, I had already started thinking about the technical aspects of the enterprise, but I have always been handy with machinery and cars, and I knew that it wouldn't involve any major worries. The only thing that might possibly demand a little extra care and planning was the question of where I should do the work. After all, I needed an hour or two undisturbed, but I was quite sure that this detail would also work out.

In the afternoon of the following day, Ewa said that she would really like to take the car the next morning, by which point, sure enough, I had solved the remaining little problems.

'Of course,' I answered without looking up from the book I was browsing. 'Listen, take it. I filled up yesterday, so all you have to do is take off.'

I remember that she also came up to me and placed her hand on my shoulder for a brief moment, but it was a very quickly passing phenomenon, and I still did not raise my eyes.

I had presumably slept rather poorly the night before I drove out to Rein's house, because even though it was only a matter of a hundred kilometres, I had to stop and drink black coffee roughly halfway there.

To keep myself awake, that is.

Otherwise it was the same high sky and spring breezes as during the past few days – it must have been almost fifteen degrees Celsius and you could feel the ground swelling under your feet. The weather had also without a doubt had a favourable effect on my state of mind and my energy; the decision to drive out and dig for the compromising letters, or whatever might turn up, in the Cherry Orchard had not been easy to make, and I needed whatever support I could get. Surely I was also searching – consciously or unconsciously – for any signs that in the slightest way could be interpreted positively and filled with implications that I was on the right path. Something I actually devoted myself to during my entire stay in A. – it just felt unusually tangible this particular day. A warming sun. White and yellow flowers sticking up by the roadside. An obliging smile from the girl at the register when I paid for the coffee. Anything at all.

Perhaps the opposite – bad omens and surly cashiers – would also have made me refrain from it all; in retrospect of course it is hard to know. It happened the way it happened, but naturally it is not an unreasonable thought that things would have taken a different path if the weather had simply been a bit more neutral that second week in March.

At the square in Behrensee it was market day. I parked outside the church and with Hoorne's sketch in hand I went out into the throng and got oriented. I still saw no sign of the sea, but could sense it quite clearly in my nostrils. Maybe hear it too: as a muffled, distant murmur under all the human voices and all the clamour that hovered over the square. In any event, a half rusted-away road sign gave notice that the distance to the beach only amounted to one and a half kilometres.

For some reason I got an irresistible desire to browse in the stalls and stands before I continued and when, half an hour later – the clock in the low, whitewashed town hall had just struck one – I took off towards the beach, I had a rather well-filled bag beside me on the passenger seat. Fruit, bread, home-made marmalade and cheese. Also a bottle of cider, which I understood you should probably be a bit careful with.

A hundred or so metres before the bank with tall grass and wind-whipped bushes, the road divided and I turned south. According to Janis Hoorne it was now a question of just over three kilometres and keeping an eye out for a dilapidated mill on the left – at that point you could glimpse the Cherry Orchard inside a sheltering wreath of pines right below the bank itself. I drove carefully along the narrow asphalt road, which was covered for the most part by drifting sand and, sure enough, after a few minutes I was at the crumbling mill. I stopped and looked around.

Yes indeed, there was a house that corresponded to the description in among the trees to the right. There was also a flaking mailbox painted blue and a lane that led up to a kind of natural garage between the trees with room for four or five vehicles.

That was also the problem. There was a red Mercedes parked under the braided roof, and I realized that the warm weather was not entirely the ally I had imagined it to be. Evidently it had also enticed other people out to the sea, and because I did not have any particularly great desire to run into Mariam Kadhar or anyone else, I released the clutch and slowly rolled further south.

When I was out of sight of the house, I drove off the road and parked in another grove of knotty pines; I assumed they were planted along the shore to bind the sand, but certainly they also served a good purpose as shady lunch spots for families on Sunday outings during the summer months. At least on these stretches between the beach houses, which were spread out rather sparsely, at a safe distance from each other. I had no clear impression of the appearance of Rein's house, but nonetheless drew the conclusion that it belonged in one of the very highest price classes.

And why shouldn't he have allowed himself that?

With my bag in hand I made my way out into the wind and down to the shore. Wandered back quite a long way north; I kept to the firm, damp sand which now and then was licked by the foaming breakers and walked at a leisurely pace with my face almost turned backwards at an angle up towards the flooding sun. Out over the water, gulls hovered and filled the air with their complaining screeches. I met a solitary jogger in a red tracksuit and a woman with a dog, but otherwise the beach was deserted; all the way over to the point outside

Behrensee, where the land started to rise, and southward as far as you could see.

After perhaps twenty minutes I climbed up over the bank again. Started making my way back through the sand dunes and when I gradually found myself level with the Cherry Orchard, I crawled down in a protected hollow and prepared to wait.

The sun warmed thoroughly. I ate a little of the cheese and bread, took a few sips of the strong, sweet cider, and within ten minutes I had fallen asleep.

When I woke up I did not know where I was.

Like many others – I have discussed the matter with both doctors and laymen – I am struck now and then by a few blank seconds in the morning. These absolutely immobile, frozen moments when you are thrown out of sleep to the mute surface of reality and could actually be anyone at all. In any time and any room at all. Ever since Ewa's disappearance I had also understood to make use of the sense of freedom in those moments of unconsciousness – and in that way, during the three years that had passed, had gathered together a couple of minutes when I still, so to speak, had her there. That is something anyway, I would think, but this time – out by the sea at Behrensee – it was not a question of something that simple and consoling. It was something much stronger; perhaps essentially different.

I was lying on my back. Above me the gulls were circling around in a high blue celestial sphere. The sun warmed. I could hear the sea and the wind that rustled in the shore grass.

Seconds passed.

Ewa? I thought. It was the first thought that usually set the conditions of life right again. I remembered Graues.

Remembered my return home three and a half years ago.

Remembered the police interrogations. Inspector Mort's green shirt with rings of sweat under the arms.

The talks with good friends and social workers.

The months at the hospital and the move out of the apartment. My new job and resumption of the translations. The failed affair with Maureen. The failed trip with B.

Where was I?

An ant crawled across my neck. The gulls were screeching. Where?

A minute or more must have passed before I suddenly regained consciousness, and what restored me was the cough.

As clear as if she had been lying there in the sand beside me, once again I heard Ewa's cough from Beethoven's Violin Concerto, and it felt . . . yes, I think that it must be the feeling you get when you are shot to death. Or when the power is turned on in the electric chair.

I survived. Closed my eyes and took the cider bottle out of my plastic bag. Took a substantial gulp and, still without opening my eyes, lit a cigarette.

While I smoked it, I lay there without moving. Started slowly calming myself down, and in order to occupy my brain with something neutral I tried to think about the arbitrary mechanisms of memory.

Or was there no arbitrariness? Is memory – or forgetfulness, I mean of course – the only truly effective medicine against life?

I think so. Believed it while I lay there in my hollow in the sand in any event, and there is actually nothing that has given me reason to change my understanding since then.

Forgetfulness.

At any rate, after a few minutes I had recovered. I made my way over the edge to spy over towards the Cherry Orchard. The house was concealed for the most part by the pines, but the red Mercedes was still there, and from the chimney that stuck up above the trees came a faint wisp of smoke, which was immediately scattered by the wind.

I looked at my watch. Two thirty. I sank back down in the sand again. Formulated two questions:

Did they intend to spend the night there?

At what time would it be sufficiently dark for me to venture over?

While I consumed a little more of my provisions, I decided that much depended on the location of the sundial itself, and that in any event I had to make my way up and locate it in daylight. Having to sneak around and search for it in the dark seemed anything but inviting.

An hour or so later I knew what I needed to know. The sundial was a truly doubtful affair, exactly as had been suggested in Rein's text – an oversized, sprawling bronze sculpture placed in lonely majesty in the middle of the large lawn. The distance to the house was a good twenty metres, and I assessed that it ought to be a rather risk-free enterprise to sneak over and dig under the cover of darkness. The Mercedes was still there; I had glimpsed a couple of people, just in passing, but it was clear that they preferred to stay indoors, despite the weather. Or to avoid being seen at least. I myself was mostly lying on my stomach with my head sticking up between two tufts of grass, and in that way had very good oversight of what was going on over in the Cherry Orchard.

Which was not very much. And nothing particularly exciting. While I lay there and waited for darkness to fall, I had time to smoke almost twenty cigarettes, which is more than my entire normal daily consumption, and my provisions were used up long before twilight.

But there was also a growing sense of calm. A rest and a recovery in those uneventful hours on the shore, which I think I needed and which I also stored in me and could benefit from later. After my memory-less minute and the shocking awakening my nervous tension levelled out, the discomfort in my body was subdued, and when I carefully started to approach the house just after eight thirty, I did not feel particularly worried. There were lights on in the windows on the ground floor, but the glow did not reach very far out on the lawn, and I understood that for any observer from inside, the sundial would presumably not even be outlined against the shoreline and the surrounding dark trees.

Crouched down, I snuck across the grass. Came up to the sundial that rested on a metre-high brick base. I groped in the loose earth around its foot with my hand. I had not bothered to bring along a spade; I knew that Rein hardly had reason to dig particularly deep, and after only a minute or so of searching I came across what I was looking for.

It was a rather small, flat package. Just as he had written, it was wrapped in a piece of canvas; it was perhaps fifty by twenty centimetres in size and a couple of centimetres thick. I brushed it off, evened out the dirt a little around the base and then slipped back in among the trees and down towards the shore. Just as I came up over the bank, the moon broke through a cloud and placed a carpet of glittering silver across the whole bay.

I understood that this was yet another one of those signs.

The return to A. took an hour and a half. My state of mind was still concentrated and neutral. Rein's package was beside me on the passenger seat and now and then I glanced at it, without it producing any excitement or many thoughts in my head.

And when later – after having returned the car and keys in the customary manner at the Hertz office – I had a few drinks at Vlissingen, I recall that a couple of times I also left it completely unguarded on my table while I made a trip to the bar or the toilet.

Perhaps it was a question of – if not challenging – then in any event giving fate a chance. To intervene before it was too late, that is.

No such thing happened, however. Fate was not on duty that evening. I came home to the apartment sometime around midnight, and after having cleaned Beatrice's litter box and given her food, I dropped the rather dirty document down behind the top row of books on the bookshelf. Also decided to let it lie there for a few days, in order to give myself at least a hypothetical chance to still leave things alone.

Clearly my afternoon sleep out by the sea had not been sufficient, because I remember that I barely managed to get my clothes off before I fell into bed.

Certain days it can feel as if you are a different person when you go to bed, compared with who you were when you got up. I know that I managed to think – before I fell asleep on this exhausted evening – that this had been just such a day.

After she drove away I returned to bed. Stayed there awhile and tried to read further in the two books I had going, but had a hard time finding the right level of concentration. Instead I got up again and took a long, hot shower, while I thought about how I would get the day to pass . . . it occurs to me that I've already brought up these small doings, but here they are in their right context.

By and by I decided to hike along the river; I clearly felt the need for movement and the weather was considerably better than it had been during my excursion up to the grotto a few days earlier. I didn't bother to trouble the kitchen staff about any provisions this time; there was plenty of development along the river and I would surely find both shops and cafes that were open.

It was a lovely day. For over four hours I wandered along the rushing river. Took short breaks now and then, sat on some stone and observed the spectacular nature and the fishermen who were standing here and there out in the rapid water with their precision rods. Altogether I walked perhaps five kilometres upstream, where I also found a little cafe with an adjoining souvenir shop. I ate a sandwich and drank two beers, thirsty from the exertion and the warm weather. Bought a couple of postcards too and conversed a little with the owner, a chubby, cheerful Tyrolean who had travelled a bit and even, it turned out, visited my home town for a few hours in the early eighties.

I returned to Graues and had dinner at Gasthof number three, walked around awhile and browsed in shops, and when I stepped in through the door of the hotel it was already seven o'clock in the evening. Madame H greeted me as usual from the reception desk, asked if I had had a pleasant day, and I answered that it had been very rewarding.

'Has my wife come back?' I asked.

'Not yet.'

She shook her head and perhaps there was a little crack there in her smile. Perhaps she could not help noticing that we spent an unusual amount of time apart, my wife and I. However, I nodded completely unperturbed and took the key that she pushed out on the polished marble counter.

But when I came up to the room something burst anyway. Without warning I was struck by very severe stomach pains; they cut like knives in my abdomen, above all in the region right below the navel, and then came the nausea. I went into the bathroom, sank down on my knees in front of the toilet seat, and soon I had emptied out of me all I had eaten the whole day.

Afterwards I staggered back into the room and collapsed on the bed in exhaustion. Through the balcony doors, which were cracked open, I heard the bells in the little chapel on the slope below strike seven thirty. Two feeble strokes that seemed to hang there over the valley for an almost unreasonably long time.

I closed my eyes and tried to think about nothing.

★

In the evening of the next day – which was a Saturday – I told Madame H that my wife was missing, and it was after high mass on Sunday that the police came into the picture.

It happened in the form of the very placid Herr Ahrenmeyer, a lean man in his sixties, who was acting police chief in Graues. In the winter he would have a couple of men to help when the stream of tourists was at its peak, but during the rest of the year the crime rate in the area was so low that – in any event according to Madame H – you might just as well do without uniforms altogether. There was something unspoken between her and Ahrenmeyer, but what it stemmed from was never clear to me. Perhaps it was failed love; they seemed to be approximately the same age.

We sat out on the balcony and he took notes in his black clothbound notebook while he smoked a pipe and now and then expressed his regret and warm sympathy. His greatest worry without a doubt was that Ewa disappeared within his district and not somewhere else, but he was broad-minded enough to grasp that my suffering was greater than his.

He asked no questions whatsoever that did not concern Ewa's or the Audi's appearance, or the time when she took off, and when he left me after barely twenty minutes, it was with a promise to have a missing person announcement sent out at once. He also promised to immediately return the photograph I had loaned him, just as soon as he had it copied.

It was not until three days later that Inspector Mort showed up, and I do not know if Ahrenmeyer sent for him, or if an assessment was made higher up within the police corps. He was of decidedly heavier calibre in any case. Short and burly with black, thinning and pomaded hair. And ice-cold grey eyes. I remember thinking that if you were born with such eyes, you are probably predestined to become a policeman sooner or later.

This time the interview took place inside the police station in Graues. Over a wobbly Masonite table and with a tape recorder rolling. I recall it quite well.

'Tell me what you think!' he started.

I did not have time to answer.

'Do you know where she is, or what?'

'No . . .'

'There must be a reason for your wife to simply take off. Do you want to deny that?'

'Yes. Something must have happened to her . . .'

'What is that?'

I shrugged my shoulders. He pointed at the tape recorder.

'I don't know,' I said.

'Can you make any suggestions?'

'No.'

He leant towards me so that I could smell his bad breath. He was sweating profusely too for some reason, even though he had hung his jacket over the back of the chair and was only in shirtsleeves.

'You had quarrelled, right?'

'No.'

'You're lying.'

'No. Why would we have quarrelled?'

He let out a laugh that sounded more like a bark.

'Frau Handska at the hotel reports that you spent almost all your time apart.'

Silence.

'Well?'

'We have somewhat different interests.'

'Kiss my arse.'

There was a pause while we each lit a cigarette.

'Did you have any reason to get your wife out of the way?'

I recall that it was right there that the smoke got in my throat, it should have been with the very first puff, that is. The coughing fit that followed was so severe that finally he stood up, came around the table and started pounding me on the back.

I realize that my sudden indisposition hardly earned me any bonus points, but at the same time I felt a kind of anger taking form inside me.

'Thanks. What are you implying?'

'Implying?'

He went back to his chair and sat down.

'You're implying that I have something to do with my wife's disappearance.'

'What do you mean, sir?'

For a brief moment I could not decide if he was an idiot or if he assumed that I was one. Or if this was simply some kind of regulation tactic. I did not say anything.

'Tell me what happened,' he requested after half a minute of silence.

'I planned to hike along the river and Ewa would rather take an outing in the car,' I said. 'When you've been married as long as we have, you allow one another that freedom.'

'Truly?'

'At least if you have an ounce of common sense.'

'And you think you do?'

'Yes.'

'And you don't know where she intended to go?'

'No.'

'Certain?'

'Yes.'

And so it went. For over an hour we sat and wrangled over the tape recorder in the rapeseed-yellow detention room. Without warning he suddenly turned off the recorder, wriggled into his jacket and explained that that would have to be enough for now.

Sure enough, he came back a few days later, the same morning that I left Graues to return home by air via Geneva. I was in a bit of a hurry and our conversation was now limited to less than fifteen minutes, but his tactics had not changed appreciably. The same clumsy attempts to take me by surprise with insinuating, rude questions . . . the same ice-cold gaze, the same sweaty shirt – or in any event a similar one – and when he left me alone, I truly felt happy to be rid of him.

No tips regarding my missing wife had streamed in during the days I stayed at the hotel. I never went up into the mountains again, and I didn't hear from Mauritz Winckler. Not then and not afterwards.

After a two-and-a-half-hour taxi drive I arrived on the afternoon of 30 August at the airport in Geneva, and a little later I would board the regular evening plane. The whole trip was paid for by the consulate, something which – as I understood – is standard practice in cases like this.

The first period after my homecoming passed without any major intermezzos. Ewa's and my socializing had been limited to a small circle of four or five persons, and to start with they showed up with such regularity that I suspected that they had agreed on a schedule. Not until towards the end of September did the visits assume more reasonable proportions, and I could start getting accustomed to – and adapting myself to – the solitude.

As for our own police department, I was kept continuously informed of how the search for Ewa progressed. For a time there was even an inspector assigned to the case full-time; I would stop by the station once a week – on Friday afternoons after work – to hear the latest news, which every time was limited to new guesses and hypotheses. At the start of October the inspector had other assignments, and we decided they could just as well be in touch if there was anything more specific to report.

Which there never was.

It was in the middle of the same month – October – that I also made my first attempt to look up Mauritz Winckler. In the greatest secrecy, naturally.

After some telephone calls I understood that he had moved for good and evidently was living in some other European country. Which one no one knew, and I was not particularly eager to find out either.

November having arrived, the majority had probably started seriously assuming that Ewa would not come back. A new girl was hired at her old job, and Frau Loewe, Ewa's mother, with whom both of us had an extraordinarily bad relationship, was in touch and wondered if we shouldn't arrange some kind of memorial service. I explained that it was not customary to bury missing persons and that I was not interested.

It was almost exactly a week after this conversation that I had my breakdown. It happened, quite without prelude, sometime between three and four o'clock the night before a Tuesday. The witching hour, that is.

The way I understood it was that I first woke up and after a few blank seconds found myself in the process of falling, or being sucked into a black hole. I fell and fell, the speed was dizzying, the feeling frightful; I tried to describe it on some later occasions, but every time the words have failed me. Over time I have also understood that there aren't any.

I was found bloody and scraped, but still with some degree of consciousness, on the pavement below my bedroom window, and it took approximately ten weeks before I could crawl back into the same bed again.

I would like to maintain that at that point I was a different person.

For the period of ten or twelve days that followed my outing to the sea, I maintained rather strict routines. I was always there when Frau Moewenroedhe opened the doors to the library; most often I had even been waiting outside on the pavement for a few minutes. We still did not exchange many words – an occasional comment about the weather at most; the early spring held up and in the afternoons through the window at my work table I could see people walking around outside on Moerkerstraat in shirtsleeves and thin, light summer dresses. Even though it was only the middle of March. Inside, among the dust in the reference department, however, the same conditions prevailed year round, and it did not concern me all that much that nature seemed to be a bit out of joint.

It was only in exceptional cases that I raised my eyes far enough to see out. Purposefully, sometimes almost with a feeling of possession, I made my way through the last forty pages of Rein's text. I took pains never to fail in precision and concentration, and my average output was somewhere between four and five pages per day. I never left my seat once I had started. Received my teacup and my biscuits at four thirty and did not finish work until Frau Moewenroedhe or one of the other two women came in and called for my

HÅKAN NESSER

attention at closing time. I could see that at least the red-haired one would like to have asked a question or two, but I skilfully avoided meeting her gaze and thus she never had an opportunity.

On the way home I would have dinner at one of the restaurants along Van Baerlestraat – Keyser or La Falote mainly – and then spend a couple of hours at Vlissingen, where I had two beers and two shots of whisky while I browsed in the newspapers or simply sat and observed people. The majority were regulars and I had already started nodding in recognition at several of them.

Naturally, I also devoted some thought to the future. Even if I still had the canvas-wrapped package lying untouched on the bookshelf, I was relentlessly approaching the point where I would have to open it, and if it turned out to contain what I thought, it would of course mean that positions were changed rather radically.

A new page. Not to say chapter. Obviously this was also what was behind my intention to be done with the translation before I took that step; true, it would not be a polished text that Kerr and Amundsen got in their hands – simply my handwritten first draft – but I had worked conscientiously from the very first page, and if it turned out that they really wanted to wait another month or so for revisions, I could of course offer them that alternative too. However, given the position that I thought things would be in at that point, I was quite convinced that they would not hesitate to publish. On the contrary, they would drop everything they were doing, rush straight to typesetting and the printers, and make sure to get the book out on the shelves as fast as humanly possible.

It was also the case – if my speculations were correct – that

222

it was all starting to get an unmistakable element of sensation. A literary scoop, to put it simply; to a much higher degree than my employers could dream of.

These were, of course, only assessments. But while I sat there in my smoky corner at Vlissingen those evenings, I knew that was exactly how things would look.

There were simply no signs to the contrary.

A question that popped up now and then, of course, was how Rein himself actually related to all this. He was the one, after all, who was the instigator and director, it was hardly possible to escape that.

So was it the case that he was twisting and turning in his roomy grave?

Or was he laughing?

If memory serves me right, it was a Wednesday that I was finally done with the translation. It was right after teatime in any event. I gathered up my papers, books and notepad. Stuffed it all into the briefcase and left my table for the last time. When I was out on the street, I went over to the florist who is always outside the entrance to Vondel Park and bought a big bouquet. Returned to the library and handed the bouquet to Frau Moewenroedhe as I thanked her warmly for the great accommodation she had shown. My work was finished, I explained, but perhaps I would still stop by another time, because I planned to stay in A. another couple of months. I saw that Frau Moewenroedhe was moved, but words did not come easily to her, and after a few ever-so-banal goodbyes we parted ways.

The same evening I went through the whole translation. It

took a little more than six hours; I made an occasional correction, of course, but on the whole the final result seemed more satisfactory to me than I felt it would be while I sat and worked on it. Despite the weight and degree of complication of the text, I seemed to have found the right tone and levels by and large, and I could not find any sections that I felt immediately dissatisfied with.

When I was done it was quarter past two in the morning. I went through to the kitchen and poured a couple of centimetres of whisky into an ordinary drinking glass. Then I returned to the room and fished the package out from the bookshelf.

Sat down in the armchair and carefully unfolded it. Just as Rein had indicated, it contained some additional packaging in the form of a yellow plastic bag.

Inside it were four white, double-folded sheets of paper. No envelope.

Before I started reading, I noticed that these seemed to comprise two originals and two copies. Typewritten. As far as I could judge, on the same machine.

I took a sip of whisky and read.

It took less than five minutes. I downed the rest of the glass and read one more time.

Leant back in the chair and thought for a while. Tried to find new approaches and solutions, but that was unsuccessful. Tried to doubt the testimony of my senses. That was not successful either.

The case was clear. Rein had been murdered.

Murdered.

I had known it for some time; only lacked this final confirmation. But now when I had it in front of me, I could not shake a rather strong sense of unreality.

Germund Rein had been murdered.

By M. Mariam Kadhar. And G.

I still did not know who G was. All four letters were signed with O, which seemed a trifle strange to me. For a good while I also let this letter bewilder me, then I picked up the phone – which was not blocked for local calls within A. – and dialled the number of Janis Hoorne.

'Who is G?' I asked when he sleepily answered after a dozen rings.

It took a moment before he found the right wavelength, but when he did, no doubt whatsoever prevailed.

'Gerlach, of course.'

The name sounded familiar, but I was forced to ask him to be a little more specific.

'Otto Gerlach. His publisher, naturally. Haven't you met him?'

I recall that I almost laughed out loud. Suddenly all the pieces had fallen into place. O and G. The hidden game. The question about the translation. The demand for secrecy. Everything.

I thanked Hoorne and hung up. Picked up Beatrice and set her on my lap. Turned off the lamp and sat there for several minutes and stared out into the darkness.

I'll be damned, I thought.

Shouldn't I have understood this earlier? I also thought.

Gradually I decided that I hardly had anything to reproach myself for. Could not see either that it would have made any significant difference, if I had been a bit more clear-sighted.

No, none at all, actually.

Ten minutes later I had put the letters back behind the books. Before I fell asleep, I tried to remember what Otto

Gerlach looked like – I had never met him, but he was quite a big name in the publishing world and I was certain that I had seen a picture of him at least once or twice. The only thing I managed to summon was a rather roughly hewn face with close set dark eyes and a fleshy mouth. Why a woman like Mariam Kadhar would fall for something like that seemed rather incomprehensible to me. But then I remembered what Hoorne had said about the nature of woman, and besides there was nothing to say that my memory was particularly reliable.

When I fell asleep it was with a feeling that I actually did not have time to sleep.

Sure enough, a few hours later I was on my feet again. I took a quick walk over to the PTT station on Magdeburger Laan and called Kerr. He was not available, it turned out, but I soon got Amundsen on the line instead.

I explained the situation. Could almost hear how he had heart palpitations while I talked, and how his desk chair creaked while he twisted back and forth from excitement. When I was finished I had to tell almost all of it one more time, and then I presented my suggestions.

Without hesitating very long he went along with them, and naturally I had never imagined anything else. The publisher would continue to pay for my stay in A. up to the middle of June. I would immediately send them my translation – after having first made a security copy, which I then had to store in a safe way.

After that I would go to the police.

★

I performed my tasks in that order. The copying took an hour at a Xerox office a little further down Magdeburger Laan. Then I sent off the original translation from the same PTT station that I called from. Went home and placed the copy on the bookshelf.

On the way to the police station on Utrecht Straat I stopped first and had a whisky at a cafe in the same block. True, there had been quite a bit of that recently, but I understood that I needed something. I had my drink standing at the bar, and while I was standing there, the whole time I remembered Mariam Kadhar's strong sensuality. Her slender shoulders and the thought of her nakedness under her clothes. I recall that it was very quiet in the place, so quiet that, when I closed my eyes, I had no difficulty imagining her figure on the empty chair beside me.

A few minutes later I stepped through the semi-transparent glass doors of the police station, explained my business to a female constable at reception, and after some ado I then got to present the whole story to a gruff but imposing detective inspector. I recall that his name was deBries and that he had an Ajax pin fastened to the lapel of his jacket.

To this seasoned policeman I also turned over – with a receipt, the importance of which Amundsen had been careful to emphasize – Rein's original manuscript and the four letters, and when I stepped out on Utrecht Straat again considerably later, it was with a hope that my one reason to travel to A. would now be settled, and that in the future I could devote even more time and energy to the other.

I must also admit that this hope would be realized to a very high degree.

TWO

For the third day in a row I wake up early. Stand in the light of dawn on my balcony and watch Mr Kazantsakis's two sturdy sons set out on the completely glassy water to fish.

It is hardly more than a ritual, like so much other work in these parts. They usually stay out for three or four hours, return in the late forenoon and with complaints and shoulder shrugs display the day's meagre catch for the tourists. Normally a dozen small, reddish mullets, which – if you assert yourself and are lucky – you can then have for lunch at the restaurant. Fried as they are, with scales and fins and without either salt, spices or very much imagination.

Thalatta, I think and go back into the darkness of the room. Get out notebook and pens, cigarettes and water bottle. Go out again. Settle down on the rope chairs to start writing. The time is still no later than twenty past six. The coolness of the night hangs on and will do so for another hour and a half. The balcony is in shadow; this is actually the only usable time of the daylight hours.

The island is so damned beautiful. Not least for that reason I hope that I can rely on Henderson, and that I really have come to the right place. In any event I intend to stay the rest of the month and not leave anything to chance.

I think about Henderson and his blurry photographs for a

while this morning too. And about the sea and the mountains and the olive groves. Then I light a cigarette and start writing.

It was on 3 April that Mariam Kadhar and Otto Gerlach were arrested. I heard the news on the radio; I had just turned it on while I stood in the cramped kitchen and made my morning coffee.

I had known about it of course, but hearing it like this from the news announcer's mouth still startled me. As if it had only now become reality; in a way it was like that too, naturally. Until this morning nothing had leaked out in the media – for more than two weeks the police had worked in the greatest secrecy; I don't know if it was simply a coincidence, or if they truly made an effort to keep things quiet.

Now, however, it was suddenly an open affair. When, an hour later, I found myself at the central station to take the local train out to Wassingen, it felt already as if everything was pulsating with the news. Pictures of all three – Rein, Mariam Kadhar and Otto Gerlach – were on the placards and front pages of the morning papers, and I remember that I thought the mood gave the impression of a movie, where the director without warning has decided to put the very knife thrust into the audience; the decisive scene when the whole thing suddenly shifts into higher gear, when all the old, murky implications become clear and you are thrown into a new tempo.

Just those moments, that is, when you often decide if you are going to leave the theatre or if perhaps it might be worth staying and watching the story to the end.

Sure enough, once I had boarded the train and we began to move, it also felt like a relief to get out of the city.

So this was my first return visit to Wassingen, that day when M and G were pilloried before the public, and it had been over a month since my last. After I had removed my hand from Rein's manuscript I had spent some rather listless evenings in Nieuwe Halle and at Concertgebouw, but naturally I had not seen so much as a glimpse of Ewa. I had not succeeded in sorting out any particularly attractive plans afterwards either, while I sat and consumed beer and cigarettes at Vlissingen and a number of other bars. Had perhaps toyed a little with the thought of simply putting out a search for her, but in the sober light of morning I had of course dismissed all such ideas.

Gradually, I thus decided on a new attempt with Wassingen. Whether I actually imagined that it would produce anything is hard to say in retrospect. To be honest, I probably did not think for many seconds that it really was Ewa that one of Maertens' emissaries had seen out here that day at the end of February. The thought had presumably occurred to me that there hadn't even been any observer, that Maertens had simply constructed the whole thing to at least give the appearance of having accomplished something. In any event, I was well aware that the Wassingen lead offered a rather thin straw to clutch at, but for lack of anything else it would have to do.

In a way, as March turned to April, I had also come to a point where I started to perceive the very search for Ewa as a goal in itself. In certain clear moments I probably sensed that I would never get hold of her again, but to continue living without having done everything in my power to find her would hardly have been possible.

At least it did not seem possible to me right then.

Besides, I had time. Until the middle of June my livelihood was secured. I had no work and no tasks that were required of me. Every day was a blank page.

So why shouldn't I search?

The same short, stubby bodybuilder was still at the bar and served me whisky with the same indomitable Eastern Bloc charm. I emptied the glass in one gulp and went out onto the square. The wind force was approximately like the last time, but it was considerably warmer. Outside the quasi-Italianesque ice cream parlour they had even set out white plastic chairs and a few tables, even though you would presumably have to wait at least a month before anyone could even think of sitting down there.

In general there were very few people; it was still early afternoon, and even if there was surely a rather large cadre of unemployed and people on disability in an environment like this, I understood that it would take a few hours before the real rush between the shops set in.

I passed through the short arcade and came up to number 36. Ewa's building.

Ewa's building? I lit a cigarette and stood and stared at it for a while. Sixteen storeys high. A greyish-brown, slightly damp-stained facade. An infinity of cold windows and built-in, diminutive balconies.

I heaved a sigh and took two puffs. A feeling of hopeless meaninglessness – perhaps spiced with a few grains of absurdity – started coming over me, but then the sun suddenly broke through a cloud and blinded me so that for a moment I just about lost my balance. I closed my eyes and recovered. Started thinking back to Beethoven's Violin Concerto and about the cough and about the series of events that made me end up in front of this apartment building in a suburb of A., and I soon noticed that it was just those types of thoughts that it was crucial to stay away from, if I was going to get anywhere at all.

Consequently I put out the cigarette and stepped in through the entryway. Stood in front of the directory of tenants and wrote down all seventy-two names in my notebook. That took a few minutes, of course, and two women – both immigrants and both with muddy kids in tow – gave me suspicious glances as they passed by.

I returned to the centre and guided my steps towards the cafe where I had sat the last time. Showed a couple of the photographs to the girl at the register; she was truly accommodating and studied them both long and well, but at last she could only shake her head apologetically.

I thanked her and bought a cup of coffee. During the next few hours I showed my photographs to another two dozen persons – both in the centre and outside the entry to Ewa's building, but the result was exactly as discouraging as I should have had reason to fear.

Zero and nothing.

I had decided on a combined ten work days in Wassingen, neither more nor less, and so as not to exhaust all possibilities already this first day, I let myself be content and took a train that departed at 4.28 p.m. back into A.

At the central station I bought three newspapers, and

armed with these I sat down a little later at Planner's to have dinner and read about the murder of Germund Rein.

The news was a bombshell, without a doubt, and evidently no one really knew how to handle it. True, the police had put out a short press release, but it was ever so vacuous, and no further statements had been made. What was known in journalist circles was that Mariam Kadhar and Otto Gerlach had been arrested, suspected of having taken the life of Germund Rein. That was all.

The rest was speculation.

About the love story. The triangle drama, as someone called it. About what happened in the Cherry Orchard during that fateful day in November. About the suicide note.

About what could have put the police on the trail.

The latter was a blank slate. The police had not let out so much as a hint, and the theories that were presented in the newspapers I glanced at had few points of contact with reality.

That they – M and G – had a relationship was generally assumed, as well as that this of course was the crux of the matter. The photos of both of them were legion, but I could not find a single picture where they appeared together. Just this struck me as a trifle peculiar, and I realized that they truly must have done their best to keep the affair concealed from the eyes of the world.

And succeeded quite well, evidently. None of the many writers who now spoke up even hinted that any rumours had been in circulation, either before or after Rein's death.

It was a bombshell, as stated, and no one had picked up the odour of the fuse that was burning.

While I sipped my coffee I studied the various photographs of Otto Gerlach ever so thoroughly. Compared with my memory of him I must say that he was to his advantage in the newspapers. I understood that he, like Mariam Kadhar, must be considerably younger than Rein, and even if it was still hard to accept that a woman like her would need such a man, I actually had even more difficulty comprehending what use she had of her husband. I thought about her slender shoulders again, and I pictured her face with the dark eyes and the thin nostrils. Suddenly I also knew that under different circumstances I could very well have been passionately in love with her.

Under different circumstances, that is. I want to emphasize that.

On the way home from Planner's I went into the PTT office on Falckstraat and acquired both of the phone books for A., and then I spent a good portion of the evening looking up the numbers of the seventy-two tenants out in Wassingen.

No less than fifty-nine of them were listed, which undeniably was a much higher figure than I had expected. Perhaps it was a good sign, all things considered. If nothing else it would keep me busy for a while, and given the situation I remember that I felt a certain gratitude about that.

It was hard to find life buoys during this time, to put it simply, and I understood to take advantage of those that were offered. It was also this evening that Beatrice went on the run. When I was going to bring her in from the balcony facing the courtyard, right before I went to bed, she was simply missing. How she set about getting out of there, and what plans she had for her action, were questions I brooded a bit about over the next few days, but when after less than a week she was sitting out there again staring at the pigeons, I understood that she had simply been hiding out in a fold of reality, to which neither I nor any other human had entry.

Perhaps I envied her a bit too. I know that I felt a rather strong sense of respect, at least.

It was Gallis Kazantsakis who made me aware of the family chapel, which is at the top of the mountain crest to the southeast. There are said to be 360 similar small whitewashed sanctuaries on the whole island; every family with self-respect has its own, preferably located as close to heaven as possible and not particularly easy to get up to.

I set off well before sunrise and after an increasingly warm hike I arrived there in an hour and a quarter. I stepped in, lit a candle on the diminutive altar and then sat down in the narrow strip of shade on the west side. The whole island was in my line of sight; the steeply sloping cliffs to the south and west, the slightly more accessible coastlines to the east and north. I noticed several small, sheltered sandy beaches outside the village that I had not seen before; an occasional isolated house too, to which you would have to go by boat, because the road ends over by Hotel Phraxos at the easternmost point on the shore. I decided to investigate who owned these – and other – private homes; there were a large number of them around the island. Perhaps it would be most probable that it was in just one of these secluded places that I would find what I had come here for.

I thought about time too. The concept of time. Over three years had passed since the events in A., but in this tremendous landscape, this early morning hour, it suddenly felt as if it shrivelled up to almost nothing. What was distant and what was past seemed to grow and draw closer to the brittle present, which for the moment only consisted of my knapsack with provisions and my sweaty body, leaning against the white-washed wall. The sky, the mountains and the sea – which was already starting to lose its horizon in the haze – were all eternal and unchanging.

A point in time and space, just as vanishing and arbitrary as the quickly fading braying of donkeys which rolled up across the olive slopes from the village below. *All the parallel presence of the flow of time*, as Zimjonovich writes about; these were of course not particularly unexpected sensations that struck me, and for that matter perhaps they were something else altogether. As usual I had difficulty with the words, and when the next donkey let out its complaint, I just felt tired and sweaty and proceeded to consume my provisions. I wisely saved one of the water bottles for the journey down, then lit a cigarette and took out my notebook to read through what I had set down in the flickering glow of the oil lamp the previous evening.

And time continued to shrink.

My very deepest hope when I started checking off the telephone list was of course that I would suddenly get to hear Ewa's voice on the other end of the line. It was this vanity that drove me forward, and during the rest of the week I got a response from fifty-seven of the fifty-nine. Thirty-nine of my calls were answered by women, only eighteen by men; if nothing else, confirmation that women talk more on the phone than we men. My tactic was simple – I simply asked to speak with Ewa, explained that I was an old acquaintance, and then in the answers and hesitations I tried to infer whether there seemed to be anything fishy.

In order to be a bit systematic, I had also introduced a kind of assessment scale, where immediately after the call I marked a minus sign by the relevant name if I considered it to be out of the running, a plus sign if I still thought there might be a possibility, and two pluses if the person in question sounded pressed or strange in any way.

Two of the women who answered were really named Ewa, and in both cases some confused exchanges arose before the misunderstanding could be explained. It was roughly the same when, after great hesitation, one Herr Weivers put his teenage daughter on the line. When I went through my notes after the last call, they showed that I had made no less than forty-two minus markings, thirteen pluses and only two double pluses.

Naturally I understood that the method was marred by almost disproportional margins of error, but I decided to direct my continued exertions anyway to the two double pluses – a certain Laurids Reisin and one N. Chomowska – and the thirteen tenants I still had not managed to make contact with. The method – loyalty to the system – is somewhat of a necessity in a holistic world, exactly as Rimley maintains in his book on being and awareness, and I had the sense to lean on just this.

I wrote down the fifteen names on a new page in my notebook and when, on the Monday of the week after the arrest of Mariam Kadhar and Otto Gerlach, I was once again sitting on the train out to Wassingen, I still felt ever so hopeful. It was now the sixth day that I was occupied with the Wassingen lead, and because I had decided on ten, I could see that in any event I had come more than halfway. I also decided to truly spend the whole week out in the suburb – every day from morning to evening – and if that still did not produce any results, I could at least feel the satisfaction of having done what was in my power, and with good conscience devote the approaching weekend to finding new paths.

My first action was to knock on doors. Even though it was the middle of the day, there were people at home in ten of the fifteen apartments; my unemployment theory held up, without a doubt. When someone answered I again simply asked to speak with Ewa, and I quickly countered the obligatory shaking of the head or the attempt to close the door in my nose by forcing my way into the hall and showing one of the photographs of her. I explained that I was a private detective and that I was searching for the woman in the picture. For her own good, naturally. There was of course a risk that Maertens' so-called emissary had already attempted such intrusive behaviour six or seven weeks earlier, but from the reactions I encountered I soon understood that such was not the case. My confidence in Maertens had probably never been lower than on that day.

In some cases I also tried to hint – without being overly explicit – that some form of reward was possibly beckoning around the corner, but it was actually only with Herr Kaunis – an elderly, noticeably foul-smelling man – that this bait worked a little. Unfortunately, however, it was obvious that he only saw the whole thing as a chance to get some money for his daily dose of stimulants. Both the apartment and its inhabitant were in a state of far-advanced decline; I gave him five gulden and left him with a strong feeling of depression.

When I was done, I realized that everything was exactly as usual. Back to zero. No one had reacted to the photograph of Ewa. No one knew who she was, and no one had seen her in the building or in the area whatsoever.

I remember that for a moment the image of the Lauern reservoir's impenetrable green surface flashed past in my mind. It was the first time in quite a while, but the force it displayed was strong, without a doubt.

I went into the cafe. Drank two beers and checked off the names on my list. Rather quickly I was about to lose heart again; a rainstorm had blown in from the west and was not making things any better. While I smoked and browsed back and forth in my pathetic notebook, I felt an insidious fragility starting to sink its claws into me. The need to be alone, away from looks and words, was growing at a corresponding pace, which of course was not a particularly desirable state of mind considering the tasks I had imposed on myself.

At the same time I knew that I had come to a point where I could simply no longer bear to carry on and confront people. Seen purely logically, it must also be the case that I was starting to become known in the building. I had been in contact with almost all the tenants – even if the majority had only heard my voice on the phone – and it was not at all unreasonable to assume that people were starting to wonder. If Ewa truly was in the building – I did not dare to think about how slight I actually deemed that possibility – it was rather likely that my snooping had come to her knowledge; perhaps in reality the chances of getting to her were shrinking the more I tried.

In any case, this was what I arrived at inside the cafe; soon

I was starting to reflect on how many possibilities I had actually ruined through my clumsy telephone calls and my door-knocking, and gradually I decided that it might be time for a little discretion.

The ideal thing, I decided, would be to find a position where I could sit undisturbed and, in peace and quiet, watch the front door and the stream of people that came and went, and it did not take long to figure out what must be the best solution to that problem.

I needed a car. There were simply no other natural places with the entry in the line of sight than a parked car. Sitting down on a bench in the rain, and then sitting there with a newspaper or a book eight hours a day, seemed inconceivable to me, with good grounds.

I finished the beers and inquired with the girl at the bar again. I thought she must have felt a kind of instinctive maternal sympathy for me, and when I asked whether she knew of any place where I could rent a cheap car for a couple of days, she immediately offered to help. Took a notepad out of her apron pocket and wrote down the address of a petrol station five minutes' walk from the shopping centre. At the same time advised me that if I said Christa sent me, then I would save a hundred.

I thanked her and set off. Half an hour later I had paid for four days' rent in advance for an alarmingly rust-covered Peugeot; the cost was not prohibitive, but I remember that I still wondered whether it was not in parity with the value of the whole car.

In any event, it worked. At four o'clock the same afternoon I parked outside my apartment on Ferdinand Bolstraat, and the following day I began my surveillance of entry number 36D out in the godforsaken centre of Wassingen.

I spent three uneventful days out there before something happened. Barely concealed, I sat behind a newspaper with a crackling car radio, cigarettes and a measured dose of whisky as my only company. The position itself was without a doubt optimal; there was never any problem finding a parking place at a distance of fifteen to twenty metres from the entrance, a point from which I had a clear view of everyone who passed out and in. I also kept notes, primarily to keep my doubt penned in and the game alive, of course, but I also think that it was through this that I became aware of a detail that until then I had not included in my calculations.

It was all explained through a person who in my notes went under the designation M6. Simply expressed: man number 6 (I also had a rudimentary description of him: about sixty, ugly, felt hat, henpecked husband, which was more than sufficient to define him with respect to all the others). What happened – late on Thursday afternoon – was that M6 passed by me and went in through the front door twice. True, with an hour interval, but without having come out at any time in between.

Because there was only this entry, and I was reluctant to believe that this anaemic gentleman had lowered himself down from a balcony on the far side, the incident stood out – for a confused minute or so before I thought of the solution – as an improbability and a mystery.

Then I understood. There must be a garage on the basement level.

I drove around the building, had to search awhile before I

found the entrance, but when I did, I undeniably felt very cheap. I also decided to change position the next day.

For a change, if nothing else.

And so it was thanks to this circumstance – this little change of parking space outside building 36 in Wassingen Centre – that the thread did not break.

That the search for my missing wife finally got the breakthrough that I had been waiting for since my arrival in A. over three months ago. It is hard to know in retrospect, of course, but I have a sense anyway that it would have been hard to continue my exertions much longer if that week too had been completely without results.

The time was a few minutes past five. A grey, persistent downpour had temporarily withdrawn and I sat with the window rolled down and a freshly lit cigarette. The gate to the garage went up and a dark blue Mazda came slowly creeping up the narrow ramp. Just as the car passed me – at a distance of only a metre – the driver turned his head in my direction to check that the exit was clear, in the same way that everyone else had done that entire day. There was never any eye contact, but even so, without worry, I could observe the face almost directly from in front. It was my pursuer.

For a brief second I could not place him, but then the mental images of him emerged. How he sneaked after me through the Deijkstraa district. How he sat behind me at the library. How he stood and stared down into the water in Reguliergracht. I started the car, turned it around and took off in the direction in which he disappeared.

With pounding temples, it will not be denied.

I have always had a hard time appreciating so-called car chases in the world of movies, and my attempt at following the blue Mazda on this leaden grey afternoon hour out in Wassingen now proved that reality scarcely exceeds fiction.

After less than a minute I had lost him. Saw him disappear towards the expressway that goes into A. while I was squeezed in between a big lorry and an expensive Mercedes, waiting for a green light. I swore and drummed on the steering wheel and smoked frantically, but it barely helped. When the light finally changed, I took off in the same direction of course, but my Peugeot was not in the best shape that day either and I soon understood that it was pointless.

Because I was on the right road anyway, I continued along the expressway, and despite everything it was with a feeling of mild euphoria that I could sit down at Vlissingen an hour later.

Even later – surely towards midnight – I returned home to the apartment. In the stairway I discovered a letter that must have escaped me earlier. I opened it as soon as I got inside the door; it was from the prosecutor's office and explained that I had to appear in court the next day to answer certain questions and receive a witness summons.

The indictment against Mariam Kadhar and Otto Gerlach had been brought the day before, apparently, and it was understood that the trial would presumably start rolling within a month.

I drank a little more whisky, even though I already felt the characteristic whirling in my temples. Stood in my dark window and observed the people who were roaming around out there. Trams that rattled past and building facades that stood there in indifferent constancy. I thought back on the day, and then came some vague thoughts about the varying density of time . . . how certain drawn-out stretches of time run past us completely unnoticed, drained of both meaning and incidents, before we are suddenly cast into swarms of bunched-up happenings. The pure lattice of significances, and presumably it is no doubt the case that events draw events to them, according to the same laws that apply for all types of magnetism.

In any case, I sensed that these vacuums and these accumulations of condensed time must have a direct counterpart in the hopeless journey through space of meteors and heavenly bodies. These dark sailings.

And similar, as stated, vague thoughts.

It was on the morning after this evening that I again heard Beatrice mewing out on the balcony.

Kerr had a new suit, and from its discreet but indisputable quality one could infer the rise in fortunes that prevailed within the publishing house. He had come on the morning plane and did not even intend to stay overnight. Just a couple of hours of discussions – that is how he explained the purpose of his visit over the phone the evening before.

We were at ten Bosch, one of the most expensive restaurants in the whole city, and Kerr nonchalantly ordered both d'Yquem and la Fitter. I really did my best to appreciate the caviar and the lukewarm duck breast, but it was still only one o'clock and it has always been hard for me to have an appetite so early in the day.

It was the book this was about, of course. After record-fast typesetting it was now ready for printing – he had galleys with him, which I did not need to bother reading, however, because they had already been proofread by others, he explained. All in all, there was only one thing missing.

The title.

Rein's manuscript lacked a title; I had noticed that in the beginning, while I was in the process of translating, but then I did not attach much importance to it. From experience I knew that Rein often wavered where titles were concerned. Would usually change them two or even three times before he was satisfied.

Now, of course, it was different. The publishers were forced to decide the issue themselves, and because I was still the one who was most familiar with the text, they thought that I could make a suggestion. It was no more than right, Kerr put it magnanimously.

I let the d'Yquem roll over my tongue.

'Rein,' I said.

Kerr nodded encouragingly.

'It should be called "Rein",' I clarified.

'Just "Rein"?'

'Yes.'

He thought for a moment.

'Yes, that's probably correct,' he said.

'How are things going with the copyright?' I asked. 'Royalties and such?'

'That will be a problem,' he admitted. 'But we do have his letter and our attorneys have looked at it. Once we've released it, we are going to contact his widow. But I think we can assert the right to the original manuscript. Do you know when the trial begins?'

'The first week in May.'

'Are you going to testify?'

I nodded. He wiped his mouth with the heavy linen napkin. Hesitated a moment.

'What do you think?'

'What do you mean?'

'Is it them? Well, it's clear that it must be, but how have they reacted?'

'I haven't seen either of them.'

'No, no . . . but are they going to confess or deny it?'

I shrugged my shoulders.

'No idea.'

'You haven't . . . heard anything?'

'No.'

'Hmm. Mariam Kadhar is a gorgeous woman, don't you think?'

I did not reply.

'Of course I've only seen her a couple of times . . . at Walker's and last year down in Nice, but you damn well can't help noticing that she's a thoroughbred.'

Kerr's imagery was what it was.

'Maybe so,' I said.

He hesitated again.

'Do you understand what it's about? The book, that is. Seems a bit murky in my eyes . . . but that doesn't have to be a disadvantage.'

'Not everything has to be easily accessible.'

'No, thank God. What I was thinking about was whether there might be more concealed messages than those . . . simple ones. After all, it is possible to hide this and that in a text . . . allegories like with Borges and leClerque, for example. Codes, actually . . . I don't know if you've thought about that?'

I shook my head.

'I wouldn't think so,' I said. 'He didn't have time to be that sophisticated. Wrote the whole thing in just a couple of months . . . and the distress signals he sent out are actually not particularly subtle, don't you think?'

Kerr nodded. 'No, you're probably right. Anyway, we'll release the news tomorrow. Amundsen has arranged a little press conference . . . what do you want to do?'

'What do I want to do?'

'Yes, you do understand that you're the protagonist in this. The spider in the web, damn it, you're the one who translated the book and got them arrested. You're going to be a rather hot item for the journalists, we thought you were clear about that . . .'

Of course I should have been prepared for that, but my anonymous existence on Ferdinand Bol had apparently lulled me into some sort of false security. The past few weeks my energy had been completely directed at the Wassingen lead and the search for Ewa, and I was already living my life more in a niche of reality than in its broad stream.

So to speak. I sat silently and thought.

'Maybe a little interview wouldn't be completely crazy either?' Kerr continued, pouring more wine. 'Exclusive, of course, and only in the right magazines. Naturally you get to decide for yourself, but if we sent a couple of guys . . . Rittmer and a photographer, maybe, so we could guide it the way we want. Maintain control, as Amundsen always says.'

I must admit that I almost admired Kerr for the lightness with which he presented it, but also for both his and Amundsen's unfailing sense of economic realities. The question was probably whether a saleable reportage with me – in the current situation or in connection with the start of the trial – could bring in at least enough that I became, so to speak, self-supporting down here in A. Speculation about the Rein case was already flourishing, and without a doubt would grow even more in the coming weeks.

And there was a shortage of real news awaiting the courtroom acrobatics. I realized that I did after all know quite a bit. I drank more of the wine.

'No, thanks,' I said. 'I probably prefer to stay underground.'

Kerr observed me in silence for a few seconds, and I think he understood that this was a dead end.

'Why are you still here?' he asked.

'I have my reasons.'

'I see. Well, do as you wish, of course. Who knows you're here?'

'No one,' I answered. 'I am a lone wolf, I thought you knew that.'

'No one?'

I thought.

'The police and the prosecutor,' I corrected myself. 'And Janis Hoorne.'

'Hoorne?'

'Yes.'

'Is he reliable?'

'If I tell him.'

He nodded. 'All right. That's what we'll do. But you do realize that you are going to be hunted once the trial gets going?'

Yes, I realized that too. But there were three weeks left until the whole thing started rolling, and as long as it was possible to stay outside the spotlight of publicity, it was my intention to do that.

We had time for a couple of cafes too, Kerr and I, and when I put him in a taxi on Rembrandt Plein he was ever so tipsy and in his very sunniest mood. The last thing he promised was to send down a little bonus as thanks for my efforts, and

I assumed that it was intended as a seal on our Gentleman's Agreement.

If I did not intend to let myself be interviewed and prostituted by my publisher, I would certainly not let any other devil over the bridge either.

Naturally that was no more than right and proper.

My second attempt at a car chase went considerably better than the first one. At six o'clock on Monday morning I was already on the scene behind 36D with another rental car – this time a brand-new, and considerably more powerful, little Renault – and I did not need to wait more than forty-five minutes before he came crawling out of the garage.

I had armed myself with glasses this time, and a silly, brownish-red fake beard, which I found in a little novelty shop on Albert Cuypstraat, and I immediately moved close behind him. Like the last time he turned down towards the shopping centre and got into the right lane to enter the expressway into A. While we waited for a green light at the big intersection, I noted the number plate – I had no idea whether it was possible to produce the owner's name from that, but the possibility vaguely occurred to me in any event.

The drive in towards A. proceeded at rather high speed, but I still had no difficulties keeping up. The traffic was not particularly heavy yet, and I could let him keep a head start of a hundred or so metres without risk of losing him. At Exit 4 after the ring road he turned towards the centre, followed Alexanderlaan and then Prinzengracht all the way to Vollerim Park, where he turned right onto Kreutzerstraat and finally parked on a narrow street by the name of Palitzerstraat. I waited at a distance of about thirty metres, saw him get out of the car, lock it, and cross the street and go into a large office building on the opposite side.

I waited a couple of minutes. Found a parking spot right around the corner and walked back to the entrance. Noted that it was open and stepped into the stairwell. On a directory immediately to the right on the wall the companies were listed floor by floor.

The two lower floors were populated by an insurance company, as far as I understood, number three by two different firms with unclear specialisms, presumably import companies of some type, the fourth – and topmost – by the magazine *Hermes*, which I thought I had heard of but could not pin down more closely by genre. I noted the names and thought a moment, while three or four persons passed me on their way up. Then I went out to the street again. Found a cafe on the corner where I parked the car; went in and sat down at a window table with a cup of coffee.

The time was quarter past eight, I noted. I had no view of either the blue Mazda or the relevant building, but I assessed this as less important at this stage.

Not important at all, in reality. I knew where I had him. His home was in building 36 out in Wassingen and he worked here on Palitzerstraat. The latter was of course not completely clarified, but I still deemed that to be a near certainty. To be completely on the safe side I hardly needed to do anything other than check whether the car was still there a few times during the day. Follow it up during the week maybe, and if it turned out that the parking was a temporary affair, it was only a matter of heading out to the suburb and the garage again. It was no more difficult than that.

No, my pursuer would not escape me again, I was sure of that. Presumably I would also succeed in sorting out his name without any major difficulties. He must be one of those I already had written down on my lists; I had not encountered him during my door-knocking raids, but I might very well have spoken with him on the phone.

The pursuer as such was thus no longer particularly interesting, I concluded, while I sipped my coffee and pretended to read one of the morning papers that were spread out on the tables. What must be clarified, on the other hand, was of course the relationship and the connection to Ewa. I had already had plenty of time to think about that. Over the weekend that had passed I had rejected numerous bizarre ideas and possibilities, and gradually decided that there was actually only one way it could be.

Maertens had been right. Ewa really had been out in Wassingen that day when his gimp caught sight of her. She had gone into building 36, but she had done it for the purpose of visiting the pursuer. Not because she lived there. It also seemed equally obvious that it must have been at her instigation that he surveilled me those days in February and early March. Thus it had nothing to do with either Rein or Mariam Kadhar. Ewa had asked him to keep an eye on me, and the reason could hardly be anything other than that she happened to catch sight of me.

By pure chance, presumably.

Somewhere in A. At a cafe. On the street. In a store while I was inside shopping. It presumably was no more remarkable than that. I had searched for my missing wife, but she had been the one who saw me before I saw her. The object became subject, if you will. The prey the hunter.

Naturally it must have given her something to think about when she discovered me, and the most important thing for her would reasonably be to find out what I was doing in A. Did my presence have anything to do with her, or was I just here on completely different business?

What was her husband, who three and a half years ago tried to murder her – and who perhaps hovered in the belief that he had succeeded – doing here, in her new city?

To put it simply.

And her first action to get an answer to that question had been to hire someone to do surveillance.

A good friend? A co-worker? An acquaintance that she trusted?

While I sat in the empty cafe, I went through this logical reasoning one more time, and I could not see any snags or weaknesses. The connection between Ewa and the pursuer was assured beyond any reasonable doubt, and I knew that the breakthrough had arrived. He was the one who would lead me to her.

Sooner or later. By or against his own will. But irrevocably.

These conclusions contained a good portion of faith, of course; I knew that it meant playing the cards right too, and it was this question that gradually forced its way in and demanded my attention and concentration.

How should I conduct myself? What was the correct move?

These damned decisions all the time. This cursed condensed time! I remember thinking.

As far as I could see there were plenty of possibilities to make a misstep, but what for the moment felt most correct was without a doubt not to reveal myself. To lie low, not let the shadow understand that I had found him. If, at a later stage, it would prove to be necessary to pin him against the wall, then naturally that must be done with both emphasis and authority – on my terms, not on his or hers.

Perhaps not without a suitable weapon in hand either.

But thus, for the time being, into the background. When I had got that far in my musings, I left the cafe. Managed to find a parking spot on the other side of the street, almost opposite the office building and in a position where I could have a rather unobstructed view of the people who went out and in.

In this way I then spent the whole day. People came and went, both men and women in more or less equal numbers. The stream was particularly dense during the lunch hours between twelve and two; the majority simply went over to a little neighbourhood restaurant right on the corner behind me, but others ventured further. A few took their cars. The shadow showed up at quarter past twelve together with another man and a considerably younger woman, and they disappeared around the corner over by the cafe. All three returned a few minutes after one thirty, and then it was not until almost five thirty that he came out again. He went directly over to his Mazda and drove off towards Wassingen. I followed him awhile, but as soon as I understood which way he was going, I let him go and made my way back to the car rental agency instead.

During the whole day on Palitzerstraat I had not caught a glimpse of Ewa, and I therefore preliminarily ruled out that she was a co-worker of the shadow. During the afternoon I had otherwise started feeling rather disheartened, and I do not think it was simply the monotony that was the cause. For the first time I also felt a hint of doubt and uncertainty prior to a possible future encounter with Ewa. So far – until that day in the middle of April – I had not been worried at all about that question, and now when I started to be, it suddenly felt incredibly hard, all of it.

Like an old trauma you successfully kept a lid on for years, but which now suddenly will no longer let itself be swept under the rug. A sick pet.

I got rather drunk that evening. Went home with a dark-skinned and very attractive woman after the last bar too, but as we stood outside her door I got cold feet and left her without a word. I hurried home along the rain-wet streets, and I also remember that I heard her open a window and scream something rather indecent after me.

I can't help thinking she had reason to.

Have not been getting up so early these last few mornings, very much due to the fact that I sit and write until far into the wee hours. Three nights in a row a full moon has hung over the bay and spread a street of silver in the water; it looks almost depressing; a drunken graffiti god, it strikes me, who painted the creation based on a garish, tasteless teenage magazine.

No subtleties at all.

But on the beach an occasional fire is burning during the nights too, and I assume that the youths who are sitting around them and singing and drinking resinated wine do not feel particularly assailed by reality either. Most of them are naked, anyway, and last night, just before I went to bed, I could observe two of them coupling right below my balcony.

It happened quietly and fervently, the girl sat on top of the boy and rode him in the moonlight and I had a hard time removing the image from my retina when I then lay down and tried to fall asleep. Presumably because I wouldn't have had anything against making love to a woman in the moonlight on a sandy beach either.

To hell with subtleties, I caught myself thinking.

One time, just one time, I returned to Graues.

Yet not really to Graues, because I stayed in Wörmlingen, the village on the other side of the pass, where I had gone that day and where I wrote postcards and where perhaps my wife's beloved had been staying.

For a whole week I stayed at Albergo Hans, and not until the next to last day did I once again drive the winding road up along the side of the mountain. It was the middle of May, down in the valley the fruit trees were in full bloom; higher up the snow was still deep. The road through the pass had only been opened a week or so before.

A year and nine months had passed. I drove past the brimming reservoir without stopping, continued all the way up to the little parking area again. Got out and looked over the landscape. Nothing had changed. Only after a long time was I able to lower my gaze down over the precipices and let it rest on the green surface of the water. It was there below me, quite even; it was a clear day, but I remember that the sun did not cast any glitter and that the faint breeze did not cause the slightest ripple.

I left the car there and made my way along the road on foot. After a while I arrived at the sharp right curve. I slowed my pace and walked out on the left side of the road.

I'd seen it already, from a distance. Snow and ice had eroded and erased during two winters, but a hole was gaping in the low stone and concrete wall. Not large, and not all the way down to the level of the roadway, but a tear – a jagged V sign, which I tried to remember but could not. Instead, a sense of fatigue and strong nausea came over me; I vomited by the side of the road towards the mountain side and then immediately started walking back up to my car.

Then I drove down, slowly and with a strong feeling of despair, and the next day I left the area forever.

Perhaps it had been my intention to look Frau Handska up too, perhaps have a few words with police chief Ahrenmeyer, but as I said, I never crossed the mountains again.

The office was on Apollolaan and was evidently parcelled out from a large apartment in the big Art Nouveau building. I rang the bell and the door was opened by a pale young man in a black suit and polo shirt. His face was sharp-featured, his eyes deep and reflective. I introduced myself.

'You were the one who called, sir?'

'Yes.'

There was not much more than a desk and two chairs in the room, which because of the interpolated wall nearest almost seemed to be edgewise. I sat down and started to explain without further preludes.

' . . . a woman who in a previous life was named Ewa, that is . . .' I took out three or four photographs. The only thing I had to go on was a man who drove a blue Mazda with registration number H124MC and who lived in building 36 out in Wassingen. Entry D . . . a man who had a horse face and brown-tinted glasses, who worked at Palitzerstraat 15 and who was the link that could lead to the woman I was seeking . . .

He looked at me and cautiously fingered the pictures.

'Why don't you do this yourself?'

'Don't have time,' I explained. 'But it is a rather simple assignment and if you don't want to take it, I'm sure I'll find someone else. I have no desire to spend too much money either.'

I had received Kerr's promised bonus by mail the same morning; it was a badly needed supplement, without a doubt, but even so there were of course no longer any great margins to speak of.

'I would like to have an agreement,' I said, 'where you promise me this woman's name and address within a week.'

He smiled.

'You don't sign that sort of agreement, even in hell,' he explained, pushing the photographs back over the tabletop. 'But I can give you a good price and promise to do what I can. It doesn't seem to be anything impossible, when all is said and done. You're sure that he knows her?'

I nodded.

'And that she is here in the city?'

'Yes.'

'Give me three hundred gulden now, and if I haven't got anywhere in a week, we'll write off the whole thing.'

I shrugged my shoulders and took out my wallet.

'Where can I reach you?'

I wrote down my phone number and my address on the pad that was in front of him. He took the money and stood up.

'I'll call as soon as I have anything. When can I be sure to get hold of you, sir?'

I thought.

'In the mornings,' I said. 'I often work until late in the evening, but in the mornings I'm at home.'

'I understand.'

We shook hands and I stepped out into the sharp sunlight on Apollolaan. It was only a five-minute walk home to Ferdinand Bol, but I realized that I had neither reason nor desire to go there.

Instead I started walking south along a canal the name of which I did not know and for which there was not a single sign at any crossing. If I was not mistaken I was heading in the direction of Balderis Park, but it was all the same to me if I ended up somewhere else. Movement as movement. I must get the time to pass, that was all; the day before I had wandered around aimlessly like this for six or seven hours, while I thought about what I ought to do, but it was not until late in the evening, when I had finished my dinner at Mefisto, that I decided to hire a detective again. I immediately rejected the thought of turning to Maertens one more time. So gradually I had settled on this Haarmann, and even if at first he seemed anaemic as anything, I must now admit that after that brief conversation I felt a certain confidence in him.

Whether I felt the same thing about Maertens after our first meeting I could no longer recall.

After about twenty minutes I came to a large, green entrance, which I assumed must be Balderis; I went in through the gates, continued in among the shrubs, among the blossoming trees and the cacophonous birdsong. Here and there people were lying spread out with picnic baskets and blankets;

mostly couples and groups of students, naturally, but also an occasional solitary woman my own age, and under other circumstances it is possible – probable, actually – that I would have approached one of these obvious seekers.

Now, however, I kept to my own ways and paths. Crossed the generously overgrown park both this way and that, and in so doing managed to make the whole afternoon pass by. When I again turned onto Ferdinand Bol it was already dirty twilight and I realized that there were only six days left before the trial of Mariam Kadhar and Otto Gerlach would begin.

On 4 May. I think it was just such a date that I repressed; refused to accept that it was fast approaching anyway, because then everything – once again – would be surrounded by new signs and unpredictable conditions. Something that only affected me and that I could in no way protect myself from.

Like a day for surgery. Or separation.

It was only the following morning that Haarmann called and revealed the pursuer's name.

Elmer van der Leuwe.

Single, but with two children from a previous marriage. For the past eight years employed at the insurance company Kreuger & Kreuger at its office on Palitzerstraat.

And it was only two days later that he explained that it was probably best to take a fourteen-day pause in the work. Van der Leuwe had just left on a charter trip to Crete along with a good friend and would not be back until the sixteenth. At this point Haarmann had not managed to expose any connection to Ewa, and – especially if I was interested in keeping the costs down – it hardly seemed meaningful to maintain a high level of surveillance for those two weeks.

I agreed. When I hung up the phone, I felt a dreadful weariness take hold of me. For several hours I just lay there on the bed, smoking cigarette after cigarette. Beatrice prowled around me and seemed seriously worried about something; at last I was forced to lock her out on the balcony. A little later Janis Hoorne called, but it was only to report that it would be impossible for him to see me in the near future, because there were still some complications with the filming.

So what remained was to wait.

What remained was to drink at the bars and keep my thoughts in check.

Night.

Sit and write and see more and more clearly what a pitiful poor stage play life is. There are no lines. No moral. The actors do not stick to their roles and the dramaturgy itself is tossed here and there like a fragile vessel in high seas.

A drunk whore in over-sized pumps. Whatever.

This evening the street of moonlight has shrunk to a narrow pavement in the water. Cicadas are chirping, a bit more delicate now in the darkness. An out-of-tune guitar is heard from down on the beach and the air is at a temperature that means you don't feel it against your skin.

Here there is no striving. No anxiety and no suffering. And the decor! I take a sip of lukewarm, resinated donkey piss and light the fortieth cigarette of the day. The oil lamp smokes as usual. Here there is no electricity. Only the moon and the fires. And the oil.

I write.

Stubbornly I spew these words out of me about these events. I am in despair the whole time, continue anyway without hesitating. This is a prison, a veritable prison with prostituted stage sets that can fool the devil himself. Twelve days have passed since I arrived. I don't know if I am going to find what I came here for, and perhaps I don't care either. To hell with Henderson's pictures! It's the road that makes the effort meaningless; I am still just one of those soulless actors in this damned play that no one is watching any longer.

That no one has written and no one directed; Gallis says that the nice thing about resinating his wine is that you can basically drink anything at all. I believe him. The bottle and the glass I have in front of me undoubtedly contain pure donkey piss, but I drink gamely anyway.

God knows I'm drunk. Can't bear to write what I was thinking when I started up an hour ago. I'm going to tear these pages out on the other side of night. My words are going to crawl underground in clear daylight. Ashamed, pale maggots.

And if I had started anyway, I would surely only have determined that:

. . . and furthest to the right sat M.

That is actually the only thing I remember.

Otto Gerlach was sitting furthest to the left. With an irreproachable fresh haircut and shave. In white shirt, tie and double-breasted suit. His hands resting in front of him on the table. A symbol of well-earned success.

To his right two lawyers were sitting. First his own, then Mariam Kadhar's. They each had one, that is, and I did not know if there was any more serious point in that, or if it was calculated simply so that they would be sitting further from each other that way.

. . . and furthest to the right sat M.

Dressed in black. One of those simple, bare-shoulder rags that only a certain sort of woman can wear and which costs a month's salary. So I've been told.

While I stood up and swore the oath, she raised her eyes and looked at me for two seconds. Then she observed the prosecutor's shoes awhile; he was standing at an angle in front of her on the dark wooden floor and there was no difference in expression between their two gazes.

None whatsoever.

I was asked to sit down and did so. The prosecutor carefully approached. He was a tall man in his fifties. Distinguished face with a sort of demigod-like, classic profile, which he evidently liked to show off. He walked around the witness stand and stood so that I only saw him from his left side, while the members of the jury and most of the audience could observe his right flank. He stood absolutely still and let a few seconds run away.

'David Moerk,' he began.

I nodded.

'Your name is David Moerk?' he expanded.

'Yes,' I admitted.

'Tell the court why you are here in A.'

I stated my own reason in general terms. It took a few minutes, but he did not interrupt me a single time. Otto Gerlach sat motionless with his hands calmly resting and did not take his eyes off of me for a second. I thought I could see his jaw moving a little and realized that, despite his appearance, he was a prey to conflicting emotions. Mariam Kadhar, for her part, kept her head lowered and seemed considerably more relaxed than her lover.

'Thanks,' the prosecutor said when I was finished. 'Tell us about your translation work. How it progressed and how you started to suspect something.'

I continued. While I talked I started to direct my gaze

around the courtroom. Lingered a moment on the members of the jury. Four men and three women, all of whom sat straight with slightly worried facial expressions. I continued in among the ranks of the public, both those who were sitting down on the parquet and those visible in the first rows up in the gallery. It was full, without a doubt. It was the second day of the trial today, the first in earnest. Yesterday – according to what I had read in the newspapers – had mostly been devoted to technicalities and to establishing the points of the indictment.

Murder. First-degree.

Both had denied it. The preliminary skirmishing was over and done with.

The question marks were legion, according to the newspapers. One of the most interesting legal proceedings since the Katz and Vermsten cases, the byline 'Laocoön' wrote in *de Telegraaf.* The evening before the first day of the trial a TV crime magazine devoted the whole broadcast to debating the situation. Or rather to asking questions. I had seen a glimpse of the spectacle at Vlissingen.

Would both be convicted?

Would either of them take all the blame? Who?

What solid evidence did the prosecutor have to present? What did the love triangle actually look like? Would they cite some kind of crime of passion?

Etcetera.

'Why do you believe Rein wanted the book published in this way?' the prosecutor asked.

Gerlach's lawyer protested. Stood up and explained haughtily that the witness was being encouraged to speculate. I kept silent.

'Overruled,' the judge decided. 'The members of the jury should bear in mind, however, that here the witness has been allowed to make his own assessments.'

The lawyer took his seat again.

'Well?' the prosecutor said.

'Will you please repeat the question?'

'Why did Rein want to publish the book in translation?'

'I guess it's obvious.'

'Explain!'

I looked at Mariam Kadhar. Through the high windows up in the gallery the sun fell in, putting her collarbone in a marble-white light. I thought about her nakedness again.

'It says in the manuscript that they intend to murder him,' I explained.

The reply triggered some concern in the gallery and the judge pounded his big gavel a few times on the table.

'Explain,' the prosecutor said again.

I told him about the passages in italics, and about what Rein had written about the letters and the sundial out in the Cherry Orchard. There was new life at once among the audience and the judge used his gavel again.

'Can you tell the court what you did when you discovered these things?'

I started to feel slightly nauseated. It was warm in the room and an odour of expensive aftershave was hanging in the air. I think it came from Otto Gerlach. Yes, in retrospect, I know that it must have been him.

'I performed a check.'

'How is that?'

'I went out to Behrensee and investigated whether it really was as he maintained.'

'You searched for the letters?'

'Yes.'

'You found them in the place he indicated?'

'Yes.'

'Did you study their content?'

'A bit later.'

'What conclusion did you draw then?'

There was protest again, this time through Mariam Kadhar's lawyer. The judge overruled again. I drank a little water. It was roughly the same temperature that prevailed in the rest of the room and my nausea did not get better.

'What conclusion did you draw?' the prosecutor repeated.

'What conclusion would you have drawn yourself?' I countered.

The judge intervened and explained that it was my duty to answer questions, not ask them. I nodded and took another sip of water.

'I drew the conclusion that Otto Gerlach and Mariam Kadhar had taken Rein's life.'

The dam burst but the judge made no attempt to call for silence. The prosecutor thanked me and went and sat behind his table.

Gradually the commotion ebbed out and the judge gave the floor to Mariam Kadhar's lawyer, who buttoned his jacket, stood up and approached the witness stand in the same studied manner as the prosecutor a while ago. He did not have the same profile at all, but assumed basically the same position anyway and let the final whispers die out before he began speaking.

'What is the name of the publisher that gave you the assignment to translate Rein's manuscript?'

I stated it.

'Do you know when the book is coming out?'

I shrugged my shoulders. 'In the next few days, I would think.'

'Reportedly today,' he specified.

'That's possible.'

'How many copies are being printed?'

'No idea.'

He took a piece of paper from his inside pocket. Fussily unfolded it and observed it with a look of feigned surprise.

'Fifty thousand,' he said.

I did not reply. He took off his glasses and started swinging them back and forth while he held them by one arm.

'Do you have any comment?'

'No.'

'Isn't that an extremely large edition? Considering the genre?'

I shrugged my shoulders again.

'It's possible. Rein was a major author.'

'Without a doubt.' He studied his paper again. 'Here I have the sales figures for his latest two books in your country . . . do you know how much they amount to?'

'No.'

'Twelve thousand. For the two titles, that is. Twelve thousand . . . what do you say about that?'

I did not reply. He put his glasses on and smiled faintly.

'Tell me, isn't this release a pretty good deal for your publisher?'

'Maybe so.'

He made a little pause while he slowly turned his back to me.

'Is it not the case . . .' He started up again. 'Is it not the case that this whole affair is pure speculation to make money on an unusually marketable bestseller?'

I drank a little water.

'Bullshit,' I said.

'Excuse me?'

'Bullshit!' I repeated in a loud voice.

'May I urge the witness to mind his language,' the judge objected.

I had no comment on that. Mariam Kadhar's lawyer sat down. Gerlach's stood up instead and came striding across the floor.

'Who is paying for your stay here in A.?' he asked.

'My publisher, naturally.'

'This manuscript that you translated . . . do you have any evidence that it really is Germund Rein who is behind it?'

'What do you mean?'

'How do you know that it was Rein who wrote it?'

I was starting to feel increasing irritation.

'Of course it was Rein. Who else would it have been?'

'How did the manuscript get into your hands?'

'I got it from Kerr.'

'Your publisher?'

'Of course.'

'And how did Kerr get hold if it?'

'Rein sent it to him.'

'How do you know that?'

'Because he told me, of course.'

'Kerr?'

'Yes.'

'You have no other sources?'

'What kind of sources?'

'That can attest that is really what happened.'

I snorted.

'Why would I need them? What kind of idiocy are you trying to suggest?'

I got a new, and somewhat sharper, admonition from the judge. The lawyer leant his elbow against the railing that surrounded the witness stand.

'Do you have anything other than your publisher's word that it actually was Rein who sent him that manuscript?'

'No.'

'So it might have been a fraud?'

'I don't believe so.'

'I'm not asking what you believe.'

'I consider it completely out of the question that my publisher would lie.'

'Even if that would mean getting the publishing house on its feet?'

'The publishing house is already on its feet.'

The attorney smiled quickly.

'But if someone else passed himself off as Rein, couldn't your honourable publishers also be deceived?'

I thought about that. Drank a little water.

'In principle,' I admitted. 'But I consider that out of the question.'

'Thanks,' said the lawyer. 'That was all.'

The judge signalled to me that I could leave my place in the witness stand and I was escorted out by the same guard who helped me in. As I passed the defendants' table, I tried once again to make eye contact with Mariam Kadhar, but she still sat motionless with her gaze aimed down at the table. Otto

Gerlach on the other hand stared hard at me, and I understood that he would gladly have killed me if we had found ourselves in somewhat more uncivilized circumstances.

When I came out onto the broad steps of the court building, I was met by flooding sunshine. I looked at the clock and could see that my effort had taken up less than an hour.

I took off my jacket. Hung it over my shoulder and started walking towards the city centre. The nausea lingered in me and I realized that I probably needed a couple of sturdy drinks to restore balance.

I rarely dream, but when she appeared I knew immediately that she was not real.

The dress was the same as in the courtroom and her white shoulders shimmered unnaturally white by means of some type of artificial lighting I could not localize. She approached me slowly, very slowly and carefully: I understood without looking that she must be barefoot, perhaps I heard the soft soles of her feet against the dark marble floor. Or felt them: the contrast between the warm, sensual and the cold, hard was razor sharp; I also recognized the floor itself, without a doubt it was that chancel in the Pierra del'Angelo church in Tusca, where Ewa and I made love one night ten years ago.

Eleven, if you want to be particular. From two steps away she stopped and let the dress fall to the floor. Her nakedness filled the whole sanctuary without inhibitions, I reached for her, took hold of her, drew her skin into my nostrils; an aroma of timothy and of sandalwood that had been left in the sun on a long, hot day in summer. And of lust. In a gentle curtsying movement she leant down and closed her lips around my stiff member; got down on her knees, I followed, she let go of me, placed herself on her back with legs parted and I entered her. And noisily we started making love, just like we had done that night so long ago. Her excitement echoed in the sanctuary, our hot bodies smacked against the smooth marble, as we like . . . like horny heathens, like unprincipled animals, made love in the Santa Margareta chancel in Pierra del'Angelo church.

Then suddenly another woman was standing in the high window oval; I saw that it was Ewa, and that the woman who was now riding on top of me and who threw her head backwards gurgling was not Ewa at all but Mariam Kadhar.

Ewa was wearing the same black dress; as soon as I noticed her I pulled out of and away from Mariam Kadhar. Ewa approached and let the dress fall to the floor and her body had the same shimmering whiteness and she approached us where we were lying on the floor. Her eyes were lascivious and while she slowly slid right next to us, she caressed herself with both hands over her breasts and in her sex. I curled up and crept further backwards, Ewa bent forward over Mariam Kadhar, who was still whimpering a little because I had pulled back, then she pressed her face in between her legs and they started making love with each other. Excitedly. Solemnly and passionately at the same time. Lay there with their mouths pressed into each other's sex and licked and sucked. I sat with my back against the wall and could not tear my gaze from them, even though my head echoed with voices that said I must get away from there. After a while they stopped and turned towards me. 'Rein!' they whispered. 'Come to us, Rein!' and suddenly one of them was transformed to a man, I don't know which one of them. Only now did I try to escape, finally understood how dangerous it all was, but it was too late. They started taking hold of my legs and arms and pulled me out to the middle of the floor where crooked beams of light shot in through the side window. The woman, whom I could now clearly identify as Ewa, ordered the man to go and retrieve something and he disappeared between the rows of pews.

'Rein,' she whispered. 'You are Rein, aren't you?'

She spoke with her face only a few centimetres from my own and I felt that the words came from her breath and were caught, not through my ears, but instead through my skin and my pores.

'No, I'm not Rein,' I said. 'I'm David. You're Ewa.'

Her nearness was strong again. 'We have time to make love before he's back!' she whispered. 'Come!'

She straddled me. Guided me into her hot sex and started slowly raising and lowering herself over me. She was tighter and hotter and more beautiful than I had ever experienced before and I was close to coming, but now at a distance footsteps were heard, they approached and echoed in the deserted sanctuary.

'Rein,' the woman moaned who was riding me. 'Rein! I love you but I have to kill you.'

'Who are you?' I asked. Her breasts were Ewa's, without a doubt, but her head was thrown back again, so I could not see her face. And her voice was every woman's.

'Come,' she said. 'Come now.'

And I came.

Then I woke up and heard a tram rattle past out on Ferdinand Bolstraat. Beatrice was sitting beside me in the bed, staring at me with yellow, reproachful eyes.

I got up and went into the bathroom.

I read about the release of *Rein* in *Gazett*. The same day Kerr also called and confirmed that all the information was correct.

The sales the first days had been quite excellent. The book and its significance in the trial just started had been noticed in more or less every media outlet all over Europe. The expected lawsuit from Otto Gerlach was not long in coming, but apparently there was no risk that the edition would be withdrawn – which Gerlach demanded immediately.

They had evidently threatened both one thing and the other, but at the publishing house they only laughed at the commotion. The only thing that possibly might be a trifle worrisome was that the text constituted evidence in the ongoing legal proceedings, but because it was not a question of closed doors, they didn't expect any problems there either.

'We've got a number of bids on the original manuscript,' Kerr explained elatedly. 'How are things going for you?'

'With what?'

'Damned if I know. The journalists, for example.'

'No problem,' I answered, but of course that wasn't really true. Late last evening I had sold myself to a young and very beautiful writer at *de Journaal*. I got two thousand gulden for the interview plus a few pictures, but naturally I would much rather have gone to bed with her for free. My sexual needs were great just these past few days.

The phone rang a few times too. I don't know how they got hold of my number, and every time I answered with surprise that no David Moerk had ever lived at this address.

A little later yesterday evening a red-nosed newshound from some obscure weekly magazine had forced himself on me while I sat at Vlissingen, but he was not particularly hard to brush off.

Back to the courtroom. To see how the whole thing developed, I tried to convince myself, but I knew of course that it was actually only Mariam Kadhar I was interested in. I had to see her again. See if she looked like she did in the dream, see if it was possible to get a little eye contact, see if her slender shoulders could retain their whiteness under any circumstances whatsoever.

Since my testimony was over there was no reason why I had to stay away. My part of the affair was now settled, and naturally I had the same right of access to the legal machinery as any other citizen. Albeit a foreigner.

As soon as I decided it became urgent. I went down to the street and realized that there were just fifteen minutes until the public would be let in. I hailed a taxi and asked the driver to take me to the court as fast as he was able.

It must have been my hope that she would wear the same bare-shoulder dress again today.

The same as the day when I sat in the box.

The same as in the dream.

Now she did not. Another dark affair, true, but it did not leave a bit of the collarbone exposed.

I managed to get an excellent place, even though I arrived a bit late; furthest to the right in the first row of the gallery, from which I had a good overview and could see Mariam Kadhar in a completely clean profile beside the lawyer.

And when she was sitting in the box, of course she simply turned the other cheek.

It was breathlessly silent in the whole room while she stood up and with restrained dignity took the few steps over to the witness stand. She sat down, took a sip of water and clasped her hands in front of her on her lap. It was impressive, simply put. I felt goose bumps on my forearms.

The prosecutor assumed his usual place, sucked in his cheeks and let his tongue run across his teeth a few times, as if he had just enjoyed a good cognac and wanted to be sure not to miss out on any of the aftertaste. Then he coughed lightly into his hand and got started.

'Ms Kadhar, how long were you married to the author Germund Rein?'

She did not answer immediately, and it seemed as if she actually sat and counted.

'Fifteen years. In two months.'

'How old were you when you married him?'

'Twenty-four.'

'How old was your husband then?'

'Forty-two.'

Just to the right of me an elderly gentleman was sitting, making notes. It took a while for me to realize that he was a stenographer, and sure enough, the next day the questioning of Mariam Kadhar could be read in *de Telegraaf*. Word for word.

'Do you have any children?'

'No.'

'You haven't been married before?'

'No.'

'And your husband?'

'Two times.'

The prosecutor nodded and made a short pause. You could feel that the court ushers, as well as the whole audience in the gallery, were holding their breath. The silence in the packed room felt like a vacuum – as if it produced some kind of acoustic negative pressure, I recall thinking; when Otto Gerlach's lawyer tapped the table two times with his ballpoint pen, for a second everyone's eyes were aimed in his direction.

'Did Germund Rein have any children from his previous marriages?'

'No. Is it really the case that you don't already know these things?'

'Of course I know about them, Ms Kadhar, but I'm not the one who is going to judge your guilt.'

She sighed, which seemed to be what was needed to allow the rest of us to start breathing again.

'Is it correct that you are the sole heir to your husband's estate?'

'Yes.'

'Do you know the value of that estate?'

'Not exactly.'

'I have information that says somewhere between five and six million gulden. Could that be correct?'

'Yes.'

New, brief pause. I found myself thinking about whether this tall prosecutor practised fencing in his spare time. And if Mariam Kadhar did. The questioning resembled without a doubt a battle on the piste: three, four, five attacks and just as many ripostes, before there was a short pause while the combatants collected themselves for the next attack.

'Did you love your husband, Ms Kadhar?'

'Yes.'

The answer came without a quiver, and I don't believe there were many persons in the hall who doubted that she spoke the truth.

'Were you faithful to your husband?'

'I don't understand the question.'

The prosecutor feigned surprise like a third-class amateur actor.

'I asked if you were faithful to your husband. How is it that you don't understand such a simple question?'

'Fidelity is not an unambiguous concept.'

He smiled quickly.

'That may be. Did you have relationships with other men?'

Her lawyer jumped up from his chair and protested.

'Will you reformulate your question?' the judge asked, and the prosecutor nodded obediently several times.

'Is it correct that you had a sexual relationship with your husband's publisher, Otto Gerlach?'

'Yes.'

Not the slightest quiver here either. The prosecutor paused very briefly to catch his breath, before he attacked anew on the same point.

'When did you start your relationship with Gerlach?'

'Two and a half years ago.'

'Did your husband know about it?'

'No.'

'Are you certain?'

She hesitated a moment.

'I think he suspected towards the end.'

'What do you mean by "towards the end"?'

'As of last summer, maybe.'

'What makes you think that?'

She shrugged her shoulders slightly, but did not reply. The prosecutor repeated his question.

'I don't know,' she said. 'Just a feeling.'

'Why were you unfaithful to your husband if you loved him?'

'I would be grateful if I didn't have to answer that question.'

'Ms Kadhar,' the judge interrupted, leaning over in her direction. 'I will ask you to bear in mind that we are trying to administer justice. The more information you choose to withhold, the greater latitude you give to caprice.'

'As far as I understand I have the right to remain silent the whole time, if I so wish?'

'Quite correct,' the judge admitted. 'You can decide for yourself what questions you will and will not answer. But if you really are innocent, it is almost always better to speak than to remain silent.'

'What was the last question?'

The prosecutor had listened to the judge's little intermezzo with lowered head. Now he cleared his throat and resumed.

'You maintain that you loved your husband. Why were you unfaithful if you loved him?'

'Our sex life didn't work.'

For the first time that day a murmur broke out in the gallery. The judge raised his gavel, but never needed to strike it on the table to get silence.

'Did you love Otto Gerlach too?'

She sat in silence for a few seconds, but it did not look as if she was thinking. Her lawyer made a sign to her with his hand – I assumed that he wanted to know if he should protest again – but she simply shook her head lightly.

'I don't want to answer that question.'

'Why?'

'Who I love and don't love is my business.'

'You are accused of murder, Ms Kadhar.'

'I understand that.'

'Did you murder your husband?'

'I did not murder my husband.'

'I have information here that says that he hit you.'

'I see.'

'Is that correct?'

'It happened two times.'

'How seriously?'

'I had to see a doctor the second time.'

'When was that?'

'About a year ago.'

'What was the reason?'

'It was my fault.'

'What do you mean by that?'

'I object!' her lawyer interrupted, standing up. 'The prosecutor is constantly asking insinuating, irrelevant questions. I suggest that he get to the point or sit down!'

The exchange was met with some approval from the audience, and the judge chimed in.

'Will the prosecutor please start addressing the alleged crime, starting now,' he instructed acidly.

'Gladly,' the prosecutor said with a smile, who evidently did not take this type of admonition particularly seriously. 'Tell the court about the night your husband died, Ms Kadhar!'

Mariam Kadhar sat silently for a few moments. Then she turned her head in the judge's direction.

'Can I speak a little with my lawyer first?'

The judge nodded and the lawyer hurried up to her. After a whispered deliberation he went over to the judge and said something. The judge wrote a few lines on a sheet of paper and straightened up.

'The court will take a short break,' he explained, pounding the gavel on the table. 'Fifteen-minute break!'

The days are getting hotter and hotter. As long as the sun is up it is basically inconceivable to be anywhere other than down by the water. I have tried to stay indoors or up in the olive slopes, but it soon becomes unbearable. Only the sea is able to give sufficient coolness; but you don't need to swim, just stay somewhere close to it, in the shade, dip your feet now and then or rinse your head.

Thalatta.

The other day I tried to make my way along the stony, rough coast around the point to the east. My thought was to reach the first of the sheltered sandy beaches and perhaps inspect the house that I had seen from up in the chapel a bit more closely. Naturally it would be simpler to get there by boat; I'm going to rent one too, within the next few days. The effort took me over three hours all in all, and even so I never really got all the way there – it was my own decision, to be sure; you see, the beach was populated by a dozen people, all of whom were running around as naked as they came into this world. Men, women and children. Two boats were also there; a rather big motor yacht that was bobbing a little way out in the water, and a smaller wooden boat that had been pulled up on the shore; roughly the same type as the Kazantsakis brothers'. The house was fifty metres up on the slope; a big, whitewashed building, surrounded by cypresses. A terrace ran around it as far as I could see; parasols and white furniture and beach towels clearly showed that the whole group lived here. I also drew the conclusion that these were not Greeks, because they appeared on the beach with such shameless nudity.

But enough about this. On a few evenings I have taken the bus to the main town and sat under the grapevines at the taverns. The street life is intense and the local population gladly mixes with the tourists in rather even numbers. I have shown my photographs a few times and on at least two occasions they have been met by nods and smiles of recognition. I am not sure, however, if that really means anything, or if it was just an expression of courtesy and general goodwill. They speak almost nothing but Greek, apart from the most common service phrases, and in the midst of it all something is also holding me back.

Something hard to grasp and at the same time quite easy.

As if I do not want to force things, it feels like. There are certain patterns, things must run their course even on this island. I have plenty of time left, and so even if I haven't received any decisive signs yet, it seems to me as if I've come to the right place. Yet of course this feeling is not particularly sustainable, and perhaps it is just that fragility that means that I don't want to burden it.

An injured bird wing, which slowly heals but still will not hold for a real flight. An embryo that is growing and growing, but that would be annihilated by the sunlight.

Especially this mercilessly flooding sun.

⋆

A bird, that is exactly how she described herself when we got together. A bird with an injured wing.

Until I am healed again I can't give, she said. Only receive.

I liked that a lot. From the start it provided the framework for our relationship and I went along with it without protest. It took almost a month before we made love for real; this too appealed to me. Gave me time to finish another affair too, which I wasn't really done with.

When we got married she was still my injured bird. Then she lost two children before they had become fully developed and viable, and this probably sealed our alliance. It was after the second miscarriage that my strength was no longer sufficient to fill the vacuum of her weakness. For a year we lived in separate worlds; I started looking out for myself as the prerogative of the strong male, Ewa kept herself enclosed behind the curtains of illness.

'Adagio,' Ewa would say during this period. 'Right now we are in the adagio. There is nothing strange about that.'

And of course there wasn't.

I only met Mauritz Winckler three or four times, and he did not make a favourable impression on me. There was a kind of reproachful self-importance in his conduct and in his way of speaking, even about the most insignificant trivialities. After Ewa was discharged we had a few splendid arguments and it came to blows a couple of times, but we reconciled and left the battles strengthened. Mauritz Winckler, however, could never understand this; even if he never brought it up, his prejudiced attitude shone through all his screens of words and smiles.

No, Mauritz Winckler never understood this morality play

about the injured bird and the rights and obligations of the stronger one, and I had an unusually hard time tolerating him.

From the beginning. Long before he became my wife's lover.

Twilight falls quickly, darkness grows out of the corners. I am lying on my bed and watch the contours of the room being erased. Try to recall them for my inner eye, my wife and her lover, but the images are false and stay there at most a couple of seconds. I fumble for the retsina glass on the nightstand. Find it and take a deep gulp.

Think for a while about the miserable drama of life I wrote a few days ago. Try to understand how it would be possible to create some kind of point and meaning, and only come up with the bitter answer I already have.

As is intended, evidently. I don't leap headfirst into just any line of reasoning. It is of course for the sake of bitterness that I am lying here in the warm darkness on this martially lovely island.

Solely and simply because of that.

Mariam Kadhar's account of the night of 19 and 20 November took – with interruptions for questions and interjections from the prosecutor, lawyers and judge – forty-five minutes, and when she was done I think it was clear to every single member of the jury that she was guilty.

Her shoulders were relaxed and resting the whole time, her voice never failed, yet even so, slowly but surely, she sowed the seeds of conviction in all of us.

Guilty.

Then nothing helped.

No sympathy. No marble-white collarbones and no murky circumstances.

Otto Gerlach's testimony followed after a very brief pause, and even though he in many respects gave a different impression than his lover, he was hardly able to straighten out the situation. In all essentials he presented the same version of events and circumstances that Mariam Kadhar had, and actually his vain attempts probably served no purpose other than to nail down and impress all the gloomy facts that framed the great Germund Rein's evil, sudden death. As could be read in any of the newspaper accounts the following day.

Both of them admitted – with no evasions – that they had a relationship; for almost three years, even if to start with it had been sporadic. The matter – both M and G emphasized – was mainly of a sexual nature, and had its roots in Rein's manifest incapacity within this field. In connection with this explanation the prosecutor asked a number of rather insinuating questions and also managed to ensnare, primarily, Mariam Kadhar a little; I could clearly see how the goodwill was extinguished in several of the audience member's faces while she tried to explain herself, and how moralistic furrows appeared between the nostrils and mouths of two of the women on the jury as they observed her. To the question of why Rein was not initiated into the whole thing, Mariam Kadhar laughed and showed with a simple motion of her head what she thought about the prosecutor's insights into these sorts of affairs.

This did not produce a particularly positive impression either.

As far as facts were concerned, Otto Gerlach had – as agreed – appeared out at the Cherry Orchard about seven o'clock on the evening of 19 November. The idea had been – it was maintained in any event – that Helmut Rühdegger, one of the editors at the publishing house, should have accompanied him, but he had a conflict – of what type, however, they were unable to specify more closely. I remember that I felt some irritation about this; it must have been the simplest thing in the world to check this piece of information with Rühdegger himself, but this had evidently not been done, either by the plaintiffs' or the defendants' side.

In any event, the three of them ate and drank gamely at the shoreline villa, and rather early on it was clear that Germund Rein was in his very worst mood – an almost adolescent mixture of megalomania and smouldering self-contempt that is not particularly unusual among authors and other creative types (according to Otto Gerlach, who evidently thought he knew what he was talking about). Neither of them felt, however, that Rein harboured any suspicions about his wife and his publisher. Neither on this fateful occasion nor earlier in the autumn. I must say that I did not really understand their persistence on this point. It was obvious after all – at least at the time of the trial – that Rein had strong, well-grounded suspicions, and what it would actually serve to distance themselves from this was hard for me to get a handle on. Both then, in the courtroom, and later. Even so, they denied categorically that the author's bad mood that evening could have been related in some way to their shady relationship.

Sometime around midnight – quarter to twelve according to M, five minutes past according to G – Rein had had enough of the company. With a cognac bottle in hand he staggered upstairs to the top floor, told both of them to go to hell and locked himself in his room. It was agreed that Otto Gerlach would sleep over, but despite this, and despite the host's obvious intoxication, they did not take the opportunity, they maintained, to share a bed that night. At about one thirty they got up from the leather armchairs and each of them instead withdrew to their own room. Otto Gerlach stated that he then read for a while in bed and fell asleep sometime between quarter past two and two thirty. Mariam Kadhar fell asleep – according to her own statement – the moment she put her head on the pillow.

That was all, by and large. The next morning Otto Gerlach was the first one on his feet a few minutes past ten, but it was not for another hour and a half that Mariam Kadhar discovered the letter in the typewriter in Rein's room. Before this she had knocked and called a few times, but had not wanted to disturb her husband if he wished to be left alone, she maintained. At last, she went into the room anyway.

The letter was no secret. The prosecutor read it out aloud and asked if it was identical with what had been in the typewriter. Both M and G testified that such was the case.

He also asked how they viewed the circumstance that there was not a single fingerprint from Rein on the sheet of paper, but here neither of them could submit any further reasonable explanation, and on both occasions I observed the frowns in the jury.

Concerning the other letters, the ones I dug out from under the sundial, both Mariam Kadhar and Otto Gerlach adopted a viewpoint that aroused some astonishment. During the trial as well as in the newspapers' analyses afterwards.

All the letters were written on the same typewriter, experts had determined; a little portable Triumf/Adler, which belonged to Gerlach and which normally was in his office at the publishing house, but which he sometimes brought with him on his travels. The prosecutor wondered with some surprise why he didn't make use of a more modern apparatus in our computerized society, but the head of the publishing house simply answered that he always preferred honourable old typewriters to word processors.

The crux was the fourth letter. That G was behind the first three was not particularly veiled, he admitted the declarations of love without the slightest hesitation, but concerning the fourth one – where the murder plot itself was outlined; the thoughts of taking Rein's life – he firmly denied that he ever would have written something like that.

Mariam Kadhar asserted the same thing. She maintained she had never read these lines before she did so at the police station – if she had, she would have immediately broken off all connections with its author, she swore that firmly. This fourth letter was, like the others, vaguely dated . . . late autumn 199–, but because the planned weekend at the Cherry Orchard was mentioned as if imminent, it was the prosecutor's understanding, at least, that it must have been written sometime during a fourteen-day period right before Rein's death.

To the prosecutor's question of whether there was any explanation for how this fourth letter ended up among Mariam Kadhar's undergarments and later under the sundial, neither of the two accused had anything to offer, and perhaps it spoke a bit to their advantage that they did not try to offer theories and speculations in one direction or another. Concerning the original and the copies in the bureau, Mariam Kadhar explained that she discarded them a few weeks after her husband's death, and the prosecutor did not seem interested in pressing her further on that point.

'Were you familiar with *Gargantua*?' he asked instead.

Gargantua was Rein's boat.

'Of course,' Mariam Kadhar answered without visible concern.

'Naturally,' Otto Gerlach answered an hour later. 'It was just an ordinary outboard motorboat. No oddities at all.'

'Thanks,' said the prosecutor.

In both cases.

No, I was certainly not the only one who had the impression that it was all decided as Mariam Kadhar left the witness stand with lowered head. The last peculiar circumstance that the prosecutor brought up was of a financial nature, and that it made her ill at ease was evident enough.

During the weeks immediately before that fateful evening, Mariam Kadhar had made two large withdrawals from one of Rein's bank accounts, to which she had right of disposal.

One hundred thousand gulden on 7 November and one hundred and ten thousand gulden eight days later. To the direct question of what the money would be used for she could only say that Rein had asked her to withdraw the amounts in question, and that she had no idea what he intended to do with it.

'Did you usually withdraw amounts of that magnitude for him?' the prosecutor asked.

'No.'

'Never?'

'Sometimes before, maybe.'

'Without you knowing what he would do with the money?'

'Yes.'

'And what do you think he used it for this time?'

'I don't know.'

'Didn't you ask?'

'Yes.'

'And?'

'He didn't answer.'

'Don't you think that was strange?'

She hesitated a little.

'Maybe. My husband was an unusual person.'

'I have no doubt of that. In any event we have not been able to establish that he made any use of the money. What do you say about that?'

She shrugged her shoulders again.

'I don't know.'

'Any ideas?'

'No.'

The prosecutor paused to make room for the next question.

'And it was not the case that you kept the money for yourself?'

'Of course not.'

'Not on any of those occasions?'

'No.'

'Do you have anything that can prove that you really turned over the money to your husband?'

She thought about it.

'No.'

And, if I remember right, it was after this simple statement that she was allowed to leave the stand.

I came out of the courtroom with a feeling of exhaustion, but also with a sense that it was over now; a sort of bitter relief like after a visit to the dentist, roughly.

The next few days this feeling stayed with me. I wandered around in the city without either a goal or urgency; sat in the parks or the cafes and read and observed people, and allowed myself to enjoy the beautiful weather fairly unconcerned. Time seemed thinned out anew; I could hardly avoid noticing that – how once again I seemed to find myself in a period of emptiness and transparency. A waiting room for a delayed train. I read in the newspapers about the various speculations before the verdict, of course, and about the ado about the book and the copyright issue, but in general I was unaffected by it all. I understood that my role was settled, and that now I could sit here at Gambrinus or Mefisto or Vlissingen and observe the drama with the same raised eyebrow as anyone else.

I didn't drink very much those days either. True, I sat at the bars in the evening, but was usually home with Beatrice long before midnight, and when Janis Hoorne called and wanted to take me out to the sea, I declined and asked to postpone the arrangement until some later time. I think we agreed on early June; I still had no idea if it ever would be June this year.

Naturally I knew that the temporary hollow of rest and distance would not last forever. On the contrary, it was rather obvious that this only concerned a period of necessary vacuity before the next concentration. The next sluggish accumulation of meteorites in the warp of time.

The intensification came – as was intended – in connection with the end of the week right in the middle of May.

On Friday, the judgement was pronounced in the Rein case. I heard about it on the radio on one of the morning news broadcasts, the same way I heard about the arrest. I had the window out towards the street standing wide open, I recall, and while the reporter slowly read the brief communiqué, it felt as if the whole city was holding its breath. For a few seconds at least, and it was a strange experience to say the least. I can still recall it without any difficulty whatsoever.

Mariam Kadhar guilty.

Otto Gerlach guilty.

Murder in the first degree.

Beyond all doubt. Unanimous jury. The length of the sentences was not yet established, but there was nothing that indicated that it would be anything other than the maximum. Twelve years for both of them.

No extenuating circumstances. Neither of them more or less guilty than the other. No pardon.

I turned off the radio and the city welled in through the window again.

About a day later – on Saturday afternoon – Kerr called and reported that the sales figures were calculated to be up to forty-five thousand, and that the second printing (of fifty thousand new copies) was now done. He asked if I needed more money, and I thanked him for another small advance.

I got drunk that evening. Also went home with a woman to her apartment on Max Willemstraat, but I don't think either she or I had very much pleasure from our meagre intercourse on her living room floor.

In any case not her.

Then on Sunday – Sunday 16 May – Haarmann reported that Elmer van der Leuwe would arrive at S–haufen the same evening, and that he intended to resume his interrupted surveillance.

Under the assumption that it was still my wish to find my missing wife, that is?

It was, I explained, and hung up. Got up, went to the kitchen and took two tablets for a rather emphatic headache. A little surprised, I then noticed that it was raining – a lukewarm and gentle spring rain – and that a growing wet spot had formed inside the open balcony door.

It was Doris with the freckles – at Vlissingen there were two waitresses named Doris, both about twenty-five, both blonde, both beautiful in that cool northern European way, but only one of them had freckles – Doris with the freckles, that is, who sometime shortly after four o'clock in the afternoon raised a hushing finger and turned up the volume on the TV, which was hanging from the ceiling in a corner of the place at the very back.

I have thought back numerous times to this brief news broadcast. The experience I immediately took with me when I left Vlissingen was that it must have been some kind of slow-motion broadcast, because afterwards it all lingered with such absurd clarity: the reporter's eyes a little too wide-open, as if she herself did not really believe what she was communicating; her voice, her occupational phrasing and professional indifference, balancing over an abyss of suppressed excitement.

And the pictures.

Of the jail. Of the corridor. Of the cell door and of the policewoman who quite dispassionately answered the off-camera reporter's questions into a blue microphone with the Channel 5 emblem.

And the words that fell still stick with me, and in the corner of my eye I see how Doris is forgetting to smoke so that the pillar of ash on her cigarette finally becomes top-heavy from waiting and falls off.

'Can you tell us what happened?' the reporter asks, coughing two times, once right into the microphone.

'Well . . .' the policewoman hesitates to start with, 'she asked for paper and pen, and there is nothing in the regulations that prohibits that.'

'You gave her paper and pen?'

'My colleague did.'

'Your colleague gave her paper and pen?'

'Yes.'

'And then?'

'Then I was supposed to tell her that she had been given time with the priest.'

'The priest?'

'Yes, she had asked to speak with a priest.'

'You went to her cell?'

'Yes. I peeked in through the hatch and saw that she was lying on the floor.'

'What did you do?'

'I unlocked it and went in. She was lying on her stomach. First I asked how she was feeling and when she didn't answer I turned her over . . . there was a little speck of blood on the floor and then I saw her eye.'

'You understood what had happened?'

'Yes. She had driven the pen into her eye.'

'The whole pen?'

'Yes. Nothing was sticking out.'

'Was she dead?'

'Yes, I called for help but we could immediately determine that she was dead.'

Brief pause while the camera focuses on a slighter darker spot on the green floor.

'How did you react?'

No response to start with. The camera slowly turns upwards to a close-up of the policewoman's face, and you can clearly see that she has a hard time knowing where to focus her gaze. But still no especially strong agitation, as stated. The left corner of her mouth twitches a couple of times.

'It was terrible . . .' she says at last, more as a concession to convention, I think.

Then the reporter says that his name is Erich Molder and the picture goes back to the news studio.

'We repeat,' the woman with the wide-open eyes says, 'that Mariam Kadhar, wife of the deceased author Germund Rein and recently sentenced to twelve years in prison for his murder, only an hour ago has taken her life in the police jail on Burg-islaan, where she was awaiting transfer to the women's prison in Bossingen. Mariam Kadhar was thirty-nine years old. We will return with more details during our regular news pro-gramme.'

Then the broadcast is over. Doris finally takes a puff on her cigarette, I observe her spotted forearm – how it rises and falls while she does that. Then she turns off the TV. I get up from my place by the window and leave the premises. Out on the street the strong sunshine strikes me like an electric shock. I stand there for a moment and close my eyes while I hold onto a bicycle that is parked against the wall. I feel a peculiar, strong dizziness and the taste of metal on my tongue is acrid and clear.

After a few seconds I have recovered and start walking in the direction of Ferdinand Bolstraat.

I read this over. Find that it is a completely correct description. It can be added that it was Monday 17 May, and that it was the warmest day so far that year.

I refill water from the scratched carafe and a cloud of mist forms on the ouzo glass. Sit alone under the parasol and wait for the siesta to be over; I have slept for an hour on a bench under the bougainvillea north of the church, but now I am sitting here with my envelope.

Hotel Ormos. There are three others here in the main town, but it is Ormos that has grandeur. Grandeur and a view. Below me, far out on the battered spit of land, is the castle, the old fortress, to which an improbably dusty bus transports tourists all day long.

Except during the hours of siesta. It is starting to end now; the heat is still paralysing, but the sun is oblique and the shadows are spreading out between the houses. As soon as Mr Valathakos comes out and unlocks the security grille to his souvenir shop, I will make my way over there. It is right across the alley; Valathakos is the only tradesman in town who uses a grille, and there are those who shake their heads at him and call him an ass or an Athenian, even though he is just as native to the island as they are and, unlike many others, lives here year-round.

When I introduce myself, it turns out that he has nothing against being treated to an ouzo at Ormos. He locks the grille firmly again, and we sit down at the same table where I had spent the last hour.

I feel some nervousness; there is only a week left of my stay and Mr Valathakos is a trump card. I have known about it for several days, simply waited for the right opportunity, and as I push the photographs over I can feel the blood rising in my temples and beads of sweat on my upper lip. They are cold and do not taste a bit like salt.

Before he observes the pictures we make a toast. Then he lifts his wide-brimmed straw hat and wipes his forehead with the back of his hairy fist. Puts the hat in place and lights a cigarette.

He proceeds meticulously. Draws his fingers across his blue-black stubble and studies long and well. Then he nods and asks if I have a map.

I unfold it. He laughs and makes a gesture towards his shop, and I confirm that I acquired it just there. He straightens it, looks back and forth across it a couple of times, as if to orient himself and check that it really concerns the right island. Then he signals for a pen. I hand one over and he draws a large, clear cross in one of the small bays on the north side.

'Boat!' he says. 'No road!'

I nod. Fumble among some bills in the chest pocket of my shirt, but he makes a discreet, dismissive gesture with his hand.

'No Italiano,' he explains. 'Greek.'

I apologize. We lean back and finish our glasses.

At Albert Hijn I buy four bottles of whisky and just as many cans of cat food. I can still distinguish a clear element of rationality in my actions during these days. I water the flowers, clean out Beatrice's litter box and fill it with new sand. Pour food into the bowl – a substantial dose that ought to last a couple of days – before I sit down in the armchair and start drinking with no purpose other than to achieve an agreeable degree of unconsciousness.

Methodically and without haste I empty one glass after another. Let the alcohol spread and take command, but without getting carried away, without falling down in hollows of dead water and indisposition. Without engagement, actually – a quiet, clinical type of drinking, where with an isolated part of my awareness I continuously keep the process under strict supervision and control. I've done it before and I know what it's about.

Sometime during the early night hours I start occupying myself with the pencil. With the pencil and the eye. Try, and really succeed, to balance a pencil between the eye and the hand. The well-sharpened tip resting against the slippery surface of the eye – a certain, albeit infinitesimal, pressure is necessary to hold it in place – the back end against a point in the very centre of my lightly cupped palm – supine position; the pencil more or less vertical, anything else is doomed to fail . . . balance in this way and let the impulses be sent out and cancelled, sent out and cancelled. It is a difficult procedure, undeniably; the tip easily slips out of position and gradually I understand that it is evidently not possible even with the most intense pressure to penetrate the eyeball itself. What instead ought to be the result is that the pencil penetrates into the brain above or below the eye, which is doomed to give way, glide around in its socket; leave free passage but hardly let itself be pierced and penetrated . . . it is an irritating conclusion in a way, a slippage from the absolute perfection that had vaguely occurred to me, but which I naturally have to resign myself to accepting anyway.

I wake up in sharp morning light. Make my way to the bathroom with a bottle and continue drinking. The first gulps come up again, but gradually I manage to keep the burning drops down. Then lie there in the darkness and the faint odour of sour gastric juice and urine and let the hours and the seconds eat their way through the day.

Another night falls. I have vague recollections of it, likewise of the next day; at some point the whisky is finished, I find a bottle of sweet wine out in the kitchen cupboard. It is a disgusting drink and towards evening I find myself in the bathroom again and have turned my stomach inside out. A cold, merciless sobriety is approaching, I am swimming in cold sweat and foul-smelling anxiety, try to curl up on the floor in a protective foetal position, but am constantly torn in two by shivers and shaking. Explosions in nerves and flesh. Spasms and sudden states of breathlessness, before I finally sink down into a black and dreamless sleep.

A series of telephone rings comes and goes. Beatrice comes and goes. Through the half-open bathroom door new daylight seeps in. I fall down into sleep again. More ringing, aches in the right hip and shoulder against the hard floor. Finally I get up.

Finally I get up. Drink water straight from the tap, rinse my hands and face. More ringing. I hurry slowly out into the living room and answer.

Haarmann.

Private detective Haarmann.

'I've been trying to get hold of you.'

'I'm sorry.'

'Really?'

'What do you want?'

'I have news.'

Silence.

'Are you still there?'

'Of course.'

'I've found her.'

'Who?'

'*Who?* Your wife, of course. How are you doing, really?'

'Just fine. Excuse me, I just woke up . . . where is she?'

He pauses, I think he is lighting a cigarette.

'If you come here I'll give you the information you need. Bring cash along so we can settle the account at once. Does an hour from now suit you?'

I look at the clock. A few minutes past ten. Morning, that is; it is no longer clear to me on what day of the week.

'In an hour,' I say.

'Life is failed. But when a door is opened, you have to go on. It is a duty and nothing else.'

That was what she said and I knew of course it was something she had read or heard. It was often that way with Ewa. She picked up phrases and sentences from every possible source: movies, newspapers, debate programmes on TV; could then conserve them for weeks and months, to reproduce them much later as her own in situations and contexts that in some way seemed to have relevance for what was said.

Like this summer morning.

Failed?

In retrospect I know that much of what she said during this particular period came from Mauritz Winckler. Perhaps I understood it even then, it was just that I didn't care all that much about it. I did not react; she was my wounded bird, I was her husband and benefactor, that was how we related to each other . . . I was the solid ground, Ewa the lost hind in the marsh. Her opinions came and went, moods and affect shifted from one day to the next, sometimes from hour to hour. But I always listened to her and I never wavered; stood there firm and unshakeable so that she could crawl up every time she risked sinking too deeply.

The rock. The fixed point.

The adagio was over now.

I thought back on these things while I wandered through A. that warm day in May. The address was far away in Greijpstraa; I could have taken the tram, of course, but something prevented me. Presumably only the time factor; I needed time, needed a long walk before I was ready to stand face to face again. Perhaps also some time at a cafe along the way. It was a warm day, as stated. Yet another one.

Haarmann had wondered if I wanted to find out the details or if I was content with name and address.

'Name?' I had asked, and he explained that her name was Edita Sobranska nowadays.

'Edita Sobranska?'

'Yes, apparently.'

I said that I could easily manage the rest myself and that I was not interested in how he proceeded to track her down. He nodded and perhaps there was a sign of doubt in his eyes, but my expression did not change. He handed over a card with name, address and telephone number. I put it in my wallet and paid what he asked. Eight hundred gulden without a receipt.

'Do you mean your life, or whose life is this about?' I remember that I replied that time.

'Ours,' she answered immediately and surprisingly. 'Our life together.'

It was out of the ordinary that she managed to continue her argument after I had made an objection.

'Our life?'

'Yes, ours. We no longer give energy to each other. We're not growing . . . we're eating each other up and falling inward the whole time. Falling inward. Shrinking and shrinking, don't you feel it? You must feel it, nothing is clearer than that right now. If we continue, one fine day we are going to be missing.'

'Those are just words, Ewa,' I said. 'Words without meaning, you must realize that. They mean nothing.'

'They mean everything,' she said.

Everything.

Who is it who decides which words have meaning and which ones don't?

For a long stretch I walk along Prinzengracht. In the viscous, brown water ducks and Cherokee geese are drifting around in timeless indolence. Between Keyserstraat and Valdemarlaan the horse chestnuts were in bloom; the massive white-green branches seemed to strive upwards and downwards at the same time. Towards the sun and towards the water; I recall that I thought about this awhile, about this duality and about the fact that I could not explain whether it concerned a both/and or an either/or. Afterwards I see, of course, that the whole thing is completely fruitless pondering, but I remember the image; after three years I can still see the trees along Prinzengracht and I can see myself wandering under them that particular day in the middle of May. Wandering and wondering about these massive trees' need for satisfaction.

Warmth and water. Warmth or water.

At Kreuger Plein I stopped. Hesitated for a few seconds

between the cafes, before I sat down at Oldener Maas. Sat there for an hour at one of the tables out on the pavement, but I drank nothing other than coffee and a glass of juice with ice cubes.

Felt strong irresolution while I sat there, perhaps it was related to the chestnuts. Now and then I took the card out of my wallet and looked at it.

Edita Sobranska. Bergenerstraat 174.

Tried to understand where she got the name from: it sounded Polish, without a doubt, but I didn't know of a single Slavic connection in Ewa's life. So why had she come up with it?

Perhaps it isn't her after all, I thought. Perhaps it's a different woman altogether, and Haarmann was mistaken. Wasn't that the most probable solution, when all is said and done?

If it were so, if the woman on Bergenerstraat were to turn out to be someone other than my missing wife, then . . . well, then the whole case would have to fall. Then that would have to be enough; I am quite certain that I took that decision with me when I left Oldener Maas. That – whatever happened – it would be over now; this was the last day, it had all been going on far too long already . . . I ought to have realized that sooner, of course, but better late than never.

Fifteen minutes later I had arrived at Bergenerstraat. It was a long and rather narrow street that went from Bergener Plein and ran in a north-easterly direction over towards the V Park and the athletic fields. Ordinary four- and five-storey buildings of dark brick on both sides. Black-lacquered entryways and close-set windows. A shop or two. Cafes at every third intersection, in round numbers.

I stopped outside number 174. Looked around in both

directions before I went up and read the name plates. Fourth
floor: E. Sobranska. M. Winck. I felt the door. Locked. I rang
the doorbell. No one answered, but a click was heard in the
lock. I stepped in and started walking up the narrow, slightly
sloping stairway.

My first knock produced no reaction and I tried again, a little
harder. I heard a radio being turned off inside the apartment
and steps approaching. A key was turned a couple of times in
the lock, the door opened and I stood face to face with . . .

I want to recall that it took a second before I realized that
it was her, but I'm not certain. She was simply dressed in black
jeans and a long T-shirt with a batik print and her face was so
familiar that I almost had to protect myself against it; yes,
I think it was this strong identification that, paradoxically
enough, made me hesitate.

I also want to recall that we stood quietly a short while and
just looked at each other before we started talking, but here I
am no longer convinced either. Perhaps in reality she started
speaking at once, in any case she was the one who broke the
silence that was now there to break.

'I see, you're here now,' she said.

She took a step backwards and I stepped into the little hall.

'Yes,' I said. 'I'm here now.'

She signalled to me to go on into the apartment. Went
ahead and sat down on one of three armchairs that were
placed around a low rattan-and-glass coffee table. I hesitated
again, but then she nodded and I took a seat across from her.

'I see, you're here now,' she repeated and her eyes oscillated
a little, as I remembered that she used to do now and then

when she was trying to concentrate on something unclear or difficult. I did not reply.

'Would you like a cup of tea?' she asked after a while.

I nodded and she left the room. I closed my eyes and leant my head backwards against the high, soft back support. Heard her bustling about in the kitchen with water, saucepan and cups; I sat there quite still and the thoughts and movements inside me were wordless and abstract far beyond the boundary of what is intelligible. But beautiful, undeniably beautiful; I know that I managed to note just that. Then I felt the presence of someone else in the room. I opened my eyes and saw Mauritz Winckler standing with his elbow leaning against a tall dresser, observing me.

I observed back. He had the same round glasses and the same short, grizzled hair as four years ago. The collarless shirt and corduroy trousers might also very well have been the same that he had been wearing the few times I met him, but you never can tell.

Neither of us uttered a word and after a minute or so Ewa came back with a tea tray. She stopped a moment in the middle of the room; looked at us in turn, first Mauritz Winckler, then me. Then she allowed herself a smile, hasty and transitory like a swallow's flight, roughly, and set the tray down on the table.

'What are you doing in A.?' she asked.

'Working,' I said.

'On what?'

'A translation.'

'Rein?'

'Yes.'

'I almost thought as much.'

Mauritz Winckler coughed and came and sat down at the table. Ewa started serving tea from a large clay pitcher.

'Have you been living here long?' I asked.

'Three years.'

'Three years. Ever since . . . ?'

'Yes,' Mauritz Winckler answered. 'Ever since.'

We drank a little tea. I looked at Ewa's birthmark on her cheek and remembered how we counted each other's marks at a hotel in Nice once during one of the very first years.

'How long are you staying?' she asked.

I shrugged my shoulders.

'Not much longer, I think. My assignment is about to end.'

'I understand,' said Mauritz Winckler, and I know that I wondered what it was he understood.

We sat in silence again. Avoided each other's gazes. Mauritz Winckler had a biscuit.

'What was it that happened in Graues?' I asked at last.

I had thought that they would at least exchange a glance with each other, but they did not. Instead both raised their eyes and looked at me with a . . .

. . . with a seriousness that I at once found to be bordering on rude; I had come as a guest with good intentions. I quickly emptied my teacup, set it down on the saucer with an emphatic bang and straightened up.

'What happened in Graues?' I repeated in a slightly louder voice.

Mauritz Winckler slowly shook his head. Ewa stood up.

'I think it's best that you leave now,' she said.

I sat there for a moment and deliberated with myself, then

I got up from the chair. Ewa went ahead out into the hall again, and as she stood with her hand on the door handle to let me out I asked for the third time, now in a low voice, so that Mauritz Winckler would not hear it.

'What happened in Graues?'

She opened the door.

'I don't intend to explain that to you, David,' she said.

'What do you mean?'

She looked at me with the same, almost nauseating serious-ness.

'You ask what happened in Graues. Yet you must very well understand that you have no right.'

'No right?'

'You have no right to find out what happened.'

I did not reply.

'Perhaps that is what is most distressing about it all,' she added, taking her eyes off me. 'That you don't understand that.'

Two completely contradictory thoughts showed up in my head; I weighed them hastily against each other, then I gave up.

'Farewell, Ewa.'

I left without looking at her any more.

Ten minutes later I had turned onto Windemeerstraat. On the broad pavement I wandered in a south-westerly direction towards the centre with the setting, but still warming, sun in my face. There were quite a few people moving about, now and then I closed my eyes for a few seconds and bumped against a shoulder or two in the throng – I remember that I thought it gave me a peculiar sense of belonging – but in general I did not behave particularly different compared with anyone else in the crowd.

I let three trams pass by before I seized the opportunity. In reality it was a very simple procedure; two steps diagonally out into the street and then suddenly everything ceased.

Everything.

THREE

Even so there was still a time to come, and I did not understand what that would serve.

A time, thinner than vacuum, more deserted than an open sea, but then one day Henderson showed up with his absurd assertions and his pictures.

A point wandered anew in the emptiness, it lingered and grew, and I had already started to follow it with my gaze.

'And you left her and slunk away like a whipped dog?'

I do not reply. Put a couple of the oily olives in my mouth and look out over the water. The sun has gone down in the usual orange haze a hand's breadth above the horizon and the stillness is almost complete. We are sitting out on the terrace, each in a rope chair that – according to what he maintains – he designed himself and had some craftsman in one of the villages on the east side make. He has also added on to the house a bit; the little core of thirty or forty square metres has, with time, grown to twice that. Modernized too: water pipe from the springs up in the mountain, electric power in a cable from the village. Terraces and grapevines on the slope on the back side and a pair of stately cypresses that he moved here from the settlement on the other side of the bay and got rooted against all odds. Two dozen of his own olive trees, which, he asserts, are over five hundred years old. Up the mountain a winding donkey trail leads to a chapel, which was also included in the acquisition; an eccentric Frenchman lived there before him, lived here for more than fifty years together with a horde of cats and a cembalo, but moved home to Rouen in the autumn of old age and died within two months. The cats are gone, but the cembalo is still there.

On the whole he does not neglect many details when he

tells, perhaps it is all pure confabulation, I understand in any event that it grants him a grim pleasure to have an audience again. Albeit just one. Albeit me. It is obvious that nowadays he does not associate with people. Takes the boat around the point to the main town every other or every third week to get provisions, but otherwise lives in sublime seclusion . . . an isolation that has made him considerably more talkative than I remember him. An acute and transitory loquaciousness, true, and the features of self-absorption and egoism have hardly been reduced. Conserved and refined a bit, possibly. His primary occupation in the solitude seems to be carrying stone: improving the terraces or adding on to the high, metre-thick wall that at the moment surrounds the house from two and a half directions.

'You do agree,' he continues, 'that it is unforgivable to fritter away a story in that way? A story that starts with a sneeze on the radio . . .'

'A cough.'

'A cough, same thing. You let it all run out in the sand like spilled milk. Donkey piss! Leave them there and . . .'

'Take off like a whipped dog, of course.'

I wait while he lights a cigarette in that affected long holder – made of ivory if I'm not mistaken.

'You are familiar with my little ideas about life scripts?'

'Naturally. By the way, they are hardly yours. So you want to maintain that your story is so much better?'

He snorts.

'The comparison is a pure insult.'

He does not even look at me. Smokes and keeps his gaze directed out over the sea. Presumably he is starting to get tired now.

'Was all this tangled intrigue really necessary?' I ask after a few seconds of silence.

'Of course,' he says with obvious irritation. 'What the hell do you think? The suspicion has to grow slowly . . . surely you don't think it would have worked if they had been exposed all at once. Don't put on airs, you know just as well as I do that this was how it had to be arranged . . . you do have the result!'

'Did you count on her death too?'

He shrugs his shoulders.

'That has nothing to do with it. What are you trying to say? Your own wife is living in the best of health together with your rival! You haven't come here to claim that you managed this as you intended, have you?'

He lets out a laugh.

'Goddamned dilettante! You didn't even manage to find out what happened!'

I observe him from the side while he sips the resinated wine . . . the heavy profile with the bushy hair that has whitened under the sun; sixty-one years old, I calculate, suntanned, hale and hearty; his reputed frailty during the final years seems to have left him completely – if nothing unforeseen happens, there is much that says he could live another quarter century here in this out-of-the-way paradise. Among his stones, his olives and his sanitized recollections.

If nothing unforeseen happens, that is.

'No, I don't know what happened in Graues.'

I have told my story in very brief terms; am not sure if he really listened while I carried on, but it seems to have stuck in him anyway. Now, however, he has no more comments.

'I was thinking about "Gilliam's Temptation" the other day,' I continue after a period of silence.

It is one of his earliest short stories: about a man who is obsessed about directing both his own life and those closest to him in accordance with certain images and signs that come to him in various ways, primarily by way of dreams. A rather bizarre story, which ends with him burning down the house with his wife and their two sons inside; the temptation in the title refers to the protagonist's hesitation before this final action, the difficult enticement to not . . . to *not* follow the instructions and his inner voices.

But then, at last, he overcomes even this.

Rein laughs.

'Oh, yes, that one!' He thinks a moment. 'Yes, one can probably say that it still holds.'

'How did you manage it?' I ask.

'Manage what?'

'Well, the escape.'

'It was no escape. Just a new passport and a simple disguise . . . and the money, of course.'

'You weren't drunk that evening?'

'A little, at most.'

'I would still maintain that you were lucky.'

'Nonsense.'

During our entire conversation I have waited for him to at least thank me for the help, show a bit of appreciation that I met his expectations and played my role as he intended, but now, when the sun has disappeared completely and the twilight quickly starts to fall, I understand that he has never even had that thought.

Should the master thank the puppet because she danced?

The marionette because she responded to the tug on the wire?

Of course not.

I look down at my boat, pulled up on the shore. It is still light enough to make my way down the uneven stone steps (which are left from the Frenchman's time) without a lantern, but in half an hour it will be undoable. Rein has fallen silent again and I assume that his relative talkativeness is now over for good. I observe him for a few seconds, and although he must feel my gaze, he does not turn his head. It is obvious that he wants to be left alone; I empty my glass and heave myself out of the chair.

'I think it's time.'

He nods, but does not get up. Just sits there and rolls yet another cigarette on his unwieldy machine.

The question comes when I have turned my back to him.

'You aren't having any thoughts about going to the media, are you? My new identity is airtight, I want to emphasize that. There is simply no point.'

'Of course not.'

'It would not be particularly becoming if you chose to behave like a sore loser too, would it?'

'I assure you.'

'Rein is dead.'

'Rein is dead. Farewell.'

'Farewell.'

When I come down to the boat, it is already so dark that I cannot make him out up there on the terrace. I do not want to light a candle and am forced to grope for a few moments for the knife under the net that is rolled up on the floor. Then I find it.

Then I sit and weigh it in my hand and feel its sharpened edge for another twenty minutes, while the darkness gets denser. Think about this and that, but nothing that would be worth mentioning and nothing that sticks with me. When I see that he has lit a lantern up there, I start to make my way once again up the uneven steps.

DEAR AGNES

Translated from the Swedish by Paul Norlen

Adapted into the film *Dear Agnes*

All in all it was a successful funeral.

The morning had been grey-minded and windless, but when we came out to the grave the sun had broken through the cloud cover and cast crooked shafts of light through the yellowed foliage of the elm trees.

Erich would have liked it. Autumn. The sky that suddenly lifted, leaving sharpness in the air. Clear without being cold. The fields down towards Molnar harvested but not yet ploughed up. A farmer burning undergrowth in the distance.

The minister's name was Sildermack, a tall, skinny, pale man; we had met during the week, of course, and decided on the procedure. He's new to the parish and suffers from some kind of deformity of the spine, which means he gets around with slightly clumsy, almost rolling movements. Makes him look older than he really is. But his face radiates light and he manages his duties without a hitch.

There were two dozen of us. The children of course. His mother with her retinue; the girlfriend and the gruff nurse.

Beatrice and Rudolf.

Justin.

Hendermaags, who had the poor judgement to drag the kids along. No older than ten or twelve; a shy boy and a girl with protruding teeth and nervous eyes, what good will it do to subject them? Neither of them had any relationship with Erich, probably haven't seen him on more than two or three occasions, as far as I can recall.

Ebert Kenner obviously and some current colleagues that I had never seen. A quartet, to be precise; two women, two men. And Dr Monsen, who gave the eulogy inside the church and could not restrain himself from saying a few words out by the grave too.

About the clarity of autumn days and our time on earth. The analytical acuity that had been Erich's hallmark and which the sun breaking through accompanied and bore witness to.

Words.

I got a little tired. Right there out in the dark-clad circle of mourners and semi-mourners and the sort who were there for quite general reasons, a wave of fatigue came over me. Maybe it was the actual grief that took hold of me. Not mourning for Erich primarily, but mourning for life.

Its unfairness and blind reflections. Falsifications that we sweep under the rug and keep at bay but that catch up with us anyway once we've turned our backs on them long enough. Haven't been attentive enough.

I didn't cry. Not a tear came out of my eyes during the whole ceremony; I don't care how people interpret this, but the medications that make us dull and mute in the soul are legion in our times, so I assume that my behaviour hardly came as a surprise. I didn't exchange a word with anyone. Tactful, confirming glances, that's all. Handshakes. Light hugs and illusory nods.

The friends from youth, from the rowing club, carried the coffin. There were four, I recognized three of them but none by name, they all live here in Gobshejm and according to the minister they came up with that initiative themselves.

And then Henny.

It was not my idea to list everyone present, but now I see that's what I've actually done.

Henny Delgado.

She was dressed in long-sleeved black inside the church, but when we came outdoors she had a dark-red poncho tossed over her shoulders. I remember that she always used to wear red, not necessarily completely, but always a splash. Something red and eye-catching. A crimson blouse or a scarf. Personally I'm blue and cold. Even when we were in high school we kept to these spheres: Henny red, yellow, ochre. Me blue and turquoise, cold colours. We could only meet in green, but at separate ends. Later, it must have been during the first autumn semester at university, we went to a colour analyst together, who also approved our intuitive choices. Held patches of fabric up against our surprised faces and expatiated on our different skin types. Pigmentation personalities, as if it were something spiritual almost.

She looked unexpectedly young, Henny. Fit and healthy somehow; I don't really know why it surprised me, but it did. She had come alone, of course; husband and children live at home in Grothenburg, yes, I've never met either of the girls, but their baptism cards are duly pasted in some album.

It feels a little funny that we didn't speak with each other, when meeting after so many years. I have a feeling, however, that she is going to be in touch. What motivates this diffuse sense I don't know, but it would surprise me if I'm wrong. After all, we have been as close to each other as two people of the same sex can be, without being related or homosexual. A long time has passed, but there are signs and small hints that hit us on a deeper level than the cognitive and linguistic. Of course it's like that.

Justin asked if he should stay overnight, but I declined. He is a good and understanding person, Justin, I've always liked him, despite his slightly uncultivated style, but I want to be alone. Just me and the dogs, a fire in the fireplace and the armchair pulled up to the window. A glass of port or two, the twilight that settles down over the garden, the gnarled, pruned-backed apple trees, the boxwood hedge and the boggy slope down towards Molnar; a few hours in absolute silence with the photo albums and the memories. Maybe I'll have a cigarette too, it's years since I smoked out of habit, but it is a special day and I have a couple of packs lying around.

I'm on sick leave next week too. Half of the classes are postponed, half were assigned to Bruun. As usual. It's a shame to have to put Keats and Byron into his clumsy hands, but there was no choice. The oral exam period is only three weeks away and everything has to be covered before the fifteenth.

It feels nice that it's over now, finally. I knew of course that one day I was going to be alone. Erich was eighteen years older than me; it wasn't fire and passion I was looking for when I chose him, but the blue. Yet he was fifty-seven, there was never any sign that he would die so young, and Monsen also emphasized in his eulogy that he had much left to do. Researchers do not belong to the category of people whom the years consume, he maintained; not in their daily activity. I understood that in this case he was referring both to himself – he can't be far from seventy – and one present colleague or another.

But Erich had to stop, as they say at home in Saarbrücken. Reached the finish line.

I'm sitting in the armchair with half an eye out towards the twilight and the garden, half in towards the room with the fire and the books. There have got to be a lot of volumes over the years. In the next few days I'm going to do some rearranging, I think. Move the heavy medical works up to the attic, and let literature take a more prominent place.

This is just one of all the little things I have to take care of. But it will have to wait until tomorrow. Right now I just want to sit here and rest.

Remember and browse in the albums. A few lines from Barin come to me.

> I miss my mother's mild odour of sweat –
> and those short pants they forced me to wear
> that first day of school.
> I miss Ursula Lipinskaja, and waking up well-rested
> to completely unwritten summer days.
> But most of all I miss the unattainable smoke
> from those cigarettes I never smoked at the cafes.

I light one now instead. A feeling of restrained satisfaction vibrates within me.

As if something long foreseen is about to come off.

The dogs are sleeping in front of the hearth and they don't seem to miss him either.

To:
Agnes R.
Villa Guarda
Gobshejm

Grothenburg, 26 September

Dear Agnes,

Forgive me for writing to you so soon after you have become alone, I hope you are not completely shattered after your difficult loss. I liked seeing you again so much, even if I wish of course that the circumstances had been a little different. And of course I should have exchanged a few words with you since I was there anyway, but something held me back. I don't know what, sometimes it's just the case that we are obstructed by forces we have no name for. Isn't that right, Agnes?

But it was a lovely and dignified ceremony, I never did know your husband, so of course I can't say whether it was also 'becoming', as the English say.

Anyhow, I would appreciate resuming contact with you, so many years have passed and I feel that you shouldn't cut off threads so casually. We were so close to each other, dear Agnes.

So, may I write to you? Tell a little about myself and my family? If you have a desire to respond?

We can probably start by mail, then we'll see. I have a hard time with email, it gets so lightweight and superficial.

If you have no desire to resume this old friendship, you absolutely must say no.

Awaiting hopefully your reply.

Yours, Henny

To:
Henny Delgado
Pelikaanallé 24
Grothenburg

                                    Gobshejm, 30 September
Dear Henny,

   Good Lord, you sound as if we were eighty!

   Of course you can write, and I will gladly write back. I'm sure we have a lot to talk about, but because you're the one who is taking the initiative, I will let you tell first.

   So feel no hesitation. Write soon, please, we have a nineteen-year gap to fill!

   Yours, Agnes

If you are simply kind and good, sooner or later you get your reward.

It is the second day in Grothenburg, and even though I am just a skinny eleven-year-old I know that she's lying.

Or maybe not lying. The red-haired girl, whose name is Henny, and who already came to visit with her mum yesterday, before we unpacked a single box, has simply misunderstood everything. Hasn't really understood what life is like and how things work.

But I don't protest. Don't have words for such things at my tender age, and besides it's not important. It's in the evening, we're standing on the bridge over the river and looking down into the brown water; our mothers have sent us out on a little walk so that Henny can show me the neighbourhood and the area. My mother has felt a so-called instantaneous confidence in Henny, despite her innate and cherished suspicion.

And Henny has by all means behaved both well-bred and charming, I won't deny that.

And plum jam was a welcome gift between good neighbours.

A clever laugh and a sincere gaze.

If you are simply kind and good, that is.

I don't remember how I answer, maybe I say nothing.

We've been taking a circuitous walk around the neighbourhood. The playing field. Hengerlaan down to the railway tracks. The shops along Klingerweg. We stopped by Smytter the butcher, who is her uncle; each of us got a white sausage and a coin from him. Bought gum in the tobacconist at the corner out toward Zwille.

And the church and the cemetery, where we strolled and looked at the graves: Henny's grandfather and grandmother are here and some day she herself will take a place here too; it's a substantial and roomy family plot with space for numerous generations.

Stumpstrasse, Gassenstrasse, Jacobs steeg and whatever they're called. And the Wallman School, where Henny has already gone for five years and where I will start in September. It is an old stone fortress with a Latin quotation above the big oak doorway. *Non scholae sed vitae discimus!* Henny intones, and then we say it together a few times so that it will be clear to me before it's time to sit down at a desk and listen to Master Pompius and Miss Mathisen and a stooped little sewing lady whose name is Keckelhänchen, of all things.

Non scholae sed vitae discimus.

We learn not for school, but for life.

But now we are hanging over the railing on the bridge; it is called Karl Eggers Bridge. Henny doesn't know why it's called that, or who Karl Eggers was, but the river is named Neckar, of course. It flows around our district, at least to the east and north, and marks the boundary with Gerringstadt, which is a completely different neighbourhood about which Henny has no knowledge other than that her cousin Mauritz lived there before they moved to Marseilles, which is by the Mediterranean Sea, because of Mauritz's failing health, but he died anyway even though he was no more than eight going on nine, so the Mediterranean is probably overrated when all is said and done.

Maybe he wasn't sufficiently kind and good, I think, but I don't say that. I spit the gum out in the flowing water instead.

'You mustn't spit chewing gum into the water,' says Henny. 'A fish might get it in its mouth and suffocate.'

The hell you can suffocate a fish, I think, they don't need to breathe.

But I don't say that either.

It's my mother and I who have moved to Grothenburg. My father and my brother are still living on Slingergasse in Saarbrücken, and even though Claus is three years older than me and we have been at odds as long as I can remember, I long for him so that my chest aches these first few days.

I found out that my parents were getting a divorce on 1 July, and we took off exactly one month later. They had planned the whole thing in detail before they dropped the bomb: we were at the Kraus restaurant, I don't know if it's usual or unusual that parents take their kids out to a restaurant when they intend to tell them that they're going to separate. But they were extremely amiable, both to each other and to Claus and me, that shouldn't be denied. Best friends in the world, but now it was the way it was, and it had turned out the way it had. It goes that way sometimes in life and this vale of tears, that's not something you can control, hey diddle diddle. I ordered the most expensive main course I could find on the whole menu, sole with white wine sauce and seasonal vegetables, and they went along with that without protest.

Dad and Claus would stay behind, they explained over dessert – citrus sorbet on wild raspberry mirror glaze with candied hazelnuts and powdered sugar – that was for the best, considering both work and school. Mum had already found a new position in Grothenburg, with a dentist named Maertens. And an apartment on Wolmarstrasse. Four rooms and kitchen, I would have my own room with a tiled stove and view of a park.

That my father had had another woman on the side for almost three years my mother only mentioned a few weeks later, when we were packing.

I cried for ten days. In any event I cried myself to sleep those first ten evenings. Then I stopped. Got that ache in my chest instead, like now when I'm thinking about Claus.

Something in my stomach too. Butterflies are dancing down there, every other day I'm constipated, every other day I have diarrhoea.

There really is a tiled stove in my room, but it's not possible to have a fire in it. The chimney flue was closed up back in the fifties, the caretaker Mr Winter has explained. There are cracks and the whole building could burn down in a jiffy if an ember worked its way out.

I think that it would be no skin off my nose if all of Grothenburg burnt down in a jiffy. I don't want to live here, I hate this city, and if we got burnt to death, it would just feel like a pleasant relief. I would never need to start in that new school and never see that silly neighbour girl again with her silly braids and clever smile.

But I don't cry in the evenings here either. It's just the ache in my chest and the fluttering in my stomach.

Her name is Else, by the way, my father's new woman. She

has already moved in with them on Slingergasse. And her daughter lives in my old room.

The worst thing of all is that her name is Agnes too.

To:
Agnes R.
Villa Guarda
Gobshejm

Grothenburg, 4 October

Dear Agnes,

Thanks for your quick reply, and thanks for not having anything against our resuming contact in this way. I don't know if it has to do with the years that run by, but however we count, Agnes, we have to admit that we're starting to approach middle age. I turn forty in February – and you, I remember it so well, on 1 May. Do you remember your first birthday here in Grothenburg, when you got the diary from me? You said that you never intended to write a line in it, but when school started in September you showed me that you already had to buy a new one.

Although I don't feel old, far from it, but I see by the girls that time is passing. Rea is eleven now, the same age you and I were when we met for the first time – Betty turns nine in December.

And David turned forty-seven last spring, he's the one who is the actual reason that I am writing to you, but I will get to that later. Soon enough, I feel that I must approach the heart of the matter in a roundabout way, that's how we function sometimes, don't you think, dear Agnes?

Where the funeral is concerned, however, I never felt any hesitation, I knew that I had to go the very moment I saw the obituary in the newspaper. It was not for your husband's sake, of course, I never knew him, but because I wanted to see you again. Over the years I have of course acquired many girlfriends – male friends too, don't get me wrong – but there is something special about those people you've known since you were a child. Don't you think so too, Agnes? Regardless of how much time has passed, how much water has run under the bridge, there is something there that connects us with each other. I truly hope that you understand what I mean, Agnes, and that you feel the same way I do. Even if words did fail me when I saw you.

Yes, David's and my socializing is ever so extensive nowadays; since he became head of TV drama the invitations rain down on us, and we have people at our house at least once a week. But one gets tired of that, Agnes, oh how one tires of it. All these smiles and talented conversationalists and confidences you didn't ask for, it makes you feel as if the theatre moved home to you and into your life, although you never wanted that. It creeps into your marrow, and under your skin somehow, so that it's not possible to wash it off . . . I don't know if you grasp what I'm talking about, Agnes, perhaps I'm expressing myself unclearly.

For my part, I put all acting ambitions on the shelf once we got married, David and I; he maintained that one clown in the family was enough and I admit that he was right about that. There weren't many professionally active years for me anyway, we have always had plenty of money and I stayed home for almost ten years to take care of the girls. But since January I've been working for Booms & Kristev, the law firm on Klingstrasse, I don't know if you remember it. Translation work into French and Italian, not a particularly skilled job, but it is well-paid and at the same time satisfying to make use of the skills you put so much effort into acquiring at one time. Likewise, naturally it's good to know *that you can actually stand on your own two feet, support yourself, if that were necessary.*

But it's the girls that mean everything to me, Agnes, I want to underscore that. From what I understand you have no children of your own, I don't know if you chose that, or if it so to speak turned out that way for natural reasons. People are different and everyone must of course seek heaven in their fashion, as old lecturer Nygren used to say. Do you remember him, Swede or Norwegian, I'm pretty sure?

Rea and Betty are so different too, even though they have the same father and same mother and have lived in the same circumstances their whole life. Rea is precise and practical and ambitious, Betty is a dreamer. Almost like two sides of the same coin – or like the principles Yin and Yang, although they are both girls. And I love them just as much, perhaps mainly because there are two of them and they complement each other so well. The last few days it has struck me that they are a bit reminiscent of you and me, Agnes, the way we are – or at least the way we were at that time. You're Rea of course, I'm Betty, isn't it strange how it's as if life can go on in long, drawn-out ellipses and how sometimes you get that frighteningly strong déjà-vu sensation of being back in the same play.

We live in a big apartment on Pelikaanallé, right next to Paul's Church; we have discussed getting a house many times, but we're so comfortable here and the girls go to school a stone's throw away. Besides, David has his childhood home up in the mountains – in the vicinity of Berchtesgaden – admittedly we share it with his brother and sister-in-law, but they live in Canada and aren't home more than a week or two every year.

I notice that I'm dwelling a lot on me and my family in this first letter, I hadn't planned that, but perhaps it's natural. As I hinted however I have a matter of considerably more specific nature, but I think it will have to wait until next time. It's past midnight, David is out with some film people; it concerns a rather large-scale production of some Pirandello plays if I understood things right – the girls are sleeping and I've been sitting in our library for a couple of hours writing and thinking. Had three glasses of wine too, I have to admit that, but it's a workday tomorrow, so it's certainly time to close.

Excuse me for having written so grandiloquently, dear Agnes, you must absolutely not feel that you have to be equally long-winded. But a few lines would make me very happy, and I promise to be more concise next time. Naturally I want to know how you are feeling. Is it just sad now when you've lost your life partner, or can there also be a streak of liberation in the loss? I'm sure you know that marriage is often compared to a cage, that you either long to go into or get out of. I hope you understand that you can be just as unreserved and frank in these kinds of questions as we were back then.

But now to bed.
Take care of yourself and write soon!
Signed,
Your Henny

To:
Henny Delgado
Pelikaanallé 24
Grothenburg

Gobshejm, 7 October

Dear Henny,

Thanks for your long letter, which – I assure you – I got a lot out of reading. Don't be afraid to tell, that's the way it was for us with words back then – you used a hundred where I used ten.

And don't think that I don't understand, even if you miss the nail head by a centimetre or so, it's so fun to hear from you again. Most likely we've lived half of our lives at this point, and both considering that and considering Erich's death, it feels like a good point in time to take account of where one stands a little.

Concerning my circumstances, I don't have as much to tell as you do, because I don't have a family. Erich already had grown children when we met, and we chose early on not to bring any more into this doubtful world. The last eight years – since I was done with my dissertation – I've worked at the university in H-berg, it's just seven or eight kilometres from here and I've been really happy with the academic life from the first moment. During the last few semesters I have really got a handle on the courses that are dearest to my heart – the Romantic period and the eighteenth-century English novel – and like you, dear Henny, I feel that I have a task to fulfil in life, even if I am never going to have children of my own and in that way continue the species.

Erich kept that marvellous house at Molnar when he got divorced from his former wife, and we've lived there ever since we got married. It is a charming old thing of timber and pommerstone with an overgrown garden and a view down towards the river. If I have any worries about the future, then it's the question of how I will manage to keep my house. Erich's children, Clara and Henry, are naturally entitled to half the estate, and how I will be able to buy them out the gods only know. I'm not sure if you picked them out at the funeral. Henry is tall, dark and arrogant, Clara a little stooped, rat-coloured and at least ten kilos overweight; both of them were sitting in the front row in the church, although on the other side of the aisle from me. To be honest I detest them as much as they detest me, but I'm sure it will be possible to find a solution to that problem too. It surprises me a little that they still haven't been in touch about the inheritance issue, two weeks have passed since the estate inventory, but I'm sure it won't be long before I get a call from some renowned law firm.

Otherwise what you suggest is completely right; there is an element of calm and relief after Erich's death. When you marry someone who is so much older, it is almost unavoidable that you will be worried about being left alone (the medical profession is of course no guarantee of a long life, rather the contrary, I think), and perhaps one should be a trifle grateful that this happens when one is forty, instead of when one is fifty or sixty. You are also right, of course, that we are approaching middle age, Henny, but I'm sure we still have something to give and something to live for. Don't you think?

You write that you have a definite reason – a specific idea – in starting this correspondence, and that in some way it has to do with your spouse. I must admit that makes me curious, and I ask you therefore not to 'move in circles and dodges in a woman's way' – but instead get to the point in your next letter, which I hope I won't have to wait too long for.

I will end with this request, it's time to go out with the dogs for their evening walk; there are two of them, you see, slender, frisky Rhodesian ridgebacks, I still haven't decided if I'm going to keep them – we've had them for almost five years, I like them a lot, but they undeniably demand both time and attention. Like now.

But as I said, Henny, be in touch again soon. I'm waiting eagerly!

Warmest greetings

Your Agnes

The school is called the Wallman School after one J. S. Wall-man, who died in war 150 years ago. There are twenty-five of us in the class; I and a nervous boy whose name is Dragoman were new when the autumn term started, but two had moved so Miss Zimmermann said it was good that we came and filled in the gaps.

Henny and I are best in the class along with Adam, who has glasses thick as milk bottles. He started reading in the crib and in that way ruined his eyes. Henny and I associate a bit with him and with his cousin Marvel, who is also in the class. Marvel is one of those who always does worst on tests, especially in mathematics and spelling, but he is big and strong and good to have around when it comes to fighting.

I am doing really well in school, last Christmas I got the lead role in *Everyone Stranger*, Miss Zimmermann said that I had theatrical talent, and I am trying not to think so much about my father and my brother off in Saarbrücken. During the whole autumn and winter I wasn't there on a visit more than two times, and my brother has been with us in the apartment a few hours one afternoon when he was in transit to a scout camp in Ravensburg. It feels a little strange that we have so little contact, but perhaps it is even stranger that I really don't care.

My mother is working quite a lot. Maertens the dentist has his practice on Gerckmarkt, I've been there too and had two cavities filled. I don't like him; he is sarcastic and incredibly hairy, his eyebrows are black and bushy and when you are sitting in the chair you see that his nostrils are so overgrown that it's surprising he can breathe through them at all.

Henny's mother has been sick a bit the past few months and we have taken care of her little brother Benjamin on some afternoons. He is a snot-nosed six-year-old who whines and is unhappy almost all the time. One time we lost track of him in Minde Park. It was cold and rainy and we searched for him for several hours. When it got dark and we still hadn't found him, Henny started crying and said that she would never forgive herself if Benjamin died. She babbled on a lot about how she would put an end to it all by throwing herself in front of the train or into the Neckar, but when she was on her knees in the sandbox on the playground where we last saw Benjamin – and prayed to God – he suddenly showed up again. Benjamin, that is, not God. He was more snot-nosed and whiney than ever and had torn his shirt, which was clean that day.

If you simply do your best and place your fate in God's hands, everything will work out in the end, Henny said, and hugged her wet and dirty little brother.

I didn't say anything; thought that basically it was good that he turned up, there would have been a lot of trouble otherwise, but in all honesty I can't maintain that I would have missed him if he'd gone and died in some way.

★

In the middle of May – two weeks after my twelfth birthday and two days after I got my first period – I discover something dreadful.

My mother has a relationship with her boss, Maertens the dentist. I happened upon them by pure chance when they came out of the Pomador restaurant on Glockstrasse hand in hand. I ran right into them, practically, and they looked frightfully embarrassed, the both of them. We just said 'hi there' and 'bye', and then I continued over to the library on Wollmarplatz that I was on my way to – but when I came home two hours later my mother told me what was going on. She said that they had started associating a little bit; she used just that expression, 'associate', and I think it sounds both old-fashioned and silly. She's not that old yet.

I tell my mother that I think Maertens the dentist is disgusting, and point out that she must be at least thirty years younger than him. My mother gets angry, says that Maertens is a very sympathetic and cultivated man, and that he hasn't turned fifty yet.

And that she certainly needs a little security after having thrown half her life away on a libertine like my father.

I repeat that I consider Maertens repulsive and lock myself in my room. When my mother knocks on the door half an hour later I turn off the light and pretend to be asleep.

It is decided that Henny and I will spend a good portion of the summer holidays together. Henny's uncle and aunt have a big house by Lake Lagomar, and we will have a separate room up in the attic. Besides her uncle and aunt there are also three cousins there, a pair of twin boys our age and a girl about five or six. I don't know if I actually have any great desire to go to Lagomar, but from what I understand I have no choice. I don't protest either, and Henny seems to look forward to the arrangement. When we compare our grades on the last day of school it turns out that we have exactly the same average. Adam is a couple of paltry decimal points better, but we agree that it's because he's a boy and wears glasses.

On the evening the day before we are going to take the bus to Lagomar I smoke my first cigarette together with Henny, Adam and Marvel. We are lying behind some bushes in Minde Park and Henny gets so nauseated that she vomits on Marvel's dress trousers. Marvel smokes two cigarettes by the way, says that tobacco makes him feel great and that he doesn't care if every one of us pukes on his pants. He has the worst grades in the whole class and is going to summer school to avoid repeating a year. When Adam has gone home, Marvel asks if Henny and I want to see his peter. Henny says that it's all the same to her if he shows it or not, and I say OK then. He unbuttons his fly and takes it out, explains that it looks the way it does because he is circumcised, and Henny and I thank him for the peek.

To:
Agnes R.
Villa Guarda
Gobshejm

Grothenburg, 12 October

Dear Agnes,
    Thanks for your letter, which I read with great interest. It makes me happy to hear that you are content with your occupation and it makes me happy that you seem to be taking your husband's death with equanimity. I know of course that you always used to keep a cool head, not get dragged down into maelstroms of emotion, and it seems like you have retained these good qualities. To what degree I myself have changed over the years that have passed I can of course not judge completely one hundred per cent, but sometimes I get the idea that deep down I am the same person as that twelve- or fifteen- or eighteen-year-old. If by and by we go so far as to meet again, you will surely have no difficulty deciding if I am right or wrong in this. Likewise I will have the opportunity to discover the same young girl in you, won't I, Agnes?
    But I have no desire to see you face to face yet, dear friend, and to explain this I must now touch on that special errand I had when I started this correspondence – and to the highest degree still have. You did urge me not to hold back this reason from you unnecessarily, but instead get to the point immediately, so therefore I will now take the bull by the horns and two deep breaths. Just hope you don't get upset, but I must take that risk; it can't be avoided.
    As I mentioned, this concerns David. You know that we have been married for almost eighteen years at this point.

He proposed only a few weeks after King Lear, we got engaged in June and were married in November the same year, yes, you're hardly unaware of this. And we have had good years together, David and I; when I look back I understand that it's been that way . . . at least the first ten. I know – you don't need to deny it, dear Agnes – that sometimes you thought I was an unacceptably naive and gullible person; I still remember many of our conversations and differences of opinion, and that you never believed in Providence and the good currents in life as I did. That we can't do much more than act according to the best of our ability and then accept the consequences, whatever they are.

That we must put our trust in the good. David and I also talked a lot about these things when we were first together, and when we swore each other eternal fidelity those were not just empty words and watered down ritual. It was serious; we decided to live together with each other and our future children our whole lives; love may not be conditional, neither on events nor on the tooth of time. It's that simple, and that hard.

But now it has happened. Through circumstances that I don't need to go into here and now, I know that David is seeing another woman. I don't know who she is, and I don't care about that either. But David has betrayed me, our children and our love pact, and I don't intend to accept that. How long this so-called affair has been going on I'm not really sure of, but it's been at least six months and probably at least twice that long. David, naturally, is keeping it secret and I respond in kind; I do not reveal by a word or an expression that I know about what he's up to behind my back. It's not through confronting him or trying to convince him – performing that whole ancient, sad act with the exposed husband and the injured and betrayed wife – that I intend to attack the problem. I have thought through all possible and impossible solutions over the past few months – with my own and the girls' best interests in mind – and, dear Agnes, there is simply no doubt. David must die.

I will understand very well if you now gasp for breath and with rising pulse reread the last few lines. Perhaps you push the letter from you and stare vacantly ahead. Shake your head and rub your right temple that way you always did before when you were thinking intensely about something.

But it doesn't help. The words are there and I am rock solid in my decision. My husband must die. He no longer deserves to live, and whatever you do, Agnes, do not try to argue with me about this point.

As far as the next item is concerned you may however – obviously – have any number of well-articulated opinions. It is namely the case that I want your help.

No, don't put the letter aside, kind Agnes! At least do me the favour of reading it all the way to the end. Completely regardless of how you react, I am going to see to it that David dies within the not too distant future. One way or another. A year or so ago I read a crime novel, I don't remember the author's name but I think it was an American – the book was about two strangers who meet on a train, and when they start talking with each other they discover that both of them would benefit greatly from the death of a close relative. Each separately and two presumptive victims, that is. Simply getting the relatives in question out of the *way somehow cannot be done just like that, however, because they would immediately be suspected of the respective murders. But then the idea pops up that they could change victims with each other. Crisscross, they call it. A undertakes to murder B's wife, B will take the life of A's rich relation.*

Do you follow me, Agnes? It was when I started brooding about David's treachery and connected it with the crisscross idea, that I happened to think of you. True, I can't help you in a corresponding way (I assume), but the point is that David must be murdered by someone who is not in my circle of acquaintances, while I myself am at another place and have an airtight alibi. That's the whole thing. And I promise you that I can pay a substantial sum for your efforts. In your most recent letter you mention that you are a trifle worried about how you will be able to stay in Erich's house – believe me, Agnes, a hundred thousand is no problem for me, and if it's the case that you need more, I'm sure we can discuss the matter.

I notice that I'm starting to get verbose again; without a doubt you have by this time understood what it is I'm asking you for. So far I haven't thought about the approach and such – we'll cross that bridge later, I like to think – but I await, as you understand, your response with a butterfly or two in my stomach. I truly ask you to give yourself a couple of days to consider my offer – and if you give me a preliminary yes, which I hope with all of my heart, that doesn't mean of course that you can't change your mind later on. Not at all. The only thing I ask for the moment is that you agree to discuss the matter. Hypothetically and with an open mind, as they say.

So, dear Agnes, have a good think about it, and then let me know the answer. Completely regardless of how you react I am and remain

Your faithful friend

Henny

To:
Henny Delgado
Pelikaanallé 24
Grothenburg

Gobshejm, 19 October

Dear Henny,

I have now read your most recent letter ten times and still don't know if I should believe my eyes.

What you propose is so horribly repugnant that I am at a loss for words. I doubt, seriously speaking, that you are in your right mind, and I've thought all evening about how I should actually formulate my response – without arriving at any acceptable alternative.

For that reason I ask you instead to send a clarifying letter, where you either distance yourself from your proposal, or explain what in the world you mean – and why you imagine for a second that I would make myself available for something so completely absurd as what you outline.

With kind regards

Agnes

The summer house by Lake Lagomar turns out, in reality, to consist of three buildings. The whole thing is located in a clearing at the edge of the forest with a lawn sloping down towards the lake and a private golden sandy beach. True, no more than thirty or forty metres long, but still.

Herr and Frau Karminen and six-year-old Karen sleep in the main building. Herr Karminen's first name is Werner but he is generally called the Chocolate King or simply the King – he has a company that manufactures chocolate pralines and after just two days we feel stuffed.

Herr Karminen is only there on weekends, evenings and nights; early in the morning he takes his blue-black Rover into Schwingen and gets the chocolate show started. Frau Karminen is named Sofie, she is a so-called mournful beauty, I think, with a willowy slim waist and long, thick hair in almost the same shade as the Rover. She basically sits all day in the shade in a reclining chair reading books, smoking skinny cigarillos in a gold holder. Karen gets a visit every day from another six-year-old from a farm in the vicinity, they stay down by the edge of the lake for hour after hour and soil themselves as best they can.

Henny, I, and some kind of relative whose name is Ruth stay in a smaller house up to the right. Ruth is in her thirties and I think she is a trifle retarded, the only thing she does is prepare food and clean up. In the evenings, when the Chocolate King has returned from Schwingen, the whole bunch have dinner together at a long table outside the middle house, and it is always Ruth who has cooked every single dish and who takes care of the dishes afterwards. But she isn't sad about that, she sings languorous ballads without words the whole day – except during mealtimes – and seems generally content with existence.

In the house to the left – which just like ours consists of a room and a teeny-weeny kitchen – the twin cousins Tom and Mart sleep. They are thirteen years old and right from the start I understand that they are the ones who are going to make the summer bearable.

They are almost identical in appearance; tall, bony boys with short dark hair and insolent eyes. The first few days I mistake which one is which, but then I learn that there is something in Mart that is not found in Tom. Something inside; I can't really formulate what it is, but one evening when they tell us that Mart is twenty minutes older than Tom I understand that this is where it is. He is the big brother, simply, presumably weighs a quarter of a kilo more and is half a centimetre taller too. Not just this summer but throughout their whole lives; I cannot understand why such petty things should be so significant, but at the same time I understand that they actually are. I have started to learn a thing or two.

'Which one do you like best?' Henny asks one evening when we have gone to bed but Ruth has not yet come and turned out the light. 'Tom or Mart?'

'I don't know,' I say.

'You have to answer,' says Henny. 'If you were forced to marry one of them, which one would you choose?'

'Mart,' I say then.

'Mart is mine,' Henny says. 'You'll have to be content with Tom.'

'Is that so?' I say. 'Well, for my part you can gladly marry both of them.'

I don't mean a bit of what I'm saying. On the contrary, this is for life and death, I know that, and I lie awake for over an hour, making plans.

A couple of days later I get Mart to myself when we are out looking for worms for a fishing trip. I tell him that Henny revealed to me in confidence that she is extremely fond of Tom, but that she doesn't like him very much.

Mart does not reply, but he gets a bullish, slightly watery expression in his eyes and I see that what I said touches him deeply. We continue hacking with our spades in silence for a while.

'But I like you better,' I say. 'Much better.'

He stops and observes me squinting.

'Come here,' he says, throwing aside the spade.

Then he kisses me hard and brutally so that I am almost out of breath.

Later, in the boat, Henny notices that I have a swollen sore on my lip, and she asks where I got that from. I say that I have no idea, but it's enough that I glance at Mart for her to under-stand. I notice it on her, it's as if her body becomes stiff and uncomfortable. My body on the other hand feels fine; a little jittery and a little sweet. I stick the tip of my tongue out and carefully lick the sore.

We spend all our time together, all four of us. The Commotion Quartet, the Chocolate King calls us. 'Now, what has the Commotion Quartet been up to today?' he asks every evening when we come to the table.

We never answer, because it is so obvious that we are not expected to. We simply exchange glances with each other, smile resolutely and conspiratorially.

And it's not that we do very much damage either. But we do things by ourselves. Swim and fish and play games. Bicycle into the village and get ice cream. Build a hut even though we are actually too big for such things, and one day we construct a raft by using two empty barrels and a lot of boards that we find under a tarp behind the left-hand house.

None of us comment either on the fact that it is Mart and I who belong together. He never kisses me again, but it's noticeable anyway. It shows by the way we always pair up when we play cards or badminton, when we row out with the boat or bicycle to the village. Or simply walk and talk.

And Henny does not ask that question again. I know that she knows, and she knows that I know. But to talk about it would be letting in something else and admitting defeat, which it would never occur to Henny to do. Nor me either. On the contrary, she and I both act like nothing has happened and she is truly a master at that, Henny. Sometimes I get the idea that she is plotting something, that she lies in her bed at night when Ruth has long since turned off the lamp and started making puffing sounds as she snores – lies there contemplating some sort of plan that I should probably try to ferret out somehow.

But nothing happens. Not until one night in the final week, when the days have got a little shorter and the nights a little darker. It is the middle of August, we have decided to sneak out when the grown-ups have fallen asleep. Take sausages and fizzy drinks with us and row out to Sort's Island and barbecue.

The island is a round affair ten minutes' row from land. It is about a hundred metres around and features – strangely enough – a single tree, a large oak, and got its name from a certain Andreas Sort, who rowed out and hung himself in the oak after an unhappy love story in the mid-nineteenth century. The girl in question was named Blanche and is said to have drowned herself shortly after.

To start with the night goes as planned, but for some reason we happen to make the fire a bit too intense and the flames work their way down into, and catch hold of, the kremtenberry thicket under the oak. We try to put it out of course, but soon the fire has spread around the whole island. The only thing we can do is to jump in the boat and set out onto the water.

And then we sit there bobbing while we see Sort's oak burn down in the mild night. I think that I have never seen anything more intense in my whole life, it's a full moon too, a big yellow August moon that has glided up over the edge of the forest, but Henny starts crying. Tom takes her in his arms, and then she cries even worse because it isn't Mart that does it. Instead Mart sneaks his hand in mine under a blanket and we don't row home again until the whole island is dark and dead.

Mart doesn't kiss me that night either, but I feel on his

warm, pounding hand that he would really like to do that. Other things too, presumably.

When we have breakfast the next morning Ruth says that there must have been a thunderstorm during the night, because lightning struck Sort's oak and both it and the whole island have burnt up.

But no one heard any thunder, it's a bit peculiar.

We are rather tired and subdued that day, it's like it passes by without leaving any impressions, and the following morning the Chocolate King drives us to the bus station in Schwingen. As Henny and I are sliding back and forth on the smooth leather of the back seat, it feels as if we have got closer to each other despite everything. As if the summer taught us quite a bit, both about life and about ourselves.

That perhaps everything isn't as it ought to be, but that you do best in adapting yourself to the circumstances. Or something along those lines. We don't talk about it while we are sitting in the Rover of course, it is only the King who holds forth there – and not during the sweaty bus ride back to Grothenburg – but two days later, when we are out in the park watching Benjamin again, Henny says:

'Do you know what I think, I think that we were actually sisters when we were born.'

'Is that so?' I say.

'But we were separated from each other somehow at the maternity ward. I have never had such a good friend as you.'

I say that I had read that there was a lot of negligence at hospitals – and to be on the safe side, a little later that evening, we mix blood with each other.

To:
Agnes R.
Villa Guarda
Gobshejm

Grothenburg, 27 October

Dear Agnes,

Thanks for your reply. I don't really know what reaction I expected, but perhaps just this. Despite everything.

I'm afraid, however, that I cannot add much to what I wrote in my last letter. But let me assure you of two things: I am in my right mind and I intend to carry out what I am determined to do. I trust that you feel connected enough to me in any event that you won't reveal my plans to anyone. If you don't want to help me that's your business, but I would be grateful if you let me know as soon as possible if you are at all interested in discussing the matter. Dispassionately and hypothetically, as stated; in no way do you need to feel that you are obligating yourself to anything, I cannot underscore that enough.

Concerning the financial aspect I stand firm by a hundred thousand, I am sure that it is possible to hire a professional hit man for a considerably lower amount, but as you understand I consider myself a bit too good for such a solution.

Anyhow, this letter will have to be brief. You wanted confirmation and now you have it. Be in touch soon, dear Agnes, and let me know what you think.

Your girlfriend, Henny

To:
Henny Delgado
Pelikaanallé 24
Grothenburg

Gobshejm, 30 October

Dear Henny,

Sometimes it is almost comical how things can coincide.
Yesterday I got two letters in the mail, the one from you, the
other from the law firm of Klinger & Klinger in Munich.
After having contacted my own lawyer here in Gobshejm,
Herr Pumpermann, and discussed the situation with him for
over an hour just this afternoon, it has become clear to me
that I really am in a bad way financially. No, don't get me
wrong, naturally I have enough to get by, and more besides
– but if I want to keep my dear house, undoubtedly a number
of rearrangements are required.

He expresses himself that way, lawyer Pumpermann –
rearrangements! – cleverly avoiding mentioning things by
their rightful name, which perhaps is some sort of
occupational injury. What he means in any event is that
money is lacking, in brief. I asked him how much, he frowned
and explained seriously that with eighty or ninety thousand
everything would without a doubt be in a considerably better
light.

So, dear Henny, after having sat in my lovely armchair
for a few hours and brooded along with your letters and four
(five?) glasses of port – scratched the dogs under their chins,
smoked far too many cigarettes and thought about old times
– so I write to you now about your specific errand, as you
call it, and . . . well, why don't we let ourselves at least
discuss it?

That can't do any harm, can it?
Signed in all haste,
Your Agnes

Maertens the dentist is dead.

He died one rainy January morning after having been in a coma at the hospital for five days. The cause of the coma was a strange fall on the stairs in our house; he had come to visit my mother one evening, they had eaten and drunk wine, and somehow he stepped wrong and fell headlong when he was on his way down the stairs, which by chance were dark as a sack of coal owing to a glitch with the electricity.

Some investigation was done of the circumstances around the death, but nothing came out except that the dear dentist broke his neck and right thumb.

Towards Easter, which this year falls in the middle of April, my mother seems to be done grieving, a new dentist has taken over the clinic and leaves have come out on the large lime trees outside my window. I feel generally satisfied with existence and my life. Nowadays I am the best in the class, Henny has lagged behind a little and Adam has been sick for part of the winter and has been unable to really do himself justice. There is something wrong with his lungs and all in all he is a rather sickly boy.

But in the autumn all three of us will start at Weiver's Upper General Secondary School on Waldemarstrasse. Five others from the class have also been admitted, but we must of course be separated from Marvel. It doesn't matter. We don't associate with him much any more, he has started smoking in earnest and most often hangs out with a couple of older boys from the vocational school out in Löhr. I think Marvel will also be going there in the autumn, and from what I understand this is a rather natural development. I have a sense that things are not going to go too well for him in life.

Henny and I talk with each other almost all the time. During breaks at school, in the afternoons when we are doing homework together or go and swim in Genzer Sportpalatz – or in the evenings when we call each other even though our mothers try to forbid us from doing that.

We discuss everything between heaven and earth, as the saying goes. What we will be when we grow up, how boys really think deep down, if it is always ugly to lie and if Miss Butts really has a relationship with the music teacher Fitz-simmons.

We talk about God too. Henny maintains firmly that he exists, personally I am more hesitant. The world wouldn't look the way it does if there was someone holding the threads, but Henny says that everything will be fine by and by, it is just the way there that is a little crooked.

Do you mean it will be fine in our lifetime? I ask, or must we be dead and wait for Judgement Day for ten thousand years first?

Both, Henny says zealously. Things will go well for both you and me in life, if we continue to be good and humble.

I say that it probably doesn't hurt to be a bit foresighted and on your guard too, otherwise it is easy to be outwitted by evil. Henny does not really understand what I mean and asks for an example, but I realize that it is best not to give her any.

Regarding our future plans, I want to be an actress or an author, maybe both. Henny changes opinion once a month – in March she wants to study to be a veterinarian, in April she intends to be a fashion designer and in May she aims to marry rich and bring up six children while she cultivates organic roses and paints pale watercolours in a little French fishing village. Her husband will preferably work for the UN and be out travelling quite a bit; in the kitchen she wants to have reddish-black clinker tiles on the floor.

I think Henny is a little naive, and rather too changeable, but we are still inseparable and when in the beginning of June she falls in love with a completely hopeless boy by the name of Dimitri, I really make sure to put a spanner in the works. Afterwards, when she has escaped with honour intact, she also thanks me sincerely for not having wavered. I personally think that I am unusually mature for only being thirteen.

During the summer holidays I go to see my father and brother in Saarbrücken. It is over with Else, and I can again take possession of my old room. I work in the mornings at Goscinski's bakery, in the evenings I bicycle down to the river and see old friends. The longer summer goes on, the more clearly I realize that I have grown apart from them – I find myself thinking that it was beneficial for my personal development that my father and my mother separated.

Perhaps I have grown apart from my father and brother too; I don't associate with either of them and when we have meals together it is often strikingly silent around the dining table. My father appears to have got ten years older and if he says anything it always has to do with the weather or the Zenit football team. My brother never tries to beat me up like in the past, but with that all communication between us seems to have ceased.

When Henny and I and 172 others are sitting in the large auditorium at Weiver's Upper Secondary School on 1 September, I feel a tense expectation about the years that are ahead of us. It seems to me that childhood is over now, and I am quite certain that I am not going to miss it.

To:
Agnes R.
Villa Guarda
Gobshejm

Grothenburg, 11 November

Dear Agnes,

I was so happy when I got your letter, even if naturally I hope that it is not simply the financial aspects that have made you go along with my proposal.

Sorry, which made you want to discuss the matter, I mean of course. In no way do I want to guide or dominate the course of events that lies ahead of us; on the contrary, I think it is important that both you and I, dearest Agnes, are in complete agreement about every step, each ever-so-little detail in the execution. We must plan everything minutely and make an effort not to take any unnecessary risks. When all is said and done it should not be particularly remarkable for two women of our calibre to murder a single man and get away with it. Don't you think, Agnes?

No, when I think about it I am convinced that we – if we decide on it – are going to find a method where we do not leave anything to chance and where the police are going to be crestfallen and left with not so much as a clue about who – and what forces – took David's life.

The first thing we must keep in mind – at least as far as I can see – is of course that I have a hundred per cent alibi. The wife of a murdered man is by definition the first person the police suspect. They are going to do so in this case too, regardless of whether they have knowledge of David's infidelity or not – regardless of whether they know about *my knowledge of it or not. Thus we must not be careless on this point, the first requirement and the first condition is that under no circumstances can it have been possible for me to commit the murder.*

The prerequisites for ensuring this condition – excuse me for sounding so formal and technical, dear Agnes, I notice it myself and it undoubtedly feels a trifle strange, but I think it would be a disadvantage for us if we start getting emotional – the prerequisites for my certain alibi are of course partly that it is possible to establish the time for David's death fairly exactly, partly that I myself at this time have demonstrably been somewhere else. So far away from the scene of the crime that simply based on this fact I can be removed from the list of suspects. Demonstrably, as stated; a witness or two should be required in this connection, don't you think, Agnes?

Oh, well, to make a long argument short, I imagine that there are two variants: either you kill my husband in our home while I am somewhere else – or else you kill him somewhere else while I am at home.

After having thought about and weighed both of these alternatives against each other, I decide that I prefer the latter. I want us to let it happen elsewhere, simply; I feel that I must consider the girls as much as possible, and without a doubt it would be unnecessarily distressing and traumatic for them if they had to have their dead father so close to them – and even if naturally it would be possible to arrange it so that they were gone somehow during the night of the murder (I seem to assume that it should happen at night, isn't that strange, Agnes?), they would surely have a hard time afterwards adjusting in an apartment where their father had been put to death.

My basic idea is thus – and I actually do not want to go further than this before I have obtained your viewpoints – that we let the murder take place at a safe distance from Grothenburg. Perhaps a hotel room in Munich or Berlin or Hamburg. David is out on trips and spends the night elsewhere at least two or three times a month, so it should not be difficult to find an opportunity.

Concerning the method, it really makes no difference to me how you conduct yourself; I definitely think you should choose what suits your temperament best. Personally I would prefer cutting his throat, but perhaps that is too risky. And extremely bloody of course. A bullet through the head seems more certain in many ways, but then of course we also have to address the question of how you acquire a gun.

Obviously there are also other methods, but here your voice must weigh heaviest, Agnes. Perhaps you have preferences in this murky area, both aesthetic and rational, it would not surprise me. Concerning the time aspect there is of course no immediate urgency, but I would probably prefer to see that we bring the project ashore within the reasonably near future. Two or three months at most; considering the planning of the girls' summer vacation and all that sort of thing it would undeniably be nice if he were in the ground before Easter at least.

Anyway, dear Agnes, be in touch soon with viewpoints, I feel that I would really like to see you again, but we must obviously avoid all contact until we have put an end to

David. Some six-month safety margin beyond that too, I assume.

But more on all that sort of thing further along.

Promises

Your devoted Henny

To:
Henny Delgado
Pelikaanallé 24
Grothenburg

Dear Henny,

Thanks for your letter. I must admit that I felt strangely disturbed after I read it – as if we already found ourselves far away down a cruel road without hope of return – but now, after two glasses of wine this evening, I have my nerves under control, and my head is as clear as a hungry nun. Do you remember that lecturer Klimke at Weiver's always used that expression, I have always wondered where he got it from. Hungry nun?

My preliminary assessment is that I agree with you on all the points you bring up. I absolutely prefer setting to work at an anonymous hotel, in preference to having to visit your apartment on such a sinister errand as this. Although I cannot help thinking about whether it really is sufficient that you stay home with the girls. Don't you need a stronger alibi? Their statements probably wouldn't count in a trial, they must be viewed as partial – if it is even allowed for them to testify for or against their parents in a court? At least those are the conclusions I draw after having seen a courtroom drama or two on TV.

Oh well, this is of course only a detail that will be possible to work out rather easily; you can always invite some friends to dinner, for example, and make sure that they stay until rather late. I am in complete agreement with you that I ought to strike during the night, that is probably when most murders take place, I assume. The most satisfactory would *probably be if he was asleep and I could send him off to the Twilight Land without him even managing to wake up first. Does he sleep heavily or does he wake up at the slightest sound? Well, of course there are a number of small questions that you will need to answer for me by and by, but we can come back to that once we have come a bit further in the planning.*

Exactly how one should proceed to make one's way into a hotel room I have also given some thought to. What do you think, can one perhaps hide there during the day and simply wait for the right hour? Or should I have a separate room at the same hotel – under a false name and in disguise perhaps? (But don't they always require some form of identification nowadays?)

Oh well, more on this later. Where the approach is concerned I would prefer to avoid a lot of unnecessary violence and exaggerated loss of blood. The fact is, I think we can decide on this point rather simply: you see, I have a weapon in my possession. It is a reliable Belgian pistol of the Berenger brand, my husband took charge of it several years ago when an old uncle of his died; it is not in any registry and no one knows that we have it. That I have it, I mean, of course. We tested it for fun a few years ago, it works just fine and I also have a couple of boxes of ammunition lying around. I think this without a doubt would be the safest method, there is no possibility to trace the gun to me, and to be prepared for all eventualities I can always bury it out in the woods when it is all over and done with.

And when? dear Henny. Yes, for my part naturally it is all the same. If you just find the right date and right hotel in the right city – then I am willing to set to work at any time.

Provided of course that we have managed to discuss everything and are certain not to have neglected any important detail.

And provided that we are in agreement where the compensation is concerned. Via lawyer Pumpermann I have given Clara and Henry a vague promise that I am going to be able to buy them out from the house – but as it were I would really like to have a small sum as confirmation of our agreement, because they will probably want some kind of earnest money before Christmas. In any event I have interpreted Pumpermann that way, good Lord, he really is a fellow that must be interpreted, Henny! Shall we say twenty thousand, then we'll decide what to do with the remaining fee as we approach D-Day?

Or D-Night, as stated.

Moving on, how is the weather in Grothenburg? Here in Gobshjem November has been unusually rainy and gloomy. Not even the dogs want to go out any longer; a trip south would undeniably perk up my spirits, but that will probably have to wait, I'm afraid.

Signed your devoted
Agnes

P.S. A terrible thought occurred to me just as I was going to seal the envelope. What if that other woman is with him at the hotel?! How do we guard against something like that?

One of those evenings.

Stayed late at the department and corrected papers until after eight. Of thirteen submitted essays I am going to be forced to fail three. All boys. Or men, or whatever you want to call these semi-intellectual pups aged twenty to twenty-two. I don't know, by the way, how old any of them are. Dietmar, the weakest of them, may well be twenty-five. Piotr looks nineteen at most, with his lopsided fringe and his pimples. Anyway, it would be best if we got them to quit at Christmas. Change to something less demanding in January. Education or psychology perhaps. Or some sort of quantifiable natural science.

It is raining when I drive home. Wet leaves cover the roadway in the lane between Münstersdorf and the castle, I maintain a low speed and think about Henny. She is truly a strange woman. Has become one, at least; perhaps all this distance was never necessary, all this silence for so many years – but considering what now lies before us it was of course just as well. As if there had been some kind of divine direction right from the start. Or choreography. Although I understand that just these thoughts easily work their way out and demand entry on such a dark and gloomy evening.

I wonder if anyone noticed her during the funeral. Naturally her presence must have been noted, but was there anyone who started – and continued – to wonder who she was? I wouldn't think so. There were quite a few of us anyway, and the majority were of course unacquainted with the majority.

The money arrived this morning. When I made a withdrawal from the ATM at Kleinmarkt, I saw that suddenly twenty thousand euros had been deposited to my account. I must admit that my heart skipped a beat. As if I was suddenly hurled from a fictional world into a real one. From a movie or a dream to a brutal reality.

Does this mean that the die is cast? That there is no turning back?

I imagine so. I don't want to turn back either. Don't want to back out of this, it is peculiar but the whole thing seems to work like a kind of sensual stimulus for me, and truly that may be needed this rainy autumn.

Just as I am driving the car into the garage, Tristram Singh shows up in my mind, and once he has dug in I of course can't be rid of him for the rest of the evening – not during the walk with the dogs and not afterwards, when as usual I sit for an hour in the armchair in front of the fire. I spend an inexplicable amount of time in this piece of furniture – as if I were an eighty-year-old woman who sits and gathers up her memories. But I am only half that old, and something tells me that the most important events in my life have not yet occurred.

Before I go to bed I read those lines of Barin that I like so much. They may be needed as a counterweight to all the constipated term paper prose I've been forced to wade through.

> At the review of Miss Beate Wollinger's life
> it was found that her heart had beat
> twenty million

eight hundred and thirteen thousand
six hundred and sixty-nine beats.
Four of these were heard by optician's assistant
Arnold Mauer one spring evening in Gimsen 1971.

Claus-Joseph.

I met him during a demonstration march; I don't recall what we were demonstrating against, presumably Apartheid. He is one year older than me, owns a Trabant and studies philosophy while waiting to report for his military service. We become a couple, but I don't love him and we don't sleep with each other.

Approximately the same time – I am speaking now of the autumn of 1981 – Henny starts going out with Ansgar. Ansgar is the son of a minister who lost his faith when his wife ran off to Canada with a coloured jazz musician and left him behind in Klubbenhügge with his parish and his only begotten son. Nowadays Ansgar's father is involved in German Shepherd breeding on a farm towards Bloemenberg. Ansgar is a rather neurotic young man, something which no doubt appeals to Henny's good heart.

Henny doesn't sleep with her Ansgar either, but not because she doesn't want to – but for some sort of murky religious reasons.

But we crowd into Claus-Joseph's Trabant and kiss a bit. Stick our hands down inside each other's waistbands, rub around and moan a little. It happens that we even make an occasional outing in the car. To Ulming or Westdorf mainly, we prefer the small villages along the winding upper reaches of the Neckar. During these excursions we look at birds with the binoculars Ansgar brings along – both Ansgar and Claus-Joseph are interested in ornithology – and talk politics. Solidarity. Cambodia. The shore starling. South Africa. Henny and I are in our last year at Weiver's. Ansgar and Claus-Joseph have their entrance exams behind them. They think they know a little more.

Cat shit, I think. When it is raining it leaks in through the side windows of the Trabant. I often catch myself not being really present.

Tristram Singh joins our class in January of the last year of high school and he actually only participates in the English classes – where he answers the scattered questions that lecturer Dibble throws out at him, with an accent that seems retrieved from some old British colonial comedy, and which makes laughter stick in our throats.

But Tristram sits in on the other classes too – unclear why, but he has come here with his parents and his five younger sisters, is going to stay for six months, perhaps a full year, his father is some sort of consul, and Tristram must have something to do, of course.

He is slightly built and humbly attentive, and has soft bronze-shimmering skin that is hard to take your eyes off – and which suddenly make Claus-Joseph and Ansgar pale into boring Bohemian sausages in shabby sheep casings. Henny uses just this epithet one evening after a debate about the red-winged shore swallow and the situation in the Chilean countryside, I don't know if she is referring to all of Ansgar or only a certain part of him.

The gentle sorrow in Tristram's eyes seems a thousand years old, anyway.

One evening in early February he goes out with us to Vlissingen, a student bar where now and then we drink beer and talk about the nature of art. We are a rather large group this particular evening, someone has a birthday, I'm fairly sure, but Tristram drinks neither wine nor beer – only tea and water. He is sitting between me and Henny and is wearing a yellow-white linen suit, he smells good and a little foreign, and is just as polite and serious in both directions. At quarter past eleven he looks at his watch and explains that unfortunately he has to leave because he promised his mother to be home before twelve. Henny casts a glance at Ansgar by her side, I cast a glance at Claus-Joseph by my side, and then we explain, Henny and I, almost in unison, that we intend to accompany him home.

It would be much too disloyal to let a mournful young Indian walk alone in the fog through the dark alleys of Grothenburg.

We need a little air besides.

Love is a force that is stronger than its actors, Henny says. You cannot control it.

I don't know where she read that, and she tries to make it look as if she formulated it herself.

For adolescent romantics and horny dogs, perhaps, I say. But if you head out and swim in the sea of emotions, it may be hard to find your way back to land, even for a sensible person.

Certain people can only love money, Henny says.

When Claus-Joseph and Ansgar are not present we like to talk this way now and then, Henny and I. Sometimes we write it in our papers for Miss Silberstein too; sometimes with successful results, sometimes less successful.

Wise, Miss Silberstein notes in the margin.

Or: *Big words, little thought.*

'Feeling and thought don't need to be enemies,' Henny now continues. 'They can go hand in hand too, you just have to dare to let go a little first.'

'Beautiful people can never understand the nature of love,' I quote. 'They are doomed to be objects. And we are both beautiful, aren't we, Henny?'

Henny thinks and browses absent-mindedly in the French grammar book. We have tests the following day; we are sitting in my room, should really be studying, the conversation is a digression.

'That's not true,' Henny says at last. 'I am convinced, for example, that Tristram Singh is extraordinarily suited to understand the nature of love.'

'Aha?' I say.

'Exactly,' Henny says.

'His skin is like pale copper,' I say. 'True, but . . .'

Henny sits quietly again and looks out the window. It is still February and it has rained three days in a row. The moments grow. Stick firmly to each other in some way, and time comes to a halt from pure weariness.

'I am thinking seriously about breaking up with Ansgar,' Henny says at last, with a little artificial sigh.

'I dumped Claus-Joseph yesterday,' I admit, and we both break out in laughter.

We laugh and laugh; fall into each other's arms, and can

almost not stop ourselves. The tears are running, the French grammar book falls to the floor and we continue until Henny gets a stomach ache and I almost pee my pants.

'Agnes,' Henny says, 'you are my blood sister. Nothing is going to be able to separate us.'

'Nothing,' I say.

To:

Agnes R.
Villa Guarda
Gobshejm

Grothenburg, 8 December

Dear Agnes,

    *Thanks for your last letter, which made me both happy
and worried.*

    *Made me happy because now I really see that you are
embracing our cause with complete seriousness (I definitely
think we can use your Belgian pistol, just so long as you
are sure it works and know how to handle it) – worried me
because your question in the P.S. must of course be taken
into serious consideration.*

    *Because of course it is on all these trips here and there
that he sees her. Occasional, hot nights in strange hotel
rooms. My God, Agnes, my insides go into revolt when I
think about it! Month after month, they've probably managed
a hundred or more fucks these years, yes, I have started to
understand that presumably it has been going on longer than
I thought at first. And I am toying with – and rejecting – the
thought of telling the girls about their father. Such cheapness!
Such a banal betrayal!*

    *I harbour no interest in her, however. Not the slightest, she
may be any tart or any so-called respectable woman at all;
her reasons and underlying motives I couldn't care less about.
The cheapness from her side is presumably no less, but I leave
her at that; he is the one that must die, not her. I don't even
want to know who she is.*

    *But how do we manage the problem that she may be on
the scene? Thank goodness you brought that up in time,*

Agnes, under no conditions do I want her also rubbed out – apart from all other complications, a double murder of my husband and his lover would immediately cast all suspicions in my direction. No, he should pay for his actions, she can escape – on that point we don't need to feel any hesitation.

On the other hand, we should not exaggerate the difficulties. If you succeed in killing David according to plan, and she happens to be the one who discovers the body – for example – well, such a spice wouldn't spoil the dish, would it? She must probably have good reason to flee the field in such a situation? Or am I thinking wrong, Agnes? If you were a married man's lover and you found him dead in a love nest, would you then call the police at once? Reveal your identity and the state of things? I don't think so. No, the more I think about this, the more certain I am that we have nothing to fear from her. As long as she doesn't become an eyewitness to the murder itself, I don't think her possible presence in the wings will play a particularly great role or need be an obstacle to us. And – as we have come so far – it should not be particularly difficult after all to make sure that he is alone when you shoot him, Agnes. Or what? It doesn't necessarily have to happen in the room either. Perhaps a shot in the back in some alley in the vicinity of the hotel will work just as well? Down into the handbag with the pistol, and then a calm walk away from there; you can shoot prime ministers that way. Yes, I'm only speculating, Agnes, and sometimes I must say that it irks me a little that I'm not the one who gets to hold the gun and give him what he deserves.

Anyway, consider these details, Agnes, and let me know what you think about it. In any event it is now crucial to find a time and a place that suits us well. I assume that we

are not going to go to work until well into the new year, so
I have peeked at David's schedule and understood that he has
at least four two- to three-day engagements during January
and February. But I will check the dates more carefully and
present them in my next letter. Christmas is fast approaching
here in Grothenburg, we have the usual family arrangements
to get started on; it can't be denied that I am happy that this
is the last time.

I hope you received the money. How we deal with the
remaining eighty thousand I don't know; I assume that you
trust me as much as I trust you, Agnes – it feels as if these
nineteen years have passed in another channel, another space
in some way, don't you think so too? I long to see you, but as
I said in my last letter, naturally that has to wait for a while.

But then, dear Agnes, can't we allow ourselves a week or
two and just be together, you and me? A little trip next
autumn, perhaps? Two merry widows in the Mediterranean,
say that it sounds enticing! I have no problem where childcare
for the girls is concerned. My brother (I'm sure you remember
Benjamin?) and his family will happily take care of them;
they live in Karlsruhe and we exchange cousins with each
other occasionally, even if his boys are of course a few years
younger.

But, as I said, Agnes, let us bide our time over Christmas,
and then strike in the new year. Enjoy the weeks off (or is it
actually a month in the academic world?) and be in touch
about everything!

Signed your devoted
Henny

To:
Henny Delgado
Pelikaanallé 24
Grothenburg

Gobshejm, 10 January

Dear Henny,

    I apologize for not having written for a while, but I've been out of town. A colleague at the department made an offer that I couldn't turn down a few days before Christmas. Two weeks in New York – his sister works for the UN and has an apartment in Manhattan – I left on Christmas Eve and came back to Gobshejm late yesterday evening, and I truly had a lovely stay over there. A three-room apartment to myself on 74th Street with a view over a frostbitten Central Park. Theatre and film, museums and a little shopping, of course we must take a trip together, Henny, exactly as you suggest. But God knows I prefer a big city . . . Barcelona or Rome perhaps, or why not New York again? Oh well, more on that in due course.

    I've been thinking about the thoughts and the risk assessments you presented in your most recent letter, and I agree with you in all essentials. I don't think we need to plan the deed itself too much in advance either – especially as we cannot be sure if that woman is going to be present or not – but I don't see this as particularly problematic. The crucial decisions must be made in any event on the scene; it is impossible to foresee exactly what circumstances are going to prevail, we must simply rely on my good judgement and my coolness in the decisive moment. And – I assure you, Henny – I am not going to shake in my boots. If I just find the right opportunity I am going to exploit it. If I find the risk of discovery too great, yes, then I will wait. When all is said and done, shooting another person to death does not take more than a second or two – reaching safety afterwards not that much longer.

So rely on me, dear Henny, I am going to manage this. Now just give me a couple of dates and a couple of places to choose from, then I promise to leave word in my next letter about how many days your husband still has left to live.

Otherwise – during my absence – we have finally got a little snow here in Gobshejm, and the river is frozen over. What is it like in Grothenburg?

Wonders your devoted

Agnes

P.S. Once again a thought pops up when I think I'm through writing. Do you know if any other people know about David's infidelity? Friends, acquaintances? It's often the case, after all, that people choose to keep silent about knowledge of this type – out of some sort of misdirected consideration, I think, which actually is only an expression of cowardice and comfort.

And does anyone know that you have found out about it? Right offhand I cannot assess whether these questions are significant or not, but you can always take them into consideration anyway.

The dogs are restless, especially Wagner. Maybe it was too much to leave them with the Barth family for two weeks, but that usually works without a hitch. Maybe it is also Erich's absence that enters into it, yes, naturally it must be that way: a sort of accumulated sense of loss that floats up to the surface when I too was away from them for a time.

For my part, I catch myself feeling a certain sense of loss too. For Erich, that is. Even if we had no love life the last few years and were actually never very close to each other, there had been good times. At long last I realize that perhaps it is only retroactively that we can understand ourselves. It was never the fire or the leap I was seeking when I chose Erich, naturally not, but life is not primarily constructed from these elements either. Requires their presence in a different way, I think. A sort of . . . well, what shall I say? . . . a sort of illusory companion perhaps? Possibilities that are awaiting off-stage and that wait to make an entrance in the event that.

If it were to be so.

Words. I am tired. Had a hard time sleeping in New York. An effect of jet lag presumably, although it is usually worse in the other direction. Woke up often at three o'clock in the morning and could not fall asleep for several hours. Tried to read but concentration failed me. Wrote a couple of letters to Henny but tore them up. In the end I mostly sat and stared at miserable movies on the TV, or listened to music on my portable CD player. Coltrane and Dexter Gordon, two of Erich's favourites that I have taken over. Sat there above Central Park's Magritte-like inaccessibility, that is, and tried to imagine how everything would work out. What life is going to look like in three or six or twelve months. I felt no worry, I don't now either, only a kind of restrained, reluctant fascination. I hadn't thought that I would need to kill again, but the conditions are clearly such – just as definitive as unpredictable, another sort of companion in the wings evidently, and once they come forward and introduce themselves suddenly you no longer have any choice. Once they have stepped onto the stage, so it is.

Two weeks still remain before classes start. It's nice. I seem to have an excessive need for rest and reflection this winter. Spend almost no time with people. Spend time with the dogs instead – with thoughts about my beloved and about the future.

We are sitting at a table in the school cafe when I see that Henny and Tristram Singh are holding hands with each other. It is a Friday in early March, the sun filters in through crooked Venetian blinds and stripes part of Henny's hair and her left shoulder; there are half a dozen of us, empty coffee cups and cigarette butts in the ashtray. Schoolbooks. A scattered deck of cards.

They are holding hands so tenderly somehow, almost shyly,

I don't think they want any of us to notice it. Halfway under the tabletop, it seems.

Or perhaps it is actually the other way around. Perhaps in reality they feel that we *must* notice it, but through this studied modesty?

I experience a moment of dizziness and then a sudden, strong nausea. The vomiting reflex that shoots up inside me is so powerful that I just barely manage to force it back. I get up quickly, my chair tips over and falls backwards on the floor, I rush out without a word.

In the toilet I empty out of me all I've eaten during the day, all I've eaten during my life, it feels like that, and while I am down on all fours retching, a splitting headache comes. Razor sharp and with white heat.

What is happening? I think.

Am I dying?

It is not death. It is something else. I dream about these two hands braided into each other, the one white, the other mildly bronze-coloured. I have not spoken with Henny in a couple of days, which in itself is unusual; after my attack at the school cafe I have been home sick in my room. I don't know, by the way, whether I am sick, I have decided to stay in bed for a while, simply. When Henny finally calls I say that I have a fever, I do not ask any questions about anything and I notice that Henny has a hard time with words.

My mother sends for Dr Moessner who does not find anything wrong with me. Diagnoses me preliminarily as over-exerted and recommends rest and fruit juices.

On Friday, after a week, I am better and return to Weiver's. I have missed a maths test, but that's not the end of the world. Henny and a few other classmates ask if I want to go out in

the evening. Vlissingen as usual, and then there is a rock concert at Embargo Club at Kleinmarkt. I decline, blame it on my
having been sick; I have my eyes on Tristram and Henny the
whole day, but see no handholding and feel no unseemly vibra-
tions.

But I am harbouring a sort of muteness and a thwarted
agitation, which I almost cannot conceal.

'What's going on with you?' Henny says after the last class.

'Nothing,' I say. 'Don't get any ideas.'

'Get ideas?' Henny says. 'What ideas should I get?'

'Don't show off,' I say.

It is an unbelievably silly conversation, but we go through
with it dutifully. Henny observes her brick-coloured nails for a
while.

'Is it because of that thing at the cafe?' she asks.

'I don't understand what you're talking about,' I say.

'It's nothing,' Henny says.

'What is it that's nothing?' I ask.

'Nothing,' Henny says with a sigh. 'Nothing is anything.
Why are you so peevish?'

'I've been sick,' I say.

Henny looks at the clock and we go our separate ways.

The following week my mother travels to Bodensee for a conference. Tuesday to Thursday. I am alone in the apartment.
On Wednesday I convince Tristram Singh to visit me in the
evening and help me with maths. Besides English, Tristram has
started participating seriously in mathematics instruction;
obviously he has both greater aptitude and more solid knowledge in this subject than any of the rest of us, and it does not

have to mean there are any ulterior motives in my inviting him. Not at all. Since my sick week I am behind; I don't tell him that my mother is away until he is sitting on the couch.

It takes three hours and a lovely acting talent that I didn't know I had to seduce him; we finish a bottle of wine that I swipe from my mother's supply in the pantry; I have never seduced anyone before and it is the first time whatsoever that I make love.

It's the first time for Tristram too. He tells me afterwards; I notice his worry but I convince him to sleep over. It isn't possible for a young Indian to come home smelling of wine and love, I say. He calls his mother, they speak for a good while in a language I don't understand. But I understand that he is lying to her. I think he says that he is at home with one of the boys in the class and that the last bus has gone.

I love his nakedness; both the nakedness of his soul and his body. We don't sleep at all that night, we touch each other as you can only touch each other the very first time. And possibly the very last. When the beaker and the content are one. Word and hand. Thought, mouth and sex. A wax candle is burning beside us in a bottle, a week later I write in an essay about fire that is reflected and shadowed and watered in soft bronze-coloured skin.

Be careful, Miss Silberstein writes in the margin.

For the remainder of the term – all the way until the family's return to Delhi – Tristram Singh does not hold any hands. Not mine, not Henny's. And not anyone else's either. Henny and I avoid each other a bit, but well into the summer we go together on a charter trip to Crete. One evening we end up at a bar, get pleasantly drunk on retsina and tsipouro and then we make love on the beach under the stars, each with our own Greek youth.

To:
Agnes R.
Villa Guarda
Gobshejm

Grothenburg, 14 January

Dear Agnes,

So nice to hear that you've been in New York. I love that city, in fact we lived there for a year when the girls were small; David had a contract with CBS and Remington's. We rented an apartment in Brooklyn Heights, and I do agree with you that we must allow ourselves a week in the Big Apple. Or some other big city. Next autumn or winter hopefully, oh, how I wish we were already there. That all this was over and done with – but I have no doubt that it won't go well and that we can soon meet again, no doubt whatsoever.

And one piece of good news is that I think I have found a date that seems very appealing. Naturally you're the one who must have the final word in this question, but let me in any event propose the weekend of February 14–16, when David is taking part in an international workshop for theatre producers (or something along those lines) in Amsterdam.

The reason that this weekend is so suitable is that I too will be away from home on those days. My boss, Dr Höffner, wants to encourage me and has sent me to a little translator seminar at the SBS Institute in Munich; like David I leave already on Friday afternoon and won't be home until late Sunday evening. What could be more ideal, Agnes? Between Amsterdam and Munich there is a good five hundred kilometres, I can never get a more certain alibi.

I have also – without David's knowledge of course – found

out what hotel he will be staying at; it is called Figaro and
is located rather centrally along Prinsengracht. I still don't
know exactly where the workshop will take place, but if you
bite at this proposal, obviously I will be able to find out both
this and all the other details that may be of interest to us.
All to facilitate your mission.

I am also sending a photo of David in this letter, it is after
all a number of years since you saw him and time has
probably left its traces, I'm afraid. The beard comes and goes,
I think it has to do with his constant midlife crisis.
Sometimes he wants to look middle-aged and distinguished,
sometimes he thinks he is twenty-five again. Well, men are
the way they are, Agnes, that's not news to you either, is it?

Whatever; if we decide on this scenario, dear Agnes –
Amsterdam in mid-February – then I am going to deposit
another thirty thousand euros in your account. As soon as
I've got the go-ahead from you, that is. Then we have half
the total – fifty thousand – outstanding until after the
murder. I think that is how it is done in those circles, at least
I've seen it happen that way on TV. Half at contract signing,
half upon delivery – agree that we are holding ourselves to a
certain professionalism in any case!

Concerning your question in the P.S. – or the questions,
more precisely – I can very well imagine that David's
infidelity is known by a few of his colleagues (the male
ones naturally), but I think none of our so-called closer
acquaintances know anything about it. And I assure you that
neither David nor anyone else has the slightest inkling that
I've become aware of the betrayal. It's part of the male
arsenal of vanities that they think we are so easy to deceive,
and in this case that is of course no disadvantage. On the

contrary, dear Agnes, David does not harbour the slightest suspicion, you are going to shoot a sitting duck, or whatever it's called.

So write to me soon, Agnes, and let me know if my outlined proposal suits you. If it doesn't, then we'll think of something else, of course. But if you accept, yes, then we have no more than a month of waiting left, which feels nice, I assure you of that. For a long time I have started imagining that David is already dead, and you have no idea how trying it is to carry on a decent breakfast conversation with a corpse every morning.

Although actually all is well, we have plenty of snow here too.

Signed
Your Henny

To:
Henny Delgado
Pelikaanallé 24
Grothenburg

Gobshejm, 22 January

Dear Henny,

Thanks for your letter. Amsterdam! So funny that city will be the stage for our little drama. Do you remember that we were there together for a few days during an Easter vacation? In the second year it must have been – Claus-Joseph and Ansgar too, yes, of course you remember. That little youth hostel on Ferdinand Bolstraat and the sand dunes out at Zandvort. Claus-Joseph, who was so jealous that I could barely even order coffee from a male waiter! Those were the days, Henny!

Or rather, they were not.

Oh well, I have been to Amsterdam a few times in later years too, and I am reasonably familiar with the city. And the time suits me just fine: it is early in the semester, no burdensome correction tasks and such. I imagine that I will take the car up on Friday, so that I have plenty of time. The Barth family will have to take care of the dogs, I'll think of some reason why I have to be gone over the weekend. I will not likely end up in any alibi situation, but I still think I prefer not to check into the same hotel as your husband. Something right in the neighbourhood perhaps, there are plenty of them along Prinsengracht. And you can trust that I am going to perform my mission in the best and most efficient way possible, Henny, the fact is that I almost feel stimulated by this, isn't that a little perverse? It elevates the sense of being alive in some peculiar way. I have also – to be prepared for all eventualities – been out in the forest and test fired my gun. It worked just fine, possibly there is a little problem in that the shot will be heard very clearly, but good Lord, a bang in a big city? It could be a broken exhaust pipe or whatever. And regardless of where I choose as the exact place for my deed, obviously I am going to reach safety immediately afterwards.

So I see no risks whatsoever, dear Henny. If you simply provide me additional details about your husband's trip, I promise to send him off to the meadows of the blessed in – yes, when I look at the calendar on my desk I see that we are actually talking about a time period of just three weeks.

Otherwise I think that he has aged with a certain grace. I recognized him immediately in the photograph – and I am one hundred per cent certain of being able to identify him even in a beardless state (twenty-five-year-old indeed, yes, talk about vanity!).

Perhaps it would also be good if I got your mobile number and your hotel address in Munich at some point – because it would surely be a plus if I could report the result to you as soon as I've struck, Henny? A necessity even? A text message or something; we'll have to agree on some sort of code, because I think we will need to have a channel that goes a little faster than letter-writing. What do you think?

Oh well, these details are naturally simple to arrange for two women like you and me. I also think your financial plan seems appealing; you must understand how much it means to me to be able to stay in the house, dear Henny, and I truly look forward to having you as a guest here within the not too distant future.

But first a trip in the autumn, as stated.
And first of all Amsterdam on February 14–16!
Signed your devoted 'sister'
Agnes

'Living together has its time, separating has its.'

Henny meets my gaze over the coffee cup, and her smile is bathed in both seriousness and mockery.

'I mean us, Agnes,' she clarifies.

It is not until we have taken our university entrance exams at Weiver's – and after the summer with the Crete adventure – that we go our separate ways for the first time, Henny and I. On 1 October Henny enrols in the Romance Languages department and starts studying Italian; I have already started studying comparative literature. We have run into each other by chance on Kloisterlaan and slipped into Kraus's cafe.

I have moved away from home. Luckily got hold of a sublease for a studio on Geigers steeg, only a stone's throw from Stefan's Church. Henny is still living at home with her mother and her brother for the first year of university.

'Life is not a hike across an open field,' I say.

'Nice to see you,' Henny says. 'But I definitely must hurry off.'

University studies pick up speed. It's over with Ansgar and Claus-Joseph. I go out for a short period with a young Finn by the name of Tapani; he is sweet and well-built in every way, but his severe melancholy, which appears as soon as he's had a couple of drinks, means that I leave him. In October–

November Henny has a brief affair with a married man; she doesn't know that he is married until his wife catches him *in flagrante* and is about to kill them both with a golf club. After that incident, Henny decides to keep to herself for a while. She got a deep gash in the head above her left ear; the scar is going to be there her whole life, but as long as she doesn't go bald no one is going to notice it.

'I had a guardian angel,' she says.

'You were insanely lucky,' I say.

'If she'd picked up an iron instead of a wood I would have been dead,' Henny says.

In early November I become part of the student theatre group, the Thalia Company, and almost immediately get a major role in the production of Chekhov's *Three Sisters*. I play Masha for eight acclaimed performances in December and January. We are only amateurs but get good reviews anyway in both *Allgemejne* and *Volktagesblatt*. Both of the reviewers also underscore that my interpretation of Masha was inspired. I continue my literature studies, but contemplate ever stronger and secret plans to apply to some drama school by and by. Here is where my fire burns, I feel it clearly; I love it when the curtain goes up and you are blinded by the spotlights, I love moving people in the way you can almost only do in the magic space of the theatre.

On 10 January my mother marries her boss, Oldenburg the dentist. She sells the apartment on Wolmarstrasse and moves in with him in his house out in Grafenswald. The same evening, as the removal van leaves, my father calls from Saarbrücken and tells me that he has cancer of the testicles.

'Both?' I ask.

'Both,' my father says. 'The whole damned shit.'

He is rather inconsolable but I do my best to make him see reason anyway.

The Thalia Company has existed since the 1700s and in 1983 it is an even 200 years since the first production – Simson de Staël's *An Offering* – took place. In connection with this, and with the Chekhov success in fresh memory, the university administration contributes funds so that the anniversary can be commemorated in worthy and artistically consummate forms. The theatre administration discusses presenting de Staël's play anew, but the piece is considered antiquated on good grounds. Instead a decision is made to invite a professional director to produce a Shakespeare play. In early February we have a group meeting and our artistic director, Marcus Rottenbühle, whose regular job is as associate professor in the philosophy department, has the pleasure of reporting that he has succeeded in engaging David Goschmann from Munich and the actor Robert Kauffner to produce *King Lear*.

David Goschmann is a charismatic director who, despite his youth, has made a great name for himself through strong productions of classics in Munich. He has also done a couple of original plays for TV, and it is truly a feather in the cap for Rottenbühle that he has managed to get him on the hook.

Robert Kauffner is, of course, legendary.

'*King Lear*,' Rottenbühle says, tugging on his grizzled black beard. 'The play of plays! Ten roles approximately plus Kauffner. Suits us exactly.'

'How will we assign the roles?' Erwin Finckel, who played Tusenbach in *Three Sisters*, asks.

'Goschmann will assign them,' Rottenbühle explains. 'He

wants to have a classic audition. Cordelia is most important, but everyone is significant. The Clown. Gloucester. Edward and Edmund.'

'Goneril and Regan,' I say.

'Naturally,' Rottenbühle says. 'Major female roles, requires careful rehearsal.'

But I have decided.

I will play Cordelia. And I do not intend to leave anything to chance.

To:
Agnes R.
Villa Guarda
Gobshejm

Grothenburg, 30 January

Dear Agnes,

So we've decided! I cannot deny that I feel an excitement that I have a hard time keeping a lid on. If all goes as it should he will be dead in two weeks – that actually works out ever so well, because the girls have a little break the following week; I mean, this way, their school attendance won't have to suffer much.

This morning as we were having breakfast it suddenly occurred to me that he suspects something. No, Agnes, don't get worried, I don't mean that in some strange way David has gotten wind of our plans, it was something else. As if a streak of awareness of death passed over him, I think; and isn't it the case that animals (and people too, I assume) can sense it when their hour is approaching? It seems to me that I read about this phenomenon not so long ago in some magazine. He sat there completely calm having his morning coffee with the newspaper supported against the toaster, just like he always does – but then he raised his gaze and looked at me for a few seconds with a quite special expression in his eyes. Then he smiled and said that he loved me despite everything and that I should take care of myself.

Despite everything, he said.

I asked why he said that, and what he meant by 'despite everything', but he simply observed me with the same serious smile, and then Rea upset her juice glass and the moment fell apart.

But it was so strong, Agnes, and it has stayed with me the whole day – maybe it's the case that I feel some sorrow that things must go this way. Don't believe for the world that I'm starting to change my mind, dear Agnes, far from it – but when all is said and done it is not a pleasure to have to get rid of a person you once believed would stand by your side all through life.

Although that's the way it is, of course, and when I think about how he has conducted himself I immediately feel something quite different. Death to that swine, I think, and then that excitement comes creeping up. Two weeks, Agnes!

Now, however, I have to leave all this emotional turmoil and focus on questions of a slightly more practical nature. The past few days I have started wondering about what the police are actually going to think when they find David's body. It is probably the case that they'll wonder a bit about the motive, what is behind it, so to speak. And here perhaps we have to think a little, Agnes. Shouldn't we make the whole thing appear like something it isn't? To be prepared for all eventualities. Serve the police a kind of motive, in other words. I think so, and the only solution I've come up with is that we have to aim for a robbery with homicide. In any case, that seems the simplest. If you can make sure to liberate David from his wallet and his Rolex watch once you've shot him, it should be in the bag. The police are going to believe that the perpetrator is some rootless wretch who was after money, an addict perhaps, and why shouldn't they think that? Especially as they have no reason to suspect anything else.

Are you with me in this, Agnes? As far as I can see it shouldn't be particularly problematic. Whatever circumstances prevail when you shoot him (in a room? in a dark alley?), it can't take much more than a couple of seconds to stick your hands in his inside pocket and snatch the wallet. And his wristwatch is really an ever-so-conspicuous affair, without a doubt it would be strange if a thief left it behind. But it comes off very quickly, so don't worry, Agnes . . . and if, by the way, he's in bed when you make your effort, then he surely has both the wallet and the watch sitting on the bedside table, he always does.

Oh well, you can think about these questions, Agnes, and let me know how you view them. But now to something else – the details about David's stay in Amsterdam! I simply went into his email and found the programme they sent him, there were no difficulties.

The whole conference will be held at some place called the Niels Franke Institute, or simply the Franke Institute; it is also located rather centrally, right at the end of Vondel Park, and it starts with some sort of welcome introduction between six and eight o'clock on Friday evening. The 14th, that is. The number of participants is 82 and right afterwards there is dinner at the institute, so I assume that David won't be back at the hotel (Figaro, Prinsengracht 112, just as I wrote in the last letter), until rather late. On Saturday they carry on between 10.00 and 6.00 with a subsequent dinner, and on Sunday between 10.00 and 3.00. Naturally, David is likely going to meet colleagues and go to a bar or two on Friday and Saturday evening . . . if it isn't the case that he has plans to meet someone else!

And if someone else hasn't already put an end to him. Yes, I don't really know the best way for you to go into action, dear Agnes. Or when. You must probably shadow him *a little in some way, sit in a car and wait outside that institute in the evening perhaps? I can't help you very much on that point, instead I trust that you will think of a plan and a method. Perhaps it's simplest if you stay hidden at the hotel, after all, and simply wait for him? But how simple – and how risky – is it to do that? I don't know how big Figaro is; the bigger the better, it seems to me – oh well, of course it will be your business to find that out too. In any event I am quite sure that he is going to check into his room before he heads to the Franke Institute on Friday; he's taking the train and will already be at Amsterdam C at 3.15, you see, there was a confirmation from the travel agency in his email too. Perhaps it would be an idea if you were also there at that time? Perhaps it is possible to strike then?*

But anyhow, as stated, I won't get involved in the execution itself. That's your job, Agnes, and I trust that you will resolve everything to your full satisfaction. I have also, as we agreed on, deposited another thirty thousand euros in your account – it strikes me that it could be hard for you to explain where these amounts come from, but of course we are never going to end up in such a situation. There is no – none whatsoever! – connection between you and David, that is of course the very prerequisite.

I also realize that we will not have time to exchange many more letters before it is time – one from each direction I'm guessing – and it is naturally correct as you propose that we must have access to quicker channels during the weekend in question. I have reserved a room at a hotel in Munich called Regina, it is on Hildegardstrasse not far from Marienplatz. My mobile number is 069-1451452, and I have a proposal:

When you are finished with your mission you call me up

and leave a fictional message, you can choose one yourself
– but don't forget to relay the exact wording in the next
letter!

If for some reason you had problems, you will say
something else instead – and if you want me to call, then
you will add something additional. (Isn't it a bit strange that
we still haven't spoken with each other, Agnes? After all this
writing and planning, it will be so nice to hear your voice
again!)

Well, say what you think? Simple and clever, isn't it? Send
me your three codes – one for OK, all clear!, one for Trouble!
and one for Call me! – in your next letter, which I assume
will be the last (or perhaps next to last?), before it is time.

Everything else is everyday, dear Agnes. Life goes on as
usual; both of the girls have had a bout of flu, but David
and I have escaped that.

And the snow is still on the ground.

Be in touch soon!

Wishes your obliged

Henny

P.S. What will we do with the letters, dear Agnes? There
have turned out to be a few; I hate to burn them, but perhaps
that would be wisest?

To:
Henny Delgado
Pelikaanallé 24
Grothenburg

Gobshejm, 2 February

Dear Henny,

    Thanks for your long letter. Yes, we are indeed approaching D-Night (day? morning?) by leaps and bounds. Like you, of course I feel a certain excitement, but at the same time deep down I am calm. Perhaps it is because I am not nearly as emotionally engaged in the matter as you are, Henny. I am completing a mission, doing a good friend a service and getting paid for it. It's actually no stranger than that. We must keep in mind that thousands of people are murdered in Europe every day, David is only going to be a small fraction in the statistics.

    Yet we must obviously proceed with the utmost care, so thanks for all the important information you are providing, Henny. As I see it I am going to have plenty of alternatives to choose from; I'll drive up to Amsterdam on Thursday afternoon (fortunately I have no teaching on Friday, the Barth family has already been informed and are happy to take care of the dogs; it is primarily their two daughters in their early teens who are so fond of Wagner and Bartok) – so I will have time to both do a little reconnaissance and be on the scene when he arrives at the central station. I have reserved a room at a hotel near Leidse Plein where I stayed once before; it is no more than a couple of hundred metres from Figaro, I've looked at a map.

    The fact is that I also know about the Franke Institute; I was there for a course once ten or twelve years ago. It has some connection to the university, if I'm not mistaken.

Where the idea of robbery with homicide is concerned, I agree with you completely. Naturally we have to make everything as understandable as possible for the police. Will you want the wallet and Rolex back, or is it safest if I get rid of them? Oddly enough my husband also had a Rolex (which the greedy son for some unfathomable reason has not laid claim to!), and I truly have no use for two.

Although the most fun of all has been to think about this thing with the codes. I definitely think that we need three of them, just as you suggest, and I think it was generous of you to leave it to me to work them out. So, here they come:

1) If David is dead and all is OK: Good day, George, this is Aunt Beatrice. I just want to say that the black hollyhocks are ordered and paid for and will arrive on Tuesday. You don't need to call me, that's just an unnecessary expense! (Naturally a wrong number like the others.)

2) If anything fails but you don't need to make contact: Hi honey! It's Maud. I'll be a little late, but we can still go out and eat when I come home. Kiss, kiss!

3) If you need to call me: Good day! This call is coming from the tax agency. Would you be please contact the administrator, Hilmer at 1716 646 960. Thanks!

Pretty clever, don't you think, Henny? And then of course you must have my mobile number – yes, you just have to reverse administrator Hilmer's: 069 646 6171!

Yes, dear Henny, I guess that's all. In eleven days I will get into the car and wend my way towards Amsterdam. We will hopefully have time to exchange a few words by mail before then, but as far as I can see there are no more details we need *to go over. It is my conviction that everything is going to go as smoothly as anything, and – a wish you expressed in an earlier letter – your spouse is going to be in the ground long before Easter.*

And – I almost forgot this – thanks for the money! In reality I only need a little more than eighty thousand to be able to arrange the house issue, but the remaining cash will of course come in handy when we are out travelling in the autumn. Don't you think, Henny? You cannot sense how much I am looking forward to that.

Hope also that you stay away from the flu even in the future; here in Gobshjem it has not yet appeared this year, but you can never be certain of course.

Signed
Your faithful girlfriend
Agnes

P.S. The letters, yes! I am afraid that it must be as you say. We'll probably just have to burn them. But we can wait on that until the very last in any event, can't we? I like going back and reading what you've written so much.

The great fear.

As I am driving home from H-berg it comes over me. A quite physical sensation of something big and unstoppable; it is so strong that I get short of breath, have to stop the car and get out for a while. Stand there smoking a cigarette despite the thin driving rain and try to calm down.

I am on the outskirts of the village of Worms, with Leuwel's valley below me and the old stone church at my back. A mass of fog settles over the landscape, twilight is about to give way to darkness. Somewhere up along the mountainside someone is sawing timber with a chain saw, in the cemetery a man walks around with a spade over his shoulder.

I stand there by the car and try to understand what is affecting me. I feel surrounded by signs I don't understand: church, car, man, spade, fog, darkness, sound, cold.

But perhaps it is just solitude. The solitude in this project; I must do everything on my own. I have no one to talk with, not even him, and how will I know that I am judging things correctly? How?

I won't be able to talk with anyone afterwards either; never get any confirmation that I acted correctly – and how can I be sure that I can live with this? That I won't just crack and everything turns out to have been wasted?

And how should I weigh this sudden fear? This weakness; if it is only something passing I will be completely right to resist it, but if it concerns something more fundamental, what happens then?

It's not yet too late, there is still room to turn around. I tell myself that is the case at least, but to be honest I cannot imagine the consequences if I were to withdraw right now. I have been aimed in this direction for so long. Weeks and months.

Nights.

I put out the cigarette. Still feel the worry in my body, it aches like nausea or an approaching fever; I see that the village bar is open and guide my steps there. Order a glass of red wine from Herr Kammerer and sit down in a corner with a newspaper.

Perhaps it's the letter writing. Before the most recent letters I felt great agony; not about reading hers, but about authoring my own. When I wrote the last ones I was drunk, it was impossible to bring the unwillingness under control any other way, and I assume that I will have to use the same means the next time too. Reasonably it will be the last, there is scarcely time for more.

I finish the wine and smoke yet another cigarette. Herr Kammerer comes and wants to refill my glass, but I say no. It was no longer needed; just this miserable drop of alcohol in the blood so that I will feel normal again. Perhaps it isn't so bad after all? I pay, thank him and walk back to the car in the dark. The rain has picked up, I get thoroughly soaked in only a hundred metres.

Once at home I prepare tomorrow's seminar on the Brontë

sisters. Browse a little in *Wuthering Heights* and think about this business of love versus morality.

Think that they belong in such separate categories that actually you can never set them against each other. Yet we do all the time. On what level playing field would a chess player meet a sumo wrestler? What a strange image, I have to smile at it.

You can't pair a duck with a fish, I also observe. None of us was right back then.

No one was wrong.

Perhaps not now either. We are tiles and pieces in a game that must proceed to its resolution. If we decide to play to the end, that is, and it is certainly here – nowhere else – that our choice is. To play or not to play.

I take only a short walk with the dogs this evening because of the rain. Drink two glasses of wine and am in bed by eleven o'clock. Pray for a dreamless night.

'And what is so remarkable about *King Lear*?'

We are sitting in the sauna after swimming. Henny lifts up her breasts, observes them and weighs them in her hands.

'My left one is bigger than the right, isn't that so?'

'Do you want an answer to the *King Lear* question or the breast question first?'

She thinks about it and lets go of her breasts.

'Sorry. What is it about this play anyway? I've never seen it.'

'You don't need to see it,' I say. 'It's enough to read it.'

'I haven't read it either. Do you think I'm ignorant?'

'No more than usual,' I say amiably. 'Pour on more water,

will you, it's not the idea that we should sit here and freeze, is it? It's about an old man and his three daughters.'

That much I actually know.

'Two of the daughters are power-hungry and selfish, the third one is good.'

'Cordelia?'

'Yes. Old Lear divides his kingdom among his daughters, but he is vain and wants to give most to the one who claims to love him the most. Cordelia loves her father but speaks in a low voice and gets nothing, the poor king puts his life in the hands of the other two daughters. He rejects the good daughter and that is the beginning of his fall . . . the final scene between the insane king and his dead Cordelia is the strongest that is possible to present on a stage.'

'Dead?'

'Yes.'

'And she's the one you want to play? The good, dead daughter?'

I nod. Point out that she is only dead in the end.

'This means a lot to you?'

I glare at her in irritation. She is sitting and fingering her breasts again.

'Of course it means a lot!' I say. 'Why would I get involved in something that doesn't mean something? If I get to play Cordelia against Kauffner and it goes well, yes, then I have no reason not to continue. Give it a real shot.'

'The acting track?'

'No, the plumbing track.'

'Hmm. But you're not the only one who wants the role, are you?'

I sigh and think. No, of course not. The funny thing is that we are playing three sisters again. First Chekhov and now Shakespeare. Both Renate and Ursula, who played Olga and Irina, want to play Cordelia of course, they would be crazy otherwise. And there are supposedly a couple of other competitors too. The Thalia Company has added new members for some reason.

'I understand,' Henny says after a moment of silence. 'Goschmann and Kauffner are not just anyone?'

'Not exactly,' I say.

'And how does the actual . . . what is it called . . . the selection process work?'

'Audition,' I explain. 'We've been given two scenes to practise. One right at the beginning, one towards the end. In two weeks Goschmann is going to sit for a whole day and assess us.'

We leave the sauna and stand under the showers. I notice that Henny is thoughtful and has started to get the point. She squints and sucks on that wisp of hair like she's done ever since she was eleven or twelve. I think that I know her better than she knows herself.

'Can I help you in any way?' she asks when we have come out to the changing room.

'Yes, thanks,' I say. 'I need someone to read and play against.'

'Me?' Henny says with a sudden infantile laugh.

'You,' I say. 'We'll start this evening. We have fourteen days.'

'*Now, our joy, although our last and least,*' Henny rumbles, '*to whose young love the vines of France and milk of Burgundy strive to be interest; what can you say to draw a third more opulent than your sisters? Speak.'*

'Nothing, my lord,' I say.

'Good,' Henny says.

'You shouldn't comment on my lines,' I say. 'You should play against me.'

'Of course,' Henny says. 'Let's do it again . . . *what can you say to draw a third more opulent than your sisters? Speak.'*

'Nothing, my lord,' I repeat.

'Nothing?'

'Nothing.'

Henny snorts. *'Nothing will come of nothing. Speak again.'*

'Unhappy that I am,' I say, lowering my eyes, *'I cannot heave my heart into my mouth. I love your Majesty according to my bond, no more nor less.'*

'That's good,' Henny says. 'I cannot heave my heart into my mouth. Super!'

'Of course it's good,' I say with irritation. 'It's *King Lear*. It's Shakespeare.'

'I understand,' Henny says. 'Sorry. Let's do it again now, I won't interrupt.'

'From the beginning,' I say.

We go swimming three times a week, and after every swim we practise. A total of six times during these fourteen days. Act I, scene 1 and Act IV, scene 7. In the latter scene Henny plays Kent, the doctor and Lear, and already after the second or third attempt we know our lines by heart. I understand that Henny must have practised at home too.

Gradually she starts to give me advice.

'Gentler,' she says. 'I think you should try to be as toneless as possible.'

'Toneless?' I ask.

'Like this,' Henny says. '*O you kind gods, curse this great breach in his abusèd nature! Th' untuned and jarring senses, O, wind up of this child-changèd father!*'

She knows this by heart too.

'She prays although actually she doesn't dare believe in any result,' Henny explains. 'I think that is the idea. You should be as subdued as you possibly can. Although you must be heard, of course.'

I think and try it.

'Good,' Henny says. 'Much better, I didn't know that theatre was so exciting.'

We do it over and over. When we think that the words and intonation are the right ones, we practise gestures and posture. Henny is enthusiastic and constantly shares ideas. The day before the audition we carry on until after midnight. I also try a dress that I intend to wear – just a simple white cotton dress, but it is long and I can be barefoot under it without it being seen. Admittedly I have no idea what Goschmann will think about it, but I want to feel the floorboards under my bare feet when I am standing on the stage. If the role allows it, of course. It gives a sort of power that is felt all the way up in your vocal cords.

'We should probably stop now,' I say at last. 'I'll be first up tomorrow. At eleven o'clock. And I have to wash my hair, too.'

'Remember to wear it loose,' Henny says.

'Are you sure of that?'

'Absolutely,' Henny says. 'You're most beautiful that way.

Beauty and goodness should go hand in hand, if that is pos-sible.'

It sounds like something we used to write in our essays for Miss Silberstein. We hug and say goodbye.

'Good luck,' Henny says. 'Trust in doing your best and be humble. I'll keep my fingers crossed for you.'

'Do that,' I say. 'I'm very grateful for your help, Henny.'

To:
Agnes R.
Villa Guarda
Gobshejm

Grothenburg, 10 February

Dear Agnes,

Thanks for your letter, it was so fun to read it. Unfortunately there probably won't be too many more now, and – which truly pains me – unfortunately it is probably also time to burn all of this correspondence. I have reread all your letters – there are nine of them actually – just this evening; David is at some meeting and the girls are asleep. But I am still waiting for a line from you before I put it all in the fire; I imagine that you'll be in touch soon before you travel up to Amsterdam – yes, can you please mail me a little greeting no later than Thursday, so I have time to read it before I go to Munich? I am leaving at three o'clock on Friday.

I have also received my programme for the translator days (as they are called); it undeniably arrived a bit late, but maybe that doesn't matter very much. In any event I am going to be occupied all of Saturday and Sunday (I am thinking now about my alibi, as I'm sure you understand); there is nothing scheduled on Friday evening however, so I guess I'll have to make sure they notice me in reception at the hotel a few times. Or if they have a restaurant I can spend a few hours there?

If it's the case that you strike that first evening, that is.

Yes, write me one more line, dear Agnes, please. I actually have nothing else on my mind right now, it is Monday and this time next week it will be over. It feels both strange and liberating; when I walked past Kemperling's store today, you know, the one that is down on Grote Square next to Kraus, I caught sight of a black dress in the window. If they still have it I will probably go in and buy it next week; I was actually about to do it today, but managed to stop myself. Perhaps it would attract some attention if the widow bought the mourning attire while the husband was still alive. Am I right, Agnes?

Anyway, may the gods support us and I trust that you have your nerves under control. I have your clever codes well preserved in my memory and look forward to a) a short letter from you on Thursday or Friday, b) a phone call sometime over the weekend.

Otherwise it is rainy and foggy here in Grothenburg, but the flu seems to have passed this time. Now I hear David's steps on the stairway, closing in all haste.

Your Henny

P.S. (Tuesday morning) Kind Agnes, do not hesitate to call immediately, even if it is the middle of the night! I feel that I must find out as soon as it has happened.

P.P.S. And for heaven's sake don't forget to burn the letters too, Agnes! It would be terrible if someone happened to discover them!

To:
Henny Delgado
Pelikaanallé 24
Grothenburg

Gobshejm, 12 February

Dear Henny,

It is late Wednesday evening. Tomorrow I have two lectures and after that I will get in the car and drive straight up to A. If there is not too much traffic on the roads I ought to be there by about nine o'clock.

After that, a good night's sleep at my hotel, and then I will be ready to meet your husband at the central station at quarter past three.

And then we'll see.

I have packed my gun and the ammunition in my suitcase. Sat and weighed the pistol a good while in my hand before I parted with it. It feels strange that this little metal object will put an end to a life, simply by means of a light pressure from my index finger. So all this planning and this effort runs out in a simple finger movement, I couldn't help thinking about it and whether it says something about our lives. I mean all of our lives, their inherent fragility – and is it not the case that after a certain point in time they narrow instead of expanding? Our lives. I think so. But when, Henny? As of when do our life paths suddenly become narrower instead of wider? When do we start – deliberately or unconsciously or both – going in a narrower direction? Because it really is like that, dear Henny, even if I feel that new possibilities will open for us after this (reunion, conversations, travel), at the same time it seems as if everything is getting tighter and tighter.

Or maybe I'm wrong. I've been drinking wine again. Maybe my thoughts are simply expressions of temporary moods and of the rain that unceasingly whips against the windowpanes. In any event I promise you to keep away from both wine and spirits in A. At least until I have completed my mission.

But I harbour no worry; on the contrary I am happy that it is finally time, I am probably not a person who is particularly good at waiting. What do you think, does that tally with your perception of me from before?

Otherwise I don't have that much on my mind either, but you asked for a few lines. I have read all your letters again this evening and ten minutes ago I saw them transformed to soot and ash in the fireplace. Am going to bed now full of confidence; I will call as we said from A and then perhaps we will meet at David's funeral.

Or do you think it is too risky for me to attend it, dear Henny? You were at Erich's after all.

In any event I want to wish you a pleasant and rewarding stay in Munich! I truly hope the weather both there and in Amsterdam is better than here, a little spring in the air soon wouldn't be bad.

Signed
Your Agnes

David Goschmann is a dark person, but his eyes are so blue that they spill over.

'For the female roles we are only auditioning for Cordelia,' he says. 'I will be in touch with the relevant person tomorrow morning. Twelve o'clock at the latest.'

I nod.

'Keep in mind that you, just like the others, are subject to considerable caprice.'

'How many others are there?' I ask.

'Four. Those who are then interested in Goneril and Regan will come here tomorrow evening.'

'I understand,' I say.

'We can possibly also let the clown be performed by a woman. You are aware that Cordelia is absent for most of the play?'

'Of course.'

'So you did Masha in *Three Sisters*?'

I admit that I interpreted Masha.

'Did you like her?'

I admit that I liked her a lot. Both her and the role.

'I've done some Chekhov,' David Goschmann says. 'Would like to do more, but there isn't that much and you have to save some things for old age.'

He smiles and that blueness shines in him. He can't be more than twenty-eight or thirty.

'Who am I playing against?' I ask, looking around. It is only Goschmann and I in the space.

'Rotten . . . What's his name?'

'Rottenbühle?'

'Rottenbühle, yes. Would you have preferred someone else?'

'Oh, no. Just so I avoid him if it turns serious.'

He laughs and promises that there will be other actors by and by.

'Do you want to lie down for a moment and concentrate first? Rottenbühle seems to be late.'

'Thanks, gladly.'

'You have a good appearance.'

'Thanks.'

'Do you intend to continue later?'

'With theatre?'

'Yes.'

I shrug my shoulders. Regret it, but it's not possible to erase a shoulder shrug.

'Maybe,' I say. 'Yes, it's not impossible.'

'I will give you a couple of names,' Goschmann says. 'Good schools. If you're interested, that is?'

'Thanks, gladly,' I repeat. 'I really am.'

The door opens and Rottenbühle comes in. He obviously has a cold and starts by sneezing three times.

'Sorry. I got delayed a little.'

'No problem,' Goschmann says, smiling. 'I don't know if Cordelia wants to have a moment of concentration first, or if we can start at once?'

'I'm happy to start at once,' I say.

★

I understand what it is David Goschmann has.

Presence. When he steps into a room a force field opens. The energy increases quite tangibly; I feel both noticed and intelligent. And significant; I have never experienced this before but I grasp immediately what it is about.

He is sitting a good way out in the auditorium. The seventh or eighth row. True, I am playing against the cold-suffering Rottenbühle, but it is impossible to avoid playing against Goschmann at the same time. It is a question of the same diagonal as usual, of course, but also something new and unproven. It feels peculiar, I can't decide if this is a good thing or a bad thing. If it strengthens or weakens my expression.

We go on for almost half an hour. Do both scenes two times; Goschmann has no comments whatsoever, but I know that he is registering every millimetre of my body and every breath I take. When I come out from Keller Theatre, where we had been – and always are – I feel exhausted and almost dizzy, as if after great physical exertion.

As if I'd been making love for two hours, for example, something that I still have never done during my twenty-one-year-old life.

I sit down at a table in Cafe Adler right around the corner and order a steak and a beer. Think that for the first time I have met a guy who seriously interests me.

Who truly . . . corresponds to me.

Later in the evening – it is a windy Saturday in February without any hint whatsoever of spring in the air – an incident occurs that I cannot readily interpret other than as a good sign.

My little studio apartment, where I have lived for over six months now, is on the top floor of an old building on Geigers steeg. Sixth floor without a lift; it is no more than a cupboard, but the sloping ceiling and irregularities no doubt have their charm and of course I don't need more space at this stage in my life.

On the same floor, an elderly couple, Herr and Frau Linkoweis, also live. They are both in their mid-seventies and a little frail, he more than her – Frau Linkoweis usually makes her way up and down the stairs once a day at least, goes to the square and selects the day's necessities and then has them sent home by courier. Sometimes I shop for them, but that is an exception, they prefer managing on their own. Herr Linkoweis, who answers to the unusual first name Sigisbard, comes out at most every three or four days. In bad weather he sees no reason to stick his nose out, and in good weather he is most often content to be out on the little balcony, which faces towards the courtyard and which I can see from my diminutive window in my diminutive kitchen.

When I come home that Saturday (after the steak at Adler's, that is, and a couple of rather ineffective hours of study at the library), I run into Frau Linkoweis along with the caretaker, Herr Bloeme, outside my door. Frau Linkoweis looks about to faint, her face is white and she is foaming at the mouth without a sound crossing her lips. The door to the couple's apartment is open; Herr Bloeme explains the situation.

Herr Linkoweis has gone crazy, he observes, breathing heavily.

Herr Bloeme smokes fifty cigarettes a day and only exceptionally visits any of the upper floors of the building.

'You don't mean that,' I say.

'I sure do,' Bloeme hisses. 'He's standing out there on the balcony, intending to jump.'

With a nicotine-yellowed, trembling index finger he waves towards the Linkoweis's apartment. Frau Linkoweis stops her foaming, takes hold of my arm and starts whimpering.

'Please,' she pleads. 'Please.'

I shake my head sceptically.

'He's climbed up on the outside of the railing,' Bloeme explains. 'He's standing there and holding on with one hand. If we approach or call for help he'll let go!'

'How do you know that?' I ask.

'He says so.'

'How long has he been standing there?'

'Ten minutes maybe,' Bloeme says. 'I just came up. Simone fetched me.'

I did not know that Frau Linkoweis's first name was Simone. But she nods in confirmation while she digs her nails into my upper arm. Sigisbard and Simone? I think.

'Please,' she repeats.

'What do you intend to do?' I ask.

Bloeme paces around and fumbles in his chest pocket for cigarettes. He has a butt behind his ear but he does not seem to be aware of that.

'I don't know,' he says. 'What the hell should we do? That this should happen today of all days.'

Simone Linkoweis starts crying loudly. I wonder quickly what Herr Bloeme meant by ' today of all days'. Maybe he has a birthday or something.

'Do you think he's serious?' I ask. 'It's possible that—'

'He's serious,' Bloeme says. 'No doubt about it. He's seventy-five, damn it!'

I don't understand what his age has to do with the seriousness, but don't bother to investigate that.

'Shall I go in to him?' I propose instead. 'Do you want . . . ?'

Simone Linkoweis is staring at me from close quarters with an expression that balances between helplessness and desperate pleading. I gingerly release her grip from around my arm.

'Stay here,' I say. 'I'll go in and look around.'

'Just don't get too close,' Bloeme says. 'Then he'll jump!'

I nod and walk cautiously in through the doorway. Come into the hall, but from here you can't see the balcony. I continue to the right into the living room, which is so cluttered with furniture and decorative objects that you almost can't move in it, and through the open balcony door I see him.

He is truly standing just as Bloeme described. The black wrought-iron railing is no more than seventy or eighty centimetres high and I understand that it has not entailed any difficulty – not even for a person with Sigisbard Linkoweis's deficient flexibility – to step over it. He is standing there, turned at an angle from me, with all his concentration aimed out at the courtyard and down. I know that it must be a fall of at least twelve metres and the courtyard is paved with uneven cobblestones. Without a doubt he is going to kill himself if he lets go.

And he is holding on with only one hand on the transverse bar. Leaning out a little too.

I remain standing in the middle of the room, at a loss. He has not yet noted my presence, but the distance between us is five or six metres. I quickly try to assess the situation. Without a doubt a hasty sortie could be ill-fated – especially as there is a rocking chair and a table in the line of attack.

I observe him. He is dressed in grey trousers and a thin tan cardigan. If he has truly been standing out there for ten minutes it must mean – if nothing else – that he is cold. The temperature is not much above freezing.

'You deceivers!' he calls out suddenly in a strong voice, and I realize that he is addressing some listener or listeners out there. I take a cautious step to the side and sure enough catch sight of a woman on another balcony right across the court-yard. I don't know what her name is, but I have run into her a few times and recognize her. She has a Dachshund that usually has a green jumper on.

'If you call the police I'll jump at once!' Sigisbard Linko-weis threatens. 'And then all of you are going to be destroyed! I am in contact with the prince of the universe!'

I understand that caretaker Bloeme has made a more or less correct assessment of his mental state. I take a step closer. Come up level with the rocking chair.

'I am so damned fed up with all of you!' Linkoweis roars. 'So damned fed up! Soon I'll jump and then you're going to die like flies!'

I hesitate. Nothing happens for well over half a minute. Herr Linkoweis's hand, which is squeezing the railing, looks desperately white and bloodless. I decide to try to come at least a little closer.

'I am in despair! I can no longer bear to be in despair!'

I round the table. There are only three metres left now, but then I happen to bump into a pedestal with an urn on it. I catch the urn but the pedestal falls to the floor with a crash.

'Beg your pardon?'

He turns his head and discovers me.

No, perhaps he doesn't discover me, because he is not wearing glasses. I know that he has rather poor vision, it is one of the things Frau Linkoweis mentions at regular intervals.

Sigisbard sees so poorly, she always says. Soon he won't be able to read any more, one day he's going to be blind.

But he is aware that someone is standing inside the room. 'Who is it?' he thunders, his voice surprisingly powerful. 'Don't come closer, or I'll let go!'

There is a streak of fear in him, I can't avoid hearing it. I stand as if nailed to the floor and do not know what I should do. Behind me I sense that Frau Linkoweis and Herr Bloeme are on their way in. I moisten my lips and brace myself.

'It's just me, Sigisbard,' I say. 'Come to me and I will console you.'

At first he does not react. Stands just as stiff as me, still with only one hand squeezing the railing. I hear the distant murmur of voices from outside; perhaps there are people standing on all the balconies, perhaps they have gathered down in the courtyard too.

Several seconds pass.

'Come closer so I can look at you,' he says.

I take three more steps and stop in the doorway. I could almost reach my hand out and take hold of him but I don't dare.

'Stop!' he says. 'No further. I'll jump!'

I don't reply.

'Who are you?' he repeats.

'It's me,' I say. 'Come to me.'

He hesitates for another few moments. Gradually adopts a completely different posture. Softer, more receptive. Perhaps he has never heard anyone say those exact words to him during his entire lifespan. Perhaps he has longed for them. He heaves a deep sigh, steps back in over the railing and I enclose him in my embrace.

He is ice-cold and immediately starts sobbing.

No, it is hard to see that as anything other than a sign.

To:
David Goschmann
Hotel Figaro
Prinsengracht 112
Amsterdam

Grothenburg, 12 February

Dearest David,

I know that it is not customary for a wife to send letters to her husband in this way (especially not in our day and when they are not apart from each other for more than a few days), but I simply can't help it. Sometimes you get a thought or an idea, and there is no way to be rid of it other than to make it a reality.

I love you, David. It is actually just this I want you to know – this, the most banal of all banal phrases, and even so the most heartfelt and weightiest thought we can entertain.

It has occurred to me that in recent times we have not been able to show the love for each other that we once promised. It's not your fault, not mine. Neither you nor I have any guilt in this. Let us in any case not reproach ourselves for anything – but isn't it the case that everyday life and the tyranny of routines have eaten their way into our lives, David? I believe it's that way, and I don't imagine for a second that it could be anything else.

But I know that it is important to break circles before they become vicious, we've talked about that so many times. It is so easy to take each other for granted, David, let's not do that any longer.

Let us realize that it is a blessing that we get to live with each other and see our girls grow up together. Let us once again give love the place in our lives that it rightly deserves.

Let us love one another until death do us part, David, just as we once agreed on.

Yes, it was only this simple – and difficult – thing I wanted to say to you with this letter, my beloved husband. I wish you a pleasant stay in Amsterdam, and I long to see you again when you come home.

Yours forever,
Henny

If the night truly was dreamless I don't know. In any case I cannot recall anything when I wake up at six thirty and it feels like I haven't slept at all.

Go out with the dogs; a long walk along the river over to Mannering's Bridge. Over it and up through the woods all the way to the horst at Gandwitz. The air is mild up here; almost no wind but the fog has lifted. I rest a while, sit on a downed tree trunk and look out over the landscape; the dogs have run free, now they are lying and panting by my feet.

My landscape. I can't own it, of course, but I feel so clearly that nothing is going to make me leave this area. Here I am at home, I would walk over dead bodies to be able to stay here, words that show up without my needing to accompany them with a thought.

On the way back the sun breaks through and I am thoroughly sweaty when I step into the shower. Then breakfast and packing. I wrap the pistol in one ski sock, put the ammunition in the other. Place it carefully at the very bottom of the suitcase; I don't know why, actually, but perhaps it is natural when all is said and done. Perhaps even a professional murderer would pack in this way.

At ten o'clock I'm ready, get the dogs into the car and drive over to the Barths'. We only exchange a few words, but friendly ones. They wish me a pleasant stay in Berlin; Herr Barth lived there for five years but he does not miss it, truly not. They are both off work for some reason, but the daughters are in school, of course.

I'll be back on Sunday evening, I promise to call when I know what time.

'We can keep them until Monday,' Frau Barth assures me. 'It's no problem.'

'Or take them over completely,' Herr Barth jokes. 'Maybe the girls would start loving us then.'

'Well,' I admit. 'I have a certain need for them too.'

'You should have a guy instead,' Herr Barth says, and his wife throws her arms out in despair.

'What in the world would she do with a guy?'

I usually try to emphasize poor Anne when I talk about the Brontë sisters, and I do that this time too.

Stress that she only lived to be twenty-five – and that admittedly both *Agnes Grey* and *The Tenant of Wildfell Hall* have their faults in comparison with *Wuthering Heights* and *Jane Eyre*, but what novels don't?

And that both her two older sisters certainly made sure to keep tight rein on her in one way and the other.

Are they possible to get hold of? someone asks, and this semester too I loan out my copies of Anne Brontë's two books.

But I feel that I have a hard time concentrating on this subject – which is actually so dear to my heart – and I end the seminar twenty minutes early. Blame it on the fact that I have an appointment in Berlin to make, and none of the students of course has anything against ending a little early.

I leave my briefcase in the office. To the extent I need to prepare Monday's lectures I can come in a couple of hours early that morning.

It's no later than two thirty as I drive out of the car park and leave the university area. After only a five-minute drive I am struck by a compulsive thought. I stop at a car park right before the entrance ramp to the expressway to check that the suitcase is still in the trunk.

It is.

I would also like to check that the gun and ammunition are truly in place, but that can't be done. Not in a car park in broad daylight.

Take it easy, Agnes, I think when I am again sitting behind the steering wheel. You have to stay calm.

But I notice that my pulse and my breathing are faster than normal. I want to convince myself however that it has nothing to do with nervousness. That instead it is that elevated sense of life, as I described to Henny, that is seeking an outlet.

There are some difficulties with finding the hotel, even though I stop and check a street map before I drive into the city centre. A couple of one-way streets make me get lost, it's the middle of late-afternoon rush hour too and there's a driving rain, but at last I end up on the right street. I stop outside the moderately eye-catching entry, go in and get instructions from the desk clerk about how to get down into the garage.

Check in, pay cash in advance without having to show ID, and lock myself in my room. Unpack the suitcase, push my gun between the extra blankets in the wardrobe and run a bath.

Lie there for half an hour in the foam with an aroma of lime and freshly cut grass and relax. Drink up the little bottle of red wine from the minibar and smoke a cigarette. It doesn't feel quite as depraved as it ought to; I think it is right in line with the key signatures of this journey. Again I compare myself with a professional murderer. Perhaps he (she?) would also choose to prepare himself (herself?) in just this way. Why not?

I have dinner in the hotel dining room and then I go out. The rain has stopped but a biting wind is blowing. I acquaint myself with the neighbourhood and with the closest route over to the scene of the crime. It's a route of no more than three or four hundred metres. A walk along barely illuminated streets, dark parked cars, a couple of poorly frequented bars. I slowly pass the hotel; it is better than I had imagined, there appears to be a real lobby, which naturally is an advantage. It surely won't be any problem making my way in unnoticed. I probably won't be stopped on the way up to the room.

I am going to be in disguise besides. Not much, but still enough. A light wig and a pair of tinted glasses. No one is ever going to connect me with this murder, so why overdo it?

I return to my own hotel. Watch a rather miserable French movie on the TV and read a couple of pages from a new dissertation about Lou Salomé.

Turn off the light around twelve thirty and think about how the situation is going to unfold in exactly twenty-four hours.

★

The following day I am awake by six thirty and I don't know if I had any dreams. But yesterday's incident with Herr Linkoweis immediately comes to mind, so perhaps I have had him with me during the night too.

I stay in bed awhile and think about him. And about the postlude after I managed to get him off the balcony. Against his will he was transported to the hospital; he cried like a child and pleaded to be able to stay at home, but both the wife and his sister – a tall, misshapen woman with bitter features, who showed up at the scene almost immediately once the drama was over – were adamant. Herr Linkoweis clung firmly to me when the two orderlies came to take him to the hospital, but it was only used as a pretext that he was crazy and must be taken care of.

'I am in despair!' he shouted so that it echoed in the stairwell on the way down. 'Don't you all understand that I am in despair!'

I suffered with him. But both the wife and the sister rode with him in the ambulance, and perhaps what happened was for the best. In any case I have a hard time seeing any more sensible solutions.

I get up and make coffee. Once I've had breakfast, read the newspaper and showered it is eight thirty. I sit down and wait for David Goschmann to call.

At ten o'clock he has still not called, and not at eleven either.

I am incapable of doing anything. Don't have enough concentration to read, start hand-washing a jumper in my narrow sink, but stop and leave the garment in wet and dirty condition over the back of a chair. Try to solve the crossword puzzle in the newspaper, it immediately turns out wrong. I need to go to the bathroom, but the telephone cord is too short for me to be able to answer if I'm sitting there. I hold it.

Twelve o'clock. I know that he said *twelve o'clock at the latest.* When it is a few minutes past eleven thirty I sit down and stare at the telephone. Change my mind, lay down stretched out on the bed. Close my eyes and count my pulse rate.

Think that Death is lying beside me in the bed, I don't understand where this fantasy comes from.

Now it is quarter to twelve. I finish the last drop of coffee from this morning and start feeling ill. A telephone never rings if you try to conjure the call, that is a good old truth. I must try to think about something else. I stare out the window and think about whether Herr Linkoweis has come home. Or got a diagnosis at least.

Ten minutes to. Nothing happens. Absolutely nothing.

Five to.

At two minutes to twelve the ring comes. I take a deep breath, place my hand on the receiver and wait for another ring. Do not want to seem eager.

Answer.

It is my father. He tells that he does not have any testicles left, but that he is going to be able to live a normal life anyway.

I hang up. The bells in Stefan's Church strike twelve.

I arrive at Keller Theatre fifteen minutes late. The others are already there. David Goschmann is sitting on the edge of the stage in a black polo shirt and black, dangling corduroy legs; he stops speaking as I push open the door at the very back of the auditorium.

Rottenbühle turns around and coughs into his hand. His cold does not seem to have got better. There are five of them sitting up there in the first row. Ursula and Vera, my sisters from Chekhov. Rottenbühle. And a new girl in the troupe, her name is Mathilde and her prospects in the industry ceased at the same time as silent film because she lisps.

I walk slowly down the sloping left-side aisle. Cast a smile at Goschmann and sit down beside Vera.

'Welcome,' Goschmann says. 'We're talking about Goneril and Regan, and about the necessity of differentiating them. Two more or less identical characters will be neither dynamic nor credible on the stage. They suck the air out of each other . . .'

'I understand,' I say.

Goschmann clears his throat and continues along the same track. During the whole afternoon I have had a clenched fist in my chest, now it is starting to move. Upwards and to the sides. I swallow and swallow. Why are both Ursula and Vera sitting here? I think. Which one of them . . . ?

'Excuse me,' I say.

Goschmann interrupts himself again. Rests his chin against the knuckles of his hand and observes me. The blue is not running over today.

'Is the role of Cordelia assigned?'

He nods. Rottenbühle coughs nervously and rises halfway out of his seat furthest to the right.

'And?'

Goschmann lowers his hand.

'You were all very convincing.'

I wait. The clenched fish is twisting.

'As I said when we started . . . you are all subject to a large measure of caprice. Unfortunately, such was the case.'

'Who?' I say.

'We decided at last on . . . I mean that at last *I* decided on a girl who is not actually part of the ensemble. Until now, that is. Her name is Henny. Henny Delgado, I don't know if . . .'

I clasp my hands and press them against my stomach. Do not have a chance to resist the enormous vomiting reflex that shoots up inside me.

All I've eaten during the day comes out of me. All I've eaten my whole life, it feels like.

Rottenbühle helps me out and puts me in a taxi.

To:
David Goschmann
Hotel Figaro
Prinsengracht 112
Amsterdam

Grothenburg, 12 February

Dearest David,

Thanks for last time and thanks for your letter.

No, I'm in no hurry at all, what makes you think that?
As a widow one ought to wait at least a year, I thought we
were in agreement about sticking to certain conventions.

So I also prefer that we keep it this way, David, believe
me. How things stand with the entirety of your life and with
your wife does not interest me, never has interested me.

But I love you and want you. A part of you. A couple
of days of you every month. Maybe more in due time.
Unfortunately I had no opportunity to come to Amsterdam,
you mustn't see that as me taking some sort of distance from
you. I was simply forced to make this trip to Berlin, that you
men should be so sensitive!

You write that you were prepared to get a divorce from her,
if I simply asked for it. I don't know how honest you are,
and perhaps one day I am going to request just this from you.
Perhaps my need is going to grow, as stated. But not now,
David, let us continue to enjoy each other sparingly, as we've
done these years. A wine doesn't get better because you drink
five glasses instead of two. Does it?

And sure, I am coming to Strasbourg in March, that I
promise. Whether I truly can stay all four days remains to
be seen, but I will do what I can to reschedule seminars and
lectures.

It makes me happy that you like my house, but it would really be a shame otherwise. It was so wonderful to have you there, and you know that you are always welcome if you're feeling hot to trot. Just let me know a few hours in advance so I have time to organize something to eat and aerate a good wine.

It is also gratifying that I am going to be able to keep living here; through unexpected circumstances my financial situation has cleared up, so everything looks bright at the moment. It is right as you always say, one should never give up hope.

Although I long for you a little, it must be admitted. I like making love hard and brutally with you, and then sleeping with you behind my back.

So next week, perhaps?

An evening and a morning, if you can?

With love,

Your Agnes

Friday arrives with an unexpected high sky over Munich. I take a long walk through Englischer Garten in the morning and catch myself missing the dogs. Dogs are made for parks, or possibly it's the other way around.

I don't yet know exactly *how* – and not exactly *when* – I am going to kill Henny. I don't even know with certainty that it will be today, but I think so. I have a plan – or several plans, rather, a gathering of alternative actions where, if the one does not work out, then the second or the third one will. I cannot proceed in any other way, must use this open method – at a certain stage seize the opportunity in flight – and that is not something that worries me. On the contrary, life itself has that structure, a fandango between chance and order, and someone who can't dance can't ask to live life fully.

But I can dance. I've always been able to.

On my way back to the hotel I go into a phone booth. Call Hotel Regina, explain that we have a flower delivery for Henny Delgado and ask what her room number is.

Mrs Delgado has not checked in yet, I am told. But she will be staying in room 419.

I say thank you and hang up. So simple, I think. So improperly simple.

No one suspected me of Erich's death, no one is going to

suspect me of Henny's. So it is. I step out of the phone booth and look at the clock. It is twenty minutes past eleven. I have nothing to do other than wait. Return to my room on Alter Wirt, but feel restless and go out again.

I spend a couple of hours out in the city. Wander along Tal and Kaufingerstrasse over towards Karlstor. Visit Haus der Kunst but soon get tired. I've seen it all before. Have lunch at Ehrengut. The weather held up the whole afternoon with a mild breeze from the south-west; there are ever so many people on the move, but as I sit with a cup of coffee at Johannis Cafe I also feel something else. To start with I can't get clear about what it is, but gradually I understand that it is a kind of presence.

Yes, *presence*.

Some sort of observer perhaps, it is a very strong and at the same time very vague impression; I look carefully around in the noisy premises to see where the sensation is coming from, if there is some person who is observing me in some way.

Why? I ask myself. Why would anyone observe me?

A guy who is out after a woman? Yes, that is naturally a possibility, but when I again move my gaze around I cannot find any credible candidate for such a role.

I pay and leave the cafe. Come out on Maximilianstrasse and buy cigarettes at a tobacconist. Continue over towards Theatiner Church and Hofgarten, but cannot completely shake off the feeling.

An obsession, I think. Certain fantasies have a capacity to

stick with you. By the way, wasn't there something in Englischer Garten earlier this morning?

I hail a taxi and return to the hotel.

At six o'clock I am again standing in a phone booth and calling
Hotel Regina. Ask to speak with Mrs Delgado in room number
419. The girl at the switchboard says one moment, and when
I hear Henny answer with a surprised and slightly worried
'Hello?', I hang up.

She is on the scene. I go back to Alter Wirt. Load my gun
and put it in the shoulder bag. Change into the clothes I have
selected; a light coat that I haven't used in years and long black
trousers. Put on my blonde pageboy wig and glasses. Just to
try them, of course, observe myself in the bathroom mirror
and see that I am a different woman. Place these accessories in
the bag too and set off.

Marienstrasse and Hochbrücknerstrasse. The bars are
empty. The parked cars are empty. A thin rain in the air. I turn
to the right onto Hildegardstrasse and then I am there. Put
on wig and glasses in a doorway and have time to be reflected
in the window glass before I step in through the front door.
The hotel lobby is large and pompous. Marble, dark oak and
heavy leather armchairs. Reception is at an angle to the left,
the lifts to the right. Further to the right is a bar and restaurant. I consider quickly, slip into the bar and order a gin and
tonic.

It is early in the evening and rather deserted here too. Just
a couple of gentlemen and a solitary woman in her sixties.
The woman looks freshly made-up and tragic; sitting there
waiting for someone, evidently. From inside the restaurant

conversations and laughter are heard from a large group. Americans, as far as I can judge.

I finish my drink and smoke a cigarette while I browse in *Süddeutsche Zeitung*. Consider calling now but let it be. Better to postpone it a little while.

Leave the bar and walk directly over to the lifts. The coat over my arm. Call down a lift and ride alone up to the fourth floor. Rooms 401–420.

401–410 to the left. 411–420 to the right. An ice machine. A shoe-polishing machine.

I follow the corridor to the right; it bends to the left after 415. 419 is the second room from the end, right across from the emergency exit stairs. I open the door to the stairway and go down half a floor. Stop in a position where I cannot be discovered either from above or below. Through a narrow window I can see a corner of the sky. Perfect, I think.

Straighten the wig and glasses and notice that I am trembling a little. Check that the pistol is ready to shoot, take out the mobile phone. Remind myself that I must remember to confiscate Henny's mobile phone when it is all over. So that the police don't find my number in her contact list.

I would like to call once more via the hotel's switchboard, but don't dare risk it. Perhaps my number would be stored there too. I light a fresh cigarette instead and stand on the landing and smoke it before I enter Henny's mobile number.

She does not answer, as we have agreed on. Voice mail is connected. I wait for the signal.

'Good day, George,' I say, 'this is Aunt Beatrice! I just want to say that the black hollyhocks are ordered and paid for and are coming on Tuesday. You don't need to call me, that's just an unnecessary expense!'

I turn off the phone. Put it deep in the bag and take out my gun. Return to the empty and silent corridor. Stop outside 419 and collect myself.

Knock two times.

'Yes?'

Her voice comes from very close by. I understand that she is standing right on the other side of the door. I do not dare push down the handle, she has just received the message that her husband is dead and presumably has locked it.

'Housekeeping,' I say, trying to make my voice lighter than usual. 'I'm bringing clean towels.'

Two seconds, then she opens the door.

I am inside in a moment. Henny retreats into the room. Looks frightened. I pull the door closed behind me. Hold my gun aimed steadily at her.

She sinks down on the bed.

'This is a mistake,' she says.

'No.'

'You're in the wrong room.'

'No, I'm not in the wrong room.'

It is obvious that she doesn't recognize me.

'Do you want my money? I don't have much, but you only have to . . .'

I take two steps closer to her. Aim at her head now.

'Who are you? It can't very well be . . . good Lord!'

I notice that I am smiling. It's impossible to hold back. I must really exert myself not to break out in laughter, it wells up inside me like an orgasm, almost. But suddenly I sense a movement behind me, and I am just about to turn around when someone

My head is flashing.

I wake up, sitting in a chair. Have a hard time breathing; a large bandage is taped over my mouth. I make an effort to tear it off, but at the same moment a powerful hand takes hold of my neck and I understand that the idea is that the bandage should stay where it is.

I take hold of the arm support instead. My wig is lying on the bed, my dark glasses too. Henny is sitting across from me in the room's other chair; she is holding a pistol aimed at me. It is not my gun, but it has a similar sound-dampening bulge over the barrel.

Somewhere behind me, next to the wall, a man is standing. The man who placed his hand over my neck. I sense that he too has some kind of weapon, but I don't bother to check. For my own part I only have my hands and a terrible headache. It is pulsing and pounding like black explosions in my frontal lobe.

Between Henny and me is a low table. On the table is an envelope. My name is written on it, just my first name, Agnes, underscored with double lines.

I raise my eyes and look at Henny. Her lips are bent in a sort of restrained smile. Her eyes are faintly glistening with triumph. Perhaps a little alcohol too. A good ten seconds pass before she says anything. When she starts talking it is all the clearer.

> Time shall unfold what plighted cunning hides,
> Who covers faults, at last with shame derides.

Brief pause. I do not recognize her voice. The right corner of her mouth twitches lightly.

'I don't intend to sit here and explain things to you, Agnes,' she says. 'And I can't bear to hear one more word from you. Not . . . a . . . single . . . word. Be my guest and read!'

She makes a gesture with the pistol towards the envelope. I pick it up and take out some double-folded sheets. Same stationery as usual, same familiar handwriting. The man behind me clears his throat and shifts his feet.

'Read!' Henny repeats. 'If you don't start reading I'll shoot you immediately!'

I nod, but just before I am going to fix my eyes on the paper I suddenly feel that presence again – it washes over me like a cold rain – the presence of the great fear that came over me like an omen in the village of Worms a few days ago. The presence I felt during the afternoon today.

I understand now that it was not just imagination. Understand that I should have taken it seriously and tried to expose its core.

Now I see it. Quite clearly between the lightning explosions in my head I see it.

It scarcely helps. I lower my eyes and start reading.

Dear Agnes,

How I loathe you. I did not think it was possible to harbour such hatred towards another person, as what I harbour towards you. But so it is.

This is also the reason that I staged this melodrama – instead of simply searching you out and killing you like a dog. I simply had to go so far to get to sit face to face with you and let you know the truth about yourself and why you must die.

Just as we're sitting now, Agnes.

No, don't lift your eyes from the paper, keep reading, and when you've come to the end and I see that you have understood I will shoot you.

Did you truly believe that I didn't know? Did you believe I was so naive that I didn't find out who my husband's mistress was? And did you believe that in such a situation I would put the blame on David?

You have misjudged me, Agnes. You have always misjudged and underestimated me. Why have you never been able to be happy about the good things, Agnes? Of course it has always been like that, that the setbacks of others have been more satisfying to you than your own successes. Of course it is cunning and calculation that have been your household gods. The overwrought.

Why couldn't you tolerate that your mother was together with Maertens the dentist? Why did you begrudge me Cordelia to that degree? Or Tristram Singh, do you remember him?

Or David? I don't know exactly what net you ensnared him in but I am convinced that you went to work with the greatest wiliness.

As always, Agnes.

But now, the thing is, I am not letting go of David. The girls need their father as well as their mother, and I have not only sworn fidelity to my husband, I have also sworn to myself and before my god, to see to it that our alliance holds. Until death do us part, I take that responsibility. I am a person who believes in fixed values, I think you can recall that it was that way even when we were young.

And I knew that I would be able to lure you here, Agnes, right from the beginning I knew that. My brother Benjamin – you must remember him, he is the one who is standing behind you now – was more doubtful. He has been my confidant right from the start; we love each other as a brother and sister should and he has been there for me in every moment. You never liked him, both he and I remember how mean you could be to him, even though he was so little and defenceless. He has been your shadow here in Munich – a few times earlier too – and once I have shot you later this evening he will carry your body out the back way (yes, he is big and strong nowadays) and throw it in the Isar. You are going to have substantial weights on you and there, on the muddy riverbed, the bodily part of you is going to end its days. Where your soul goes we hardly need to entertain any doubt about.

You are never going to be found, Agnes. You are going to be reported missing; I don't know what destination you indicated to the Barth family, but I am certain that you did not say either Amsterdam or Munich. Benjamin is also going to take care of your car and make sure that it disappears.

You are going to be obliterated, Agnes. Obliterated.

As you understand, I am enjoying this. Right now, while

DEAR AGNES

I watch you read your death sentence, I feel a warm, strong delight. It has cost me money to bring about this arrangement, you know that, Agnes, but I am well off and it has been worth every euro. Perhaps there is no more complete satisfaction than this – to get to punish a person with your own intelligence and your own hand who has done so much evil. Killing someone you despise and who tried to turn one's own life to ruins.

To take revenge.

You intended to kill me; I knew that you would not be able to resist the temptation, and now you are sitting here in your own trap. It all came to naught, I think you must agree that you are actually getting exactly what you deserve.

You are now approaching the end of my last letter, dear Agnes. Not much remains; you will simply follow the lines, read word for word, and when you come to the last word you will raise your eyes and I will shoot you with two or three shots in the head.

Or perhaps I will shoot you in the chest, I will grant you a little pain before you die.

Yes, look up now, and you will see that I have a silencer on my gun, similar to what you had, Agnes. Why did you maintain that your pistol would go off so loudly? Did it seem much too improbable that you would have a gun with a silencer in your possession, or could acquire one? I don't know, Agnes, but I know that your gaze is now wandering, no, don't seek eye contact with me already, there is a page left, you still don't know how much is on it, but soon you will see, and when you have come to the last word on that page then you will die. No, don't go back and try to reread, I know that everything is clear to you, completely clear . . .

So, now there are just these poor lines left, isn't it strange how one can linger with every word, as if clinging tight to every
little letter
simply to stay
alive.
That a short second should mean
so much, Agnes, but now I see
that you are there.
You must raise your eyes soon, Agnes.
Cannot keep them there on
every word.
This is the last page,
this is
the last
moment
of your life.
Raise your eyes, Agnes.
Look at me
now.

THE FLOWER FROM SAMARIA

Translated from the Swedish by Paul Norlen

Adapted into the film *Samaria*

1

It wasn't me who got the whole thing started. Who dug up the Snake Flower again. I just want that said. In no way was that my object or intent; life is so full of alarming and cruel happenings that it's bad enough to have to stand by and watch.

I know what I'm talking about. During my forty-nine years here on earth I haven't made more than four or five important decisions, but each time I've done so they've had the most unforeseen consequences. As a result I've learnt to abstain. Over the years I've increasingly understood to avoid the sorts of things that in any way can jeopardize the balance and stability in existence, my own and others'.

Don't get me wrong. Certain people can commit the most astounding stupidities and still land feet first. For my part, all that was needed to find myself with a twenty-five-year marriage and two daughters around my neck was a little wink of the eye. For example.

I live in Grothenburg. The wife and daughters do too, although we are no longer under the same roof. Hilde and Beatrice are two and a half years apart in age, but there was only five months between their weddings. Both events took place in the winter just passed and Hilde, and quite possibly the other one too, is pregnant. I still have one year left until my fiftieth birthday, yet I'm well on my way to becoming a grandfather.

My wife's name is Clara and she no longer loves me. She announced this quite recently, just four days before the summer holidays started, and that was the real starting point. Yes, in a way it was actually Clara who got the ball rolling. I wash my hands, I always do that when the opportunity offers itself.

Yes, and not without reason.

Perhaps she never loved me at all and when I winked at her that evening by the Aegean Sea in 1972, my head was full of this, that and the other, but hardly full of love.

That absolute flame has only burnt in me a single time. It was thirty years ago now, but that time I truly acted based on my passion and what I'm now going to recount is about the consequences of that.

About the consequences and about their peculiar, late-occurring interplay with my wife's announcement on that particular warm, promising evening in June of 1997. The announcement that she no longer loved me.

I lowered the newspaper and sat quietly a moment. Clara kept pottering with the tomato plants, as if she hadn't said what she'd said at all. For a moment I got the idea that it had only been an illusion, that I'd heard wrong.

'Do you want a divorce?' I asked anyway.

'I think I do,' she said without looking up. 'I'd like to have the summer to myself anyway.'

'Have you met someone else?' I asked.

'In a way,' she said.

I thought that was an unusually dubious answer, even coming from my wife. Thought for a while about who the guy could be, but soon found I didn't really care and continued on with the newspaper instead.

Less than two hours after this conversation Urban Kleerwot called. It may seem peculiar that this happened on the same evening that my quarter-century-long marriage came to an end, but as I've tried to explain: this is the way it goes – and has gone – in my life. Events are simply drawn to events, a kind of psychic magnetism that I don't really know how to relate to or explain. Consequently I keep from trying.

'Henry Maartens?'

'Yes.'

'Hi there. Urban Kleerwot here. Do you remember me?'

I thought about it and said that I remembered.

'Long time.'

'It wasn't yesterday.'

'Thirty years to be exact.'

He laughed. I didn't recognize his voice, but I recognized his laugh. It had been a force of nature during our high school years and seemed to have been refined with the years and the kilos.

I hadn't yet seen Urban of course, but if there is anything that is unable to conceal a considerable weight gain, it's a laugh.

'How are you doing?' he asked.

'Doing OK,' I answered. 'Getting a divorce, I think, but I shouldn't complain.'

'Oh, boy,' he said. 'So you've been married?'

'You hit the nail on the head. Haven't you?'

'Haven't had time.'

'I see. What do you want?'

He faked a cough before he got to the point.

'You work as a language teacher?'

'How do you know that?'

'I heard.'

'From whom?'

'Max. You'd seen each other, he said.'

I thought about it and recalled that I had run into Max Sterner at a book fair a year or so ago.

'And?'

'I need a little help. You were some kind of linguistic genius back then and it can't very well have gone away completely, right?

I didn't answer. This was starting to smell like work.

'What kind of work do you do yourself?' I asked.

'Psychotherapy,' said Urban. 'But forget about that. The thing is, I've written a book. A real winner, to be honest, although I need someone to look through it. Grammatically and such.'

I didn't doubt that at all.

'Where do you live?' I asked.

'Aarlach. But I still have a cabin outside K–. Completely isolated out by the lake. Thought about asking if we couldn't spend a couple of weeks down there this summer. I'll take care of the food and lodging. You read and make corrections. We'll talk about old times. A glass of cognac and a cigar. Fish a little. Are you in?'

I thought for two seconds.

'When?' I said.

'The sooner, the better. I can be there as of the tenth, just have to finish up some work first. What do you say?'

I looked at my calendar. It was as open as can be.

'Two weeks starting the eleventh,' I said. 'Those are the only weeks I'm off.'

'Excellent,' said Urban Kleerwot, laughing again. 'In just seven days. Well, I'll be damned, it's going to be fun. You haven't been to K– that often since we graduated?'

'Not one time.'

'What the hell are you saying? You haven't set foot there in thirty years? Why is that?'

'There are reasons,' I explained.

'You mean . . . that thing that happened?'

I didn't answer.

'Oh, well,' Urban continued after a while. 'It is what it is. Maybe we can talk about that too.'

We exchanged addresses and telephone numbers, then we hung up. I sat there a good while in the study and thought. Felt how time, those three decades – more than half of my life – seemed to shrink together into just about nothing.

What is life really? I thought. What becomes of all these days?

Then I went and made up the bed in the guest room without saying goodnight to my wife. It was several hours before I could fall asleep, and what then pursued me in the world of dreams was by no means thoughts of Clara and our soon to be separated ways, but instead what it would mean to re-establish acquaintance for the first time with K– and with the paths I wandered in my late teens. The high school years.

It felt generally disquieting and I understood that under no circumstances would I have said yes to Urban Kleerwot's proposal if it hadn't been for my wife's surprising move earlier in the evening. That she no longer wanted to be with me.

So it wasn't me who dug up the Snake Flower. Might just as well underscore that one more time.

2

When I set off early on Saturday morning – the day after school broke up for summer – my wife was not awake yet.

At least that was the impression I got, but it's possible of course that she was only pretending to sleep to avoid any sort of uncomfortable farewell scene. We had come to an agreement not to discuss the situation until August. After twenty-five years of marriage between two language teachers it's still not words that will save you. I had told her that I intended to go away, but that was all. Would presumably be back for Midsummer; she said that suited her just fine, because she herself had a trip booked for the twenty-fourth.

Were we to cross paths, it wouldn't need to be for more than a day or two.

I had packed the evening before. A soft suitcase with a few changes of clothes, a half-dozen books and an old baitcasting rod that was presumably both antiquated and useless. I thought it showed a little goodwill anyway.

Because the meeting with Urban Kleerwot was not set until Monday, and I really wanted to get away from Grothenburg as soon as possible, I had called and booked a room at Hotel Continental in K– for two nights. It was the only hotel I could recall from the sixties, and when I contacted directory enquiries it turned out that it was still there under the same name. I remembered Continental as a rather imposing fin-de-siècle building across from the railway station; I'd had dinner twice in its dining room, both times in the company of my parents and my brother, and both times with a sense of finding myself in a different kind of world. Not necessarily a better or finer world than the usual, just different. Parallel.

Whether the Continental would make the same impression on me thirty years later was of course an open question as I wended my way towards K– that beautiful June morning. We'd had a late spring in our part of the country, bird cherry and lilac were both still in bloom and the open landscape that spread out on either side of the road still had some of the delicate greenery of innocence. No saturation, no heavy sweetness, just the promise.

I was not primarily focused, however, on experiences of nature as I sat behind the wheel and cruised southward. Of course not. I thought about K–. About the Charles Church. About the Mefisto restaurant. About the river with all the bridges. About Doggers Preparatory Academy and my years of high school – which should have been three, but which had had an undesired extension thanks to the unmistakable pitfalls of that era: freedom, revolution, pop music, general immaturity and the smoky existentialist cafe the Grubby Bun.

Four years instead of three. I was fifteen when we moved to K–, I was nineteen when I left. My father took the position as acting postmaster on 1 August 1963; it wasn't the first time we came to a new place, but this time it was intended to be permanent. K– was going to be our city, my parents', mine and my brother's. Georg was six going on seven when we arrived, but was still wetting the bed. My mother thought it had something to do with all the moves. And the moves had to do with my father's career. His postal promotions.

Even if you're in the postal service you don't have to be passed around like a bundle of second-class mail, my uncle Arnt put it, adding to the criticism.

But K– would be enough, that was the thought. The postmaster function was sufficiently grand, my father strove no higher.

So it surely would have come to be – all signs pointed in that direction those optimistic years in the mid-sixties. But suddenly, and against all odds, the regular postmaster, Strunke, recovered from his alcohol-related liver disease, and in August of 1966 it was time to pack again.

That was when I refused. The year before, when I had regained my aptitude for studies, there was only one year left until graduation, and for good reasons jumping into a new third-year group in a new city felt both unreasonable and simply annoying. I think it was the first important decision of my eighteen-year-old life. It was somewhat trying, but at last my parents gave in. First my mother and three hours later my father too.

I got a rented room.

The woman's name was Kuntze and she was the widow of a butcher who'd died from a blood clot. The house behind the athletic field down on Pampas had become a little too costly, for that reason she rented out spare bedrooms.

I got a room under the eaves with a view of an old apple tree, a spruce hedge and the very top portion of the brick-red preparatory school roof. If I had the window open and was waking up, I could hear the first bell from bed and still be in school no more than four minutes later. It was kind of ideal.

In the other room lived Kellermann, an introverted optician's assistant, thirty-something and ninety-something. Kilos, that is. He had no social life, busied himself with philately and chess by mail. We shared a toilet and bathroom, but that was all.

The widow Kuntze herself had two malicious cats, a Slingbolt brand hearing aid, and a lover by the name of Finckelstroh. He usually arrived one Saturday a month on a black motorcycle, stayed half the night and was always mysteriously gone on Sunday mornings.

Otherwise I didn't bother much with any of those in my physical vicinity, be it Kuntze, Finckelstroh, Kellermann or the cats. I was in the final stage of my teens, in my last year at Doggers, and naturally had more noble interests.

Such as pop music. Such as politics and poetry and philosophical issues. From whence and where to? Hellhound on my trail.

Such as girls. It was 1966 and skirts were starting to get short. It wasn't easy to be young, pimply and peach-fuzzed, truly not easy. Desire, unbridled and unsatisfied, climbed in tempo with uncertainty and awkwardness. In my language class at Doggers the gender distribution was uneven: twenty-three girls and twelve boys. In round numbers, two ladies per man, but what did that help?

No doubt one or two of the peach-fuzzed ones had started to taste the forbidden fruit, but for the majority of us all such things were still the stuff of fantasy. True enough, in the select company with whom I usually associated – Niels Bühltoft,

Urban Kleerwot and Pieter Vogel – the conditions of art, the Communist manifesto, the situation in Cuba and deontological ethics were discussed, but about how you actually might get on with a woman, we knew nothing. Not a thing.

Perhaps it was in the nature of a small town, a small town just as prudish as its high school students. When my last term started I'd been in love with half a dozen girls from the class, I had held hands with three of them and I had kissed one. Her name was Marieke and she had a passable right hook that made me sober up at once.

That's the way it was. Woman was a mystery. Despite the spirit of the times. Despite pop music. Despite the existential questions. I can't get no satisfaction.

It was a gorgeous day, this year's first summer Saturday, and I took my time. Indulged myself in a couple of hours rest at midday by one of the lakes outside Wimlingen, and it wasn't until almost seven o'clock in the evening that I cruised in through the old, well-preserved East City Gate in K–.

I felt at once that I was lowered into the well of time.

Thirty years? I thought. Was it truly possible that thirty years had passed since the last time I saw these narrow, pastel-coloured houses along the old shopping street? Wasn't it yesterday – or last week at least – that I stood and observed the quietly purling water from the familiar bronze figures of the fountain on the cobblestone square? And, in reality, weren't those young girls who sat having ice cream on one of the benches in front of city hall a couple of my contemporary classmates?

*

A glance in the rear-view mirror made me return to the tundra of reality. The year was 1997. I was forty-nine years old; true, I'd lost the pimples, but acquired liver spots, wrinkles and bags under my eyes in return. Elephant skin on my neck. *C'est la vie*, I thought, and I drove on through the tunnel to get on the right side of the railway tracks. *Ou peut-être la mort*. There's a time and a place for everything. Young girls in the square, travel-weary middle-aged folks at the Continental.

The girl in reception was red-haired and had a ponytail. She smiled with a full set of flawless teeth, gave me the key to room number 39 and informed me that the dining room served dinner until eleven o'clock.

Because it was Saturday. If I wanted to wash the travel dust off myself first.

I understood that I reeked of sweat. Quickly said thank you without revealing my breath. Took my bag and hurried over to the lift. Ten minutes later I was standing in the shower, wondering why in the world I travelled back to this hole two days sooner than I needed to.

It was a question I would have reason to come back to.

I had dinner at the hotel – Saltimbocca alla Romana, to be exact – that first evening. Briefly considered plans for a walk through the city before night too, but two glasses of heavy wine teamed up with my accumulated fatigue and sent me straight to bed. I heard the bells in Charles Church strike quarter past eleven through my open window, but I do not recall the half hour stroke.

Evidently I had ordered breakfast in my room, because I was wakened at nine o'clock on Sunday by the redhead, who came in with a well-loaded tray and a morning paper. She showed all her teeth again in what resembled a conspiratorial smile, and for a moment I had the feeling that she had something on her mind.

I was too sleepy, however, to get any conversation started and she left me without any comments other than to wish me *bon appétit* and a pleasant day.

After breakfast and a shower I took possession of the city. K–. Wandered around the old city centre, which felt strangely unchanged since the sixties. Krantze's bookshop was still in the same location; the pharmacy, the police station, Grote Square with all the pigeons . . . everything seemed to be there, exactly where it had always been and was always going to be. The Grubby Bun, the existentialist cafe, was just a memory however; the whole block had been razed, now it was glass and concrete and postmodernism that prevailed. Boutiques and shops.

And Doggers. This Gothic colossus of knowledge. Pinnacles and towers. Steeply sloping roofs. Jackdaws and black brooding windows; I had slight palpitations.

The Pampas residential area – on the other side of the river seen from Doggers – was also fairly intact, rows upon rows of old wooden and brick houses with moss-grown lawns, fruit trees and lilac hedges. My old apple tree was blooming so opulently it seemed to be almost singing in tune with the sunshine, and I noticed how I got a lump in my throat while I stood outside on the pavement and stared up at the attic window with the red-checked curtains.

Hasn't she changed curtains in thirty years? I thought. Is she still alive, old Mrs Kuntze, can that even be possible?

I never investigated any of these questions. This mild late-spring day was nonetheless filled with all the unexpected and mysterious memory strokes of reunion, and when I returned to the Continental rather late in the afternoon, my head was so packed with impressions and recollections that I felt both dizzy and overstimulated.

What was awaiting me in reception hardly made things better. The redhead was replaced by a stick-thin youth with stubble and a nose ring; he stopped me just as I was about to step into the lift.

'Excuse me. There was a message too.'

'A message?'

He handed over an envelope with the hotel logo. I thanked him, put it in my pocket and went up to my room.

Kleerwot, I thought, removing a piece of paper folded in two. Of course he can't make it. The lout.

But that's not what it was. The message was brief and handwritten. I stared at it a good long while.

About time you came back. I'll be in touch.
Vera Kall

I sat down on the bed to counteract the vertigo. Felt a slight but noticeable taste of metal on my tongue, and wondered how in the hell a woman who had been dead for thirty years could know that I had returned to K–.

3

Of my four years at Doggers, I came to spend two in the same class as Vera Kall – the last two. The reason was my so-called victory lap in the second year; hardly an honourable victory lap, naturally, although on the other hand I had skipped a year back in primary school because I was considered precocious, so as far as age was concerned, towards the end of high school I was on a par with my classmates.

I have already touched on how my Platonic flame wandered between a handful of the girls in this congregation. Love is eternal, it's the objects that shift. That may be, but there was one object that was constant. Vera Kall. I loved her simply from the first moment, and I was hardly alone in that predicament. I think all of us desired her equally strongly. The whole male dozen. Even someone like Carl Maria Erasmus van Tooth, who otherwise was a real bookworm and only liked literary figures.

That my closest brothers-in-arms – Urban Kleerwot, Pieter Vogel and Niels Bühltoft – worshiped Vera Kall I knew with certainty; we had talked about it at the Grubby Bun on more than one occasion. That Niels had fallen was obvious, by the way, to anyone and everyone; he could not talk intelligibly if Vera was within his field of vision. When he was supposed to read or present something during class he was forced to demonstratively turn his back on her to keep from stammering. Everyone has their problems.

Pierre Borgmann and Thomas Reisin, who had a reputation for being a bit more advanced than the rest of us, had both – each one separately – tried to approach Vera in a slightly more manly, Mediterranean way. But, to everyone's great relief, they had been amiably but firmly brushed off.

Vera Kall didn't run around with boys. Especially not those kinds of boys. Vera Kall was not cut from that cloth. Could they accept that?

No, they couldn't, but they did anyway.

Yes, we probably all loved her. And maybe deep down we were grateful that she didn't give in and choose one of us. Better to be part of the admiring dozen, the yearning flock, and still have both your yearning and your lot.

Better no one than someone who wasn't me. I think we thought that way. I know of course that I did.

Urban too. Pieter and Niels.

For Vera Kall was a revelation. A goddess in female form. The words fail, but yet . . . her hair, dark and thick as the night, her half-almond eyes, her smile and irresistible half-millimetre gap between her front teeth. Her slender body and her lithe way of moving, as if gliding along through existence, indolent and effortless as a female panther. She was a symphony. Or a sonnet. Or any damn thing at all. Completely natural and completely unaware of all this perfection, who could even make a double class in Latin with senior master Uhrin pass by as if in a transfigured shimmer. That's how she was. The Snake Flower.

'Send Vera Kall into the UN General Assembly,' Niels

Bühltoft proposed on one occasion, 'and we are going to have peace on earth within half an hour. Or a world war.'

Presumably he was completely right.

Presumably senior master Uhrin was also completely right when he could not take his eyes off Vera while he contemplated the final sentence during the double period the last Friday in the month of April in 1967: *Quem di diligunt adolescens moritur.*

Whom the gods love dies young.

Unapproachability played its part, of course. Vera Kall was not someone who went out dancing. Vera Kall didn't hang out by the jukebox at the Grubby Bun existentialist cafe and smoke crinkled Lucky Strikes. Vera Kall didn't stand in front of the stage at the Grotto, rocking in time when the area's pop gurus executed their mediocre interpretations of 'Satisfaction', 'My Generation' and 'Do-Wah-Diddy-Diddy'. And when they played 'I Saw Her Standing There' she was never the one you saw standing there . . . other than in the deepest space of imagination.

And she didn't take part in the picnics or the class parties in the temporarily parent-free houses, where we tried to smoke ourselves high on dried banana peels in corncob pipes and drink ourselves intoxicated on premature, half-fermented gooseberry wine that tasted like it had already passed through one or two digestive systems. My God, what rotgut. It was Bühltoft who would always steal it from his dad's cellar.

No, Vera Kall stayed at home.

Her parents kept her at home.

The latter seemed most probable, at least it was seen that way in the inner circle. In my circle. She was an only child, her house was out in the sticks – out in the forest even – in the vicinity of Kerran and Maalby. The father, Adolphus Kall, was pastor in the congregation Aaron's Brethren; known for their strict, sometimes Old Testament rules of living. Which made them all the more unfamiliar with anything else. One of those sects simply, there were a few in K– and the surrounding area at that time; the countryside had been known for freethinking since the 1800s and that's the way it was.

That Adolphus Kall's daughter would run to dances or pop concerts or shady high school parties was naturally beyond the horizon of what was reasonable. It was what it was. Seemed to be part of the conditions, in some obscure way.

And beauty flourished and desirability grew. 'It's so annoying,' said Pieter Vogel. 'It's like showing Niagara Falls on film to someone thirsting in the desert. Like a sunrise on the radio, I'm going to castrate myself.'

Our metaphors seldom made much sense.

Not Pieter Vogel's and not anyone else's either. Possibly senior master Uhrin's.

Quem di diligunt . . .

A prophesy with a month-long fuse.

The Snake Flower.

It was actually just Pieter Vogel who gave her that name, but it had nothing to do with metaphor. The name originated from an old detective novel – *The Snake Flower from Magdala*, by Richter-Frich, I think – that he hadn't read, but came across along with ten others in the same genre for a song at Will-mott's Used Books.

The Snake Flower from Samaria, thus, because the Kall farm was named Samaria. There were plenty of farms and villages with Biblical names in the countryside around K–. Jerusalem. Cana. Capernaum. One of the district's biggest and most notorious hog farms was in Bethlehem. If it is Our Lord's intention to be everywhere present, then he seems to have been so to the highest degree in this seedy part of the country.

In this seedy time.

Now Pieter Vogel's invention was no common name for Vera Kall; we only used it now and then in the inner circle, but someone must have said it in front of some journalist, because when the newspapers started writing about it, that was exactly what they called her. The Snake Flower from Samaria.

And when you saw her beautiful, slightly mysterious face in all the pictures, you understood that it was a rather appropriate name.

But I'm getting ahead of myself.

Graduation that year was set for 29 May. Two days earlier, on Thursday, the tradition-encumbered exam party was held. By custom it took place in the Limburg dining rooms, a venerable establishment with an abundance of stucco, cornices and non-descript chandeliers – plus experience of similar events since the early thirteenth century or something.

In principle, the programme was divided into three parts.

First, a leisurely arrival in the new graduation suit or dress. Drinking of bubbly beverage in the formidable foyer with columns of black granite and five-lane staircase of polished pommerstone up to the magnificent dining hall. Witty conversation between teachers and students; this exceptional evening was the first time you stood on any sort of common footing with your mentors and tormentors, hopefully also the last.

After this slightly anxiety-filled half hour the long dinner itself commenced, where as far as possible the students were placed next to some pedagogue and had to show themselves practised in the arts of conducting table conversation, not spilling, not drinking wine to excess, honouring their father, their mother and their school, and behaving themselves in the most general terms. You did not talk about Vietnam and not about the situation in Gaza. The hell you did, God forbid.

Three courses, coffee, brandy and an endless number of brilliant speeches. 'O Jerum' and the scent of blossoming fruit trees through wide-open windows. Student songs and 'Oh See My Youth' and for the most part an inspired evening.

Third, there was a dance and bar service. The Doggers school band played, with a mixture of jazz and inoffensive pop tunes in the repertoire. The Hollies and such. Rounding off about one o'clock, deadline one hour later. The faculty were expected to start trooping off at the end of dinner, this year like every other.

This year like every other attendance was good. Almost one hundred per cent, both among the older as well as the younger set. Even moss-grown old lecturer Krüggel, who could barely stay awake during his own classes, was on the scene. Even double adjunct Bisserman, who was said to be both homosexual and alcoholic.

Even the Snake Flower.

Forty-two teachers, both male and female, if you want to be precise, one *rector magnificus* Laugermann, 196 students.

One hundred and ninety-six hopeful male students and blossoming female students on their way out into life. One of them on their way out of it.

She had arrived early in the afternoon by bicycle, as usual. In the winter you took the bus from the country, but in the summertime velocipede was the norm. Dress, shoes and accessories in a cardboard suitcase on the carrier. Shower and preparation in the customary manner with her girlfriend Claire Mietens, over in the Deijkstraa block. Then in company to Limburg's, the festivities and journey home. It had not been agreed that Vera would sleep over at Mietens, even if that would have been a simple matter.

Simple for the Mietens family, that is, not for father Adolphus. Vera Kall would sleep at home. Would bicycle home to Samaria when it was over at Limburg's. Over ten kilometres through the forests and the summer night, that was nothing to fuss about. God holds his hand and watches over his . . .

A lot was written about this in particular.

About the unreasonable and antiquated attitude of Aaron's Brethren to youth and morals. About Pastor Adolphus's stubbornness. Letting a young, beautiful girl travel alone through the forest in the middle of the night. Was that wise? Was that Christian?

What was it other than a sign, when it later turned out the way it did?

That was how it was written about in the newspapers, although no one really knew what happened. Other than possibly Our Lord, and if he did, he kept silent.

It was written about and it was investigated. Because Vera

Kall was never seen again after that night. She participated in the springtime of youth together with her 195 classmates. On 27 May 1967. Drank bubbly beverages and conversed on the steps. Sat at the table. Had her three courses, listened to the speeches, sang along with the rest, shed lustre on the party, especially over her table companion, lecturer Lunger, but in the break between dinner and dance she disappeared.

Sometime then. According to the police investigations and calculations, the Snake Flower from Samaria left the student party right after eleven o'clock. That was right before the time when the last witness – a certain Beatrice Mott – saw her out in the women's bathroom; the last of these 251 (serving personnel included) witnesses, who the police in K– (reinforced with half a dozen detectives) spent the first weeks of June 1967 in questioning.

Questioning and questioning and questioning. Once, twice and even three times.

Thus, in the minutes after eleven o'clock (presumably not all that many, because Vera Kall was a girl you noticed), she leaves Limburg's dining rooms, takes her bicycle from the bike rack under the chestnut tree out on the yard, pedals out into the summer night and disappears without a trace.

One knew this the next evening. One knew this after a month and one knew this thirty years later.

I use the word 'one'. There are reasons for that.

4

The redhead did not come with a tray on Monday morning, so I had breakfast in the dining room instead. Contrary to habit I had two cups of black coffee. I had slept restlessly during the night; presumably dreamt a bit too, but nothing that let itself be recalled. In general I seldom remember my dreams, but this morning of course it was not particularly difficult to speculate about their content.

Vera Kall, naturally. While I sat there at a window table, browsing a little indifferently in the morning papers, I tried to somehow get this straight.

About what it could conceivably mean that a woman who died thirty years ago now wanted to make contact with me, that is.

Or maybe she hadn't died? Had she been alive all this time without making herself known?

Or had the mystery of her disappearance been solved without my knowledge? Five or ten or fifteen years ago, perhaps – without my having found out about it? That was naturally not completely impossible, I had lost contact with K– completely, yet it seemed quite improbable.

I had always assumed that Vera Kall was dead. That she met her murderer that mild evening thirty years ago. How she would have acted in order to simply take off and then

485

stay away . . . well, both I and many others had wrestled with that question for a long time without finding a hint of an acceptable answer.

And why? Why would she have chosen to disappear without the slightest warning? Two days before high school graduation.

Unreasonable, as I said. Out of the question.

That was, at least, what I thought until that Monday morning in June 1997.

I left my breakfast table and made my way out to reception. It was vacant behind the polished counter, but when I rang the bell the skinny youth showed up from an inside room.

'Excuse me,' I said. 'I'm wondering a little about that message I got yesterday.'

'I see,' he answered, yawning.

'How was it delivered?'

'Huh? What do you mean?'

'Did it come by phone, or did someone drop it off?'

He hesitated a moment and observed me with sleepy eyes. 'No idea.'

'Why don't you have any idea?'

'Because I wasn't here to receive it.'

'Who was here when it was dropped off?'

'How would I know that?'

'Perhaps you could ask one of your colleagues?'

He pulled on the nose ring and tried to frown. 'Maybe. I'll have to see.'

I couldn't think of anything else to ask about. Thanked him and took the opportunity to pay my bill. Ten minutes later

I left Hotel Continental and could tell that the coffee had given me heartburn.

As agreed, I met Urban Kleerwot on the big staircase to Doggers at exactly twelve o'clock. It was Urban's idea of course, this nostalgic choice of place for the reunion.

He was a couple of minutes late, I guessed that it was on purpose. He simply wanted to see me standing there. Wanted to stroll in through the old squiggly cast-iron gates. Pretend to discover me. Let out his thundering laugh and throw his arms out in a big fraternal gesture.

It happened according to this plan of his. He almost turned me into pulp by throwing his bear paws around me and squeezing.

'My God, Henry, I'll be damned,' he snorted.

'Urb . . .' I got out. 'Let go.'

He had truly not shrunk. At 190 centimetres tall and approximately just as many kilos heavy . . . oh, well, maybe not really, but well over a hundred in any event. Despite bushy, slightly greying hair, beard and glasses, he was easy to recognize, and when he released his introductory grip and held me at arm's length he noted the same.

'To the dot. I'll be damned, Henry, you haven't aged a week.'

'Not you either, Urban. Same fresh little flower you always were.'

'I'll be damned.'

'You bet.'

We expressed an additional dozen phrases with approximately the same degree of finesse. Then he pulled out a bottle with green-glistening content from his jacket pocket. The label was missing, he screwed off the cap and tossed it over his shoulder. Handed the bottle to me with a solemn expression.

'Nectar from sixty-seven,' he explained. 'Room temperature vodka-lime. You remember, don't you? Cheers and welcome back.'

I drank. 'My God,' I said, handing over the bottle.

Urban drank. 'Oh, man, that's some bad shit,' he admitted. Searched for the cap and screwed it on again. 'But I have slightly more noble goods in the car. Thought we should just have a little memory jogger. When did you get here?'

I explained that I had been in K– since Saturday. Urban looked a bit surprised, then pounded me on the back.

'Then you've seen the old dump, huh? We don't need to waste time on sightseeing?'

I said that I'd seen what I needed to, and we decided to make our way to the cabin without further delay.

Lake Lemmeln is an oblong brown-water lake, whose southernmost end turns into the black, nameless river that runs through K– and continues out over the plain. I don't know how common it is that obvious geographic phenomena lack a name in this way, but where this waterway is concerned the circumstance is recorded all the way back to the fifteenth century. It is mentioned in a variety of writings over the years, but is never called anything other than the river, or possibly the River. The explanations are legion, but none I've come across seems more probable than any other.

In the other direction, northward, Lemmeln is surrounded by forest-clad shores, here and there broken up by scattered settlements; isolated farms, an occasional fishing cabin, but no actual villages or communities.

Urban Kleerwot's nest was a simple, extended fishing cabin right on the edge of the lake, a hundred or so metres down from the main road. It consisted of a larger room with an open fireplace and four rattan chairs around a table, two smaller bedrooms and a kitchen with running water but no electricity. Stove and refrigerator were run with butane; a simple sauna was around the corner and an outhouse a little way up in the forest. Towards the lake side it was clear-cut; an overgrown grass field that sloped down towards the water. Under tarps and a scanty tar paper roof was a flat-bottom plastic boat and some irregular woodpiles.

'*Et voilà*,' said Urban, hitting me on the back. 'Welcome to Urbanhall. I was here at Easter, but it may be a little stuffy.'

It was. We opened windows and doors wide and cleaned out mouse crap for a while. Carried in baggage and necessities. So far the day had been cloudy, but now towards afternoon the sun started to break through. When we finished with the practicalities – got the fridge going, put the beer in the water barrel, lifted the boat into the lake and found the oars – we took a dip from the rickety dock. Urban preferred floating on his back near the dock with a skinny cigar in his mouth and a beer in his hand, I myself swam a good way out in the dark water. The cool water and the strong silence, broken only by the calls of scattered birds and someone chopping wood far away, felt undeniably invigorating. Rather soon I had a sensation that time – these years and decades that had elapsed – had a different meaning in this stillness. A kind of new dimension; seeing Urban Kleerwot again after so many years had actually not been a particularly strong experience, apart from this. It could easily have been the case that we had been away from each other just a couple of weeks, it seemed to me, and I suddenly felt quite tangibly what this business with the relativity and varying density of time can actually mean.

Seconds, days, years? I thought again as I slowly circled around in the water and observed the surrounding forest. In the rear-view mirror of life the one is no larger than the other. Perhaps not in the telescope of the future either.

Then I started to swim back, because I was hungry.

During the entire day Urban had not said a word about his book – the reason that we were meeting in this way – but after dinner (a splendid veal ragout that he prepared with pickled onions and cucumbers and all on his own, despite my serious attempts to get involved and help out) it came out. With a solemn expression he took a thick bundle of papers from a black, worn briefcase, and explained that now it was high time that I made myself a little useful.

I smiled and took the manuscript. The sheets were not numbered, but the whole thing seemed to amount to 250–300 pages, as far as I could see. I looked at the title and browsed a little; to my surprise I realized that it was a mystery. I don't know what I'd actually expected, hadn't thought all that much about it, but in any event, that Urban Kleerwot would have written a crime novel came as a surprise.

It was called *The Fly and Eternity*, and it did not take long before I had Vera Kall coming back. In some semi-conscious way I had managed to keep her at a distance the whole afternoon, but now she was back with unreduced force. I consulted with myself for a few seconds.

'Vera Kall,' I then said in as casual a tone as I was able while I gestured towards the manuscript. 'Speaking of mysteries, that is . . . there was never any clarity in what happened to her, was there?'

Urban Kleerwot did not answer immediately. Just sat and twirled the cognac glass in his hand and observed me over the edge of his steel-rimmed glasses. Suddenly I felt the sweat breaking out on my palms.

'You know,' he said. 'I've always had a feeling that you knew more about that story than the rest of us . . . No, there was never any damned clarity, no.'

I swallowed. Gulped down the cognac and tried to quickly consider how much I could rely on Urban. And if I really had the desire to open the lid on something that had been closed up so long.

If it hadn't already been opened, that is? The envelope with that brief message was in the pocket of my jacket, which was hanging on a hook inside the door. Did it matter if I let my host read it? I wondered. What would he think about that?

Urban cleared his throat. 'If it's that way . . . that you know something about it, that is, you can go ahead and tell me. It was prescribed five years ago. If you were the one who killed her, you'll go free in any case.'

He laughed out loud and the wicker chair complained. That decided things.

5

The suit was a prison.

No doubt it was stitched according to all the rules of the art; my mother came for a visit one week in March and dragged me to Suurna the tailor, who measured and gauged and poked me in the crotch. I retrieved the result the day before the student dinner at Limburg's. Positioned myself in front of the mirror and gasped out loud at all the finery: white shirt with tie, black crepe nylon socks, shoes with edges like Polish tin cans. And the hellish suit. A waistcoat!

A prison, as stated. From outside it was possibly acceptable, from inside it felt as alive as a casket. False. Tame monkey in borrowed plumes. Miserable.

The next evening, when Niels and Pieter and Urban were waiting for me a couple of blocks from Limburg's, they didn't look much happier, but that was meagre consolation. 'Christ,' said Niels. 'My whole body is itching, do you all have starched undies too?'

'Sure,' Pieter said in an English accent with a gloomy sigh. 'Every inch.'

Pieter was already an Anglophile at that time.

★

The Limburg foyer was a new trial. I ended up for almost twenty minutes with the wife of *rector magnificus* Laugermann, chemistry lecturer Hörndli and the twin Siewertz sisters, who were both known for being tongue-tied, but were good at laughing in a way that was heard. I spilled a little bubbly on one of them, but Hörndli expertly explained that it would presumably evaporate and in any event there were two of them, so people could at least stare at the one who was spotless.

'Ha ha ha ha,' Ada Siewertz whinnied.

'Hee hee hee hee,' Beda filled in.

'What do you think about the theatre's operetta programme this year?' the rector's wife asked.

At the table it turned out that I had drawn yet another blank. To my left I had old Miss Glock, lecturer in mathematics. I never had her as a teacher; the only thing I knew about her was that she was single and had tried to commit suicide during Christmas break. To my right side was a Doric column that was just about as talkative and across from me sat a shy and nervous boy from one of the biology classes. His name was Paul and he had eczema. Both on his neck and as a special interest.

By force of age and maturity it was Miss Glock who took the first, and only, initiative in conversation. It happened after about ten minutes. 'So, what are you going to do this summer?' she asked, glaring at Paul, whom she had either had in some class and recognized or perceived as a kindred spirit.

'Huh?' said Paul.

'What are you going to do this summer?'

'I don't know,' said Paul, looking down at the table.

Then nothing more was said. As long as the food lasted I

could keep my gaze on it. Neither Paul nor Miss Glock drank wine, so I had to be content with toasting with the column. Beside Paul sat Marieke van der Begel – the one that I kissed and got a slap from – but because of a substantial flower arrangement I could not even make eye contact with her. Maybe that was just as well.

When dinner finally ended after two and a half hours, I had long since decided to go home. True, the remainder of the evening could hardly be worse, but I was done, to put it simply. Mentally and physically; enclosed in a horrendous Dacron casket (plus 20 per cent pure wool) in a depressing corner among suicides and eczema researchers . . . You student bold, Spring of life . . . kiss my arse, I thought.

The evening was warm and redolent as I walked into the yard. So as not to be too hasty, I decided on a cigarette and a walk around the block first, and it was when I had made it halfway around this block that I ran into her.

First her bike, then Vera Kall herself.

The black-painted lady's bicycle was parked a bit carelessly on the pavement, leaning against a grey pad-mounted trans-former. The small suitcase on the carrier. Vera first became visible as a white speck inside the overgrown garden on the Gillberg lot. The Gillberg house had burnt down sometime right after the war, and ever since then it had been overgrown. An excellent refuge in general: when you wanted to sneak a smoke. Or have a gulp of lukewarm vodka-lime out of the way. Or just pee.

It was presumably the latter Vera had been engaged in, but I didn't ask.

'Hi,' I simply said.

'Henry? Hi, Henry,' she said, smoothing out her dress. 'How are ya doing?'

'How are you?' I countered, and at the same moment I understood what was going on with her.

She was drunk.

Vera Kall, the Snake Flower from Samaria, the consolation of our German classes and the Valkyrie of our wet dreams, had had a little too much of a good thing and now she was standing there staggering on her heels. Not stiletto, to be sure, but still. Good Lord, I thought. This can't be true.

'I feel so funny.' She giggled and supported herself against the bicycle. Pushed back the thick, dark hair and looked at me with her green eyes.

'Where . . . where are you going?' I asked, feeling the suit tighten up again.

She turned serious. 'Home,' she said. 'I have to go home. It's eleven . . . although . . .'

'Although what?' I said.

'I don't feel so well . . . or I'm fine, but I feel so strange.'

'Did you have a nice time in there?' I signed towards Limburg's.

She lit up again. 'Very nice. We talked and laughed and sang . . . I'm not accustomed . . . didn't you have a nice time?'

'Not too bad,' I admitted. 'Ended up a little awkward.'

She nodded vaguely and took a couple of exaggerated deep breaths.

'I have to go now.'

She was making no effort, however, to get on the bicycle. Just kept looking at me. I suddenly felt the blood rush up in my face.

'Uh . . . you don't want to go back?'

'No.' She shook her head energetically. 'No, I can't . . . it feels so strange.'

Suddenly voices were approaching. I quickly consulted with myself. Then I made the decision. 'Come,' I said. Took hold of the handlebars of the bike with one hand, put the other on Vera's shoulder. When I felt her bare skin the world turned black before my eyes for a brief moment, but I regained control. 'Come, I'll walk with you a bit.'

She did as I asked without protest and let my hand stay there. Before the merry gang managed to catch sight of us, I had guided us into Günders steeg, a narrow, dark alley smelling of jasmine. I have to say something, I thought. Have to think of something. Talk, talk, talk.

'Why do you have to go home?' I finally managed to squeeze out. I knew the answer, of course, but it was the only thing I could come up with to ask after my hours at the mute corner of the dining table.

'Daddy,' she said simply, and sounded so mournful that I thought that now the angels are crying.

'So that's how it is,' I said.

Then the Snake Flower hiccoughed.

Then she started crying. I pressed her a little closer to me and it went black before my eyes again.

'What's going on with me?' she said, sniffling a little. 'I don't understand what's going on with me.'

Two hundred thousand thoughts went through my head. None of them stayed.

'I know what's going on with you,' I said. 'You've had a little too much wine. I think it's best if you wait a while before going home.'

She stopped and looked at me.

Her glistening green eyes were brimming with tears and I understood that this was the most beautiful thing the earth had ever managed to produce. Those eyes in this moment. Thanks, I thought. Thanks that I get to experience this moment.

'Do you mean . . .' she said. 'Do you mean I'm drunk?'

'A little,' I said. 'Just a little, but I don't think it would be a good idea to go home right now.'

'Do I smell?'

She got on tiptoe, opened her mouth and breathed carefully over my face.

I don't know if there really was wine on her breath. I just know that I kissed her.

When we went up to my room it was quarter to twelve. We hadn't said much the past ten minutes. After the kiss we just went there. Close to each other in the summer night, and several times I caught myself wondering if it really was just us walking there. If it was me and her. Henry Maartens and Vera Kall.

And if those were the sort of thoughts all lovers were struck by. If that was how it felt and if it truly was for real.

Would the earth continue its orbit tomorrow? Would the sun come up? It was all the same to me. It was all the same to us. I loved her. She loved me.

I took off my jacket and tossed it onto my red rented-room armchair.

'I think we should lie down and rest, Vera,' I said. 'For a while anyway.'

I don't know if I had expected it, but she didn't protest.

'Yes,' she simply said. 'Let's do that. A while.'

Then she slipped out of her dress. Turned her back to me while she undid her bra strap, took off her panties and crawled into bed.

I tore off my clothes hurriedly. Got a strong and irrepressible erection that I did my best to conceal, but Vera just smiled at me. I didn't see it, but I felt it. Her smile in the thin summer darkness.

'Come here,' she said.

And I suddenly knew that making love was no more difficult than eating an apple.

A warm, fully ripe Gravenstein apple.

When I woke up she was gone. It was twenty minutes past four. She had left a note on the desk.

I'm leaving now. Don't know how it's going to turn out, but know that I love you.

Vera

I read the words a hundred times. The blackbirds were singing out in the garden. I read a hundred times more. Then I fell back asleep.

6

Urban Kleerwot sat motionless for a long time after I stopped
talking.

'That's the damnedest thing,' he said. 'I hardly believe my
ears. Sure, I've had a feeling all these years that there was
something, but that . . . but that . . .'

He couldn't finish the sentence. Stuffed a new skinny cigar
in his mouth instead and poured more beer in our glasses. I
didn't say anything. Felt exhausted like after a case of gastritis;
as if I wouldn't be able to squeeze out one more word after
getting this out of me . . . this burden that had finally been
let loose after thirty years. Yes, it was like giving birth, I think.
You get a little tired. Urban took a gulp and lit the cigar.

'The message?' he said. 'The note from the hotel. Where
is it?'

I stood up and retrieved the envelope from my jacket
pocket. Handed it over to him. He read the brief text a few
times with a frown. Leant back in the chair and looked at
me.

'That's the damnedest thing,' he repeated. 'But why . . .
why the hell didn't you say anything? Why didn't you come
forward?'

I sighed. 'Let's deal with that tomorrow,' I said. 'Can't take
any more right now.'

He looked a little disappointed, then he put on an understanding expression and nodded paternally. 'All right. But what does the message mean? It says Vera Kall. My God, you don't think that she . . . ? No, I don't understand a thing!'

I took a deep gulp of beer so that the bitterness brought tears to my eyes. Blinked them away and looked out over the dark, absolutely mirror-like water of the lake.

'Me neither,' I said. 'You were talking about putting out nets?'

I rowed, Urban sat on the thwart and let out the net with expert, careful hands. I shouldn't get my hopes up, he explained, but there was usually a perch or two and one or two bream.

We didn't say much as we slowly glided across the black water. It was a little past midnight and the stillness was complete; it felt as if we were sitting in a painting and I started wondering again about that business of the actual nature of time. How poorly our experience of it really fits with our way of measuring it.

How poorly our feelings fit with our thoughts.

Urban respected my wish to save the discussion of the Snake Flower until the next day, but I could see that it wasn't easy for him. He smoked intensely and muttered now and then when the mesh got caught; a couple of times I caught him sitting and observing me with a deep frown and narrowed eyes. As if he suddenly no longer knew what to make of me.

As if this thing with me and Vera Kall was something basically incomprehensible, something he couldn't imagine.

Or else he just sat there and thought about whether it

would be possible to write a crime novel about it. When we were done casting nets and came on shore, we did a hasty evening toilet, wished each other good night and went to bed. I took *The Fly and Eternity* with me as reading matter, but only made it a few pages before sleep was hanging in my eyelids.

They weren't bad pages, however. On the contrary: the story started in a little village out by the sea, unclear where; two little girls are digging in the sand and gradually find a dead body. The language was simple and pared back, I don't know what I had expected, but that my efforts as copyeditor would not need to be all that burdensome seemed apparent in any event. Always something, I thought, and turned off the lamp.

'Well, what do you intend to do?' Urban said as we settled down at the breakfast table next to the south wall the next morning.

'Do?' I said. 'What do you mean?'

'Come on,' said Urban. 'You don't intend to just sit here and stare after all this? For Christ's sake, we're sitting on the key to a crime mystery that baffled the police for three decades!'

I took a slurp of yogurt with honey and thought.

Partly about his subtle gliding from *you* to *we*. Partly about how wise it had actually been to initiate him in my secret. The mystery writer in his schizophrenic soul seemed to have taken command completely this warm, cloud-free morning.

'Henry, damn it, answer me!' he insisted. 'If you've said one thing you have to say another. Why have you kept quiet all these years? I promised to wait until today to ask, and now it's today. Why didn't you tell the police that she'd been at your place that last night? Good Lord, you made love with the Snake Flower the same night she disappeared, that changes everything—'

'It doesn't change a thing,' I interrupted.

'What do you mean?'

'Just what I'm saying. It doesn't change a thing. Everyone knows what the Snake Flower was doing up to eleven o'clock on 27 May 1967. What time she got to the party, who she sat next to, what she talked about and when she left. I happen to know about what she was doing three, four hours more. What does that matter?'

Urban thought a moment.

'Do you think she bicycled home when she left you?'

'What else would she have done?'

He shrugged. 'And why did you keep silent?'

'Why shouldn't I keep silent?'

I said that in a light tone.

In reality I still didn't know why I chose that track. Had never been clear about that; actually it probably hadn't been a considered decision. When the first shocking news came that Vera seemed to have disappeared, I hadn't said anything about our night together, and then in some way it became more and more impossible the longer it went.

I simply kept it to myself. No one knew about it, no one had seen us together; it was of course a game of coincidences, but that's how it was.

That was how it remained.

In retrospect, of course, I tried to justify my actions; it wasn't particularly difficult. For whatever happened to Vera that night after she left me, I had no part in it. This was the crux of it. I had no guilt. My own frustration and despair, when I started to realize that she wasn't coming back, was punishment enough. There was no reason to start making myself a suspect as the cherry on top of everything. No reason at all.

A hopeless dream had come true in fairy-tale form for a few hours – only to change key and be transformed into a hopeless nightmare for the rest of my life. That was how it came to appear. How it felt.

To fly and to land.

And her parents? What reason was there to add a stone to their burden by letting them know that the last thing Vera did was get drunk and go to bed with a boy . . . even if I never harboured any sympathy for Aaron's Brethren and their teachings, it was hard to see what good that would do.

'All right,' said Urban after sitting and chewing the threads of thought and a bite of sausage a while. 'I guess you had your reasons. But even so . . . sure as hell this puts the whole story in a new light.'

'Hardly,' I said. 'Some lunatic killed Vera that night. The only thing my effort changes is that it presumably happened a few hours later than was thought. Let's talk about something else.'

'You're forgetting one thing,' said Urban.

'What's that?'

'The message at the hotel. Have you already had sunstroke?'

I sighed.

'A joke,' I said.

'Joke?' Urban snorted. 'That's the dumbest thing I've ever heard. Have you told anyone else about your and Vera's night?'

I reluctantly shook my head.

'You see,' said Urban. 'Who in that case would write such a message?'

I didn't answer. We kept eating in silence a few minutes.

'If deep down you didn't want us to talk about this, you never should have told me,' Urban observed with a therapeutic sneer.

'Fucking two-bit psychologist,' I said. 'Just go examine your navel or something, I'll take care of the dishes.'

The good weather held up. After the dishes were done I devoted a couple of hours to sitting in a reclining chair in the sun and reading Urban's book.

It held up too, I thought. Slowly and deliberately he unravelled an old, dreadful story with incestuous undertones. He had truly succeeded in exploiting the double movement of time – forwards and backwards – that is so characteristic of a good crime novel, and the story was exciting. Here and there I made notations with a pencil when I thought a linguistic correction was justified, but overall I had few objections. Not to the plot and not to his way of presenting it.

Urban, for his part, sat in another reclining chair and worked with a number of files he had with him; we had both coffee and beer within reach, but by one o'clock it was too hot to sit in the sun. My host moved into the shade under a horse chestnut, I myself took a dip in the lake and had another swim.

When I came back, Urban was sitting on the dock with a beer in one hand, a cigar in the other and his feet in the water.

'I've been thinking about something,' he said. 'Would it actually be so strange if she was alive? If she simply took the chance and ran away that night . . . it could have been one of those occasions in life when a door is suddenly opened. She got an opportunity to leave through it and start a new life . . . and she did. Can't very well have been all that great to live out there among all those fanatics . . .'

'I don't know,' I said. 'I've thought about it for thirty years . . . hoped for that for thirty years, maybe, but if I'm going to be honest, I don't believe it.'

'Why is that?' Urban asked, taking a puff.

I got up on the dock. 'Where would she have gone?' I said. 'If it had been London or Paris or New York, maybe, but a farm girl from Samaria outside K– . . . no, it's not so easy to just bicycle into a new life.'

'The bicycle?' said Urban. 'Her bike was never found, right?'

'No,' I said. 'Not as far as I know.'

Urban smoked, drank and thought.

'So the murderer would have buried both her and the bike, huh?'

I did not reply. Took the beer bottle from him. 'Oh, well,' he said. 'The last word is probably not said. We'll have to wait and see. It's good to be a bit prepared, in any event.'

'What the hell do you mean by that?' I asked.

I got no answer from Urban, but a few hours later in the afternoon there was grist for his mill. Plenty of grist. I had taken a walk south along the edge of the lake, while Mr Mystery Author devoted himself to the six perch that he had taken out of the net in the morning and which would be our dinner.

When I returned he was standing out on the lawn and welcomed me with his beard parted in a crooked smile.

'The mystery deepens,' he said.

'Fat man speaks with forked tongue,' I said.

'She's coming on Saturday. Vera Kall.'

'What the hell . . . ?'

It turned white inside my head and I sank down on the reclining chair. Why white? I thought in confusion. Why not black, like usual? Urban observed me with interest, then he waved a mobile phone; one of the very latest models, evidently, not much bigger than a pack of cigarettes.

'She phoned,' he explained. 'On this. Vera Kall. She's coming here on Saturday and wants to speak with you.'

'That's impossible,' I spit out.

'Nothing is impossible,' said Urban Kleerwot, stuffing a new cigar in his trap. 'Would you like a beer?'

7

We sat outside and carried on quite a long discussion that second evening. The air was warm, the mosquitoes buzzed, of course, but a couple of smoking kerosene lamps kept them at a distance.

And then Urban's cigars. Pfitzerbooms, the sweeter sort; he had changed from Luugers fifteen years ago and never regretted it, he maintained.

We talked both about old recollections from the high school years and about Vera Kall. In some way I had dropped my guard after the news that she intended to come here and see me; it was simply no longer possible to defend myself against Urban's attacks.

Perhaps I had no great desire to, either. In certain respects, it felt almost nice that there were two of us in this, despite what I had previously muttered about amateur psychology and the like. If the Snake Flower truly was alive and wanted to talk with me, I presumably needed all the support I could get. Even from someone like Urban Kleerwot.

If it was good or bad that he started to fall back into his professional therapist role, I had a hard time deciding. In any case, now and then while we sat there and argued I had the feeling that he viewed me much more as a client than as an old friend from youth.

Although perhaps it was just imagination, and actually I didn't care about that. To the degree it was necessary to make decisions before Saturday I was rather grateful to be able to leave it in Urban's hands. At least it felt like that this evening, and I soon understood that if you'd let the camel's nose under the tent, then that was it. Despite his profession, Urban Kleerwot was not much for discretion and tactical retreats.

The questions were given, in any event. Especially mine about the telephone call: How did she sound? What did she say? Did you recognize her voice? How the dickens could she know that I was right here?

Urban explained in an orderly fashion.

Yes, she had sounded calm and collected on the phone. Introduced herself as Vera Kall, simply, and asked for me. Urban had said that it had been a long time and that unfortunately I was on a walk along the lake shore at the moment . . .

Then she had hesitated a moment, evidently. Answered that it didn't matter and explained that she intended to come and visit on the following Saturday to have a conversation with me.

At lunchtime, if that was acceptable.

Of course it was, Urban had assured her. She thanked him and then hung up.

No, he hadn't recognized her voice, and didn't have a chance to ask how the hell it happened that she was alive and knew where she could find me besides. That's how it was with that.

'And you didn't try to find out anything else?' I asked, a little irritated.

'Of course,' said Urban, blowing smoke in my face. 'I asked a number of intelligent questions, but she was no longer on the line. As I said.'

'Why does she want to talk with me?'

'She didn't say.'

'Do you think it was her?'

'How the hell should I know that?'

'Intuition, for example.'

'I forgot to turn it on.'

'You damned idler.'

'I'm on holiday. Cheers.'

So, gradually, when we had just decided to forget about the net-laying this evening, we started to direct focus towards a particular point: namely how she – Vera Kall or her representative – could be keeping track of me like this. Could know where I was staying and how she could get hold of me. Both at the Continental and out at Urbanhall. Here at least it was possible to speculate a bit, Urban thought.

For regardless (he maintained) of whether Vera Kall was alive, or if this was merely someone passing herself off as her, then it was clear as day that it all must have to do with my showing up in K– again. My return to the scene of the crime, so to speak. It could not just be a time-related coincidence that someone – Vera or Miss X – had waited for thirty years and then happened to decide to strike right now. Impossible. Out of the question. It was my journey here that started the stone rolling, lit the beacon. As sure as . . . amen in church.

He glared at me to convince me that I ought to agree. I nodded a little vaguely.

'And who knew that you were coming here?'

I thought about it. 'My wife . . . no, actually,' it occurred to me. 'I never talked about my plans. Hmm, no one . . . nobody, in other words. Other than you and me, that is.'

'Ha!' said Urban triumphantly. 'Same here! I haven't spoken with a soul about you . . . I've probably mentioned that I was going to the cabin, but the name Henry Maartens never crossed my lips.'

'Thanks,' I said for lack of anything else.

'So . . .' Urban Kleerwot continued, digging in his beard, 'so someone happened to catch sight of you. The Snake Flower or someone else.'

'The Snake Flower or someone else . . .' I repeated. 'Damn it, Urban, it's not possible that she's alive, you have to get that out of your head.'

He snorted. 'Listen, you take care of your head, I'll take care of mine! Now, what conclusions do you draw?'

I pondered a moment. 'None at all,' I said.

'Weak,' said Urban. 'But hardly surprising. How old are you?'

'Forty-nine. What does my age matter?'

'How old were you when you moved from K–?'

'Nineteen. Get to the point.'

'I'm sorry if this wounds your vanity, but how great a chance do you think there is that someone would recognize your student mug after three decades? Hmm.'

He took a deep puff on the cigar and leant back. Looked as if he'd just made the decisive thrust in the prosecutor's crown witness in his next mystery.

'All right,' I said. 'I understand. The hotel.'

'Exactly,' said Urban. 'You've left your name in just one place. Hotel Continental. There we have the crux of the matter.'

And how the hell does she know we're sitting out here in the woods then? I thought, but didn't say anything.

Then I suddenly felt something flash inside my head, but it passed much too quickly for me to be able to perceive its content. One of those passes from the subconscious that perhaps I could have managed to catch twenty years ago, but which now just fell down into the indolent marsh of middle age.

To speak metaphorically.

'What are you thinking about?' said Urban. 'You look cross-eyed.'

'Nothing,' I said. 'Nothing you would understand.'

That night I dreamt about how I woke up.

Woke up that morning and sensed the aroma of Vera's body in my bed.

The taste of her tongue in my mouth. The feeling of her warm skin, of her hands, her breasts, her womb. It was twenty past four, the blackbirds were singing and she was gone. An absence that pounded in every cubic millimetre of my pitiful rented room. My love nest. Our love nest. I got up, read her message, crawled back down into bed. Lay there and held my inexplicable, fragile warm happiness; recalled all we'd done during those inexplicable hours. Everything we'd said, everything we touched. That she loved me.

Then dreamt about how I woke up the next time late in the

morning. How I went out in the summer, how the day passed by in a sun-entangled haze. How late in the afternoon I met my parents and my brother at the railway station; they came because of the graduation reception the next day, put up by the Reims family, where we also had dinner. I left them about eight o'clock, here the dream starts to fall, here everything is drawn slowly downwards in a relentless surging spiral, a maelstrom; twilight in the air, a cooler wind; I take the road past the Grubby Bun, there's where I hear about it. The first rumour; Vincent Bauer and Clemens de Broot are sitting and smoking out on the steps, I stop and bum a couple of puffs and hear that Vera Kall is missing.

Went up in smoke. Vera Kall, of all people.

She's gone; no one knows where she is, it's Ellen Kaarmann who knows about it, her father is a police officer.

At first I have some kind of short circuit. Vincent Bauer and Clemens de Broot shrink up and disappear in a whirling narrow tunnel. The same maelstrom, the same vortex, both in the dream and in the model for the dream. Their voices are distorted to an incomprehensible chatter. I smoke and smoke and hold onto the railing so as not to fall. The world totters and me along with it. The nausea comes in waves; I don't fight it, little by little it ebbs out. 'What the hell is going on with you?' says Clemens.

I go into the cafe and get the story fleshed out. Yes, Vera Kall left Limburg's sometime around eleven, Fritz Neller and Elizabeth Muijskens talked with her just a few minutes before; Fritz is playing pinball right now. There is some indication that she may have been a little tipsy, but who wasn't? Hee-hee. Must have taken off homeward in any event, no one saw her the rest of the evening. Her bicycle is gone from the rack. Papa

Adolphus reported to the police at eleven thirty in the morning. Before that all her classmates had been called, asking about her.

All the female classmates.

No one knows a thing. It's a confounded mystery. What should one believe? What the hell happened? What happened to her? Vera Kall, of all people.

What do I think?

I don't think anything. I smoke two cigarettes in rapid succession; glare down at the pinball machine and try to keep from screaming.

I was still sitting in the Grubby Bun of my dream when Urban woke me up.

'You screamed,' he said.

'The hell I did,' I said.

He observed me with a professional frown.

'Must have heard wrong then. Breakfast is ready. Then we have a few things to accomplish.'

I took two deep breaths and woke up for real. Saw that it was ten o'clock in the morning. I don't usually sleep that long. Cleared my throat and tried to raise the curtain again.

'Accomplish? What do you mean accomplish?'

'I have a plan,' said Urban Kleerwot. 'We can't sit here with our arms crossed. Can we? You really did scream.'

I sat up. Pulled back the curtain and noted that the sun was shining this day too. Summer went on; thirty years had passed, they didn't seem to weigh anything.

'Do you want to know?' said Urban.

I shook my head. It didn't help, he initiated me anyway.

'First a good, nutritious breakfast. Then an offensive against Hotel Continental. The more straightforward, the simpler. What do you say?'

'I'll take a swim and think about it,' I promised.

8

I stayed in the car – Urban's old, splotchy green Audi – while Urban visited the Continental. As I was hanging my elbow out the rolled-down side window, I caught sight of my face in the misdirected side mirror. Discovered that I looked ravaged. Almost hunted. Circles under my eyes, two days' stubble. Fish eyes. My temples were pounding too, as usual the morning after; I got out of the car and bought a bottle of mineral water in the kiosk across from the hotel. Best to take care of my water balance at least, I thought.

Urban came back after just a few minutes.

'Nada,' he said, sinking down in the driver's seat. 'No progress.'

'How did you proceed?' I asked.

He shrugged. 'Inquired at reception, of course.'

'Who was there?'

'Callow youth with nose ring. I said that I was looking for a certain Vera Kall. He didn't react. I explained that I thought she was employed at the hotel, he explained that she wasn't. He knows everyone who works there . . . in all functions, he maintained, wonder if they have a couple of whores too? There's no Vera Kall, anyway.'

'Didn't he know about the story?'

Urban shook his head and lit a Pfitzerboom. 'Apparently not. I never asked.'

'And you didn't speak with anyone else?'

'Didn't see anyone.'

I finished the bottle of mineral water. 'I see,' I said. 'So what do we do now?'

He spat out a few tobacco flakes and started the car. 'Plan B. We follow her footsteps . . . or bicycle tracks. Get the map out of the glove compartment.'

It was not particularly hard to find the way out to Samaria. First, just under ten kilometres along a reasonably wide asphalt road through the open landscape. Then, at the junction in the village of Kerran, a couple of kilometres on a winding gravel road through the forest. After a while we came up to a yellow, flaking sign with the name *Samaria* on it, and stopped for a brief discussion.

The new side road had a strip of grass in the middle and seemed barely navigable by car; no houses were visible, just warm, aromatic coniferous forest and an abundance of lupins, Queen Anne's lace and chamomile by the roadside. Two mail-boxes were hanging on a post, one with the name Clausen on it, printed in fresh yellow letters. We drew the conclusion that there was still life in Samaria.

Urban got out of the car, stepped across the ditch and peed against the trunk of a pine.

'Let's turn around,' I said when he was done. 'What good will this do?'

'Reconstruction,' said Urban.

'You're delirious,' I said. 'We're driving on Vera's bicycle route thirty years later, and you call that reconstruction? Let's drive home and fish instead. Plan C.'

'In due course,' said Urban. 'We'll just turn up and take a look since we're here anyway. We'll go with the journalist shtick.'

'Journalist?'

'Exactly. I'm in the process of writing a series of articles about unsolved crimes. We're out looking for a little atmosphere. You're my photographer.'

'I don't have a camera.'

'There's one in the bag on the back seat.'

I reached across the back support and dug in the worn shoulder-strap bag. Brought out a little red automatic camera.

'This one? Do you think a professional photographer goes around with one of these little toy cans?'

Urban threw out his hands. 'You get to be my chauffeur, if you prefer. Now let's go.'

Samaria consisted of a yellow, newly renovated farmhouse and two run-down, grey annexes. Apparently it was an old homestead; numerous acres of cultivated ground were cleared around it in two and a half directions. To the north and northwest the forest continued untouched. It was just as apparent that the ground had been fallow for quite some time; brush of aspen and birch grew man-high out on the fields and on the farmyard were two fairly new cars, evidence that it wasn't the surrounding earth that gave a livelihood for today's inhabitants. Urban drove up to the farmyard and parked alongside the larger of the cars, a shiny red Volvo. We got out. Two children, a boy and a girl of about eight and ten, came to meet us with furtive expressions.

'God's peace,' Urban greeted them. 'Is there a mama or papa at home?'

There was both. A man and a woman in their thirties had soon been lured down to the white garden furniture that stood in a shady corner of the lawn. Urban praised in turn the house, the grass, the flowerbeds, the jasmine bushes, the children, the Volvo, the discreet location and Mrs Clausen's batik-print T-shirt. I sat silently and tried to pull in the beard stubble.

When Urban got to the point, the woman went in and put on coffee.

'Of course we know about it,' the man said, lighting a cigarette. 'We're not from this area, but the estate agent told the whole story when we bought the house. Three years since we moved in.'

'You bought from the Kall family.'

'Mrs Kall,' Clausen corrected him. 'She was almost eighty and had lived here alone since her husband died. Ten years, if I remember right. She didn't have the energy any more, moved directly to some kind of nursing home . . . died just this April, by the way, we saw the obituary in the newspaper.'

'Did you speak with Mrs Kall?'

'A little,' said Clausen. 'She was still living here when we came out and looked the first time. Had a hard time moving around, it's not easy for old people to live like this.'

'She didn't say anything about her daughter?'

He shook his head. 'No, why would she have? It was the agent who informed us, as I said. Terrible story, right before graduation and everything . . . it's supposed to feel even worse if you don't really know, I've heard. Harder with uncertainty than with the grief, they say. Although she was quite certainly murdered, at least Jessmar, the agent, maintained that . . .'

Urban nodded. Kicked me on the shin under the table, I understood that it was time to photograph a bit.

I did my duty. Took a few pictures of the house from various angles. Wondered a bit vaguely about which could have been Vera's room and soon had a lump in my throat. Then went back a little way along the road and tried to capture an overall impression. The boy and the girl followed me at a safe distance and at last I had to snap a few times at them too.

Then we had coffee and talked about the advantages of living out in the woods. Both Mr and Mrs Clausen seemed to have a rather great need of being reminded of this. Both by themselves and by others.

After half an hour Urban had eaten up all the cookies and we took our leave. He promised to send both text and pictures, noted down name and address and patted the children on the head.

'Successful operation,' I noted as we took off. 'It's hard not to be impressed, Holmes.'

'Bah,' said Urban. 'You never know. This was the road she cycled on anyway.' He signed meaningfully towards the forest on both sides. 'If . . . I say if . . . she truly was murdered, then it's quite likely that she's lying somewhere in here. Buried along with her bicycle in some bog . . . well, perhaps there's not that much left at this point, of course.'

'Shut up,' I said.

'Sorry,' said Urban. 'My thoughts run away with me.'

'Thoughts is saying a lot.'

'Hmm,' Urban said sullenly. 'Do you want clarity about this, or what the hell do you want?'

'The clearer, the better,' I said. 'It's mostly the methods I'm wondering about. Why don't we look in a phone book, for example? If there is a Vera Kall in K– . . . she may have come back quietly.'

'Nonsense,' said Urban. 'Why would she come back, if she got away from here so elegantly? There is no Vera Kall in the phone book. Not in the census register either. Not in K– or anywhere else in the country either.'

'How do you know that?'

'Because I've checked. You know, if you get up in the morning it's possible to get a few things done. No, it's possible that it didn't produce that much, but in any case we know that her parents are dead.'

I thought a moment.

'If there's anything else to know, we'll find out on Saturday.'

Urban nodded thoughtfully a few times. 'I'm not so sure of that,' he said. 'After all, we have no idea who it is we're dealing with, right?'

I sat silently for a moment. 'Doesn't matter,' I said. 'Either it comes to nothing, or else something happens. It's all the same to me.'

Urban slowed down and looked at me. 'You don't mean that,' he said. 'You screamed in your sleep last night, I'm no idiot. Anyway, we need to talk with someone who knows something about this.'

'About what?'

'The Snake Flower, of course,' he snorted. 'The case of Vera Kall. He's coming to see us tomorrow, I promised him some new information and he actually sounded really interested. Even though it's past the statute of limitations.'

'What are you talking about?' I asked, although I'd already started to suspect it.

'Inspector Keller,' said Urban, picking up speed. 'The one who was in charge of the investigation in 1967. He just turned seventy, but on the phone he sounded sharp as a forty-nine-year-old.'

I heaved a sigh and closed my eyes.

9

While Urban prepared dinner on Wednesday evening, I took the boat and rowed out on the lake for an hour. Sat out there in the great solitude and tried to put my thoughts in order.

What did I really think about all this? There were only two conceivable courses of action, but when I started analysing the consequences of these courses – one at a time, in order – I felt that I was very quickly sliding out on slippery ice.

If it really was the case that Vera Kall was alive, then she must have decided to disappear right after our marvellous night of love thirty years ago. My first, her first. Two days before graduation.

Why?

I knew for certain that she experienced our hours together just as strongly as I did; if nothing else the message she'd written showed that.

And where would she have gone? Was it actually possible to pull off such a manoeuvre at that age? Nineteen years old. At that time, in that little town?

Or could she have been abducted? By who? Abducted but still alive?

And why show up in K– again? Right now. As stated.

The questions were legion and I found no acceptable answer to any one of them.

So she is dead, I decided. Just like everyone believed and assumed. She died that night.

So who was this new Vera Kall who wanted to talk with me? Someone who knew something?

But no one could know anything. I pondered. The only one who could know anything about Vera and me must be a person who either spied on us, or who saw Vera before she died.

I ruled out the spy alternative. One possibility remained. Just one. Vera had met someone after she left me in the middle of the night.

Could this someone be someone other than the one who . . . ?

I sat absolutely motionless in the boat for several minutes while I pondered this conclusion; gave it an honourable chance to take hold in my volatile awareness.

Maybe it succeeded, maybe not. In retrospect it's hard to decide. I looked at my watch, took hold of the oars and started to row back.

We had venison stew with rice and mortadella. Drank a full-bodied Burgundy with it. Lemon parfait for dessert. Coffee, cognac, chocolate macaroons and a cigar. I had one too, haven't smoked for fifteen years, but the mosquitoes were stubborn and Urban insisted. It didn't taste bad at all.

I did the dishes and then read three chapters of *The Fly and Eternity*. It truly held its style, I expressed my appreciation to Urban; he chuckled self-consciously and picked at his beard.

Then we sat there and talked about old teachers for a while – lecturer Bluum, language adjunct Lingonstroem, senior master Uhrin, of course – but we let the Snake Flower rest. As if we had an agreement. A little later we fired up the sauna and spent numerous hours with hot steam, leafy branches, beer and quick dips in the night-dark water.

Plus a considerable quantity of old bullshit.

I think it was past two when we went to bed.

Inspector Keller arrived in an old Buick at eleven o'clock on Thursday. I didn't recognize him, but then I didn't have much of a recollection either. Didn't speak with him during the investigation, only saw his face in the newspaper. I had been questioned in the same way as everyone else – in two rounds, both times in the care of a ruddy and rather anonymous constable. And a tape recorder.

My first impression of the inspector this warm morning was that he was in the process of shrinking out of life. Everything seemed too large for him: the suit, the glasses, the car, the brown briefcase that with some exertion he tossed up on our rickety outdoor table. I wondered whether he could even come up to a third of Urban's weight, but also thought that you shouldn't judge a person by their shell. *Homo Bananicus non est*, as Uhrin used to say when he made a joke every other semester.

'Brought along a few old papers from the case,' Keller explained. 'Are you Henry Maartens?'

We greeted each other and settled down. Urban took three beers out of the barrel and opened them. Keller hung his jacket on the back of his chair and started rolling up his shirt sleeves; it was clearly noticeable that the old dead policeman had come to life inside him. He leant forward on his elbows and moved his gaze between me and Urban. There was something birdlike about his physiognomy, especially the head and his way of moving it on the slender hymenopteran of a neck that stuck up from a collar four sizes too big. He smoothed out his thin moustache and his even thinner greyish-white hair and started.

'Facts in the case of Vera Kall. What the hell do you two have to say?'

After a good half hour he was content. Leant back and emptied his beer glass; the pointed larynx went up and down a few times like an overheated tachograph.

'I'll be damned,' he then summarized. 'So you've been sitting on vital information for thirty years. The case is prescribed, of course, but if I weren't so old I would punch you on the jaw.'

'I didn't want to scandalize her,' I said.

'Bullshit,' said Keller. 'After-the-fact construction. The dead don't care about scandals.'

'I was thinking more about the survivors,' I attempted. 'Her mother and father.'

'You were thinking about your own hide,' said Keller.

'Hmm, yes,' Urban interjected. 'Anyway, he kept quiet. There's not much we can do about that now. The question is, what would it have meant for the investigation if Henry had come forward?'

Keller observed his empty beer glass and wiped his moustache clean. 'Depends on what you mean by that,' he muttered, glaring at me. 'You would have been a suspect in any event, you should be clear about that.'

I didn't reply. Urban lit a cigar and exhaled a diversionary cloud of smoke. 'Did you ever have a suspect?' he asked.

'Not so much as a hen,' Keller snapped in irritation. 'We

expended thousands of work hours, but if you don't even have a corpse, suspects are hard to come by. We dug up a couple of conceivable characters; a rapist who'd been let out six months earlier and an old swindler who lived along her travel route. Both of them had alibis.'

'Witnesses then?' Urban asked. 'Who saw her somewhere during the night, or something.'

Keller opened the briefcase and started rooting in a folder. 'No one reliable,' he noted, taking out a sheet of paper. 'Just some hysterics and nitwits. This one, for example.'

He remained silent a moment while he studied the information he was holding in his hand. 'A certain Miss Paisinen,' he explained. 'Maintained that she'd seen an angelic figure on a bicycle at quarter to four in the morning. Baarenstraat on the outskirts of Pampas. A dark-haired angel on her way westward, to be precise . . . the lady came forward after a month when she'd read forty column kilometres about the case in the newspapers . . . but sure as hell she may have been right. We dismissed her mostly on the basis of the time. If Vera Kall left the party at eleven o'clock, she ought to have made it further in five hours, we thought . . . if she wasn't doing something else during that time, that is. Harrumph.'

'I understand,' I said.

Urban served more beer, while Keller kept digging in his briefcase. I took a substantial gulp and wondered about what actually would have happened if I had come forward and told at once. What would my parents have said? And Vera's? The teachers at Doggers? Would I have even got the white graduation cap? It was hard to find any bright spots in such a scenario, and in silence I thanked my lucky stars that I'd had the sense to keep my mouth shut.

Although perhaps it didn't have that much to do with sense. If one were to be honest.

'Theories?' said Urban. 'What theories did you have? There must have been a few things that didn't come out to the general public.'

Keller sighed. 'Of course I had theories. Two tons of theories and half an ounce of facts. You should know that I didn't let go of the Snake Flower for years. But I never got any wiser . . . it was at a standstill from the very start and it continued that way.'

'I can believe that,' said Urban. 'You assumed that she was killed in any event?'

Keller thought a moment.

'One thing I was sure of,' he said. 'If it was the case that she simply ran away, then she must have planned it. It can't have been a moment's impulse . . . although the only thing that speaks for that alternative is those damned Aaron's Brethren. I talked for hours with that Bible-thumping father of hers, and this I will say, if I'd grown up under such a numbskull I would have run away on my first tricycle.'

Urban and I nodded. 'Are they still around?' Urban asked.

Keller shook his head. 'Dissolved a few years later. There were never more than thirty or forty members. The high priest's nerves got a bit delicate after this thing with his daughter, and, well, it fell apart in any event. Nothing bad that doesn't bring something good with it.'

We sat silently for a few moments again.

'And this . . . new development?' said Urban. 'What do you think about that, inspector? Who is this Vera Kall who wants to make contact with Henry after three decades?'

Keller undid the top button on his green nylon shirt and observed us in turn. First Urban, then me.

'I believe what I believe,' he said. 'One thing I know, and that is that someone is lying. Either her or the two of you.'

'Or all three,' he added after a short pause to think. He finished his beer and stood up. 'Be in touch after the visit on Saturday,' he said. 'Regardless of how it goes. If you don't do that, I'm submitting a report to the police.'

Then he turned on his heels, crawled into his gigantic car and rumbled off.

I looked at Urban Kleerwot. He suddenly seemed to have a problem with the suspension of his lower jaw.

We did not leave Urbanhall for two days. Urban had stocked up provisions properly; we ate, drank, discussed, talked nonsense, fished and sat in the sauna. The weather was a little worse those days, but it was quite nice. I finished reading *The Fly and Eternity* and congratulated my friend for the particularly surprising – and yet completely credible – resolution. We decided that I should go through the whole thing one more time the following week. With an eagle eye and a sharpened pencil.

The night between Friday and Saturday I almost didn't sleep a wink. I lay there, twisting and turning in the narrow bed while I listened to the thunderstorm that shuttled back and forth overhead. On Saturday we had breakfast inside for the first time, but by late morning blue patches started showing up in the sky. I hoped that would be a good sign.

★

It was almost two full days to the minute after Inspector Keller left us in his Buick that the next car came crawling along the bumpy road.

It was a white Renault with a few years under its belt. It parked next to the woodpile, the engine was turned off and in the brief second before the door was opened and the driver got out, my life passed before my inner eye ten thousand times.

10

The man who got out of the car and stretched was in his mid-thirties. He was at least 190 centimetres tall and looked physically fit. Wore jeans, running shoes, T-shirt and a thin windbreaker with rolled-up sleeves.

Suntanned face, blond hair cut short. A handball player who is just coming home after becoming a world champion, approximately. I cast a glance at Urban. He was standing five metres from me with an unlit Pfitzerboom in his hand and a question mark on his face.

The man observed us a moment without changing expression. Then he walked around the car and opened the door on the passenger side.

A woman of about forty-nine got out.

She was dark. Dark and beautiful. Slender, with clean features, dressed in a simple, dark-green cotton dress and a cardigan the same colour over her shoulders.

It could be her, it could be someone else.

I don't know how much time passed before we came out of this frozen second, but I managed to decide numerous times both that it was Vera Kall and that it was not Vera Kall. And I had time to think that God – on his side – must have decided to photograph just this moment and put it in his big album, but that he had problems setting the focus and that was why it was taking so long.

And that it was damned strange that such thoughts could pop up.

At last Urban broke the silence. 'Welcome,' he said. 'My name is Urban Kleerwot. This is Henry Maartens. I don't believe we've met.'

'Adam Czernik,' the man said, shaking hands.

'Pieters,' said the woman. 'Ewa Pieters.' Something let go of something else inside my chest. Suddenly it was easier to breathe, but at the same time more boring.

Infinitely more boring.

'It was you who called?' Urban asked. She nodded.

'Yes. I gave the name Vera Kall.'

'What reason did you have to do that?'

'I had very good reasons.'

She looked resolute and serious the whole time. The man too. Urban gestured us down around the table. 'We seem to have a few things to talk about,' he said. 'Beer or coffee?'

The woman shook her head.

'Neither,' said the man.

There was silence for a few seconds and I sensed that this was some kind of tactic. A game of bridge. To start conversing was to give away the first trick. I had a little difficulty understanding why.

'May I suggest that you explain what the hell your intentions are,' Urban said when he was unable to wait any longer. 'You've subjected us – especially my good friend here – to a little discomfort the past few days.'

'Your good friend Henry Maartens?' said the woman.

'Exactly,' I said. 'Who are you, ma'am, and why do you maintain that your name is Vera Kall?'

An unconscious smile limped across her face, and I started to suspect that the attitude she tried to stick to was not particularly natural for her. She coughed twice into the crook of her arm.

'May I first explain that Adam has nothing at all to do with this,' she said, signalling towards the handball giant. 'He is only here with regard to my safety. I have also notified a number of other persons where I am. Just so you know.'

'What the hell?' said Urban.

'What do you mean?' I said.

She took a cigarette out of her handbag and lit it. I looked at Mr Czernik. Bodyguard, I thought. Good Lord.

'I'm her cousin,' said Ewa Pieters. 'Vera Kall's cousin. Do you understand?'

Urban shook his head. I shook my head.

'I've found out certain things.'

'Certain things?'

'Yes. That the police never figured out.'

I felt myself starting to get angry. Or else it was fear.

'Will you please say what it is you know,' I requested. 'What happened to Vera, for example? Is that what you know about?'

She hesitated. 'What makes you think that?'

'Because why else would you carry on with these silly mystifications?' Urban interjected, looking increasingly irritated.

She held back the answer for two seconds. 'Because I know that your friend had something to do with my cousin's death,' she then said.

'What the hell are you babbling about?' Urban roared. Adam Czernik adjusted his glasses and leant forward.

'Excuse me,' I said, to soften things. 'But I can assure you that those are pure fantasies. We don't have the slightest idea what happened to Vera, neither Urban nor I. I think it's best if you explain yourself now.'

She sat quietly a moment and smoked while she appeared to be debating with herself. Never sought eye contact with Adam Czernik; it was evident that he was not particularly initiated in the whole thing. That he was only there as some kind of security measure, just as she'd said. I observed his upper arms and understood that he was presumably a rather effective one. Especially if you contemplated resistance. Urban went over to the barrel and fished out four beers.

'All right,' Ewa Pieters said at last. 'I'll tell you what I know and I hope you can provide a satisfactory explanation. May I have a glass, too? I'm not used to drinking from the bottle.'

Urban got up again. 'You'll get an explanation if you just say what it is I'm supposed to explain,' I promised.

Finally she started.

'I liked Vera very much,' she started, and now her tone was considerably softer. It suited her better, much better. 'Even if we were only cousins, we were almost like siblings . . . even though we lived a long way from each other. Both of us were only children and there is no more than two months differ- ence in age between us. I think that what happened affected me just as hard as it affected her parents . . .'

'Where did you live?' I asked.

'Linden. Sixty, seventy kilometres from here. But we saw

each other every summer holiday and at weekends. Our mothers were sisters . . . the fathers who married into the family didn't have that much in common. Well, that was how it was.'

I nodded. Urban poured beer.

'It was a shock when she disappeared. I've brooded about what happened just as much as everyone else . . . for thirty years. Then gradually I started to understand that we would never get the answer. I guess I thought, like most, that she must have encountered a rapist that night. A lunatic who attacked her and killed her and hid the body when he was done. But then last spring . . .'

She paused. Took a gulp of beer and lit another cigarette.

'Then last spring Aunt Ruth was on her deathbed. Vera's mother, that is. The dad, Adolphus, passed away more than ten years ago.'

'We know,' it slipped out of me.

She observed me with surprise for a moment before she continued.

'She had many illnesses, Ruth, but a strong heart, which kept her alive even though she was bedridden – more or less bedridden anyway – the last three years. That day in April, it's only a few months ago, I got word from the nursing home where she was that she wanted to talk with me. I went there . . . Ulmenthal, out by the sea, I don't know if you're familiar with it . . . I saw a doctor first and he explained that she probably didn't have many hours left. If I understood him correctly, it was the case that she had simply decided not to struggle any longer, but that she had to exchange a few words with me before it was time. I was her only living relative, both of my parents passed away several years ago, and, well, there was something she wanted to say—'

'Was this unexpected for you?' Urban interrupted. 'That she wanted to talk with you, that is . . . did you used to visit her?'

'Not that often,' Ewa Pieters admitted. 'It's a really long way out to Ulmenthal and it wasn't easy to talk with her. She had difficulty speaking after a stroke a couple years ago . . . '

'What did she want?' I asked, a little irritated at Urban's interruption. 'Why did she have to talk with you?'

Ewa Pieters suddenly looked self-conscious. Smoothed her dress across her knees a couple of times and looked down at the table.

'I don't actually know,' she said. 'I don't know for certain what it was she wanted. If I'd understood that, naturally I would have gone to the police . . . maybe I would have done that anyway in time, if you hadn't shown up here in town.'

'What the dickens are you trying to—' Urban started, but I raised a hand and silenced him.

'Tell us,' I said.

Ewa nodded. 'She was very weak when I came into the room,' she explained. 'The only life that was left in her was in her eyes, they were full of . . . well, what should I say? Eagerness? Eagerness and gratitude, I think . . . gratitude that I'd come and eagerness at getting to say what she wanted to say before it was too late. I wish she hadn't waited so long. That she'd had a little more energy left, but then she didn't. I sat down on the edge of the bed and took her hand as usual. She looked at me with a burning gaze and her lips started moving . . . but no sound came out. I leant closer and listened, right next to her mouth, but nothing other than a weak hissing was heard. I called a nurse and asked if it was possible to do something, but she just shrugged and looked apologetic. When we were alone again, Aunt Ruth made a final exertion. I leant close to her again and now I heard.'

'Then you heard?' I said. Saw that Urban's jaw had dropped again and that Czernik too had actually pricked up his ears.

'Yes,' said Ewa Pieters. 'Then I heard. Rather clearly, actually, and she repeated the name two times: "Vera . . ." she said . . . "wrote . . . Henry Maartens, Henry Maartens' fault." That was all. Then she closed her eyes and fifteen minutes later she was dead.'

There was silence around the table. The sun broke through a cloud and cast a sudden, wandering pattern of light and leaf shadows across Ewa Pieters' dress. I swallowed. Adam Czernik crossed his arms over his chest.

'Can you say that one more time,' Urban asked.

'"Vera . . . wrote . . . Henry Maartens, Henry Maartens' fault." The name two times. And I promise that I heard right.'

I leant back in the chair. The sun changed its mind and went behind a cloud.

11

I made my decision in half a minute, but it took half an hour to tell my part of the story.

Or our part. There was of course no reason to hold back about Urban's and my visit out in Samaria or the conversation with Inspector Keller. Ewa Pieters listened and smoked and asked questions, and it seemed ever so clear that she believed what she was hearing. Why shouldn't she? She didn't seem to have very much to reproach me for either. It felt a little awkward to have to relate Vera's and my love encounter, but it was necessary and I think Ewa saw a little bright spot in that her cousin got to taste the fruits of love at least once before she died.

Or did she not die after all? Was Vera Kall really dead? The absurd thing was that we still didn't know. New facts in the case had come to light for both parties, both for us and for Ewa Pieters, but while we were still sitting out there on Urban's garden furniture having a discussion, we were far from coming to clarity about the crucial point.

What had happened the night of 28 May 1967? Or the morning, rather; those early hours that at the same time seemed so near and so unattainably far away?

Concerning Ewa's behaviour after my arrival in K–, the mists soon dispersed. Ever since Mrs Kall's death in April she had tried in a slightly amateurish way to straighten out the question marks around her aunt's final words. She knew, thus, that a certain Henry Maartens had been in the same class as Vera during her last two years of high school. She had also cautiously inquired with a couple of other classmates if there could have been anything between Vera and me, but only got head shakes and negative answers in response. She didn't know where I lived nowadays nor how to go about finding that out . . . yes, that was more or less how things stood, when I suddenly showed up at the Continental a week ago. Ewa Pieters had been working at the hotel as an accountant for the past four years. At least one point for Urban, I thought. She had seen my name on the room reservation, it was no stranger than that.

Because she didn't know what was behind Mrs Kall's intimations on her deathbed, she – after a couple of nights of brooding and rejection of various strategies – had decided on the bold move with Vera Kall's name. To be able to observe my reaction, if nothing else. She had initiated a good friend, Adam Czernik, younger brother of her ex-husband, in the plans. At least semi-initiated. On Monday they had followed us from K– out to Urbanhall, and then it was just a matter of retrieving Urban's mobile number by way of the vehicle registration. Simple and painless.

That she waited until Saturday for the visit was simply due to the fact that Adam wasn't available earlier. She didn't dare attack us on her own, that was obvious.

So that's how that was. Suddenly all the cards were on the table and we soon realized that we were sitting in the same boat. It felt like a relief to start with, at least for me personally, but gradually frustration got the upper hand.

Frustration that we still weren't there. Hadn't found the answer to the question of what happened to Vera. I had been incredibly tense before the meeting with Ewa, and naturally it had been like that for her too, but now, when I knew who she was and we had settled the supposed animosity, once again the basic problem itself reared its ugly head.

What had happened to Vera that night thirty years ago? Same old question as always.

'Thundering typhoons,' said Urban. 'I made a bet with myself that we would have the solution today. I'm starting to think I'm going to lose. All the cards on the table and just as confounded . . .'

'We have one more card to turn,' I reminded him. 'What the heck did she mean?'

'Who?'

'Ruth Kall, of course. If we understand what's behind her final words, then we have the answer.'

'You assume that she knew about it?' said Urban.

'Don't you?'

Urban did not reply. Observed his cigar with a worried expression.

'Go on,' said Ewa Pieters.

'Hmm,' I said. 'What conclusions did you draw yourself? When you started thinking about those words, that is.'

'Nothing certain,' Ewa Pieters said after a brief pause. 'At first I thought you must be the one who killed Vera and that her mother knew about it. But then I asked myself why in the world she kept quiet about it in that case, and I haven't found an answer there.'

'Because there isn't any answer,' I said. 'I didn't kill your cousin. I loved her.'

'A certain distinction,' Urban muttered.

It was at this point that Adam Czernik took off his glasses and started getting involved in the debate. 'You all seem a bit confused, if you excuse me for saying so,' he said, showing that he had brushed his teeth properly. 'Do you or do you not think that Vera's mother knew what happened that night?'

I thought. Urban scratched his beard.

'She knew,' said Ewa Pieters. 'Let's assume that she actually did.'

'How?' said Czernik. 'How could she know that?'

A cloud of silent thoughts flew across the table.

'Because the murderer wrote to her and confessed,' Urban suggested. 'Thus the word "wrote".'

'And signed with the name Henry Maartens,' I added.

'There are other alternatives,' said Czernik. 'Say those words one more time, Ewa.'

'Vera . . . wrote . . . Henry Maartens, Henry Maartens' fault,' said Ewa for the fourth or fifth time.

'Wrote . . .' Czernik repeated. 'There's something missing before that. What if it's an "I" that's missing? In that case, what would that mean?'

'That she wrote down something she knew,' Ewa replied. 'I've thought about that, but I haven't found anything . . . of course, words are missing in her message, I just don't know which ones.'

'Have you searched?' Adam Czernik asked. 'For something she may have written, that is. You took care of her estate, right?'

'Just a little bit,' Ewa admitted. 'I haven't had time, it's half a basement storage room's worth of stuff, but if you're interested . . .'

Urban looked doubtful. 'If she wrote down something that concerned Ewa and really wanted it to come to the eyes of the world, wouldn't she have left it in a place where it could be found?'

'She may have written it a long time ago,' Ewa Pieters pointed out. 'Her mind wasn't completely clear at the end, we can't demand just any amount of logic . . .'

They continued the discussion along these lines awhile, but I noticed that my thoughts were slipping away in a different direction; I was starting to see Vera in my inner eye again, recall her figure that night . . . her enchantingly beautiful body in the pale darkness of the summer night . . . how we caressed each other, how we made love, how she received me with her legs around my back . . . how later she must have sneaked out of our love bed so as not to waken me. Got dressed and wrote her final message to me, that she didn't know how it would turn out, but that she loved me . . . how she tiptoed down the stairs, out into the June morning and up onto the bicycle in her white dress and her abundant dark hair . . . pedalling through the fair landscape in the virginal dawn; early summer of 1967, the summer that would be the great Flower Power summer, the summer of freedom she would never get to experience, I could no longer conceive that she got to, and I understood, no, didn't understand . . . sensed, started to sense, that there had never been any attacker on her path, that she never encountered a lunatic . . . for if what had now finally come to light added up, then that could only mean one thing . . . Good Lord, I thought, it can't have happened like that.

★

We spent three hours going through the property left behind by Ruth Kall in Ewa Pieters' basement storage room on Langvej. What remained of it, that is; all the clothes and textiles had been given to fundraising and charitable purposes of various types, and much had been taken care of in the final years Mrs Kall was alive. Like many lonely old people, she had planned for her departure. Got rid of things and had not intended to leave too much behind.

But there was quite a bit. Mostly storage furniture and boxes filled with books, old magazines and papers. Pastor Adolphus's handwritten sermons and theological reflections, for example. Vera's exercise and arithmetic books all the way from first grade; it felt strange and almost awe-inspiring to stand with them in hand. Registers and attendance lists from the meetings of Aaron's Brethren. Etcetera. It was no dream job squatting down there and rooting, and when Adam Czernik departed about halfway through, I for one had difficulty granting credence to the meeting at the sports association that had suddenly come up.

Whatever, it was not until we were basically done with the whole dust trap that Urban saw the light and added his two pennies' worth.

'Wasn't there a will?' he asked.

Ewa Pieters straightened up. 'Will? No, I was the only one with the right to inherit, so I got it all, it was just this and a few hundred in a bank account. Although there was actually a lawyer . . .'

'A lawyer?' I said. 'Why is that?'

Ewa wiped sweat and dust from her forehead with the back of her hand and looked thoughtful. 'I don't know,' she said. 'Think he'd been around since Adolphus's time. Attorney

Hegel. He was in touch, in any event, and explained that there was no will.'

'That there wasn't a will?' I asked. 'He got in touch and told you that?'

'Yes.'

'Was that all he wanted?' Urban asked.

'Yes,' said Ewa. 'That was all.'

Urban pushed aside the pedestal drawer he had just looked through. 'Was it Hegel you said?' he asked. 'Let's go up and call him, I've had enough of this.'

Attorney Hegel had his office on the south side of Grote Square among the well-to-do turn-of-the-century bourgeois houses. Even though it was Saturday and it was already six o'clock, he agreed to receive us there.

If I hadn't already sensed the resolution, this was probably as good a sign as any. That he took the time. While we stood there and waited outside the richly ornamented Art Nouveau facade, I suddenly felt that I no longer had any desire to be part of this.

No desire at all.

12

'Unusual terms?' Urban Kleerwot says, raising his eyebrows. 'What do you mean by that?'

We are sitting submerged in leather furniture in Attorney Hegel's spacious office. Urban and I on the couch. Ewa Pieters and Hegel himself in the armchairs. Hegel has just accepted one of Urban's Pfitzerbooms and leans back during the first puff. I look at him furtively: he is somewhat reminiscent of a Good Guy from an American courtroom movie, which is no doubt his intention. Presumably a few years over sixty, but with a trim figure and distinguished grey temples. Dark suit, light-blue shirt and subtle tie. I feel dirty and sticky after the rooting around in Ewa's basement storeroom, and hope the cigar smoke is sufficient to overpower the odour of sweat.

'Terms,' Hegel repeats. 'Unusual, as stated. Can't recall anything similar right off hand, but one naturally has to accommodate the client's wishes. Rules of the game.'

He thumbs the brown envelope and observes us in order, as if he can't refrain from keeping us on tenterhooks a few more seconds.

'For Christ's sake,' Urban exclaims. 'What kind of wishes?'

'Uh-hm,' the attorney clears his throat. 'I have had this in my safekeeping for almost thirty years; twenty-eight, if you want to be precise. Mrs Kall handed this over two years to the day after her daughter disappeared . . . turned over both the letter and the instructions, that is.'

He pauses yet another time, but no one breaks the silence.

'Which are as follows,' Hegel continues. 'Under no circumstances could the letter be passed on or opened as long as either Mr or Mrs Kall was alive. After the death of both I had to safeguard it in a satisfactory manner, until the day when someone – whoever that might be – came and asked about it. However, for ten years at most, then it shall be destroyed. Unread.'

'Huh?' says Ewa Pieters. '"Someone, whoever that might be"? You didn't have orders to hand it over after her death?'

Hegel shakes his head. 'That was what the condition was. The client's wishes are law. Unusual, isn't it? I think she wanted to leave it in God's hands somehow, but one may have differing opinions about that . . .'

'But . . .' says Ewa. 'But now we've come and asked about it?'

'Exactly,' Hegel agrees, taking a puff on the cigar. 'Now you've come and now I will do my duty. Be my guest. It's fine to read the contents.'

He hands the envelope over to Ewa. She takes it, weighs it in her hand and inspects it.

'No addressee?' she says.

'No addressee,' Hegel confirms. 'Just the date and her own name.'

There is silence for several seconds.

'Open it!' says Urban. 'Read it!'

Attorney Hegel contributes a thin letter opener. Ewa slits it open and takes out the contents – two double-folded sheets, filled with handwritten text. She sets them in front of her on the table, smooths them out and looks at the first page.

'Out loud!' says Urban. 'Read out loud for God's sake, otherwise I'll explode.'

Ewa Pieters takes a deep breath and starts to read:

'Lord God in heaven, You who rule over everything. I don't know what to do, but this is my confession . . .'

It was not until Monday morning that we set off. Urban and I spent all of Sunday out at the cabin, but we were kept informed about the preparations by way of Urban's mobile.

It was a strangely quiet day, that Sunday; no wind, a pale sky and a temperature that meant you don't feel the air against your skin. We went out on the lake and fished for a couple of hours without getting so much as a nibble. Ate ready-made food that we brought with us from K– on Saturday evening. In the evening we sat in the sauna and discussed the plot in Urban's mystery. We talked very little about the Snake Flower.

It was certainly not standard protocol that we were allowed to go along during Monday's police call; I think Inspector Keller obtained some kind of special permission. It had more to do with patterns and style than with the usual police procedures; besides, he had been retired from all regulations for several years. We all drove together in his big Buick, Ewa Pieters as well as Urban and me; we had a police car in front of and behind us in the caravan, and I could see on Keller's face that it was his last major operation that was ahead of him. He seemed more shrivelled than ever, sitting there behind the wheel and chewing on a match; even more resolute and concentrated. No wonder, I thought, and again regretted that I hadn't asked to stay at home.

Ewa Pieters sat with me in the back seat and felt self-reproach. 'I should have figured this out sooner,' she complained. 'Should have understood what it meant that she knew.'

'It doesn't matter,' I consoled her. 'It wasn't easy to grasp.'

'Yes, it was easy,' said Ewa. 'If Ruth knew something – regardless of what – that must mean that Vera came home that night.'

'Yes, she did come home, always,' Urban muttered from the front seat. 'But it's really awful that someone takes the law into their own hands and keeps quiet like this.'

'Some people have more than one law,' Keller noted acidly. 'It's popular to have a little private ethics sometimes. Especially among the Bible-thumpers, believe me.'

Ewa squirmed. 'I don't think, anyway, what Aunt Ruth did was so indefensible. They probably got their punishment, nothing would have actually been gained if she had come forward, would it?'

Keller grunted in irritation. 'There were a few too many who never stepped forward in this story,' he said, catching my gaze in the rear-view mirror. 'What do you think the investigation work cost the taxpayer, for example?'

That was, of course, one way to look at it. I had no comment and no one else did either.

We got to Samaria just after eleven o'clock. Mr Clausen was standing out on the grassy field and greeted us guardedly as we got out of the cars. I noted that the red Volvo was not there and understood that Mrs Clausen had taken the kids somewhere. Unnecessary to subject them to traumatic experiences in the rural idyll, naturally. Completely unnecessary, it was bad enough as it was.

Six policemen in overalls quickly took shovels out of car boots and took off under the leadership of the commander and Inspector Keller to the indicated place. The rest of us kept our distance and, once the digging had started, Mr Clausen went inside and put on coffee. We sat down in the same plastic furniture as the last time, and after a while I noticed that Ewa had started crying. I stroked her arm a little awkwardly, she took out a handkerchief and blew her nose.

'It's too much,' she said.

'Yes,' I said. 'It's a lot.'

'And so unreal,' she continued. 'I can't believe that it's true . . . yet I know that was exactly how it happened. He could be so hot-tempered.'

Urban cleared his throat. 'I've been thinking about something,' he said. 'If she hadn't been so confoundedly honest, this never would have happened.'

'What do you mean?' I said.

'Just that she should have lied instead,' Urban said with a sigh. 'She comes home at five o'clock in the morning and confesses that she both got drunk and that she went to bed with a boy, what the hell was she expecting?'

'He didn't need to hit her,' said Ewa. 'If she'd known that he would do that, maybe she would have kept quiet. Although Vera was always honest . . . and don't forget that it was an accident. If it hadn't been that she fell so unfortunately . . .'

She fell silent. Urban nodded and then no one seemed to have anything to say. The only thing to do was wait. I closed my eyes and started playing out that scene inside my head.

I don't know how many times I'd done that since Saturday evening.

Father and mother sitting at the kitchen table and waiting. Worried and tired from lack of sleep.

Vera, who comes in and stops in the middle of the room. Strengthened – I imagine in any case – by her love for me, she starts to tell them. Everything she's experienced. Straight-backed and frankly.

The father, the uncompromising preacher, who stands up and without a word doles out his punishment.

Vera, who falls against the sharp corner of the stove.

Vera, who dies within a minute. So her mother has written. Within a minute.

Man and wife, who then stand there, the man, the man of God, who through his anger killed his daughter . . . it is a beautiful summer morning, the sparrows are fluttering out in the blossoming lilac thicket, her red blood darkens slowly on the cold kitchen floor, and they stand there . . . they have desperately tried to get life in her, but her heart has stopped and now they stand there . . .

Quem di diligunt adolescens moritur.

They must have prayed. Hundreds of prayers they must have sent up that morning to their incomprehensible god, who in his great mercy let their only daughter die.

Die by her father's hand.

And perhaps, perhaps the unfathomable god of Aaron's Brethren answered them and said that he forgave them and that they shall bury what they have done in the earth and sweep away the traces.

Whom the gods love . . .

And that the guilt, the enormous guilt, is raised from

their shoulders and placed on . . . Henry Maartens'. Henry Maartens' fault . . .

I am startled when Ewa places her hand on my shoulder. Suddenly notice that I am sitting there shivering in the summer heat.

'They've found it now,' says Ewa, almost whispering. 'They've hit rotten wood, it must be the casket.'

Yes, they gave her a casket, she also wrote that in the letter.

And now she is being dug up. I'm not the one who is digging up the Snake Flower, but I go over and watch.

Ewa Pieters too. I am crying and I hold her hand in mine. It feels as if it belongs there.

ALL THE INFORMATION IN THE CASE

Translated from the Swedish by Paul Norlen

Adapted into the film *Samaria*

It came to pass in those days that a young man by the name of S was living in the university town.

His parents died early, his only sister moved to Australia a year or so before the story begins – but despite his obvious lack of living, present relatives, outwardly S is a well-mannered and capable person. After several years of mixed but successful academic studies he has decided to possibly become a teacher. Because he is a conscientious individual, and does not want to risk ending up on the wrong path in life, he applies for – and gets – a temporary job for a spring term at a high school in the community of H–. If it turns out that he likes the profession, after this trial semester he is prepared to complete the teaching programme where, considering his good academic record, he should have no problem being accepted. This is his plan.

He finds a room to rent in the vicinity of the school in H– where he got his position, he leaves his girlfriend and his two-room apartment in the university town, and in early January he gets started on his educational activity. The rest of the faculty consists of forty-odd teachers of varying age and character, the school is beautifully located with a view towards a lake, and almost immediately S finds that he is adjusting very well.

H– is an old mill town with just one major industry, a steel plant, where practically all the able-bodied inhabitants make their livelihood. The school is strictly a secondary school with about 400 pupils, two-thirds from the town itself, one-third from the surrounding countryside, in round numbers. On the school grounds is a bronze statue of the school's most prominent student over the years, a successful cross-country skier with a dozen national medals to his credit.

S teaches Swedish and English in three different grades: one class in seventh, one in eighth, one in ninth. He soon discovers that he enjoys the teaching job, in all its aspects. He likes the students, he appreciates the interaction with his colleagues, he finds the instructional process itself – teaching and practising skills – inspiring. Especially where the ninth graders are concerned, who are of course only eight or nine years younger than himself, the situation feels very satisfying, and he also gets the idea that the young people appreciate him as a teacher. He is also the form teacher for this class; he has taken over the role from a crabby old woman with failing kidneys, and realizes that it is rewarding to follow just such a run-down, worn-out educator.

The semester goes by and in the month of May it is time to assign grades to the students. Only three weeks before the end of school, however, a very sad accident occurs. A girl in the ninth grade class in question, Sofia, perishes in a traffic accident. She is run over by a motorist as she is on her way to school early one Wednesday morning. The incident is observed by a couple of independent witnesses, but the driver flees from the scene of the accident, and despite an extensive investigation the police are unable to capture him.

Sofia's death puts a gloomy damper on schoolwork in the final weeks before the summer holidays. More than half of the pupils in the school are present at the girl's funeral in the beautiful church in H–, and at an extra meeting the day after the burial the school administration and all the teachers gather to solemnize the girl's memory. At this meeting it is also announced that Sofia will receive her final grades, even though she is no longer present among the living.

The decision has been made by the school administration in consultation with the department chairs, and no open criticism of the directive is voiced. The girl has spent nine long years working towards them after all, before she was torn away so tragically. No decisive tests remain; it seems as if there might be a certain logic in all this.

When S comes home to his rented room on the Friday of that week, he feels inexpressibly sad. Normally he travels down to the university town and his girlfriend at the end of the week, but he has decided to spend this weekend in H–. He needs a couple of days of peace and quiet to finish the grading; everything must be entered in the proper forms the following Tuesday, and because S has never before found himself in a similar assessment situation, he wants to be extra careful and have plenty of time available.

But this thing with Sofia weighs on him. Now, as he sits in solitude on Friday evening, he has a hard time finding the point of having to assign a grade to her. *What will a dead girl do with grades?* he asks himself. *What's the use?*

And according to what criteria should he assign them? The principal has made it clear that Sofia should receive exactly those grades she would have got if the accident had not occurred; the customary pale-brown envelope with the school seal – two stylized swans in flight over a lake – will be sent to her parents on the last day of school. The viewpoint that it might be nice for her father and her mother to think that she nonetheless managed to finish school has been expressed.

It has also been pointed out that it is even more important to be fair, because this concerns a dead pupil. A dead pupil has no possibility to speak on her own behalf, the grade will stay as it is, unchallenged for all time.

Little by little, S manages to push aside these feelings of dejection and frustration. He decides to be done with all the other pupils first, and leave Sofia until last. Thus it is not until late on Saturday evening that he starts going through the dead girl's results and performance.

For English this is relatively simple. Sofia has been among the two or three best in the group on every test and quiz, and her oral performance has also been top-notch. For the autumn term she had an A, and it is with good conscience that S can enter the same letter as the final mark for ninth grade.

For Swedish it is more doubtful. When she left eighth grade, Sofia admittedly had an A in this subject too, but it went down during the autumn term of ninth grade to a B. During the spring she has struggled to regain her A; it has truly gone back and forth. Even without these tragic circumstances, S would have had a hard time making the right assessment, he knows that. On the so-called standard test in February Sofia reached 91 points – one below the limit for an A; two essays have been written, which S rewarded with a B and an A; and on the grammar test in April the girl had 62.5 points out of 68, a strong B or a weak A, the threshold for the higher grade being exactly 63.

S checks all these numbers one more time and reminds himself that the old, irascible teacher with leaking kidneys, when they met in the days before Christmas, informed him that Sofia was a pupil who was right at the boundary between B and A – and that she chose the lower grade because it was the autumn term and that it possibly might inspire the girl to really put her back into it during the spring.

I'll give her an A, thought S, raising the pen to enter the mark in his grade book. But then it was as if something – perhaps his sense of justice – took hold of his arm, and he stopped himself. There was another girl in the class who found herself in the exact same situation as Sofia – and he had just given her a B. Should Sofia be favoured simply because she was dead?

Shouldn't he rather give the other girl, whose name was Elinor, the higher grade? She at least had turned in her final project in literature (about the author C. S. Lewis, weak A or perhaps a strong B; he had deliberately, following the advice of an old and experienced colleague, avoided grading these projects officially) – while he hadn't read Sofia's project on the poet Karin Boye. She had presumably had it in her schoolbag the morning she was run over; it was the final day to turn in the assignment, but there had been no opportunity for S to read the work.

Of course it's the case, thought S, that there are questions in life that you simply cannot decide. But which you have to decide anyway.

He made more tea and called his girlfriend. They talked about everything imaginable that they planned to do over the summer, but after a while he brought up his grading difficulties.

His girlfriend was studying psychology and was a good listener. When he was finished explaining his dilemma and had given her all the information in the case, she said that he definitely had to make an effort to be fair, but that she obviously had too little knowledge of the girl's proficiency to be able to offer any more exact advice.

'B or A?' asked S.

'You're the one who has to decide that,' the girlfriend answered. 'I'm sure you're going to handle this in the best way. You've always been a fair-minded person.'

Then they ended the call. S had three cups of tea and smoked six cigarettes.

That final project would have decided the issue, he thought.

He had another two cups of tea and smoked four cigarettes. Then he made a decision and went to bed. The grade book was still open on his little desk under the window, which faced right towards a blossoming apple tree. An aroma of late spring slipped in through the curtain and drove the cigarette smoke out into the fresh air. S fell asleep after only a minute or so.

The following morning he had breakfast and read the Sunday paper. Then he took out his school directory and looked up the telephone number for the dead girl's home. Called them up and got an answer after four rings.

A woman, he assumed it was Sofia's mother. He told her his name and explained that he had been Sofia's teacher in Swedish and English during the spring term.

'I see,' the woman said sadly. 'I'm her mother. What is it you want, sir?'

S explained that he was working on assigning grades and that he was a little uncertain about Sofia's performance.

'But the girl is dead,' said the mother.

'She should still get a grade,' S explained. 'That was decided by the school administration.'

'Why is that?' asked the mother.

'Because it was considered most correct that way,' said S, suddenly feeling unsure whether it really had been right to call the girl's home. Yet he had slept a whole night on the decision, as he usually did in difficult cases.

'I see,' said the mother. 'So that's how it is.'

She sounded sad, but that was understandable and he could not perceive anything in her voice that indicated that she thought the school administration had made an incorrect decision.

'Of course we want the grades to be as good as possible,' he continued. 'And fair, of course, even if Sofia unfortunately is no longer alive.'

A sound was heard on the line. He could not decide if it was a sneeze or a sob.

'As perhaps you know, I'm rather new to the school and don't have any great experience in grading, but—'

'What is it you really want, sir?' the mother interrupted him.

'Only if it's not any trouble, of course,' said S.

'What is it?' the mother asked.

'Well, I would really like to read an essay that Sofia was supposed to hand in the same day that she . . . well. It's about Karin Boye, I'm sure it was in her schoolbag, when . . . yes. And I assume you've saved it.'

There was silence on the line for a few seconds.

'Sir, can I call you back in a bit?' the mother then asked. 'I think I have to consult with my husband about this first.'

'Of course,' said S. 'I apologize for having bothered you like this. But I didn't know what else to do.'

'Don't mention it,' said the mother. She got his number and hung up.

After this call S showered and got dressed, and when he was done the phone rang. It was Sofia's father.

'My wife got a little upset over that conversation you had with her an hour ago,' he explained.

'I'm very sorry,' said S. 'It was truly not my intention to—'

'Although naturally it's not your fault if the school administration has made a decision.'

'I really want Sofia to get as correct a grade as possible,' S elaborated.

'Naturally,' Sofia's father agreed. 'On that point we are in complete agreement. And we've found the project on Karin Boye. Although we are a little reluctant to give it up . . .'

'What do you mean?' S asked.

'You're welcome to look at it,' the father explained, 'but our suggestion is that you come here and read it. If you understand.'

'I understand. But . . . ?'

'It's fine if you come in half an hour. In the afternoon we're a little busy.'

'I don't really know . . .'

'The address is Rosenstigen 12. So we'll expect you at eleven o'clock, OK?'

'Thanks, yes, thanks a lot,' said S. 'Of course I'll come. That will be nice.'

Rosenstigen was a short street in a rather recently developed townhouse area on the southern edge of H–. Low, white-brick buildings with diminutive front gardens and flat roofs. S parked his bicycle in a little rack where there were two women's bicycles, and knocked on the door by means of a heart-shaped metal clapper.

A red-haired boy answered the door. Eight or nine, S guessed. He was dressed in a blue tracksuit and was intensely observing his bare, ever-so-dirty feet. Sofia had red hair too.

S asked if mum or dad were home. The boy answered, without looking up, that they were waiting for him out on the patio.

'You must be Sofia's brother,' S said, stepping into the hall. The boy sniffled and disappeared into a room to the right, closing the door behind him. A woman of indefinite age came to meet him. She was dressed in a worn, light-blue housecoat and moved without raising her feet. Her hair was thin and colourless, and her posture made him think of a wounded bird that he had once taken care of when he was a little boy.

'We're sitting out there,' she said, motioning with her hand towards an open glass door. S followed her out to a small stone patio. An oval, white plastic table was surrounded by four plastic chairs. In one of them a thin-haired man in his fifties was sitting. He was wearing dark trousers, white short-sleeved shirt and tie. His upper lip was covered by a sparse, reddish moustache and looked slightly deformed. S guessed that there was a harelip involved. The man half stood up and shook S's hand.

S sat down on one of the other chairs and looked around. There was a birdcage with two motionless budgies, a lawn-mower, a narrow flower bed with red and white flowers, and a stone-paved walkway out over a lawn with a sagging badminton net. Two rackets were stuffed into a plastic case, which was leaning against a spindly young fruit tree. A thermos of coffee and cups were set out on the table. The mother went back into the house and came back with a small plate of biscuits in one hand, a yellow folder in the other.

'I'm sorry about your loss,' S said. 'It must be terrible.'

The mother nodded and sat down.

'You can't imagine,' the father said. 'My wife hasn't slept since it happened.'

S observed her a little more carefully. She had large, dark circles under her eyes, and he thought she didn't really look quite present. She filled three cups from the thermos without asking.

A greyish-white poodle came out on the patio, looked around and went back into the house.

'Fifi,' said the mother. 'Sofia got her on her tenth birthday. She doesn't understand where Sofia has gone.'

'I'm sorry that I need to bother you like this,' said S. 'It's just this business with the grades.'

'We understand,' said the father. 'We have Sofia's project here. Margareta, perhaps you'd like to . . . ?'

His wife handed over the yellow envelope. 'Go ahead and read,' she said, her voice trembling. 'We'll be quiet. And have a biscuit. They're left over from the funeral.'

'Thanks very much,' said S, taking six handwritten sheets from the folder.

'Have a biscuit,' Sofia's mother repeated.

S picked out an almond biscuit with a small cross on it, sipped the coffee and started to read.

The introduction was excellent, he noticed that immediately. Karin Boye's life story was drawn concisely in distinct, well-formulated strokes. And Sofia had beautiful handwriting. True, that was not included as an official grading criterion nowadays, but obviously it didn't hurt.

'How does it seem?' the mother asked, trying to smile.

'It seems quite excellent,' S affirmed without taking his eyes off the paper.

'She put a lot of work into this,' said the father. 'Sofia was an ambitious girl, no one can say otherwise.'

'Talented too,' S added, and continued reading. 'She could have gone far.'

The mother took hold of the father's hand under the table, but neither of them made any further comment. S was done with the read-through after seven or eight minutes. Normally he would have gone to work on a second, more careful reading at once, but he didn't feel that was necessary in this case. The work was quite brilliant, he hadn't needed to make a single mark with his correction pen. There could be no doubt that the grade must be an A. A completely crystal-clear A, which happily enough also caused the pendulum to swing in the right direction where Sofia's final grade in the subject of Swedish was concerned. With a contented sigh, S put the pages back in the folder and nodded sympathetically at the parents.

'This was a very fine piece of work,' he explained. 'You have every reason to be proud of your daughter.'

'We are,' said the father, stroking his moustache deliberately with his thumb and index finger. 'And she put a lot of work into this, as I said.'

'It shows,' said S.

'Probably sat up half the night with it the day before the accident. I almost think . . .'

He paused and exchanged a glance with his wife.

'A lot of work,' the wife said sadly.

'She was an ambitious girl,' said S.

The father changed position in the chair.

'Thorough and ambitious,' said S.

The father cleared his throat. 'Yes, I actually think that was why,' he said slowly, while he observed the mute budgies in the little metal cage. 'That it happened the way it did. It was almost impossible to get any life in her that morning. She was worn out and unfocused, to put it simply.'

S sat silently.

'She walked the same way to school for three years,' the mother said.

The dog came out on the patio again. Observed those present with a sad expression and went back into the house.

'It's not easy for the dog,' said the father. 'She doesn't understand. Well, I saw that the lamp in her room was still on at two thirty in the morning that night. I got up to use the toilet.'

Suddenly S noticed that he felt cold. Under the late spring sun, he sat there shivering with goose pimples on his arms.

'Sir, you're welcome to write a grade on the project too,' said the father. 'It would be nice to know that the last thing she did in this life turned out . . . – Yes.' He interrupted himself. Took a handkerchief out of his trouser pocket and blew his nose.

'I haven't graded the other pupils' special projects,' S explained. 'But I'm prepared to make an exception in Sofia's case.'

'We're grateful for that,' said the father.

And then S took out his correction pen and wrote the A grade and his signature at the very bottom of the last page.

An hour later he wrote the same letter in his green grade book, but the rest of the day he spent in his rented room. Hour after hour he lay on his back in bed, looking up at the ceiling, even though it was a beautiful, late spring day with a mild, promising breeze and light clouds. He didn't smoke any cigarettes, he didn't read anything, but the aroma from the blossoming apple trees sneaked in through the open window and surrounded him like a mourning veil.

In the autumn of that same year S was accepted to the teaching programme in the university town, but he declined the position. Instead, the following spring term, he started studying at the library school in B–, and ever since 1982 he has worked as a librarian in a small city in central Sweden.